ORANGEBOY

ORANGEBOY

PATRICE LAWRENCE

Hodder
Children's
Books

HODDER CHILDREN'S BOOKS

First published in Great Britain in 2016 by Hodder and Stoughton

7 9 10 8 6

A CIP catalogue record for this book is available from the British Library.

ISBN 9781444927207

Typeset in Berkeley Oldstyle by Avon DataSet Ltd,
Bidford-on-Avon, Warwickshire

Printed and bound in Great Britain by CPI Group (UK) Ltd, Croydon, CR0 4YY

The paper and board used in this book are from well-managed forests
and other responsible sources.

MIX
Paper from
responsible sources
FSC
www.fsc.org   FSC® C104740

Hodder Children's Books
An imprint of Hachette Children's Group
Part of Hodder & Stoughton
Carmelite House
50 Victoria Embankment
London EC4Y 0DZ

An Hachette UK Company
www.hachette.co.uk

www.hachettechildrens.co.uk

*To Josephine, for love, gaffer tape
and the extensive selection of tea*

*To the family, UK, Trini and Jamaican,
who fill me full of ideas*

1

Man, I couldn't stop looking at her. When I closed my eyes, I still saw her. Her hair was thick and blonde, and a curl looped over her ear to her shoulder. She wore black mascara and green eyeliner and her lips looked shiny and sticky.

Sonya Wilson was right there next to me and it made my brain buzz.

The fairground was doing its thing around us. Every family in Hackney was out today, every eight-year-old in the world come along just to squeal at each other. The queue for the dodgems stretched out past the barriers and on to the grass. Legs dangled from the top of the Tower of Power as it shot halfway down to Australia and back up again. The Octopus was swinging screamers towards us and away.

All that noise was fighting with the music and the music was fighting with itself. It was the usual crappy mashup, The Beatles mixed with Frank Sinatra mixed with Michael Jackson. But underneath was a bass beat, thump, thump, thump, like my heart.

What if I reached over and touched Sonya's chest to see if her heart was thumping too? Damn, she'd slap me from Hackney to Hawaii! I laughed.

She looked around. 'What's so funny?'

'Nothing really.'

She smiled. 'Yeah, it gets you that way.'

She finished paying for the hot dogs and offered me one. She'd squirted mustard *and* ketchup, an 'S' on mine and two straight lines on hers. I should have told her I hated mustard, but it was an 'S' for Sonya, like she was giving herself to me. My brain cells were glowing, all lit up with bubbles of serotonin. That's what Ecstasy does to you; it tickles your brain's insides. I grinned, at the hot dog seller, a steward, anybody.

Sonya said, 'Try it.'

I took a bite of hot dog and the claggy bread stuck to the roof of my mouth.

'You like?'

'Mmph.'

I forced myself to swallow. A big lump of mustard dropped to the bottom of my stomach, bread and pink sausage churning up together. My gut jumped, ready to seal itself shut. Sonya was looking at me, so I took another bite and she nodded her approval. My brain circuits were flashing like Switchback lights.

'Better stuff it in now,' she said. 'When the pill kicks in proper, you won't want nothing to eat. Except, maybe me.'

I felt myself blush. She couldn't have meant *that*. Those South London girls must use words differently. She grabbed

2

my hand and I was grinning again. I must look like Pac-Man. I wrapped my fingers round hers, not too tight or she'd feel them all sweaty. That must be the drugs again . . .

Or just being skin to skin with her.

We stood side by side, looking across the fair. Could she see it too? The world a bit gold and glittery?

I said, 'I think it's working.'

She shrugged. 'You only had a quarter, Marlon. But it's your first time, and the first time's always the best.'

Ha.

Maybe I should have kept my mouth shut. I could have been like Yasir or those other wide-mouths. If everything they said was true, they'd smoked their weight in weed by time they were six.

I poked my tongue across the roof of my mouth. 'Should I have another drink?'

She rolled her eyes. 'You're all right. A quarter's just dust.'

It looked like I was heading towards sad-case country, so I took a deep, silent breath and put my arm round her shoulders, not too much pressure, keeping it all light. She didn't move away, but *her* arm stayed by her side.

'You're right,' I said. 'This is much better than revision.'

'Yeah.'

'My mum'll go mental.'

Sonya pulled her lips down into a sad face. 'You're going to tell her?'

"Course not!'

'So what's the problem?'

My mother's a secret god and she can see everything.

'Nothing. Look!' It was the pick 'n' mix stall. I still had a twenty in my pocket. 'Fancy some?'

'No. Let's go around before it gets really mad. You don't want too many people about if the pill sends you loony.'

I blinked. The world had turned dull again. 'It doesn't do that, does it?'

She gave a little sigh. 'I was joking! I've done it loads of times and I'm all right.'

Yes, she was. More than all right, but I'd be a slick creep if I told her straight.

I said, 'What do you fancy doing after?'

'I dunno. We haven't finished here yet.'

She sounded flat. I had to stop being so para. Girls like Sonya picked up on that stuff quick.

I smiled and said, 'Cool. It's up to you.'

But she must have heard something in my voice. She wriggled out from under my arm and moved round so she was facing me. Sonya's face was different from this angle and when she smiled, her cheeks were big and round like a young kid. She held my hand between hers and squeezed my fingers. Oh, yes! Now my whole head was one giant light bulb. You could probably see it from the moon, no, even further than that. Thirty trillion miles away, an Alpha

Centaurian astronomer was wondering about that bright new speck blazing through the Milky Way.

Her little finger moved up to my mouth and stroked the side. Thirty trillion miles away, a lens shattered from the heat.

'Ketchup,' she said. 'Seriously *not* cool.'

She unravelled her other hand from mine, took a tissue out of her little bag and dabbed my mouth. Even after she stopped, it felt like her finger was still there.

'Why think about later when we're here now?' she said. 'And even if we don't do anything after, we're definitely on for tomorrow. Today's like, I don't know, the starter. And tomorrow's the main course.'

Our fingers were twisting together again, black and white all mixed up. At least Mum wouldn't be funny about me going out with a white girl. Sonya's family might not feel the same way about me, though. I'd have to find a way to ask her. Not now. Next time, or the time after that.

And Tish? What's she going to say when she finds out? She should be happy for me. We'd be equals.

I scanned the crowds. Imagine if big mouth Yasir or double-thick Ronnie were here. Or Amir or Saul, or any of them other idiots. I played it out in my head. They'd swagger off some ride and catch sight of me and Sonya. Their mouths would drop open in shock. I'd slip my hand out of Sonya's and slide my arm round her waist, all in real slow-mo. And we'd walk away leaving them staring.

I know that sounds shallow. And yeah, she turned heads, but there was more to it. I wanted to make her laugh. I wanted to touch her arm. I wanted her to know how my breath kept getting stuck when she looked at me.

'It's the Dizzy Drum!' She pulled me towards it.

'We've just had hot dogs!'

'So what? Come on!'

Say 'no'? Not happening. I just had to stop thinking about the chaos that'd follow if I threw up in there.

I handed the yellow tokens to the fairground guy and we went through. Sonya pressed herself against the wall and I moved in next to her. Our fingertips touched as the drum began to spin.

'Here we go!' She squealed.

I was slammed against the metal like a dead fly, my hot dog squeezed into mush. The floor fell away from us and Sonya was just a blur of screams and pink jumper. Our fingers slipped apart and now I couldn't turn my head to see her. She was shouting or was that the girl across from me? Or me? The blood was pumping through my head like it was looking to burst out. And that mustard. I swallowed, swallowed, swallowed.

It slowed down, then stopped. Sonya grabbed my sleeve, laughing.

'You all right, Marlon?'

'Yeah. Perfect.'

We stood there looking at each other, just for a second. Our hands locked again and we staggered off together, her shoulder nudged against mine so her hair brushed against my face.

If we have kids together, what will their hair look like?

Kids? I haven't even kissed her yet!

If I did kiss her now, she'd taste of hot dogs and fun. All I had to do was bring her towards me, put my other hand on her back and stoop down a bit.

She was looking at me.

'What are you thinking, Marlon?'

'Spaceships.'

How the hell had that been in my head?

She didn't run away though. She giggled. 'Why?'

I had to get this back, but my mouth had become an independent life form. 'The fairground. All the noise is like when the spaceship takes off. The flashing lights are when the engines go online and the gravity goes, and . . .'

Quick as it came to life, my mouth died.

'Er . . . right.' She stopped and let go of my hand, but it was okay. She was stroking my back now. The spine. Dead centre. 'They must have cut these pills with something really good.'

My stomach blipped, but I made my voice casual. 'Like what?'

She giggled again. 'Fairydust.'

I waited for her to walk away, straight on the phone to her mates about the moron she'd dumped in the park. But that didn't happen. Her hand worked its way up my back until she was tickling the hair on my neck. My follicles tingled, and my skin was straining up to her fingers like a happy cat.

And she said, 'Go on, Marlon. Tell me more about the spaceship.'

Kiss of life to my mouth. 'I know it's kind of geeky, but my dad was a Trekkie. Not just *Star Trek*, all of it, *Next Generation*, *Wrath of Khan*, everything. And *Star Wars* and *Blade Runner*, he was into that too. Even the really old stuff, like *Space 1999*.'

She stuck her fingers under my cap and twisted one of my plaits. 'Maybe everyone here's really an alien and we're the only humans.'

'Some people really think that,' I said.

She widened her eyes. 'Serious?' Her finger moved back down my neck until its path was stopped by my t-shirt. 'Go on, then!'

She was tracing shapes across the fabric, drawing circles on the knobbly end of my spine. *Speak, Marlon!*

She said, 'Come on! Tell me about all the abduction stuff!'

'It's not really abduction. Some people have got this

thing wrong with their brain, which means they never remember faces. It's called prosopagnosia.'

Luckily I managed to miss her with the bucket load of spit that came with saying that.

She raised her eyebrows, like she was impressed. 'So they don't recognise no one?'

'Kind of. It's more like they don't really remember what a face is. They think it could be an umbrella, or a hat, or, I don't know, a banana. So they might think their mum was an alien or something.'

Sonya breathed out heavily. 'Yeah, I can understand that. I sometimes think my mum's from another planet. How do you know all this stuff?'

'You know I told you about my brother?'

She nodded.

'When he was in hospital, the doctors gave me and Mum loads of neuroscience stuff to read. And then, I don't know, I just kept reading.'

'That's cool. Maybe you can be a brain surgeon.'

I laughed. 'How many brain surgeons do you know from Hackney?'

She poked my back. 'There may be some. Or you could be the first. You could really do that, Marlon.'

This was it. Now. With her face tilted sideways, looking at me with that smile. She had dimples! Why hadn't I noticed before? Perhaps she hadn't smiled this way before.

My throat was all sandy and my mouth tasted of metal, but I could just touch my lips against hers. Starters.

I reached my arms around her and she moved towards me, like she knew the routine. She wouldn't let me if she wasn't happy about it. But she was happy, because her fingers were stroking my neck again. She was looking right at me. Around me. Behind me.

She stepped back, taking her hand away. My bare skin seemed to stretch out to her. I needed her to touch me again.

'Sorry,' I said. 'I thought you wanted to—'

'Not now.' It was like she'd put a forcefield up all around her.

I touched her arm. 'What's wrong?'

She shook her head and pulled away from me, stalking across the fairground. I stood there staring at the roughed up grass and rubbish. Was this a game for her? Had she got a mate filming this for YouTube? No. I was getting para again.

'Sonya!' I called. 'Wait!'

Her flash of pink jumper was disappearing through the crowds. I squinted. She wasn't by herself. There were three boys, brushing round her, much too close. One was a black kid with cane row. Him and a skinny white kid with a bike were on one side of Sonya. I reckoned that they could be the same age as me, but I didn't recognise them.

The last one wore an old Stussy cap with his hood up, so the shadow made it hard to see his face. He was taller than the others, maybe a bit older. Then the black one turned around and stared right at me, a proper, hard screwface look.

What the hell?

It's her boyfriend. He's come for her.

I let my eyes drop, then looked again. He was walking away, the others sloping after him. Something far back in my brain started itching. Who was he?

'Sonya!'

I pushed towards her. All the dads out with their kids were looking at me, at her, then at me again. None of them were getting out the way. She was up ahead, standing by the Ghost Train, rubbing her face. Her eyes were shut. I stopped in front of her, went to touch her shoulder, but let my hand drop.

I said, 'Why d'you run off like that?'

She opened her eyes and stared right through me.

'I thought I was going to throw up,' she said, at last. 'But I'm okay now. It must have been that ride.'

'Those kids, were they hassling you?'

'I know them.'

'Yeah, the black one, I thought I recognised him too.'

She shrugged. 'Maybe you do. I don't know your life.'

Sonya?

'It's just, I thought, one of them might be your boyfriend, or something!'

'You what? You think I pass between boys? You really think that?'

No! The words came out wrong!

'Serious, Marlon! If you think that, you can just fuck off now. Actually, maybe it's best if you do.'

Her face was pale and she was screwing up her eyes like the air was too bright.

I waited a second, like I did when Andre went off on one, and kept my voice low. 'D'you think the pill's making you feel a bit dodgy?'

'No, Marlon! I don't!'

'Are you sure?'

'Just clear off and leave me alone!'

She was loud enough for people in the queue to turn around and look at us.

'Okay,' I said quietly. 'I'll go.'

But neither of us moved. Then Sonya jammed her knuckles into her eyes and her body hunched. When she took her hands away, green eyeliner was smeared down her cheek.

'I'm really sorry.' She rested a hand on each of my shoulders, with her forehead on my chest. 'I didn't mean to be such a bitch. My head feels like I've been shot between the eyes.'

'We can go somewhere quiet, if you want.'

'No, I'll be fine. It's sort of like a migraine and they come and go dead quick.'

Don't breathe too hard. Don't jog her head. Don't start her off again. Just—

I wrapped both my arms around her, breathing in slowly like I was drawing her into me. I closed my eyes and let my chin touch the top of her head. A massive group of kids swarmed past us, jumping around and singing the chorus to 'Thriller'. But it was okay, because I could hold her steady.

'Thanks, Marlon. I feel a bit better now.'

'Cool.'

'Do I look okay?'

'Yeah, great.' *Perfect.*

She grinned. 'You wouldn't tell me if I looked shit, though, would you?'

It would have been good to run through some of this stuff with Tish first. She'd have told me the right answer to that one.

Sonya was scrabbling in her little bag, probably looking for her tissue again. She glanced around quickly and pressed something into my palm. She was squeezing my fingers shut around a plastic pouch.

I looked down at my hand. 'What are you doing?'

'A present,' she said. 'We can share them.'

'What is it?'

She rolled her eyes. 'You know what it is. There's six there.'

Six Ecstasy pills, clenched in my fist. 'I can't take these.'

Her face clouded over. 'Why not?'

Because Mum thinks I'm at home with my nose in a book and she'll have a breakdown if she knows what's in my hand.

Because boys like me don't walk round Hackney with a pocket full of drugs.

Because . . .

'I just can't.'

She shrugged, then covered my fist with her palm.

'Aren't you enjoying this, Marlon? Me and you being together?'

'Yeah . . .'

'We can have a picnic tomorrow, if the weather's nice. Take another half each and just lie back and enjoy it. But it's okay,' she said brightly. 'I know you're supposed to be doing your revision. I don't want to get you in trouble.'

'Sorry. I just can't.'

She blinked two, three times, quickly, then smiled. One hand covered my fist, the other moved round my back, fingers pressing my t-shirt against my skin.

'It's not fair I take all the risk,' she said. 'If I'm a bit bad, you have to be a bit bad too. We can be bad together.'

Tomorrow, on a blanket lying side by side staring at the

clouds, her blonde hair like sun. I'd lean over her and she'd close her eyes, reach up and pull me towards her. She was looking up at me again. Her lips were still shiny. If I kissed them, would my mouth be shiny too?

'Well?' she asked.

I shoved the pouch deep into my jeans pocket. I moved to put my arm around her, but she wriggled away.

'Come on!' she said. 'Let's go on this!'

'The ghost train? They're always crap!'

Her thumb stroked the backs of my fingers. It was like pressing a lever; a dam opened and all my endorphins came rushing out. She moved her lips close to my ear. 'It's dark in there. You can balls it.'

'What?'

'The pills. You know, stick them down your pants. Make sure they're safe.'

How'd she know about that? I only knew because that was one of Andre's old mates' tricks. Sometimes they'd even wear two pairs of joggers to make sure their stash was good and snug.

I said, 'Yeah. Sure.'

I handed over more yellow tokens to a kid in a red jacket. Even he did a double-take at Sonya. I smiled right back at him.

It was a tight fit in the carriage, even though neither one of us was fat. The bar pushed down on my thighs. My jeans were rubbing against Sonya's, the pouch in my pocket squeezing against her hip. I was never going to get it out and in my pants here, not unless she was going to help me.

Jesus, Marlon. Show some respect! My brother may have worked his way round two local sixth forms by the time he was my age. But I didn't want *gyals*. I wanted one girl, this girl, sitting next to me. I'd risk the Portaloo afterwards and stash the pills then.

I rested my arm along the back, my fingertips in Sonya's hair. Just a few millimetres away, Sonya's head was full of thoughts. I wished I could see them.

The carriage slammed through the door into total blackness and the air seemed to wobble with the noise.

'Mum and Dad used to take us to Littlehampton,' I said. 'I was only four, but even then I knew the ghost train was pretty crap.'

She didn't answer me, but she probably hadn't heard. It was hard to hear anything with the mad volume soundtrack, groans and shrieks, rattling chains and banging doors, probably ramped right up to stop us thinking about how sad everything was. I peered into the gloom. Light flashed on and off grey witches with enormous noses and plastic bones the colour of old butter. An ogre shrieked in a corner and somewhere far back, a kid screamed. They didn't sound like they meant it.

But the light was weird in here, like they'd sucked every

16

bright colour into a hole. I looked down at my hands; they were grey. Sonya's fingers jerked on the bar, then she relaxed back. I covered her hand with mine, the same way she'd done with me.

A zombie poked its head out of a hole and bellowed at us.

I laughed. 'Look at that one! You can see the strings holding it up!'

Sonya didn't reply, didn't even look at me. Maybe, and my chest hurt thinking this, maybe she really didn't want to be with me after all.

We bumped to a stop. I flexed my arm, my fingers catching for a moment in her hair. Still no reaction. I turned to her, but she was staring straight ahead. A fairground guy released the bars of the carriage in front. He was waving a severed head, making the little kids squeal. It was a rubber and plastic thing, with eyes that rolled up and down.

'Sonya?'

The severed head was coming our way now. What would she do if I just dropped the pills in her lap and went off and left her?

'Sonya?'

The fairground guy was standing in front of us, the head drooped in his hand. His lips were moving, like he was singing her a song.

'Sonya!' I nudged her shoulder. Her head slumped

forward, her hands still gripping the bar. A smear of bright mustard blazed on her sleeve.

God . . .

Her neck was all bent over, not the way bodies should be. If I turned away, if I blinked long and hard, she'd sit up and laugh at me. This was her joke. It couldn't be real.

The bar yanked up, the men pulling Sonya from the seat, me trying to stumble after them. Strangers laying Sonya on the floor, hands pumping her chest making her body jolt around. A man's mouth pushing air through her – *shiny* – lips. The silence when the first aider leaned away from her.

And that kid with the cane row, just there behind the barrier.

No, all this must be a brain glitch, the Ecstasy tickling way too hard.

The shriek building in the bottom of my throat, that was real.

2

A bloke in a high-vis jacket had his arm round my shoulders, pulling me. I couldn't walk; my legs kept rolling away.

'Easy,' he said. 'I've got you.'

I strained to look back, past the wall of people, at the shape lying on the ground. A coat was spread across Sonya's chest. A man was kneeling beside her with his face in his hands. The woman standing behind him shook her head. And the kid with cane row – nowhere.

'Where are we going?' My words were lost in the sirens blasting towards me. An ambulance pulled up close to the ride, followed by police vans and police cars.

'You need to sit down.'

The steward had gone and I hadn't noticed. I'd been passed on to the coppers. The policewoman put her arm round my shoulders, gently, like the way I'd tried with Sonya. Her copper mate looked like he should be rowing a Viking longboat. He was scanning me up and down.

'What happened?' The words crumpled, but they must have understood.

The policewoman said, 'We need you to help us find out.'

They led me to one of those stalls where you throw a hoop to win a prize. Viking pulled together three red plastic chairs. I needed that seat badly.

The woman said, 'I'm PC Bashir. What's your name?'

'Marlon. Marlon Sunday.'

She nodded towards Viking. 'This is PC Sanderson. Marlon, we need to ask you a few questions. Before we start, do you need a drink? Water? Tea?'

'I . . .' The copper fuzzed out for a second. All those lights across my brain had snapped off and I was in deep darkness. I gripped the edges of the seat to stop myself pitching forward. As I shifted, the pouch of pills pressed into my side, a proper 'here-I-am' poke. The police must be deaf if they didn't hear that.

'Marlon? Are you okay?' Bashir looked concerned. Viking didn't seem bothered at all. If I collapsed on the floor, he'd probably complain about the trouble of stepping over me.

Sick joke. You're sitting here, alive. And Sonya . . .

Something heavy and sour was rising in my throat. I swallowed hard.

I said, 'Can I have some hot chocolate, please?'

Viking gave me an annoyed look, but Bashir smiled. 'I'm sure we can find some somewhere.'

She called over a yellow-coater. I looked across the park. The police had come quick; they must have been here already, checking out the crowd. I suppose they had to since that bloke got caught in gang crossfire in London Fields. Now they were making themselves busy. One copper was talking to the fairground guy who'd had the severed head; they looked over at me and the copper made some notes. A load of them were cordoning off the ghost train, leading the people still in it out the other way. The kids must have thought it was part of the experience.

All the other rides were stopping and turfing people off, the crappy songs cut off one by one until the only loud voices were blasting through the megaphones, mixing with a new lot of sirens. The proper numbheads had their phones up so they could capture this moment forever.

That had been my plan for later, a picture of me and Sonya together, first thing I'd see when I woke up.

She'd been right next to me when she—

I should have rubbed her fingers to keep the last warmth. I should have stroked the hair back over her shoulder. Because life can't jump away from someone that quick, can it? Not so you can't reach it. In hospitals they bring people back all the time.

My fingers were ice cold now, my toes too, like the day had shoved itself back into January. But the sky was still bright blue with skinny clouds and I could see the tip of the moon.

'This for you?' A fairground worker was standing over

21

me, holding out a plastic cup.

'Thanks.'

It was dark brown water, scalding hot and it tasted like chocolate toothpaste. It must have come from a sachet. But the heat and sugar made my brain focus.

'Just a second, Marlon.'

Bashir and Viking were being summoned over by another copper and they stood in a little huddle nearby. Viking stared at me over Bashir's shoulder. My brother, Andre, would have stared right back, disappointed if he wasn't offered the challenge. But I *wasn't* Andre. I turned away from Viking and dug into my jacket pocket. I wasn't under arrest or anything. They couldn't stop me from making a call. As soon as I hit eleven years old, Andre made sure I knew the rules.

I had less than a quid of credit left and a tiny bar of battery. Mum or best mate?

My fingers felt like they belonged to a drunk tramp.

Please, not voicemail. Please pick up.

'Marlon?'

Thank you! Thank you! Thank you!

'Marlon? Where are you? What's that noise?'

'Sirens. Tish, I'm at the fair—'

'Me too! But they're doing some idiot thing, closing everything down. I was having a crap time anyway. I was supposed to meet a friend, but he's not answering.'

'Tish?'

'Who d'you go with? Why didn't you ask me?'

'I was with Sonya Wilson.'

Silence.

'The one from school? With the big blonde hair?'

'I think she's dead, Tish.'

More silence, then a scream of laughter.

'Hilarious! Sick, but hilarious. It would have worked if you'd used someone else. Melinda, maybe, or Bryn. But Sonya Wilson? I'd have to believe *that* first.'

'Yeah? Thanks, Tish.' I hung up and tried to stand, but my legs still weren't working.

'Take it easy!' Viking Sanderson had finished his conversation. He sauntered over and leaned back on the counter watching me.

I sat down again. Bashir was talking to a paramedic by the ambulance. Behind those screens, they must have lifted Sonya on to a stretcher, taken her in and closed the door. I buried my head in my hands and squeezed my eyes shut, though I had to open them quick again. Sickly yellow was swirling through the black, Sonya's hair, the counters, the mustard smudge on her sleeve. I could smell it too, like old rancid hot dogs. My forehead prickled with sweat. I retched, but nothing came up. Viking just stood there, still watching.

Bashir came back as my phone started vibrating in my pocket.

23

Viking raised his eyebrows. 'Not going to answer it?'

I shook my head.

The coppers settled themselves down, Bashir leaning forward. 'What's your girlfriend's name?'

My girlfriend. 'Sonya. Sonya Wilson.' I took a little sip of minty chocolate.

'Any others? A middle name?'

I promised not to tell . . .

'I don't know.'

'Her date of birth?'

'I don't know.'

'Was she the same age as you, Marlon?'

'She's seventeen.'

'And how old are you?'

'Sixteen.'

Viking and Bashir looked at each other.

Viking said, 'Do you have her address?'

I shook my head. 'She was staying in Streatham, that's all I know. She's really . . . ? Is she . . . ?'

Bashir bit her lip. 'We need your address, Marlon. And a phone number.'

I told them. Viking even rang my number from his phone to make sure it was right. He sat back. 'What did you do to Sonya?'

'What? Nothing!'

'You sure about that?'

Pressure behind my eyes, my nose.

Not here! I can't cry here!

Bashir cut in. 'It must all be an immense shock for you.' She dropped her gaze for a second, then lifted her head and met my eyes full. 'Marlon, we've heard reports that Sonya was shouting at you by the ride. Is that true?'

I nodded, sniffed hard, and again.

No. Not in front of the coppers and everybody. Not with all those idiots hovering by the barrier ready to get a good look.

I breathed in hard, held it.

Bashir offered a tissue. 'I think we should call your parents, don't you?'

I wiped my nose, scrunching the wet tissue in my palm.

'Your mum, Marlon. Can we have her number, please?'

I just about managed to stutter it out.

'Her name?'

'Jennifer. Jennifer Sunday. She's working today. At the library in Willesden.'

'And your dad?'

'He's dead.'

'Oh. Sorry.'

Everyone always was. Even though they'd never met him.

'Anyone else?'

'No.'

'So, Marlon.' Viking was never going to be the one

handing out tissues. 'What did you say to Sonya to upset her like that?'

'Nothing! She had a headache!'

'A headache?'

'Yes.'

'Had she been drinking?'

'No!'

Bashir's pen was poised over her notebook. 'Anything else?'

'Like what?'

I clenched my lip between my teeth. Bashir was scribbling hard. Why? I'd hardly said anything.

She balanced her notebook on her lap, lay the pen on top. 'Do you know if Sonya took anything that could have hurt her?'

Fairydust.

The pills must be calling to the coppers like Frodo's ring. Viking was right on the edge of his chair.

He said, 'A complete stranger tried to save your girlfriend's life. He was in the queue with his kid when he saw what was happening and he came to help her. You saw him afterwards, didn't you? You don't forget that stuff quickly.'

I knew that.

Bashir again. 'If Sonya took something that hurt her, you may have taken it too. You might need medical care.'

Viking was shaking his head. 'Think about Mr Ibrahim, Marlon. He has to go home and tell his wife that a young woman died in front of him. He'll tell her that he tried as hard as he could to save her life. Maybe he'll always be wondering if he could have tried harder.'

'We need to know what you know, Marlon.'

The coppers' eyes weren't moving off my face. My heart was straining so hard my skin must be one big pulse beat.

'It was nothing!' The words burst out of me.

Bashir said softly, 'What wasn't anything, Marlon?'

'She – we – took some Ecstasy.'

Now my hip was jumping with the pulse – six little beats in their plastic pouch. My fingers brushed my pocket and I jerked my hand away.

Viking narrowed his eyes. 'How much Ecstasy?'

I couldn't look at him. Anything else but him. My best Pumas, Bashir's sensible shoes, the muddy wheel tracks leading up to the ghost train and the ambulance with Sonya inside.

'One pill? Five pills? Ten?' Viking was almost shouting. 'How many, Marlon?'

'Nothing much! Just a quarter!'

'Just a quarter?'

'Yes.'

'You got the rest on you?'

'What do you mean?'

'Marlon!'

The coppers looked towards the voice. I stood up, Viking just as quick. Tish was ducking the cordon, sweeping past the copper who was trying to block her way. She ran straight up to me and threw her arms around me. My eyes were stinging and I had to swallow hard, keep swallowing, so I'd be able to talk.

'Jesus, Marlon! What the hell's going on?'

I tried to say her name, but just over her shoulder I saw two tall coppers striding over.

Bashir said, 'We have to search you, Marlon.'

Tish faced the cop up. 'What you on about?'

'Tish.' My tongue was thick with dry spit.

'Marlon?' Tish moved back from me. 'What's going on?'

'We took Ecstasy.'

'Who? You? You're kidding me, right?'

No. I wasn't. She could damn well see I wasn't. My body, my hands, everything was shaking. The coppers told me to turn away and I held out my arms and stood with my legs apart. I closed my eyes, but it made their hands stronger, patting me up and down like they were trying to clear away dust. The pouch squeezed against my hip. The patting stopped and their fingers were in my pocket, yanking it out. My arms were pulled behind and the handcuffs slammed on.

3

It was a cell on wheels, bars, grille, metal, jammed into the back of a transit. No Tish, though she'd been close to getting thrown in too, under arrest.

Under arrest!

They thought I was responsible. Sonya Wilson asked *me* out. It was the best thing that ever happened to me. I was buzzing about the picnic with her tomorrow, seeing a film with her next week. And they think I killed her.

The van suddenly stopped and I slid along the seat.

Once I got to the police station, I'd have to face Mum. After all the other stress, I'd promised I'd never make her come to a police station for me. Promise broken. Big time.

First thing this morning, though, when the door clicked shut and Mum went off to work, I'd made myself squeeze any promises to her out of my head. I'd taken a good, long shower and put on my jeans. They were the ones I got last year in American Apparel. But today was special. I took them off and put on the Nudies. I'd been saving them for an occasion like this. Did I need a shave? Keep the stubble or crank up new razor bumps? Mum hadn't moaned at me yet, so I'd save the shave. I tried three t-shirts, holding each one up to the light, just in case there were forgotten stains. I was pretty sure Andre knocked some juice over the green one, but I couldn't see any marks now. It didn't matter. The grey one looked best. I needed a haircut, but I'd have still been sat at the barbers until midnight, listening to them talk crap about their girlfriends. So I'd used a slick of Daks to smooth down the rough edges between my plaits, creamed my face and I was ready to go.

Except I was three hours too early.

Some of my promises to Mum were creeping back into my head, so I'd laid out my revision books. I put on some Stevie, then some Donny Hathaway, then Chaka. But the Chaka was Tish's favourite so that came off. I didn't need her in my head. I hadn't told Tish anything about Sonya and she was going to be vexed when she found out I hadn't shared. Roberta Flack? No. That was like slow-dancing in your bedroom by yourself. So back to the usual, from Dad's old vinyl, Earth, Wind and Fire's *Faces*. The blonde girl in the top left of the cover – if her hair was longer, that could be Sonya. And me? Maybe the bloke with the beard and 'fro, bottom left at the back. But without the beard and 'fro.

All that time in my bedroom, willing the minutes to flick past quicker, could have been a year ago.

The police van stopped and stayed stopped. The back doors opened. A short, thin copper, Sikh-looking, eyed me

30

up like he was waiting for an excuse. They'd probably done a search, thrown up Andre's name and rubbed their hands together when they saw little brother was coming in. Andre was off the street now, but he'd stamped his name hard into the territory.

They led me into the station. It must be the small red brick one near home. I'd passed this place so many times and never been in, not like Mum, who probably had a seat with her name on it. The medical examiner checked me over, asking me a few questions. She said the drug should have worked its way through me if it was just a quarter and nothing else. I shouldn't drink too much water, or any alcohol, tell someone if I started feeling sick.

And then they said Mum was here. She could come into that little room if I wanted, while they searched me. Proper searched me. Yeah, my mother could watch me pull down my trousers, and my pants. No, I didn't want that. How would we ever look at each other again? I had to pretend I was a different person, in a different time and space. And all the time, they were calling my name politely like they were checking me into a VIP suite.

Except next stop was the cell. The stink hit me as soon as I entered the corridor. It was drunk puke and sewers, like every scrap of something nasty had been scraped out of Hackney gutters and smeared across the walls. My mouth greased up with stench stew.

The copper shrugged. 'You shouldn't be in here too long.'

The door clicked shut. I sat down on the skinny plastic mattress, then lay down and curled up. Hundreds of people's sweat must have rubbed against it, spit too, if they were dribblers. And the air conditioning was blowing so hard it could take off my skin. I pulled the blanket up over my face.

That last copper was having a laugh. One day, two days, they could keep me here. Or maybe it was more. I tried to breathe but the air was too heavy. I pushed my nose into my hand. After four minutes or so with no oxygen, brain cells were permanently destroyed. Maybe I could hold on for five.

No! I had to stop this. Every day, all over the world, in London, in Hackney, people did worse. Six pills. That was all I had on me. Except, it didn't have to be about the number, did it? Those guys who died over in Wales, it probably took just one of those shabby pills, dissolving crap through their system. The dealer was getting slammed inside whether he sold one or twenty of them.

So what was I going to tell the police?

'Nut'n.' That was Andre's number one arrest rule. 'Don't say nut'n, then mandem can't say nut'n 'gainst you.' Don't admit, don't deny, shut your mouth like the FBI . . .

Let the police do all the work. Make them prove their case.

I had six pills in my pocket. Was I going to deny that?

And a dead girl next to you. Are you going to deny that?

I needed to calm down and get my thoughts in order, or else when they put me in that interview room, my mouth would go mad. I folded down the blanket so the cold air hit my face. That helped. Now for calm thoughts, sensible thoughts, in neat columns. Make a list. Parts of the brain? No, not that one, not now. The periodic table, the one left spread open on my bed. No, that was just coming up a page of blank boxes.

Music, then.

Faces. I'd been staring at the cover – it could have been months ago, years. It was Earth, Wind and Fire's tenth album. Dad had them all, in vinyl, stacked up in order of release. He got the first one, *Earth, Wind and Fire*, specially sent from America and played it, Mum said, until the grooves smoothed out. First track, side one – 'Help Somebody'. Name all the tracks, all the albums, in the right order. If I ran out of EWF, who next? James Brown? Maybe. He was a man who knew the inside of a cell.

The police interview room was small and hot and the cell stink had wound itself inside. No matter how hard I scrubbed, I was never going to smell clean again. The copper told me that the duty solicitor was on the way and shut the door.

She was there. Mum. She jumped up so quick her chair fell back, her hand raised up. And she must have seriously wanted to knock me into orbit.

'Oh, Marlon!'

We stood there looking at each other. Then she came to me, hugging me to her, and the stupid part of me was ready to smile as the smell of her cocoa butter blanked out the cell rot.

She said, 'Did they treat you okay?'

'Yes.'

'The search? You didn't want me there?'

I shook my head. She tilted up my chin to make me face her. She looked much older than this morning, like she'd opened a jar and rubbed ten years into her skin.

'I'm sorry, Mum.'

She wiped her eyes. 'Jonathan said I should use his solicitors again, but . . .'

You were hoping it could be cleared up quick.

I said, 'I didn't hurt Sonya, Mum. I don't know what happened, but it wasn't me.'

She nodded. 'I want to believe you, Marlon. Like I believed you were in your room bent over your chemistry books. Because . . .' Mum sighed. 'Well, you understand, don't you?'

'Yes.'

'Do you know what happens next?'

'The duty solicitor comes and they interview me.'

She sat down on one of the hard wood chairs, all business now.

'Yes,' she said. 'That's part of it. But you know they'll do tests on . . .'

'Sonya.'

'They'll see what's in her blood and match it to yours. Is there anything I should know?' She took my hands. 'This is hard, Marlon. But if I'd asked your brother these questions the first time I was sat here with him, maybe things would have turned out different.'

She was trying to drill into my thoughts. I let my hands go slack, but she held on.

'So is there anything? Talk to me, Marlon.'

I looked around her, at the wall. 'We took some Ecstasy.'

'I know. Anything else?'

'No.'

'Look at me, Marlon.'

'No, just Ecstasy. It was a tiny bit, a quarter each and she gave me a few pills— '

Mum dropped my hands and they thumped to my side. 'So she wasn't the one getting caught if you were stopped.'

'No! It wasn't like that!'

'Where are you now?' Mum sat back sharply, making a point of looking round the interview room. 'You're in a police station! You did get stopped! You have to tell them the pills weren't yours, you hear me? Jesus! Why did you agree?'

Because tomorrow me and Sonya would be lying back in the grass together and both my arms would be around her.

The door opened. It was a young white guy in the kind of clothes they wore in Mum's Sunday magazines. He introduced himself – Damian or Daniel, or something. I pushed my brain to concentrate, but it kept swerving away, back to Sonya and her streak of pink jumper as we spun round in the Drum, her fingers all mixed up with mine.

The solicitor offered his hand for Mum and me to shake and sat down behind the table.

'Okay.' He unbuckled a large satchel and dropped some papers on the table. 'Intention to supply.' He read a few lines, breathed out really slowly. 'And a death.' His voice was quiet. 'You'd better tell me what happened.'

When me and the solicitor were done, the coppers came in. The sergeant was big, too much policeman trying to fit into a medium-sized uniform. His sidekick looked like Ol' Gil in *The Simpsons*. They started the tapes, did the introduction stuff and warned me about watching my words. If my mouth opened the wrong way, I could put myself in jail.

The solicitor had been clear – the cops wouldn't go easy. This was a first offence and for straightforward possession,

Damian, or Daniel, or it could even have been Darren, said, I should be coming out of here with a caution. I hadn't got any previous and no matter how much they tried to link me to my brother, they were going to fail. Even Andre didn't want me getting caught up in the life he was living. If they wanted to go tougher and make a point, they'd push on the intent to supply, but they'd have to prove that the drugs were mine and I'd given them to Sonya.

Maybe – and the solicitor had looked a bit embarrassed when he'd said it – Sonya might be on the police records. He'd caught my eye and looked at Mum instead. As Mum nodded back, I wanted to shout at her. *Sonya's dead! She can't even answer for herself!*

For a moment though, I saw inside Mum's head. A pretty blonde girl had died. And me, I was the Hackney youth with the gangboy brother. The papers would be quick to pick up on it, probably scanning Facebook for a photo already. *Drug-Toting Gangboy 'Kills' Innocent Girl*, with pictures of us both underneath for compare and contrast. Things hadn't been that bad with Andre, but it had got close. He'd been named and shamed in the local paper once and Mum had just wanted to die.

I glanced round at her; she was sitting rigid and upright, like she was waiting to pounce. The solicitor was next to me, ready if I wanted to stop the interview and ask for more advice.

Want to give me some advice? Tell me how to make Sonya come alive again.

They started with all the easy stuff – what time I got to the fair, what me and Sonya did there, how we ended up on the ghost train. They nodded like they believed me when I told them about the headache.

The sergeant sat back behind the desk. 'Are you a regular drug taker, Marlon?'

Sly git!

Mum shifted in her chair and I felt her hand, steady on my shoulder.

'No,' I said. 'I've never taken drugs before.'

The sidekick gave a little nod, a half smile. 'Nothing? I thought everyone smoked a little weed these days. Isn't it a bit like a rite of passage? Instead of a fag behind the bike shed, everyone has a little spliff, don't they?'

This time Mum leaned right forward.

'My son does not take drugs.'

The sergeant leaned forward too. 'Unless you're with your son every minute of every day, Mrs Sunday, how can you be sure? His girlfriend just died after taking Ecstasy with him. You weren't there then.'

Mum moved her chair until I was sandwiched between her and the solicitor. She faced the copper square on. 'I do know, because I take the trouble to talk to my son and find out what's happening in his life.'

Sidekick raised his eyebrows, turned back to me. 'So did you tell your mum about the Ecstasy, then?'

I felt my cheeks heat up. Lucky, brown skin's good for hiding that.

The sergeant said, 'So it was your first pill?'

'It was my first anything.'

The words bounced off the table, strong, just how I needed them. Mum's eyes were hot on the side of my face. She leaned back, then the sergeant leaned back, like they were playing 'Simon Says'.

'What about Sonya?' The sergeant said. 'Was it her first time too?'

'How do I know?'

The sergeant frowned. 'That's not very helpful.'

'No, Marlon, it's not.' Mum was glaring at me. 'Just tell them what you know, okay?'

She unzipped the pocket in her little leather bag and took out the plastic pouch with the pills. I bought a can of Coke to wash away the taste, letting her drink first because I wanted to follow, knowing her mouth had touched it. Want to know that, Mum?

'It's the first time we've . . . we'd been out,' I said. 'I didn't really know her that well.'

Sidekick nodded, like he was trying to be my mate. 'Sonya Wilson was a pretty girl. Bet you were pleased to get a date with her.'

Out of the corner of my eye, I saw Mum's foot jerking up and down. She only usually did that when she was trying not to be stressed about Andre.

It didn't bother Sidekick. 'You got the drugs to impress her.'

'I didn't get the drugs.'

The bouncing blip at the edge of my vision – Mum's foot, moving faster.

'A good-looking girl like that . . .'

How the hell would Sidekick know what Sonya looked like? Did he lift the blanket and have a peek? The thought made me shiver.

'So what was the plan, Marlon? A few thrills at the fair, then what? More pills? Maybe she had some friends you could sort out too.'

'What the hell do you mean by that?' Mum looked ready to be arrested herself.

The copper didn't break a sweat. 'You're Andre Sunday's mother. You should know.'

'Seriously?' She shook her head. 'It's been more than three years. Don't you lot let anything go?'

Sidekick opened his mouth, but his boss kicked in. 'It gets busy round here on weekends, Mrs Sunday. In the eighties, it was heroin, all around the estates. Now we've got the trendy clubs starting up. If you walk down Kingsland Road, there seems to be a new place every week. And along come a load of kids who think they're brave just by taking a few steps over the border from Islington. They want something to make their night have a bit of sparkle. What do you think, Marlon?'

'I don't know.'

The sergeant was fiddling with his wedding ring, like he'd pull it off if his thick knuckles weren't jamming it. 'I heard the E15 lot are serving up Dalston now.'

'I don't know.'

'They were your big brother's mates, weren't they, Marlon? They must be like family to you.'

Sidekick made a great show of thinking. 'What were their names? Dibz? Watchman? Ring any bells?'

'I am my son's family.' Mum's voice was almost a hiss. 'He is not part of any so-called gang. And those hooligans were not Andre's friends.'

Sidekick tried out his sad face. 'Of course. I'm sorry.'

Mum pushed her chair back, breathing out loudly.

The sergeant blew out his cheeks. 'So, Marlon, your story is that you took a tiny bit of Ecstasy and that's it.'

I checked with Damian who gave a tiny nod.

'And the rest was just for you and her.' Sidekick sounded weary.

'Yes.'

Then the sergeant said, 'Did you and Sonya sleep together?'

You what?

They just didn't get it! She was Sonya Wilson! I was Marlon Sunday! She wouldn't even let me kiss her.

The chair scraped beside me, but Mum didn't say anything. The coppers were sitting back, watching, as if the answers were scrawled across my face.

I said, 'What's that got to do with it?'

'The pathologist will examine her, Marlon.'

They were going to poke her and prod her, scrape out things and look at them. Maybe cut her up and sew her together again. Oh, Jesus. I gulped back half my glass of water.

Damian snapped to attention. 'Do you want to pause the interview?'

'No. It's okay.'

The sergeant continued. 'So you slept together then?'

'No.'

'She was your girlfriend, though?'

'Yes. No . . . Sort of.'

The coppers glanced at each other. The sergeant said, 'That's not a hard question, Marlon. Was she your girlfriend or not?'

Mum clapped her hands together, like she was praying. 'He told you. The answer is 'no'.'

Sidekick said, 'She wasn't your girlfriend. Is that right?'

I nodded.

The sergeant was twisting his ring again. 'How did you know Sonya?'

I kept my eyes on the copper's fat finger. 'From school.'

'Were you friends?'

I shook my head.

'So you just admired her from afar?'

Idiot! But I breathed in slowly. I wasn't going to give him the pleasure of seeing me stressed out.

I said, 'She was a couple of years above me. She was only there a few months.'

Sidekick nodded. 'The different age groups don't really mix, do they?'

The age groups? I didn't mix so good in my own year, forget about the others. The cool black boys stuck together, with a few white boys thrown in with them. The Turkish boys did their own thing. The kids with an eye on a university place lived in a parallel universe where the teachers smiled and seemed pleased to see them.

And where was I? Not cool enough, not clever enough, not street boy enough for anyone to take notice. I read books about the brain and listened to old funk. I was the kid people looked straight through. But last Thursday, things suddenly changed.

'So?' Mum's voice was quiet. 'How did you and Sonya finally meet?'

'She knocked on our door.'

43

'What?'

And I felt like I was falling through space when I saw her there.

'What the hell did she knock on our door for?'

Why didn't Mum just cross over the table and join the coppers?

I turned to face her. 'She said she knew Andre.'

'And you let her in?'

Sidekick looked like he was trying not to smirk. 'So, there's a blonde girl you know from school standing at your door. You let her in. Then what?'

'We talked.'

'Talked.' Mum spat it out like a swear word.

'Yes. Talked. She said she'd met Andre through a friend, but she'd only just found out what happened. So she thought she'd come and see how things were.'

'Three years late. That's nice of her.'

'Yes, Mum. It was.'

'Talked.' Still sharp in her mouth.

'Yes.'

Except it was me talking, and Sonya asking questions and listening like she was really interested. She wasn't even embarrassed when I told her about Dad dying and Andre's accident. She said there were weird things in her family too. She'd told me her other name, the one only her Mum called her.

44

We agreed to meet again at the fair on Saturday.

The sergeant wiped his face with his hand, stretching the skin so I saw the raw pink behind his bottom eyelid. 'Who gave you the drugs, Marlon?'

Andre always said you never grass. Not ever. I bit my lip.

'Your brother's mates?'

My teeth were going to break through the skin soon. I'd taste blood.

'Who supplied you with the drugs, Marlon?'

'Marlon.' Mum's hand was on my back again, like she wanted to press the answer out of me. 'Tell them the truth.'

Grass up the dead girl? Push all the blame on someone who isn't even around to defend herself?

Mum was pressing harder on my spine, so close to where Sonya's fingers had been.

'Tell them what you told me, Marlon. Tell them where the drugs came from. Please.'

'Please.' Like it was coming from the corner of Mum's soul.

I nodded and the pressure on my back eased. I made myself look the sergeant in the eye. 'The pills weren't mine. They were Sonya's.'

The coppers looked at each other.

Sidekick said, 'You're going to blame the girl who died, Marlon? Think how her mum and dad are going to feel.'

Mum couldn't hold herself back. 'You want my son to lie to make it easier for the girl's parents?'

The sergeant said, 'I'd say that's rather harsh, Mrs Sunday. A young woman died in your son's company and he was carrying a bag of Class A drugs. We need to be sure of the truth.'

I reached back and took Mum's hand. It felt as light as paper.

'I'm telling you the truth,' I said. 'I am not a drug dealer. I've never bought drugs and I've never sold them. Not even a little weed *as a rite of passage*. Sonya brought the pills with her. She asked me if I wanted to do some. And do you know what? I did. I really did.'

4

Sonya. With a 'y'. It was her middle name, but the one most people called her. Her real first name was something she reckoned her mum had made up – Siouxza. She'd written it down for me when we were in the sitting room, talking. Because yeah, that's all we did. Talk. She said only a few people knew about her proper name, so I was never to tell anyone. She even made me look her in the eye and promise silence.

And I'd kept my promise, even when the coppers were asking me questions. Siouxza was just for me.

Mum got us a cab home. We sat there, either end of the backseat, not talking to each other. There was no point; our words would have just fought with each other. As soon as we got home, I went straight upstairs.

Down below my bedroom, Mum was on the move. Doors were clicking open and shut, her footsteps tapped from the sitting room to the kitchen, the kettle fitted back on to its stand. I heard these noises every evening, but it was all sharper tonight, like my bedroom floorboards were a hologram and there was really nothing between me and downstairs. If I poked the floor, Mum might see my finger coming through the ceiling.

Siouxza. When she'd left, I'd picked up the scrap of paper and stared at her writing. Her 'x' was like two 'c's, back to back. Then I changed her from 'Sonya' to 'Siouxza' on my contacts.

My phone rang. What? *Siouxza?* I rolled off my bed and on to the floor, pulling the phone out the charger to check the name. My heart slowed to normal.

'Milo?'

Only one person called me that. I lay back on the floor.

'Tish. I was going to call you.'

''S'okay. I reckoned you had other stuff on your mind.'

'Yeah, you could say that.'

'Your mum's going mental, isn't she? She's been crying and everything.'

'Crying?'

'Yeah, that's what Mum said. Mum's vexed, Milo, hearing her friend all cut up like that. You better avoid her, man.'

Aunty Mandisa and the rest of the world. I lifted my head and let it thump back on the carpet. My thoughts felt sharper.

I said, 'The police tried to make out I was a drug dealer, Tish. Going on like I was hooked up to Andre's old lot.'

'Shit. Reckon your mum's going to put you on lockdown?'

'Probably.'

'Steamy shit. What are you listening to?'

'Donald Byrd.'

'That's the trumpet bloke, right? Don't start on the slitty wrist stuff.'

'I don't listen to slitty wrist stuff.'

'You forgotten the one about the pimps and junkies in Harlem? That's seriously slitty wrist.'

I laughed and a tiny bit of heaviness lifted. Tish was good at doing that. 'Okay. No Bobby Womack.'

She said, 'Still shaking?'

'A bit.'

'I bet the police had a real go.'

'Yeah. I mean a girl died next to me and I had drugs on me.'

'God, Marlon. It's really weird hearing you say stuff like that. You got bail, right?'

'Yeah.'

'They'll need to do some tests.'

'That's what the solicitor said.'

'Could be supply or possession.' I could almost hear her brain ticking. 'How many pills did you have on you?'

'Six.' Pulsing away in their pouch in my pocket.

'Could go either way, especially with Andre's record. Thing is, I reckon Sonya knew what she was doing. She'd already spotted the cops and wanted to make sure she was safe. That's why she gave them to you. Think about it, Milo.'

'Tish! Not now!'

'Yes! Now!' I could almost see her face, screwed up and vexed. 'If this comes to court, they'll probably throw all sorts of stuff at you. What if they find drugs in her system? What if they say you gave it to her and killed her? You have to get your story sorted, Marlon. The police are going to be prepared. You need to be too.'

I rubbed the bridge of my nose. My eyes felt like they were being hooked back into my skull.

'Marlon? You still there?'

'Tish, Sonya's dead. I was sitting right next to her and she died. One minute she was alive and the next minute . . .'

The ache in my throat again, the weight behind my nose and eyes.

Tish sighed. 'You weren't to know, Marlon.'

'I know. But then the police were asking me all these questions and I couldn't answer any of them. I didn't know if she had any brothers or sisters, nothing.'

A cough and muttering in the background.

'Tish? Where are you?'

'Out. I better go.'

'Is that . . . ?'

'Shaun, yeah. We're just sorting stuff out.'

'What about that girl who said she was pregnant?'

'Look, Milo, come round tomorrow. We'll talk about it, okay?'

The line went dead. Except, now Mum was knocking. I forced myself to sit up. 'Come in.'

She pushed open the door, carrying two mugs. She held one out to me. 'Hot chocolate. Sure you don't want something to eat?'

'No, thanks.'

She placed my mug on my bedside cabinet.

'Must admit, I haven't got much of an appetite either,' she said. 'But if you fancy anything later, there's some of that dhal in the freezer. If you nuke it for a couple of minutes it should be all right.'

Hot, yellow dhal. My stomach lurched.

'Can I stay?' she said.

'Yeah. Of course.' *Just please don't start on me.*

She sat down on my bed, hunching over her drink. I watched her ease the milk skin aside with her fingertips. Finally, she put the mug down beside mine without drinking from it.

'I trusted you, Marlon.'

'You can still trust me.'

'You lied to me. That's the hardest thing.' She sighed. 'I want to try and understand what you were thinking.'

Sonya held my hand and touched my face. She was

51

beautiful and wanted to be with me. That was what I was thinking.

I said, 'Sonya was special.'

Mum didn't show she'd heard me. 'I'm always telling them at work what a good boy you are.'

'Maybe we shouldn't always worry what other people think.'

'No?' She picked up her mug and took a sip. 'Every time I got another call about your brother, I told myself that. "It doesn't matter what other people think, he's still my son." Now I see some of the kids in Brent, the ones round here, on their bikes with their hoods up. Even if they're not doing anything, they're trying to look like they are. A boy was stabbed to death in Victoria Station, Marlon. Broad daylight.'

'I'm not . . .'

'They say it's as easy to buy a gun as a pint of milk.'

Or a book, or a comic.

'I'm not part of all that, Mum. You know that.'

'I thought I did.' She leaned over to touch my shoulder. 'Andre wasn't part of it all, not at first, was he? Not when he was five, not when he was nine, or ten. Then what happened?' She shook her head. 'Sorry, Marlon. I'm not being helpful, am I? Maybe you need someone else to talk to. Another man.'

'I don't . . .'

. . . need some stranger looking me in the eye and asking about my problems.

'I don't mean Jonathan.'

Good. How could he ever understand?

I reached up for my hot chocolate. Just a tongue touch though, because anything bigger was going to bounce off the knot in my stomach and come right back up again.

'Just think about it, Marlon, okay? There's a few projects around. I know I've put up some posters about them in the library.' Mum stood up. 'I'll probably be up before you in the morning. I've promised to help Jonathan with some paperwork first thing.' Her laugh sounded tired. 'He's completely ignoring the system I set up for him. I'll call you around ten to see if you're up for visiting Andre. He's already been on the phone twice to check I'm coming.'

'Sure. Thanks for the hot chocolate.'

'No problem. Sweet dreams.'

'I'll try.'

Midnight. I lay down on my bed and turned off the light. Three hours on FRANK and all those other drugs sites – none of them convinced me that quarter of a pill could kill you. The papers weren't going to print that bit, though. There wouldn't be enough room after they'd pulled me and my family to bits. All the old stuff mixed in with this, served up for Mum to read about over breakfast.

The day flashed through my head. It was like my thoughts were stuck in the Drum. As the ride stopped, two faces became clear. One was Sonya, the slick of blonde hair brushed over her shoulder. The other was the boy with the cane row.

The tree in front of the streetlight was making shadows across the walls. When I closed my eyes, the knocking in the radiator pipes was louder, like bony fists pummelling my head. I twisted on to my side, had to move again as my arm went numb. Then round on to my back. It felt like my bed was trying to get rid of me. And my head, if I could shine a torch into my brain, I'd see my neurons all tetchy and yawning.

If this was bad, on Monday I'd have to deal with all the numbheads at school.

I shoved off the duvet, climbed out of bed and lowered the needle on to Bobbi Humphrey's jazz flute. Tish thought this kind of music was deeply weird. Nudging the curtain aside, I looked out across the road, past the lit-up bus stop to Tish's house. Her bedroom window was dark, curtains drawn.

I kneeled down by my bed and looked underneath, at the sweatshirt and jeans I'd scrunched together there. I untangled the sweatshirt and held it close to my face.

Cell-stink. But across the shoulder, so close it looked like a rope, there was a blonde hair. I flipped off Bobbi and climbed back in bed, holding the sweatshirt close to me.

I woke up heavy and groggy. My dreams had been pretty full on; I'd tasted the pill's bitterness on my tongue, felt the cold gulp of the Coke and watched bony white fingers threading through mine. The fingers grew brown patches of skin that spread across to me and crawled up under my sleeve. It wasn't my sleeve, though. And as the skin crept its way across the face, it wasn't my chin or my nose or my forehead. The face twisted and gave me a hardface stare, dark spaces where the eyeballs should be.

I sat up. The sweatshirt was still crumpled beneath me. I stood up and drew back an edge of curtain, squinting at the brightness. Across the road, Tish's old-lady neighbour was being helped into the Rose of Sharon Ministry minibus. The guy on the other side of Tish was fiddling around in his garden. Further down the road, a Tesco van was pulled up, with a skinny bloke unloading crates.

Everybody had their Sunday plans. Sonya's mum and dad, maybe they'd had something arranged for today, something with their daughter. Maybe they were the sit-down-to-dinner type. Or the walk-in-the-park type. Or maybe her parents just plonked themselves in front of the *EastEnders* omnibus while Sonya did her own thing in her bedroom. But they would have known she was there. And now she wasn't going to be there ever again.

Downstairs, Mum had left a note tacked to the cereal cupboard, reminding me that she was round Jonathan's. She'd signed it with a big kiss, two strong diagonal lines, one over the other. Not two 'c's back to back.

I returned to my room, grabbed yesterday's clothes, and threw them all into the washing machine. I checked the sweatshirt first. The blonde hair had gone.

The click and whir of the washing machine motor on a Sunday – that was normal. I needed more of that. More normal. I turned on the radio and fiddled with the dial. Hymns, talking, Rihanna. The news came on, wars, murder, sports stuff. The weather – more heat. Now the local news. I didn't move, listening hard. There'd been a stabbing in Catford. Two men from Hillingdon were arrested at Heathrow airport. And yeah, there it was, tucked in afterwards. A 17-year-old girl died on a fairground ride in east London. Police were investigating the circumstances. The girl had not been named.

Yes, she had. She was called Siouxza.

I waited, but they moved on. I hadn't been named either. I turned off the radio. My phone was ringing upstairs. Tish, or Mum. As I started up towards it, it rang off. Then it started again. For God's sake! I was on the landing now . . . and the phone stopped. Silence.

Who's going to keep trying like that? Probably Yasir or one of the other school idiots. They'd keep giving it a go until they got me. Or it could be Sonya's parents, because now— Jesus! Someone was hammering the door like they wanted to smash through the wood. Who'd knock my door like that? Police? Journalists? There was a whole mob of coppers at the station, veterans from run-ins with my brother. Their eyes must have lit up when they heard my name. That Sikh one, he looked like he had history. He'd probably set up a direct line to *The Sun*.

I crept down from the landing, along the hallway to the front door. I squinted through the spy hole – nothing but the path. The letterbox flap sprung up and a finger jabbed my knee. I almost fell over backwards.

A mouth appeared in the space. 'Hurry up, Milo. I haven't got all day, you know.'

I breathed out slowly and opened the door. 'What the hell are you—'

Tish grabbed my arm and pulled me out, the door clicking shut behind me.

'Tish, man! I haven't got my keys!'

'Mum's got spares. You know that.'

'Where are we going?'

'Back across the road.'

The sunlight hit my face. It was going to be hotter than

yesterday; there were no clouds at all. It would have been a perfect day for a picnic.

'What's across the road?' I said.

'Me. What else do you need?' Her eyebrows shot up. Tish kept hers thick, not plucked to a thread like the other girls at school.

'You're welcome, Tish,' she said.

'What for?'

'My generous time.'

Tish twisted her key and bumped the door open with her shoulder, me following. Her house defied the laws of physics. Light bent through the windows and landed in different colours, though Tish's mum said the colour scheme was because she'd only had enough money to buy paint ends. The purple hallway led to stairs down to the kitchen, which was painted grey and covered in collages of photos. Their giant fridge-freezer was red, though you could barely see the original colour between the ticket stubs and cut-out newspaper faces. Mum wasn't so keen on the decorating. She complained that she needed sunglasses to go in and Nurofen when she came out, and it was nothing to do with the wine she always ended up drinking when she went over.

I said, 'Where's your mum?'

'Gone to the flower market. She's meeting up with some friends from her old school.'

'The one you used to go to?'

'Yep.'

Tish took a couple of glasses from a blinding green shelf; I poured the juice.

'You put in the pizzas,' Tish said. 'I'll get my laptop.'

'Pizzas? For breakfast?'

'There's no law against it.'

'Tish . . .'

'Pizzas, Marlon. I'm starving. Shaun took me to some crap restaurant last night and tried to make me eat bone marrow.'

I opened the freezer, burrowing past the ice cream tubs and lumpy plastic bags. I managed to manoeuvre out the pizzas without triggering an avalanche. I slammed the door shut, cold air puffing out on to my face.

Dead bodies in chilled drawers, click, pull open . . .

I rested my hot forehead against the fridge door.

'You all right, Milo?'

'Yeah. I didn't sleep much last night.'

'Not surprised. I tried to call you this morning. D'you see?'

'I haven't checked my phone yet.'

As I pushed myself away from the fridge, a ticket stub caught my eye. Hackney Empire panto three years ago; me, Mum, Tish and her mum had gone together. Next to it was the newspaper picture of me. A couple of days after Andre's accident, a *Gazette* journalist knocked on our door and asked me loads of questions before Mum came screaming down the corridor and dragged me away. God knows how they got the photo they used, an old school one, where I had a serious, knotty 'fro. Tish said she kept it in case I became famous and she could blackmail me.

I peeled away the green ticket next to it.

'Was this from the Year Seven talent show?'

Tish looked up from her laptop. 'Hmm.'

'I'm surprised you kept it.'

'What you trying to say?' But she was smiling.

'You got hammered by the Arethas.'

Tish shook her head slowly. 'I was pretty pissed off. It took me three months to learn those tricks and a fortune at Hamleys. But you saw what I was up against. Four refugee girls doing 'Say a Little Prayer' in harmony. Beyoncé couldn't have won that match. Second was cool.'

I nodded. She'd deserved first. I turned on the oven and took the pizzas out their wrapping.

'Stick them in now, Milo, and come over here.'

I slipped in the pizzas and pulled up a stool next to Tish. We were ear to ear, almost cheek to cheek. *You were this close to Sonya, and you didn't see her die.* Tish, though, was very alive. Her eyeballs twitched side to side and her eyelashes fluttered. Her fingers moved over the keys and her breathing became quicker as she clicked and scrolled.

'What are you doing?' I said.

'Checking out the stories. You know, about you and Sonya.'

'Jesus, Tish!'

'Aren't you curious?'

'No!'

'So why are you looking so hard?'

I turned away from the screen.

Tish shook my arm. 'Come on, Milo! This stuff doesn't happen to us every day!'

'Us?' I stood up so quickly my stool fell back. Tish was supposed to be my mate, but she was acting just like a standard school mankhead, digging around for all the juicy bits. It wasn't her who'd been sitting next to someone when they died. It all might as well be a plotline on *Eastenders*. 'It wasn't *us*! It was me!'

Tish slid off her seat, picked up my stool and sat back down again. 'I was just trying to help.'

'Help do what?'

'I don't know, Milo! Like I said, this sort of stuff doesn't happen to us – *you* – every day. I just don't want you going all mad over it.'

'Mad? Someone dropped dead next to me, Tish. And I didn't even notice!'

'Yeah . . .'

'I didn't see. Right, there, next to me!'

She was staring at me now because I was laughing. I was the nerdy loser, chatting away to a super-hot girl who died! It was funny! Really hilarious! And Tish's face, her mouth hanging open like a fish, her nose wrinkled like she was smelling something rotten, that was making me laugh so hard I wanted to throw up.

'Stop it!' Tish's voice cut through me.

I was panting. My cheeks hurt, my throat as well. I wiped my eyes with my sleeve.

Tish said, 'That's scary.'

I sat down. There was no noise now, except the fridge and the oven and a motorbike shooting past outside.

Tish said, 'You gonna tell me what's funny?'

I shrugged. 'I can't explain.'

'You looked a bit mental.'

I'd felt it.

'Maybe you should go to the doctor's,' she said. 'Get something to help.'

I shook my head. Mum said that stuff made you feel like a paper bag with a lit firework inside.

'Well, Milo, don't try that laughing crap at school tomorrow.' Tish was tapping on her laptop again. 'Remember *Trisha*?'

'Yeah?'

'Ever watch it?'

I was going to say 'no', but Tish narrowed her eyes.

'A couple of times,' I said. 'Dad used to have it on in hospital. Mum pretended to disapprove, but I reckon she secretly liked it.'

'Yeah, she's a chat show snob. My mum too.' Tish sat back. 'Anyway, they were showing some old *Trishas* on ITV once, when I was off school with tonsillitis. She interviewed this girl whose fiancé died when he was on holiday with his cousins. He got really drunk and tried to dive off his balcony into the swimming pool. His room wasn't all that high up, but he landed all wrong. Nowhere near the water.'

A body smashing to the ground, lying there all crumpled. The picture shone in my head. *Thanks, Tish, for that.*

'So she came on the show with one of the cousins,' Tish carried on. 'She said how much she'd hated them all. You know, proper hate, wanted them to die and everything.'

'Then what happened?'

'She stopped hating them. She talked to them and found out how crap they felt. Then she went to the place where it happened and laid some flowers there.'

'And?'

'I don't know, Marlon! You have to do something, or you're going to be laughing like a nutter all over the place!'

Tish was right. It was still there, just bubbling under.

63

I said, 'What if I went to see her mum and dad?'

'What?' Now Tish looked like she was ready to start laughing. 'That's a bit extreme, isn't it? Maybe we should just get some flowers and take them to the park.'

It all felt so clear now. 'I was the last person who saw her alive. There's things they'd want to ask me.'

'Like "Did you give her drugs?"'

'Then I'd have to tell them the truth.' The dullness was shifting inside me. 'Yeah . . . I'll go and see her mum and dad. The only way they'll know about me is from the police. It might help them if they see me properly.'

'They'll see you all right. The black kid with the gangsta brother who had a bag full of pills he's pinned on their daughter.'

'No, Tish. It really helped Mum when people talked to her about Dad. She said half her friends avoided her, like they were going to catch dying.'

'Sorry, Milo. It's a really crap idea. What happens if they call the police? What if you get arrested again?'

'It was your idea!'

'No! It wasn't!'

'You don't have to come.'

She sighed. 'Know anything about them?'

'No.'

'So when you find them, you're just going to knock on their door and introduce yourself?'

Yes. Like Sonya did to me.

Tish frowned. 'What?'

'Nothing.'

'You kind of smiled. I thought you were going to start nutter-laughing again.'

I shook my head.

'I'm not going to encourage you in this.' Her fingers bounced off the keys. 'Well, I am. But it doesn't mean I approve. So you don't know anything about her mum and dad. Name, nothing.'

'She said her mum's a bit weird.'

'Well, she can join the club on that one. Let's see what we can find.' More speedy finger work. 'Nothing on Instagram. Not in her name, anyway.'

'Would you use your own name?'

She laughed. 'It wouldn't matter. There's probably more than one Sonya Wilson . . .'

What about Siouxza? How many of them would there be, Tish?

Tish carried on talking. '. . . but I'm the only Titian Harding-Brooks. And there's a whole load of people I never, ever want to connect with again, so no. You don't know if she had a middle name or nickname, do you?'

'No. Well . . .'

Tish looked up, fingers poised. 'Did she?'

'No. Nothing.'

'Okay. Then it's back to the obvious then, isn't it?'

More clicks. Facebook.

'Let's hope she's not all private.' Tish looked at me. 'Do you still use it?'

'You'd know if I did.'

Eyes back on the screen. 'We all have our secrets, Milo.'

'What do you mean?'

She gave me a quick, surprised look. 'On Thursday afternoon, Sonya Wilson knocks on your door, completely out of the blue. Not worth mentioning, right? There any more secrets you want to share?'

'Probably not as many as you.'

'Yeah, funny, Milo. Here she is.' Tish pointed to the screen.

I breathed in, too loud, because Tish stared at me. But Sonya, in this picture, she really was stunning. It was a head shot and she was slightly turned away, still looking directly at the camera though, and smiling. She was at a party, with a couple of dressed-up people milling in the background. Her hair curled over her right shoulder, the blonde turned gold by the lighting.

The thing was, I'd tried to look for her before, after she came to see me. I just couldn't find anything in her name.

I looked away from the screen at Tish.

She said, 'It's funny how blokes still go for blonde girls.'

I felt a blush creeping up my neck. 'Yeah, the same way girls go for dumbheads.'

'Thanks for that.' She turned away. 'Only twenty-three friends. That's strange. Don't you think so, Milo?'

'Maybe she didn't want people to know who her friends were. Andre never really bothered with it all because he didn't want people to find out stuff about him.'

'Do you think she was mixed up with dodgy stuff?'

'I don't know. She had to get those pills from somewhere. Then there were these kids in the park. She said she knew them. But it was like she didn't want to know them.'

Tish looked up, interested. 'What d'you mean?'

'There were three of them, kind of dodgy, like they were after something. They sort of closed in on her and one of them stared at me. You know, proper gangman look. And it was kind of like I recognised him.'

'From school?'

'No. I don't know. Maybe he just looked like someone.'

'Did you ask her about it?'

'Yeah. She didn't say much.'

'Did you tell the police?'

'I saw three shifty kids at a fairground?'

'Yeah.'

'I might as well tell them I saw Batman.'

'It could be important. Maybe they can find some CCTV or something. Just a thought.' She was studying the

Facebook page again. 'It's weird, though. Someone like Sonya Wilson was always going to have more than twenty-three friends.'

I scanned the screen. 'Look at the comments. "Gorgeous sweet girl, never forgotten." "I was so shocked when I heard. Will miss u, hun." Four people liked that one. 'It's a memorial page.'

It was all upside down. Sonya didn't share anything about her life, but these strangers could 'Like' her death. All they had to do was click. In the picture, her smile was definitely a real one; it shone in her eyes.

'Perhaps there's another page for her,' I said. 'Before she died.'

'Who knows? Someone's put up some photos though. That's pretty quick. They must know her well.'

Tish clicked on an album. Thirty pics. Sonya as a kid with thin, brownish hair and a tooth missing, pretending to play a big guitar. Sonya on a bicycle. Sonya, twelve or thirteen years old, crouched by a Christmas tree, holding a bauble.

'What do you think?' Tish said.

'Haven't seen any parents yet.'

Back to the main page, with her beautiful face and the people below saying how sorry they were that she'd died.

Tish jumped off the stool to go and rescue the pizzas. I clicked on Sonya's Friends list. There were two people

I recognised from school. None of the other 'Friends' had proper profile photos. 'Aunty Bliss' used a photo of a poppy and 'Skunk' wasn't going to earn originality points for the black and white tail.

Tish put the pizzas face down on each other and cut them into gooey wedges. 'Margherita sandwich.'

One by one, I checked out her 'Friends'. 'I wonder who set this up.'

'Find the earliest comment and see what it says.'

'It's from someone called Bitter Rose: "I'm truly sorry. I wish I could change. I wish I could put the clock back, but it's too late. Sing me a song from heaven. M x"'

Tish bit into a slice of double-pizza. 'Whoo! Hot!' She fanned her mouth. 'Here, have some.'

Red and yellow. Ketchup and mustard. 'Later, thanks.'

'If you want some meat, I'll put some bacon on or something.'

'No, I'm fine, thanks.'

'Okay. What are you doing?'

'Looking up Bitter Rose.'

'Why?'

'M. That could be her mum.'

'Or it could be Michael. Or Maria. Who knows?'

'Yeah. That's why I'm going to have a look.'

Google offered teen novels and gaming vampire rituals.

'I'll try Yasni.' Tish took over, skimming the results,

scrolling the pages at high speed.

'You'd make a great hacker,' I said.

'I'd go into school records and mash them right up. Turn Mrs Ocean into a porn star. Hey! This looks interesting.'

A small scanned newspaper report. 'Bitter Rose, Faded Petals'.

Tish zoomed in on the grainy photo and the print below. 'They were a South London band. No good, unless you think "wild girls screaming" is a compliment. This was in the back of a pub in Highbury. 1989. Move on?'

I bent forward. Four girls, two with crew cuts, one with a Mohawk of dreadlocks and another with a big hat, half-hidden by a drum kit. A bassist, two guitars and the drummer. I squinted hard at the faces. Not a hint of Sonya.

Why should there be? They could be anybody.

Tish said, 'What is it?'

'It's just . . . well, there's that photo of Sonya with a guitar and this lot are from South London. I thought there might be some connection.'

'Don't get your hopes up, Milo. It's probably a coincidence, but it's the best thing we've found so far. Hang on a sec.' Tish tabbed back to the Facebook picture of kid-Sonya, one arm strained over the fret, other hand picking at the strings. Tish squinted at the screen, zoomed in and pointed. 'Look.'

I moved next to her, ear to ear.

'There,' she said. 'On the guitar.'

I saw it. Scrawled on the guitar body in black marker – *Bitter Rose*.

'So that must be her mum,' I said. 'On Facebook.'

'You don't know for sure.' Tish clicked over to the newspaper article. 'This is a rubbish picture. Even if one of them is her mum, you won't be able to see it. But look at this bit. Seems like they had one fan, at least.'

'"Where are they now?"' I read.

'Yep. Some people do have a lot of time on their hands. Where are they, then?'

I started with the half-hidden figure with the hat. 'Reeta Peter on drums.'

'Well, that's going to be her real name, isn't it?' Tish bit down hard on her pizza slice. 'What happened to her?'

'Became a social worker and moved to New Zealand.'

'Next.'

'Gloria Skank on vocals.'

'Oh my God!'

'Married a record executive and set up a music magazine. According to this, she now runs a small chain of health clubs.'

'Skanky health spas?'

I laughed, making sure I kept it light. 'Could be! It doesn't say. Then there's Melody Harmony, lead guitar.'

'Obviously taking the piss. Did she become a ballerina or something?'

'No.' I sat back from the screen. Tish moved forward, her greasy fingers curled into each other.

'A drug addict,' she said. 'In and out of prison.'

'Right.'

'And the last one. What does it say, Marlon?'

'Ruby Stunt. Now a midwife.'

The whole room was filled with the stink of hot cheese. How could Tish want to put that in her mouth?

She wiped her fingers on some kitchen roll. 'So we've got a midwife, the health spa woman, a social worker and a druggie. Any of them could be her mum. Or none of them at all.'

'The social worker's in New Zealand.'

'Okay. Rule her out then.'

'And no one who owns a load of health spas is going to send their kid to our school.'

Tish shrugged. 'You never know. That MP's son was in my year for a bit. But even so. That still leaves two. And there's loads more stuff to look through. Hang on while I wash my hands and we can do a bit more searching.'

'It's her.' I zoomed in to get a better look, but it just made a bad picture worse. Back out and there she was again, crew cut, glaring at the photographer, half hidden behind an amp. 'Melody. 'M'. It could be that, it doesn't have to be 'Mum'. It's got to be, Tish. All that stuff Sonya told me about moving school and her family being a bit weird. And who's embarrassed if their mum's a midwife?'

'Unless they've poisoned a load of babies.'

'Seriously, Tish!'

She rinsed her hands and dried them on her jeans legs. 'A bit extreme, I know. But you hear about it on the news. What about the other one?'

'The social worker in New Zealand?'

'Fair enough. So Sonya's mum's a crackhead.'

'Tish!'

'Well, that's what you want to believe, isn't it?'

'Jesus!' I stood up. 'What's your problem?'

'What's yours, Marlon?' She was standing too, pointing at me. 'It's like you want to build up this whole story about poor little Sonya with her druggie mum and . . . and it's horrible that she died, but she made you hold those drugs for her and it's got you into all sorts of crap. You don't want to see things as they are. Come back to the real world!'

'The real world.' The words wouldn't lie still. 'Where you smooch up the bad boys then run away when it gets too hot.'

Tish opened her mouth, then closed it. She marched out the kitchen, me right behind. The purple corridor wasn't funny any more; it was like being inside a big, meaty vein.

She took a key from a hook over the radiator and jammed it into my hand.

'Remember to give it back,' she said, and strode back down to the kitchen.

I crossed the road to my own house, put the key in the lock and turned around. A curtain flashed in Tish's window. I stayed there for a while, leaning back against the door. What the hell had happened back there? That's why most of the other girls hated Tish; too much mouth. Too much Tishness. She didn't just cross the line, she kicked it to crap and spat on it.

And this time, she'd . . . I opened the door, went upstairs. She'd . . . I slumped down on my bed. She'd . . . done what? It's what she hadn't done – kept her mouth shut. It was like those people who have bits of their intestine blocked off to make the food drop into their stomachs quicker. Tish'd had a tact bypass. The words dropped out of her head straight into her mouth. Usually, I could handle it, but not today. M. Melody. Mum. I had to be right.

My phone was ringing. *Yeah, Tish. I'll accept your apology.* I picked it up and it went dead. I checked the screen. I'd missed thirty-two calls.

Thirty two.

I checked back over the call list. That was Tish's number, twice. Then 8.20 a.m., private. 8.21 a.m., private.

8.22 a.m., two calls. Private. Private, private, private. Thirty all private. Voicemail? Two messages. Tish at 0.47 a.m., all sleepy, just got home and offering herself for a chat. Voicemail number two, 8.53 a.m. I listened to it, and again, pushing the phone close to my ear.

'Tell Mr Orange, I'm coming.' Caller – Unknown.

What the hell did that mean? I pressed loudspeaker and listened again. Street twang, slow and deliberate to make sure I understood, with a cut-off laugh at the end. It could be a mistake. Along with twenty-nine other mistakes.

The phone started ringing in my hand. Jesus! *Tell Mr Orange* . . . I checked the number and accepted the call.

'Marlon? You're up?' Mum sounded surprised.

'Yeah.' Long breaths, in and out.

'I opened your door to check on you around eight and you were out for the count. I tried the landline earlier, but you didn't answer.'

'Sorry. I was over by Tish's.'

'That's okay. Are you up for coming to visit Andre? I'll understand if you'd rather . . .'

Sit around staring at my phone?

'Yeah, that's fine.'

'We'll be home in half an hour or so.'

Mum ended the call. I scrolled down to Tish's number. Thirty private calls. She'd want to hear about this. It would probably make her scream with excitement. She'd know exactly how I should deal with it, popping out a plan from the back of her head.

Not this time, though. I dropped the phone on my bed. Tish was in her real world and I was in mine.

Jonathan was right on time. He always was. He gave a little hoot on his horn and leaned back to open the rear passenger door. He had that solid smile that made his head look like a beach ball with a happy face painted on. Though it was only me who seemed to see that. Tish thought Jonathan wasn't bad looking. She used some stupid word like 'princely'.

I left my phone on my bed. If I brought it with me, I'd be looking at it every few seconds and that would make Mum even jumpier than she was. I locked the front door and walked towards the car.

'Morning, Marlon.' Jonathan could speak without moving that smile.

'Morning.'

I slid in the back, but I must have shut the car door a little too hard because Jonathan's body went rigid, just for half a second. Then he gave a little 'ha' and said, 'Don't forget to belt up.'

I caught Mum's expression, fierce, in the rear view mirror and my lips stayed sealed. Funny how she'd never got round to stopping him from saying that.

East London rolled out in front of us, our own special scenery. Nail bars and barbers, adverts for cheques cashed and SIM cards unlocked, in running red and gold lights, even in daytime. The traffic lights bounced between stop and go as cars raced cyclists to get through on amber.

Jonathan kept his eyes on the road, Mum too, as if she was driving the car with her mind. Nobody was saying much. Jonathan was probably under manners, ordered to stay 'schtum' unless otherwise advised. He slid in a CD, the one with four beardy blokes and a banjo in a field.

Knowing Jonathan, he'd probably chosen today's music specially; something to soothe Mum's mind after her outing to the police station.

As we reached Tower Bridge, Mum turned round and touched my knee. 'Are you okay, Marlon?'

'Yeah. Thanks.'

'I'm not sure we should tell your brother about what happened. What do you think?'

I think you're scared it'll spark up the one bit of his brain that you're pleased he's lost touch with.

'No,' I said. 'You're right.'

'Thank you.'

As she turned away from me, the CD finished and she flipped on the radio. A vicar was talking about how his life had changed when his daughter was blown up on a plane. We listened for a few seconds until Mum jabbed it off.

'Not right now,' she said, under her breath.

Jonathan stuck in another CD and rested his hand on Mum's knee. I looked out of the window, quick.

There were free spaces for a change, right across the road. And the pots of bright flowers and twisty-looking trees outside the door still hadn't been stolen. They'd be gone in seconds if they were outside my house, along with the paving stone they stood on. Any thieves were probably put off by the cameras over the door.

Mum rang the bell, and a bleep sounded inside. I took my usual place next to her, but as the latch clicked, the tightness returned, as if every nerve in my body was trying to catapult me in the opposite direction. The door was answered by a tall woman with clipped back greyish hair. I hadn't seen this one before, but people came and went quickly. The staff, that is. Not the residents.

She smiled. 'Can I help you?'

Mum smiled back. 'I'm Jennifer Sunday, Andre's mother.'

The woman stretched out her hand. 'I'm Deidre Arnold, the new family liaison worker. It's nice to meet you. Come in.'

I held the door open for Mum and Jonathan; I wanted to close it with me on the outside, but made myself go in. It was warm inside, as if the heating thought it was still

December. School was like that – the wrong temperature at the wrong time. Somebody must have done a study about keeping people in places they didn't want to be and reckoned that if they can't work out if they're hot or they're cold, they're going to be too confused to do anything else. Mum was asking if one of the other staff members had had her baby yet, then the talk went on to birth plans, water births, childminders, as if Mum was trying to delay the moment too. Eventually, baby talk finished.

'I'll get Andre,' Deidre said.

Mum sighed. 'It's a shame to be inside on such a lovely day.'

Deidre nodded. 'I know. We're lucky to have some green. Some of the lads have dug up a patch. They're planting salad and we'll probably put in a few flowers. But Andre won't have anything to do with it.'

Mum laughed. 'Well, that's one constant thing, then. He'd never have touched a trowel before.'

And he had a whole load of names for the people who ended up in places like this too.

I looked around. The noticeboard above the radiator was full of leaflets that never seemed to change; something about personal safety, a cooking class, a book group, a number to call for advice on safe sex. Book group? The funny thing was, Andre's street name was Booka. Not because he read stuff. Someone's dad reckoned Andre

79

looked like the musician, Booker T. Jones.

Andre didn't look anything like that now. He was trailing behind Deidre Arnold, still in his pyjama bottoms with a stain, maybe baked beans, down his t-shirt. My brother. Gangboy. Street thug. Car-crash survivor. He'd been wearing his big sunglasses to watch television. Pyjamas, baked beans, shades. Sign of a crap day ahead for everyone. But he must have been to a barber because his beard was neat and his hair trimmed down. Even his scar seemed more settled in his skin, less churned up and lumpy. Underneath the dark lenses, though, Andre's eye would still be all drooped down.

He said, 'You're early.'

'Eleven-thirty, honey,' Mum said softly. 'Just as we agreed.'

Andre frowned. 'It's time now? Them people must change up the clocks here.' He was looking at Jonathan with interest. 'You came back, then?'

'Yes,' Jonathan said. 'If you don't mind.'

''Course not, man.' Andre held his hand out to Jonathan and pulled him into a hug. 'Join the party.' He let Jonathan go and stared at me.

Hi, big brother.

Andre scowled. 'Sharkie?'

'No, it's me. Marlon.'

Andre shook his head hard like he wanted to dislodge

me from his brain. 'Yeah, it's Marlon. Yeah. Okay.'

But it wasn't okay, this time or any of the other times. After all those years I'd followed him around like a spare tail – not all his memories of me must be mashed to a pulp. It was like saying the first twelve years of our life together didn't really happen.

Andre suddenly turned and limped away down the corridor.

Mum called, 'Andre! You need to go up and change!'

Andre looked down at his t-shirt and pyjama bottoms. 'What for?'

'We're going out, remember? I sent you a text this morning to remind you.'

Andre's face screwed up in rage. 'Damn phone's got no battery!'

'Did you remember to charge it?' Mum kept her voice chatty. I tried to catch her eye to show I wanted to support her, but she was tilted towards Jonathan. He moved closer towards her.

'I ain't no crip!' Andre was yelling now.

A girl, maybe just older than me, came out from the gym. 'Just shut up, won't you?'

Deidre stepped forward. 'Saleema, that's not helpful.'

Saleema jabbed her middle finger up at Deidre, then at Andre, before disappearing back where she came from. Mum walked towards Andre holding her arms open.

My brother stood his ground, then smiled. 'Sorry.'

He was always tall, but recently he'd been getting wider and he almost swallowed Mum into him as he hugged her. She stretched up and kissed him on the forehead.

'Are you going to get changed then?'

'Yeah.'

He let go of Mum and shuffled towards the lift. As soon as the lift door shut, she folded her arms and strode back towards Deidre Arnold.

'His leg looks worse. Is he having his physio?'

'The physio, yes. But he's not exercising as much as he should.'

'And the antidepressants?'

Deidre shook her head. 'Not every day. He says they make his brain feel wet.'

Mum was biting her lip hard, as if she needed it to keep her face from crumpling in. 'There must be something we can do.'

'There are good days and bad days,' Deidre said. 'I suppose it's like that for most of us.'

Mum glared at her. 'Personally, I prefer more good days than bad. Don't you?'

Yeah. A few hours with an angry stranger dressed in my brother's broken shell. A phone full up with anonymous calls. Some kid playing gangsta, stabbing words into my voicemail. And Sonya. Her fingers on my neck, her face close to mine. The ambulance pulled up to the ghost train.

No one was calling today 'a good day'.

Andre had one of his lightning mood changes and came down from his room looking cheerful.

Mum said, 'Front or back today?'

'Front.'

Yes, he was definitely feeling more perky. On bad days, he climbed in the back and sat there, scowling. It helped that Jonathan's car was big and solid. The seatbelt slipped across easily and Andre slotted it in without too much trouble.

'All ready?' Jonathan said.

'Yeah, man. Ready.'

Andre dozed all the way over to Richmond and next to me, Mum looked like she was doing the same. She wouldn't have slept well last night either. I tried to close my eyes, but the car smell or the backseat motion made me feel sick. I opened the window a crack, not enough for the draught to disturb Mum. I leaned forward so the breeze blew across my face.

In spite of everything, the day went okay. Andre was happy by the river, chatting away to Jonathan and sometimes even to me. He didn't even freak out when his leg did that spasm thing. He just waited for it to finish and carried on eating his chips. He went back into the house happy. The times when he screamed that we were abandoning him with strangers were the worst. It used to happen every time when he first moved there.

It was classical music on the way home and the usual routine. Mum took a tissue out her bag and wiped her eyes. Then she stared at her knees until we crossed Tower Bridge. As soon as we officially touched down on the north side of the Thames, she breathed in and sighed as if the familiar air gave her new energy. Even Jonathan knew better than to talk to her until she was ready.

As he parked up outside our house, he said quickly, 'Are you okay, Marlon?'

Before I could answer, Mum ushered me away and got back into the car with a set look on her face.

I could have kissed Jonathan for the delay. I ran upstairs and grabbed my phone off the bed, pressed the button and watched the screen light up. There'd been no more calls. No voicemails. Nothing. I shook it. A pretty densehead thing, I know, but it felt like something was lodged in there and needed help getting out. Of course, nothing happened. Just the same thirty missed calls and the voicemail. *Tell Mr Orange, I'm coming.*

Outside, Mum and Jonathan were having a heavy conversation. Mum threw the car door open, climbed out and slammed it shut. That bang couldn't have hurt Jonathan more if his fingers were in the door.

'Marlon?' Mum was inside now, hanging up her coat. 'You hungry?'

I called down from the landing. 'Not really.'

'Me neither. I forgot to put the chicken to defrost this morning. Just as well. Jonathan's not coming in after all.'

Mum stomped down to the kitchen and the fridge door rattled open. I stood by my door, holding the phone close to my ear listening to the message again. *Mr Orange.* It definitely wasn't Amir; his voice was higher. Taneer? No. His 'street' sounded like some posh comedian, pretending. I closed my eyes and concentrated. That boy in the fairground, Cane Row, his lips were moving along with the words. I opened my eyes. That voice could be anyone's. It was too easy to close my eyes and see him.

The fridge alarm was going off. The door had been left open. Mum always blasted me when I did it.

Ting, ting, ting.

She must be clearing the manky stuff out.

Ting, ting, ting.

A whole ton of manky stuff. Our fridge isn't even that big.

Ting, ting, ting.

I ran down the stairs. 'Mum?'

She was standing by the open door, dead silent, but I couldn't miss her shoulders going up and down. I closed the fridge door and moved towards her, but she waved her arm, like she wanted to push me away. I watched her, heart beating.

I said, 'I'm sorry.'

I yanked off a piece of kitchen roll and handed it to her. She rubbed her face.

'Sorry. God. It's not just you, Marlon. There's you, there's Andre, there's everything, all knocking together in my head.' She sighed. 'And now I've taken everything out on poor Jonathan. I told him not to mention last night because he's helped me enough already. He's not your father and I don't want him to take on that responsibility. But . . .' She turned on the tap and splashed cold water on her face. 'But sometimes it's all a bit too much.' She gave me a watery smile. 'Promise me, Marlon. No more bad surprises. No more trips to the police station. And please – no more drugs.'

I nodded, like my head was being tugged by a rope.

She leaned towards me and kissed me on the forehead, the same way she'd kissed Andre.

'Thank you, honey. Thank you.'

5

'The Circle Line is suspended because of a person under a train.' Someone else hated Mondays then. I slammed the button on to snooze, though I wanted to slam the whole clock against the wall. I'd had another night of weird dreams full of yellow. Not sunshine or daffodils. Not even stupid rubber ducks. It was that mustard puffing up and dissolving into smoke.

No house sounds. Mum must have left for work already. I could lie back down, never get up, never bother about the consequences. Other kids managed to do that, no problem.

I thought of Mum in the kitchen, wiping her face with kitchen roll. If I didn't make it to school and she found me out, then everything we were building back between us would just collapse.

A clean shirt and trousers were hanging from the doorframe. My tie was drooping out of an open drawer. Fresh socks were balled up next to the tie; a jumper was ready in my cupboard and I knew my blazer was thrown across the banister. Mum had been nagging me to put it away for the whole half-term. All I had to do was put them on.

Mum had pushed a note under my door. I heaved myself out of bed and went to get it. She was at a conference in Birmingham and wouldn't be back until late.

School been on the phone, want to check you're okay. Told them to be sensitive! Good luck! Stay calm! Make sure you have some breakfast! And call me if there are any problems at all.

Mum xxx

I managed two mouthfuls of cornflakes before the rest of the cereal landed on top of Mum's toast in the waste box. We might as well just dump our meals straight in the compost until our appetites came back.

Mum had made me tack a lesson plan to my wardrobe and this morning it warned me about double maths revision, first thing. That was going to be a couple of hours silently staring at old exam questions with hawk-eyed Wisbeck walking up and down between the desks. Last week, that was my idea of hell. Today, though, it'd be two hours guaranteed where no one was going to bother me.

I pulled out my books from the stack under the coffee table and shoved them in my bag. And then my phone. No more calls. Nothing.

Maybe that was it, a stupid prank by some stupid kid looking for cheap laughs.

I opened the front door and stepped into the street. I

almost closed the door and went back inside because this was different. I wasn't just going across to Tish's house or into Jonathan's car. I had to walk past houses and shops. Cars and buses were driving past me. Someone, somewhere must have been at the fair on Saturday and knowing round here, they weren't going to stay quiet about it.

I kept my head down, walking quickly to the top of the road. The weekend sun was gone, but the air was warm and heavy and thick with car fumes. Time had slipped and I was running late, heading for a detention.

'I'm sorry about Saturday.'

I must have jumped higher than Superman. 'What?'

'I'm sorry. About Sonya Wilson.'

Melinda had appeared out of thin air, her face smug with the knowledge that she'd got to me first.

'You'd better bugger off then, in case it's catching.'

Those weren't my words, though I wished they were. Tish's timing was perfect. She'd crept up on my other side and was standing with her hands on her hips. Melinda wrinkled up her face and trotted off.

'I didn't see you,' I said. 'I thought you'd gone.'

'That's because you didn't bloody look. Good job I was watching out for you, eh, Milo? Catching up was hard, man.' She gave me an enquiring look. 'You still vexed about yesterday?'

'Yeah. Sorry . . .'

'Apology accepted. Special circumstances.' Tish waved her fingers towards the direction of school. Her green nail polish was getting her a detention, even if we did make it through the gates on time. 'You ready for this?'

'Not really.'

We walked side by side in silence, Tish's blazer rubbing up against my arm. Did she always walk that close to me? All that man-made fabric and soon we'd be starting a fire. I gave her a sideways glance. Gold loops spiralled up her left ear and there was a small hole above her nostril. She turned suddenly, catching me looking.

'What's the matter?'

'Nothing.'

'You seen earwax or something? You have to tell me, Marlon. I can't go around with globs all day.'

'I was just – I was just wondering what happened to your nose ring.'

'Oh!' She smiled. 'I never knew you'd noticed it. Shaun asked me to take it out so we could go to that posh restaurant. Then the bloody hole just filled up again.'

'Shaun?'

'Yes.' She glared at me. 'Shaun.'

We carried on walking, though you could drive a bus between us now. As we waited for the lights by the Chinese to change, Tish said, 'So you're not going to do it, then?'

'What?'

'Give me your wise opinions on Shaun.'

'Do you want me to?'

''Course not. But then you weren't impressed by Jaheem, neither.'

'Tish—'

'Nor Salvi.'

'I didn't mean . . .'

We crossed the road, Tish slightly ahead.

I said, 'You can go out with who you want.'

'I know that.'

More silence, until we reached the turn off to the park.

Tish nudged me. 'It might not be that bad.'

'What?'

'School today.'

'You reckon.'

'Lots of stuff happens around here. Maybe no one will be interested.'

'Yeah? If you heard Billie, or Leda, or someone, went to the fair with a boy that died right next to them, you'd want to know more.'

Tish slung her bag higher up her shoulder. 'I didn't even know you knew Sonya Wilson. I mean, for her to come knocking on your door . . .'

I tried to stare her out on that one but she looked right back.

I said, 'What are you trying to say?'

'You're not her usual type, Marlon.'

'What do you mean?'

'I thought we agreed. Girls still go for numbheads, don't they?'

There was an edge to Tish's voice.

'Not all girls,' I said.

'Yeah,' she said. 'Not all girls.'

Through the park, under the bridge and we'd be there. Now detention was definite, there was no point in rushing, so we stopped to watch two fat guys slugging the ball to each other on the tennis court. They were much fitter than they looked. Much fitter than me.

I said, 'Why do *you* think she knocked on my door?'

'I don't know. She said she knew Andre, didn't she?'

'She's three years late.'

The fattest man missed his serve and ran to get the ball.

Tish shrugged. 'Andre had his own life. She could have been a friend.'

'But?'

'I didn't say "but".'

'You didn't have to, Tish.'

'Okay. But. She'd have been fourteen when he had his accident, younger when he was on the street. Reckon your brother hung out with twelve-year-old girls?'

'No!'

'And the pills and stuff. Look how she made you carry

them. She knew what she was doing, Marlon! Those kids at the fair probably did know her. Maybe they were carrying stuff too, or checking up on her, or something.'

'That's the official Tish Analysis, then. Sonya Wilson was using Marlon Sunday and didn't really like him at all.'

Tish smiled. 'Of course she liked you, Milo. It's hard not to.'

Really, Tish? So far every girl in the universe disagrees with you.

The main gates were closed and we had to wait for one of the learning mentors to come and get us.

'God,' Tish grumbled. 'I hope it's not Celia Mae.'

'Who?'

'Remember *Monsters Inc*? She was Mike's girlfriend, the one with all the snakes on her head.'

'Jesus, Tish! Do you mean Miss Hedder? That's racist!'

'It might be interpreted that way.' Tish looked up at the sky, mock-thoughtful. 'By morons. But it shouldn't be. I was referring to the way one look from her turns you to stone. Not the length and width of her dreads. And,' she grinned at me, 'I resent the accusation!'

I laughed. 'Thanks, Tish.'

'What for?'

'I don't know. Just helping.'

A sideways smile. 'Someone's got to look after you.'

It wasn't Miss Hedder who came for us, but some new bald bloke I hadn't seen before. He already looked like he'd given up. He gave us the standard 'not in lessons, not learning' lecture like he was reading it from a board over our shoulders and led us through to the main reception, waiting while we signed in. Me and Tish separated, heading towards our different tutor groups.

'Good luck,' Tish said.

'Thanks.'

I sloped up the stairs, stopping on the third floor to look out the window, at the park. The fat guys had finished their tennis and were talking and laughing, zipping away their racquets. They must do this every week, a regular thing that they looked forward to. Funny how I'd never noticed before. I suppose I was nearly always on time.

Along the corridor, past Mr King's, past Ms Reznic's, to Mr Habato, my tutor. Through the glass panel I saw Simeon sneaking a blast on his DS under the table and Alexandra and Mattie doing homework catch up. Yasir was sitting with a stupid look on his face, as usual. Habato was at his desk reading *The Economist*. Nothing different.

When I opened the door, Habato's head snapped up. He frowned, then nodded. 'Sit down, please, Marlon.'

No second chapter of the 'not in school, not learning' lecture? He must know. Yeah, he was peering at me over his magazine. When he saw I noticed, he dropped his eyes. I kicked my bag under the table and raised my head; Alicia, Beau, Yasir, all of them were staring me out.

Alicia must have pulled the straw to say she was going first. 'You oversleep?'

Yasir sniggered. 'He was dead to the world.'

Not bad, from Yasir's bulging intellect.

Alicia was impressed. She thumped Yasir's arm. 'That's sick, man.'

And she was smiling, ready to repeat the joke later. So this was how it was going to be.

'She was gorgeous!' Beau said. 'How d'you meet her, Marlon?'

'What you asking him that for?' Yasir's thicko face shone with joy. 'You want to snog a corpse, then?'

Alicia giggled. 'Yasir!'

My fists curled tight. I jammed my hands between the table and my knees. Their eyes were on me, Yasir, Alicia, watching for the reaction. And all the kids, chatting or scrawling their late homework, they were waiting too. Even Habato, his face in *The Economist*, his ears twitching.

The bell rang for first lessons and all four of them on my table stood up.

Yasir shook his head. 'You were desperate, man. You had to drug up the girl before she let you touch her titties.'

Alicia's eyes were wide. 'Yasir! Stop!'

My heart was pounding now, probably a thousand times harder than the fat blokes on the tennis court.

Yasir bent towards Alicia. 'You know how she really died?'

Giggle. 'No.'

'Our boy's so boring, she topped herself!' Gun-fingers pointing to his own thick head. 'Boof! Self-destruct!'

I punched him. My bag thumped to the floor, my fist crunched against his nose, microseconds before my brain kicked in. And when it did, it yelled, 'Do it again, mate, harder!'

'Fuck!' Yasir fell back on to the table.

My hand balled, my arm snapped back and I hit him again, my fist glancing off the side of his head as the maggot tried to squirm away. Air was fizzing in my ears and words, my own words yelling into his ugly moron face. All the other kids were laughing, egging us on and somewhere in the rumble, Habato was shouting.

Yasir grabbed my arm and tried to use it to lever himself up. He was flailing around with his other arm, missing me every time. Everything packed deep inside me was springing free. And God, it was good.

'Stop it now!'

I managed one more punch before Habato yanked me up and shoved me into a corner. My throat was sore, my breathing coming hard. Yasir was rolling on the table like a flipped turtle, blood smeared across his face and down his shirt. There was blood on my hands too, beneath my nails and in the lines of my palms.

'All of you! Get to your classes now!' Habato's voice was slightly shaky.

My audience broke up, chattering and looking back. The story was going to be around school by first break. Habato handed Yasir a wad of tissues to mop up his nosebleed, glancing at me all the time. What did he think I was going to do? Take on both of them? Though I felt like I could.

Yasir was muttering something Arabic, probably hoping I'd end up in the same state as Sonya. But I didn't care. For the first time since Saturday, my head felt crystal sharp.

'What happened?' Habato folded his arms, looking from one of us to the other.

The man was here. Didn't he see?

'Well?'

I stayed still. Yasir dabbed his nose and looked at the floor.

'You both gone mute?' Habato shook his head. 'Fair enough. Yasir, are you dizzy? Fine to walk? Go down to the medical room.'

Yasir slouched out, banging the door behind him. The teacher leaned against the closed door. 'Is there a problem, Marlon?'

'What do you mean?'

Habato cocked his head sideways. 'Your mum and I had a chat this morning. She said you'd prefer to keep things low key. But I'm here, if you want to talk.'

To my teacher? He'd watched too much *Glee*.

He said, 'There are going to be many more Yasirs.' Habato was using his kind voice, the even-though-I'm-a-teacher-I-understand voice. When Dad died, when Andre was in a coma and no one had a clue what was going to happen . . . I got to know that teacher tone well. It was the one that broke into you.

The next class was outside, scuffing against the door, faces pressed against the glass behind Habato's head. I wasn't going to crack up. Me, of all people, had hit that idiot Yasir, who reckoned his uncle was a gunman who set up the Hackney Turks! Half the school would have paid to clout Yasir, including loads of the teachers. Habato should be congratulating me, not trying to break me down in front of the Year Eights.

Habato said, 'Do you want to talk about it, Marlon?'

'No, sir. I don't.'

Not to him. Not now. Not here. I pushed past Habato, opened the door and ran through the waiting kids and down the corridor. Someone was shouting after me. It could have been some of the big mouths or even Habato. Who cared?

I hurtled down the steps and through the foyer. The

receptionist lifted a hand, but I ran past her. A second later, I was in the park dropping on to a bench. Now what?

The sky had turned dirty grey, ready to tip it down. A train rumbled over the railway bridge and I counted four, five, six carriages heading out to somewhere that wasn't here. For a second I wished I was in one of them. But then I remembered that moment when my fist connected with Yasir's chin – that had felt so good. And so had the moments after that. I ground the knuckles of my right hand into my other palm. I must be rubbing Yasir's blood into my skin, just like Mum's cocoa butter. I wiped my hands on my trousers.

A figure was walking towards me. I stood up.

'What are you?' I said. 'My conscience?'

'Yeah,' Tish said. 'I'm gonna sit on your shoulder and poke you with a pitchfork.'

'What are you doing here?'

'I saw you Usain Bolt out the school. Thought I'd follow.'

'You'll get in trouble.'

'Really?' She held out her hands. 'Green nails. The wrong socks. Late. They're running out of room on the detention slip. I suppose they can put "leaving school without permission" on the other side in really small writing.' She picked up my bag and offered it to me. 'Let's get out of here.'

We headed back along the path through the park.

Tish said, 'Was Habato trying to counsel you?'

'Something like that.'

'Honest, Marlon, I'm sorry. I don't think I've properly said it, but I mean it.'

The first drops of rain were hitting the branches. A pair of joggers flashed past us, trying to outrun the downpour. They were going to be disappointed.

'I'm sorry too, Tish.' Drizzle was dripping down the neck of my blazer. 'A girl dies right next to me and I can't even do anything to – I don't know, make it better. Mum was with Dad, right until the end. She told me she closed his eyes. She was probably all psyched up to do the same thing with Andre. And me? What was I doing when Sonya . . . when *she* died? Laughing at a stupid zombie.'

'It wasn't your fault, Marlon.'

'But I didn't know her, Tish. They asked me questions about her and I didn't have a clue. She could have been anyone.'

The sky cracked open and the rain hammered down on us. Tish grabbed my arm and pulled me towards the bus stop.

'Of course you didn't know her. You'd only been out once.'

I felt a twang of anger. 'It doesn't matter! She listened to me, Tish! She sat down in my house and let me talk about my dad and Andre and everything! That was special.'

100

Tish cut her eyes at me. 'Right. So it's not special when I listen to you!'

'I didn't mean that.'

'Bloody better not. So, what next?'

'I'll go and see her parents and talk to them.'

'You still seriously think that's a good idea?'

'Yeah.' *Kind of.*

'It's just as well, then. When you sulked off yesterday, I carried on looking. Sonya didn't live with her parents. She lived with her grandmother on her mum's side. Violet Steedman.'

Mum and Dad waiting to hear about their daughter . . . All that crap the police had spun me and let me keep on thinking, even though they probably already knew different.

'Tish, do you know where Violet Steedman lives?'

'Yup. I followed a load of court reports then checked 192 to find her. Dead easy.'

I stepped into the rain. 'Let's go.'

She hesitated, then said, 'You've got blood on your collar. Sort that out first.'

I got my train ride after all, right across the river. As we climbed the steps from Streatham Station, Tish pinched her nostrils together.

'South London air! Can't. Breathe. Too. Much.'

'At least it's not raining,' I said.

'The rain's probably too scared to come here.' Tish took out her phone and looked at the map. 'Reckon it's this way.'

We headed left, down the road running alongside the station. Soon it widened into a residential street, odds on this side, evens on the other. The houses were all small semis with bay front windows and a patch of concrete outside for the bins.

Tish said, 'We need to go halfway down. Keep an eye open for a road off the right.'

I scanned ahead. She touched me.

'Why did you do it?'

'What? Go on a date with a dead person?'

Tish stopped walking. I plodded on. I reckoned I could see the turn ahead.

'It's just here!'

She didn't move. 'You're not funny, Marlon.'

'I wasn't trying to be.'

'Yes, you were. And it's pathetic.'

Maybe I should have told her other stuff that wasn't funny. Like waking up with the smell of fairgrounds filling your head, thinking your fingers are stroking grey skin. Not funny at all.

'The pill, Marlon,' she said. 'That's what I meant. Why did you do it?'

I walked quicker, so she could only see the back of my head.

'She was Sonya,' I said. 'And I'm me. I can name all of Earth, Wind and Fire's albums in order. You surprised no one sits next to me in Humanities?'

'I would.'

'You know what I mean.'

She was looking at me like there should be something more. But what else could I say? Sonya Wilson, blonde and beautiful, had knocked at my door. Why would I want to say 'no'?

I pulled Tish's arm. 'Come on. Before I lose my nerve.'

'How did you feel?' she said. 'Was it good?'

Before the bar squeezed our knees, before Sonya's body slumped forward. 'Maybe. I don't know. I was just, you know, I didn't expect to be at the fair with Sonya. Nothing felt real.'

Tish's eyes were shining. 'I've always wondered what it's like. If I had a chance, I might try it.'

'You stupid?'

'No, Marlon. I'm not.'

Security doors blocked our way up, but someone didn't care, or really believed I was delivering a pizza, and buzzed us into the block. We started up the stairs.

'A little bit's safe,' Tish insisted. 'I've done loads of research. There's loads more deaths from alcohol than Ecstasy.'

'Safe? How do you work that one out, Tish? Did you miss out the bit about being suffocated by your own blood? Or your kidneys packing in? Or your heart stopping? People die from it, Tish.'

'And people get drunk and throw up in their sleep.' Tish sounded breathless. 'There's this new kid in my year called Scott Lester. I've heard he can get them.'

'Don't.'

'You're not my keeper!' She tried to storm past me up the stairs, but I stretched out my arms so my fingertips touched each wall.

'You're like my sister,' I said. 'That's why I care about you.'

'Your sister?' She glowered at me. 'Thanks, Milo.' Suddenly she smiled, and her fingers shot up and tickled my armpits. Damn! How did she know that? She must stash bits of info about me in some secret, indestructible brain pouch.

'Remember! I know all your weak spots – little brother!'

Yes. Secret indestructible brain pouch.

Mrs Steedman's flat was right next to the stairs, by the rubbish chute. The window on the left of the door was bumpy glass. That must be the bathroom. The curtains were drawn tight on the other side. All the other flats showed people, windows open, old boots and scooters stuck outside. But this one just had a doormat with a curry menu dropped on it.

Tish shifted the leaflet aside with her toe. 'Maybe we shouldn't have come.'

And maybe she was right. But I said, 'Well, we're here now.'

I knocked on the door twice and stood back.

'She's not in,' Tish whispered.

'She hasn't had any time to get to the door.'

And she could take as long as she wanted. All day, all year. Some time round my thirtieth birthday would be fine. What the hell was I thinking? I'd just turn up out the blue, tell her who I was and everything would be all right? She probably thought I'd murdered her granddaughter.

Tish said, 'Look through the letterbox. Just in case.'

'There's someone staring through your letterbox. You'd open the door, right?'

'Yeah. And throw pepper in their face.'

We laughed together, a bit too loud.

The door to the neighbour's flat opened. An African woman bumped out, with two bulging checked laundry bags, clanking like she was heaving around her own restaurant. She put them down to lock the door.

'Excuse me,' Tish said. 'Do you know if . . .'

The woman studied us. Not in a friendly way.

She said, 'I hope you've come to pay your respects.'

I'd never got that phrase, though I heard it so many

times about Dad. Respect for what? That he'd died? Why not come and see him before then?

Tish nudged me.

'Yes,' I muttered. 'We've come to pay our respects.'

The woman looked unimpressed. 'Were you friends?'

'She went to my school.' I couldn't look her in the eye, but I could still feel her examining me.

The woman frowned. 'There are too many troublemakers coming here. My poor friend Violet, she has been broken down. The Lord will look after the child now and my church is praying for Violet too.'

She looked up over the balcony as if God was walking his dog on Streatham High Road. I bowed my head and Tish did the same. The woman nodded in approval at us. 'Yes. I can see you have a good background. You're not like those other thugs who turned up here.'

Thugs?

The woman shook her head. 'Perhaps Violet can be left in peace now.'

I said, 'Do you think Mrs Steedman's in?'

'The police called on Saturday to say her granddaughter had passed. Then they took the poor woman to identify the girl. She walked into her house and shut the door.'

'What about Sonya's mum?' Tish asked. 'Is she here?'

The woman screwed up her face in disgust. 'Even the Lord will lose patience with that one. But you two, I believe you're here for good reasons.' She pounded the knocker. 'Violet? Open the door, my dear!'

The racket should have brought everyone out their flats, but this seemed the sort of place where they'd be used to it. Tish was looking even more uncertain now.

Bang! Bang! 'Violet! It's Agnes!'

The curtain twitched in the window and the door latch clicked.

Agnes said, 'Violet, my darling. These young people have come to see you. These are good ones.'

I jumped back from the door straight into Tish. I couldn't help it. Tish was holding her place, though. Now the door was opening, she wasn't letting me go anywhere.

Sonya's grandmother looked like a living waxwork. Her eyes moved slowly from me to Tish.

Agnes picked up her rattling bags. 'I'll bring you food later, Violet.'

Tish was clasping her hands in front of her neatly, waiting. Mrs Steedman stared at us.

'I'm sorry to bother you,' I said. 'We've come from school. We were Sonya's friends.'

Mrs Steedman narrowed her eyes. 'What friends? She didn't stay long enough at any school to have friends.'

I wanted to take another step back, and another one, drop over that balcony and float away from this place. It sounds pathetic and selfish, I know, but I'd seen my mother with that look for years after Dad died. Seeing it fresh dug right into me.

Tish prodded me with her elbow. Mrs Steedman was closing the door.

'No. Please.' I stepped forward. 'I had to come and see you, because . . . because it was me.' I made my eyes stay on the waxwork face. 'I was sitting next to Sonya at the fairground. On the ride.'

Mrs Steedman's chin twitched up. Tish poked harder.

'You.' A whisper of stale cigarette breath. She was looking right at me now. 'Why were you with her?'

'We were just out together. It was the first time.'

Mrs Steedman wiped her eyes. 'You were with her when . . . when it happened.'

'Yes.'

The word hung there for a while, then Mrs Steedman sighed and the door opened wider.

'Thank you.' My voice didn't sound so sure.

The heat inside almost pushed me back out again. Incense was burning and every window was closed, every curtain drawn. The air was so heavy I could wade through it. Standing in the hallway, I saw a sitting room at the end. The television was on, an American talk show by the sound of it.

'This was her bedroom.' Mrs Steedman opened a door on the left.

Sonya's own space. Pale pink walls. A dark pink carpet. Last time she was in here, she was getting ready to see me. I wanted to stare at things, touch things. But it didn't feel right with Sonya's gran standing there.

'It's funny,' she said. 'Because she never used to let me come in, not even to clean. I said I'd hoover for her, but she wouldn't have it. Now I can come in all the time if I want to. It's stupid the things you argue about.'

'Yes.' Like me and Andre, yelling at each other about who got to be Michael when we did the Jackson 5 for Dad.

About why I looked in the box in Andre's wardrobe.

Mrs Steedman said, 'I'll go and put the kettle on.' She walked out and left us.

'She sounds like a robot,' Tish whispered.

'They've probably given her all sorts of drugs to calm her down. That's what happened with Mum after Andre's accident. It might have been the same after Dad died, but I don't think so. She was more expecting it.'

Tish bit her lip, as if she was trying to hold something back. Instead, she looked round. 'This room's a bit . . . just not her.'

I knew what she meant. Mrs Steedman must have tried really hard to make things good for Sonya. The curtains were bright and flowery and her bedcover matched, though it was thrown off like Sonya had just jumped out of it. There was a bedside table rammed with stuff. She must have been collecting little glass ornaments, sea things, like mermaids and dolphins. There were bottles and jars, cream for her face and body. Nail varnish. Hairspray. Straighteners were thrown in the corner, still plugged in, though the power was off.

Tish pointed to the bookshelf by Sonya's bed. 'They're fairy tales.'

'Maybe they were presents or something.'

I was still standing just inside the door. The incense smell curled round from the hallway and caught in my throat. Underneath was the thick hum of cigarette smoke.

Tish straightened up. 'What now?'

God knows.

'I thought you might like to see these.' Mrs Steedman pushed the door back, her arms full of photo albums. 'If you've got time.'

'Thank you.' I held out my arms for them but Mrs Steedman balanced the books in the crook of her arm and opened the top one. I looked at Tish, she nodded back as if to say, 'This is what you want, isn't it?' We moved into place, either side.

'These were Sonya, when she was a baby.'

'Oooh,' Tish cooed. 'She was beautiful.'

'She was about a month old, there. And I think that one was a couple of weeks later.'

There were hundreds of them, under their plastic

covers. It was hard to tell some of them apart, but Mrs Steedman knew the time and place every one was taken. She showed us Sonya at her christening, in a long, dangly robe. And Sonya at her First Communion, in a white frilly dress and silver shoes.

'That's her.' Mrs Steedman pointed her out. 'Verruca Salt.'

As we flicked through the books, Sonya was getting taller and blonder, Mrs Steedman thinner and greyer. There was no sign of Sonya's mum or dad, though sometimes there was a miserable-looking old man who must have been Sonya's granddad.

Tish was really good at smiling and saying the right things.

'I remember my sixth birthday party.' She was pointing to a photo of a load of kids round a table. Sonya was blowing out the candles though her eyes were on the camera. 'That was the first one you came to, Milo.'

I remembered it well. It was a couple of months before Dad died, though I still thought he was getting well. Somehow, I won most of the party games.

Mrs Steedman flipped the page over. Sonya must have been twelve or thirteen in this picture. She was with an older woman and they were wearing identical red puffas, arms round each other.

'Is that Sonya's mum?' I kept it casual. The woman

was smiling towards Sonya, creamy brown hair falling over her shoulders. I stared hard. Was she Melody Harmony? Could be.

'Yes.' Mrs Steedman's voice was flat. 'That's Hayley. She gave Sonya some silly name that nobody had heard of. But she was always Sonya to us.' A new page. 'This was Nativity. Year Two, I think. Sonya was a shepherd, though I told her teacher she should have been Mary. That was a picnic we had just after Hayley went again. We thought we'd take Sonya's mind off it.'

'Where did she go?' Tish asked.

Mrs Steedman turned the page. 'Prison.'

'Oh.' Like Tish couldn't have guessed.

Mrs Steedman ignored her.

School photos. More birthday parties. Trips down Southend. My eyes wandered round the room again. Mrs Steedman had *tried* to make it pretty, but it didn't seem to match Sonya. Maybe Sonya had been that kind of pretty when she was a kid and then just grown out of it. Now the bed was all mashup and her slippers were in different ends of the room, like she'd been doing a cartwheel out the door. A t-shirt and leggings were flung over the back of a chair. She'd been like me, trying on clothes and taking them off again before she came out. Suddenly my chest hurt and it was hard to breathe.

Mrs Steedman was pointing to another photo. Sonya

was with another blonde girl, in bikinis on a beach.

'She went to Ibiza,' Mrs Steedman said. 'I thought she was too young, but her mum said it was safe and let her go.'

The photos and the room and the incense. The walls were shifting closer and closer.

'Mrs Steedman?'

She looked towards me.

'Do they know what happened to Sonya?'

Tish drew in her breath, but Mrs Steedman just shook her head. 'They're doing the tests today, but it might take a few weeks to get the results.' Another page flapped down, then the album slammed shut. 'Maybe you should tell me what happened,' she said. 'You were there.'

Mrs Steedman was so close to me. It was make-up that made her look like an old plastic doll, a thick layer of pale powder.

'I don't know that much,' I said. 'Not really. We had . . . there was . . .'

'Drugs.' A sharpness in Mrs Steedman's eyes that wasn't there before. 'I know that. Were they yours?'

I shook my head.

'That's what the police told me you said.'

'It's true.' I managed to keep the anger out my voice. 'They weren't.'

'I believe you.'

'You do?'

After the speech from the coppers about upsetting Sonya's family, about them not wanting to hear bad things about their daughter? After they'd virtually accused me in front of my mum of dealing drugs and killing someone?

'It wasn't the first time.'

Tish poked me in the leg. I ignored her.

'She may have kept her door locked,' Mrs Steedman continued. 'But that doesn't mean I'm stupid. In the end, I didn't do any better for Sonya than I did for her mother. Trouble always found Hayley in the end.'

'What trouble?' The words came out of me and Tish together, same time.

Mrs Steedman turned a page, but didn't look at it. 'The usual.'

Tish said. 'What's that?'

'Drugs, prison, drugs, prison. You could set your clock by it.'

I said, 'Do you think she got Sonya involved?'

Mrs Steedman frowned. Her granddaughter wasn't even buried yet and I was standing in her home, accusing her daughter of the same things the police tried to lay on me. I opened my mouth to say sorry, but she was talking.

'You got involved in Hayley's life whether you wanted to or not. Even when she wasn't here, social services brought the babies to us. Her stepdad wouldn't have them in the house. Sonya only got to stay because he was too sick to fight about it.' She flicked back to the photo of Sonya on the beach. 'This was her first trip to Ibiza. Her mother arranged it. Hayley was supposed to go but couldn't. They'd stuck her in Styal prison over in Cheshire, too far for us to go and see her.' She looked from me to Tish. 'And after that, Sonya started locking her bedroom door.' She tucked the albums under one arm and put her other hand on my shoulder, so light I could hardly feel it. 'But the last person she was with was you.'

'Yes.'

'Thank you. I'm glad I know that now.' She let go of me and opened the bedroom door.

Tish made it to the front door quick. 'It was very kind of you to let us in.' Her eyes were telling me to hurry up and get out.

I didn't move. Mrs Steedman looked like the draft from the front door would blow her apart. I took a deep breath, scrabbling for words and touched Mrs Steedman's arm.

'Sonya was beautiful,' I said. 'I mean, not just her face. The way she was with me. She treated me like I was important.'

'Did she? Yes . . . My little girl . . .' Mrs Steedman's voice came out in a whisper like it took all her energy to talk. 'There was still some of that left in her.' Her arms dropped to her sides and the photo albums crashed to the floor.

115

'I'm sorry.' She bent down, trying to push the mess of photos together.

'Don't worry.' Tish took her arm and helped her up. She gave me a hard look. 'We'll sort this out.'

Tish led Mrs Steedman down the hallway to the living room. I tidied the albums into a pile, seven, eight books, all heavy with Sonya's life.

'Marlon?' Tish's voice.

I left the books in the bedroom and went to her.

The sitting room was large and dark. An electric fire was blasting, with candles burning on saucers around the fireplace, cigarettes stubbed out on the side of them. The incense sticks were prodded into a spiky pot plant next to the television. The mantelpiece was covered with more pictures of Sonya.

Mrs Steedman was lying on the sofa.

'Are sure you don't want us to call someone for you?' Tish said.

'No, I'll just lie here for a bit. But I wouldn't mind a cup of tea. The kitchen's opposite Sonya's bedroom.'

'Sure.' Tish headed out and shut the door behind her.

'I'm sorry,' I said. 'I didn't mean to come here and make things worse.'

'There isn't a worse.' She closed her eyes. 'But I'm glad you came. I keep asking myself what I could have done. Could I have banned her from going out? Called the social worker? Though all they say is that at her age, there's nothing you can do, not unless you want to lock her up as well.'

I thought of Andre and all the times Mum tried to talk to him. 'I don't think there's anything you could have done.'

'Thank you.' Mrs Steedman propped herself up. 'Have you ever lost anyone close to you?'

'My dad.' *And my brother.*

'I thought so. Only someone who understands would have been brave enough to knock on my door.'

'I was wondering something too.' I tried to push it away, but the question bounced back. 'Why me?'

Mrs Steedman rubbed the balls of her palms into her eyes. 'What do you mean?'

'It's like she chose me. It was like – I don't know. Girls like her don't usually speak to me, but she knocked on my door.'

I glanced towards the door. If Tish came in, she'd slam her hand over my mouth and drag me out.

'Please, Mrs Steedman. If you know why she chose me, tell me.'

'Sorry. I don't know.'

I prayed that there was no milk or teabags, or that Tish had to wash up some mugs. Anything to stop her walking in right now.

I said, 'All this stuff's happened to me, but I still think

Sonya was a good person. I don't really know anything about her. I just want to understand.'

Mrs Steedman was looking at the mantelpiece full of framed photos. Some of them were school photos and a couple were those ones taken at theme parks, when the camera catches you with your hands in the air, screaming.

'You can't understand,' she said. 'People do what they do. The police gave her a chance, but she didn't take it.'

I checked the door again. 'Sometimes people do what they do for a reason and if you find out why, it makes things – I don't know. It helps.'

She sat there, still staring at the pictures. Maybe she could see through to another world where Sonya was still alive.

I said, 'My brother was driving a car. It smashed into a wall and killed his best friend. Everybody was trying to say my brother was drunk or on drugs, but he was being chased.'

She was looking at me now.

I carried on. 'They arrested the guy who was chasing them. They found all this stuff at his place, guns, drugs, loads of things. My brother did some bad things, but not that time. Him and his friend, Sharkie, were coming back from the chemist with some Calpol for Sharkie's baby. That was all. I think the only way my mum got through it was because she knew the guy was sent to prison and this time my brother did nothing wrong.'

Mrs Steedman shook her head. 'What do you want?'

'I want to understand more about Sonya. She had those pills on her, but the more I think about it, the more it seems that she was going through the motions, like she didn't really want to be the person she was. I know there were good things in her.'

Her eyes were sharp again. 'You saw good things in her?'

I looked straight back at her. 'Yes. And, Mrs Steedman . . . I have to know . . . there were these boys at the fairground. I only saw them for a few seconds, but it looked like Sonya knew them and she didn't want them to be there. Then, just now, your neighbour said something about thugs coming by.'

'There's always thugs.' Mrs Steedman gave a sour laugh. 'Sometimes they're on this side of the door, sometimes the other.'

'Maybe if I find out who they are, I could help.'

'You saw good things in her?'

'Yes, Mrs Steedman.'

She pushed herself up to standing, shuffled over to the mantelpiece and slid her hand behind the barrier of pictures.

'I found this in Sonya's room.' She was holding a Blackberry, one of the cheap ones, plain, with no case. 'After the police went, I just . . . I had to go into her room and touch everything. It was like a part of her was still there and I had to catch it before it went too.' She blinked hard, resting a hand against the mantelpiece. 'I found this on top of her fairy tale books. I've never seen it before. I helped her pay for her other phone monthly, just so she could always call me to let me know she was safe.'

She pushed it into my palm and my fingers closed around it.

I said, 'Do you know what's on it?'

'Just a list of silly names.'

We stood there looking at each other.

'Milo! Can you get the door for me?'

I slipped the phone into my blazer pocket and let Tish in. Mrs Steedman sank back on the sofa and closed her eyes.

Tish carried in the tray. 'I wasn't sure if you took sugar so I brought a bowl.'

She'd brought the teapot too, a mug and a glass of milk, even found some biscuits.

'Thank you,' Mrs Steedman said. 'You're so kind.'

After Tish poured the tea, we let ourselves out. We stood for a moment on the balcony breathing in the grimy London air, stinking of bins and other people's cooking. But it was better than that incense.

'I'd forgotten it was day time,' Tish said.

'Yeah, I know what you mean.'

We walked down the stairs in silence. Tish pushed open the door. 'Did you get what you want?'

'Kind of.'

But I didn't look her in the face.

6

The Blackberry made my blazer hang different and when the train jiggled, it bounced around in my pocket. Any time soon, it was going to wriggle against the seams, drop through the lining and land by Tish's feet.

I glanced at her; she was lost in her own thoughts.

She said, 'Did you find out anything about the funeral?'

'No and I wasn't going to ask her. I suppose they have to wait until the coroner's happy.'

'Yeah, probably. What if she wants you to go? Would you?'

'Maybe.'

'That's good. But I won't come with you. I didn't really know her and there'll probably be loads of kids from school seeing who can cry hardest. I bet Melinda's up Boots right now looking for waterproof mascara.'

I must have looked shocked because Tish sighed. 'You know them girls, Milo. Shallow.'

I turned down my path first. Yeah, I should have invited Tish in and she lingered just a bit, before walking off, but the Blackberry was going to burn through to my skin if I didn't deal with it. As I twisted the key, my other hand was already in my pocket fishing it out.

I stood in the hallway turning it over and over in my hands, then switched it on. Nothing. The damn thing was completely out of charge.

The landline was ringing in the sitting room. I dropped the Blackberry back in my pocket and went to answer it.

'Marlon?' It was Mum. 'Why have you been ignoring your phone?'

'Sorry, it's upstairs and I've been—'

'Been what? I've been trying this number for ages. How do you think I felt when the school got on to me? And then I couldn't get in touch with you!'

I felt a prickle of guilt. But at least she was calling from Birmingham. Better than standing opposite me right now.

'The school thing,' I said. 'I didn't mean to . . . It wasn't . . .'

'I heard the school's version, Marlon. And even then I was on your side. But I've been killing myself worrying about you. Where were you? Please, Marlon, make my day and say you were revising.'

I held the phone away from my ear. Like that was going to make the lies better. 'I've been with Tish.'

'Oh hell.' Mum would be rolling her eyes. 'Seriously, Mandisa does not need any more grief from the school about Tish's attendance. But I'm glad you're all right.'

'Thanks.' That was it?

'Something else has come up, Marlon.'

My hand was in my pocket, cupped round the Blackberry. 'What?'

'Andre's walked out again.'

My attention snapped back to Mum. 'When?'

'About three hours ago. Deidre Arnold called. Apparently, he had some run-in with that Saleema girl and stormed out. It's happened before, she said, and they're not too worried. But she thought she'd call me just in case he's been in touch.'

'Has he?'

'No.' Mum sighed. 'I've tried his phone but I bet the battery's dead. Can you have a look, Marlon? Usual place.'

'Sure.' And I owed my brother one big favour when I found him. If it wasn't for him taking the heat off me, Mum would be pulling me apart, tendon by tendon.

I ran upstairs, dropped the Blackberry on my bed and slammed out again. I caught the bus just as it was about to leave the stop, puffing my way upstairs and slumping into a seat at the very front. This was the seat I loved when I was a kid. Andre would slink to the back, hood up, iPod on, pretending me and Mum didn't exist. He didn't want to play word games with us or make up stories about the passengers. He wanted to earn money and hang around with the boys Mum hated so much.

Up here on the top deck, I was higher than the traffic lights. I was above the law. Andre would have appreciated that.

I got off by the playground. The council did it up a couple of years ago and it was still looking good. I turned into the estate. They'd done this place up too, but it was still three blocks around a tarmac square. At half-term, kids would be racing around on their bikes and skateboards, playing chicken with the pizza boys on mopeds. Today, there was just a woman washing her car, the hosepipe trailing back through the window of her ground floor flat. Music blasted from a radio on a chair, The Temptations.

I could stop and ask her. Andre wouldn't be hard to notice, even in a place like here that threw all sorts together. Maybe she'd been here a year ago, when all the crap kicked off, and seen what was happening to him and ignored it. All those 'friends' who'd never visited my brother in hospital but came slinking back into his life when he first came out. Andre's flat was the easy place, good for hiding things – drugs, junkies, money, who knew what else. It got so full, there was no room for Andre. Right up there, corner flat, third floor with the red curtains across the kitchen window.

'Ball of Confusion' finished and it was straight to the next song.

Those first notes. The Jackson 5, 'I Want You Back'. It

was like they started a pulley in my head heaving out hidden things. I had to stand there, just listening.

Andre had seen something on *The Cosby Show*, when the family mimed to a Ray Charles song for the Huxtable grandparents' anniversary. He reckoned that we should do a performance for Dad to cheer him up. It was soon after Dad had started chemo and the treatment was really wiping him out.

Andre reckoned that we could do a Jackson 5 song because there were five of them and five of us, if you counted Sunflower, the cat. Dad, though, was the audience, so he couldn't be part of it. Mum said she'd help with the costumes, but wasn't up for dancing. And Sunflower always bit Andre any time he went near her. So in the end we roped in my action figures – Buzz Lightyear as Jackie and Lando Calrissian as Tito. Jermaine was played by Mr Potato Head. I even made some guitars out of cardboard for them. That left Marlon Jackson and my hero, Michael. I had to be Marlon Jackson, Andre said, because of my name. Seriously? He knew I was named after Superman's dad in the film.

Two days later, we were still arguing about it. *I* was the youngest, I should be Michael. It was Andre's idea, so it should be *him*. Andre wasn't used to me standing up to him, but he was ready to fight for it. So was I. He was eleven. I was six. He would have won. In the end Mum

126

threatened to call the whole thing off if we didn't sort it out, so we split Michael in two.

Andre set to work. As soon as I got home from school he made me practise. If we were singing along with the Jacksons, it had to be proper. I had to know every word. He dragged Mum round Dalston for afro wigs and made big, flappy collars out of paper and pinned them to our school shirts so we'd look the same. Even Lando, Buzz and Mr Potato Head had mini versions.

We had to wait until one of Dad's good days, when he was able to keep some food down. Mum helped him downstairs and into an armchair in the living room. Even Sunflower came in and curled up on his lap.

Mum dropped the needle and as soon as the intro hit, Dad was grinning. Our choreography was tight. Leg forward, bend, leg back, chin flick, arm roll. My squeaky little voice, Andre's just starting to get deeper, then Mum and Dad, singing along.

It was like you could see all the colour creeping back into Dad. And because he was happy, so was Mum. She took a photo, me and Andre, Dad and Sunflower. It's the last one in Dad's album.

I pushed the door to the stairwell. The lock was still busted and I went straight through. Andre was sitting on the bottom two steps, his arms wrapped around his knees and his face buried in his lap. This was my big brother now, bad boy Andre, slumped on concrete that stunk like park toilets.

For a second, I stood there looking down at him. All that stress, that didn't even let up when Dad was in hospital. All the yelling and arguing, that only stopped when Mum threw Andre out. This flat he set up like his own private fortress, and me and Mum never visited until after the accident.

'Andre?'

My brother looked up. His glasses were crooked and in spite of myself, I was staring at the scar that almost cut his face in two.

I held the door open. 'Can you hear that?'

'I don't hear nothing.'

Michael's voice, pleading to be forgiven . . .

'The Jackson 5. 'I Want You Back'. Remember? We did that thing for Dad.'

'I don't remember nothing.' He rearranged his shades and pulled the peak of his cap low. 'And I don't remember any time I liked Michael Jackson.' He laughed to himself. 'Yeah. Me and Michael Jackson. Jokes.'

The pulley in my head jammed then spun backwards, Dad, Sunflower, Mum all happy, all falling away.

Andre nudged his glasses high over his eyes, then let them drop. 'What's your name, again?'

'Marlon. Your brother.'

'Yeah, yeah. You look like my friend.'

'I know. You tell me all the time.' I offered him my hand and helped him stand up. 'I was worried about you.'

Andre clamped my shoulder in a kind of half-hug. 'I try and remember you but you're gone and I'm seeing Sharkie. I don't know.'

Me neither. You remember Mum and even Jonathan, but you're letting me drip away.

'What happen to Sharkie? He doesn't come and see me no more.'

'Let's talk about it later.' I was bottling it, but I couldn't deal with all that now.

'You've already told me,' he said. 'Yeah?'

I nodded.

'Some man chasing us, yeah?'

'Yeah.'

'Bastards!' He pushed the door hard.

I followed him out into the courtyard. 'I'll take you home.'

'This is my home! Not the other place! I told them other people. That skinny little Indian girl, man! Boy, she better not mess me up. I tell her I got friends!' He was shouting now. The woman washing her car looked up at us, then turned up her radio, bass coming hard through the crackles. She must have changed the station.

'That!' Andre pointed up. 'That's my flat! But the bitch won't let me in!'

'Andre, you don't live there any more.'

'You think I'm stupid?' Andre's body stiffened and he clenched his fist. 'You think my head's all cripped up and I don't know nothing?'

I stepped away from him. Sad Andre, bad Andre, mad Andre all clashed together. He'd smashed the front of his brain against his skull. All the itchiness and anger already in there got bigger and madder.

Mum always kept calm; I had to too. 'You don't live here any more, Andre. Remember what happened when you came out of hospital? All those people kept passing by and locking you out your own place? You got picked up by the police and they brought you home to Mum's.'

Andre was eyeing me like I was the enemy. 'You called the police on me?'

'No. They found you up by Hackney Central. You'd been sitting on the platform for hours.'

Andre tapped his head, body relaxing, instant mood change. 'The computer's still not working properly. Hard drive damage, that's how one of them people put it. Updates won't stick.'

Except you could reboot computers with the information you wanted. You could service them and replace failing parts. Junk them, get a new one.

'I'm just going to call Mum,' I said. 'And let her know I

130

found you. Then I'll take you back. Try not to let Saleema bother you.'

'Who?'

'The girl you had the argument with.'

Andre frowned, then smiled. 'Oh, you mean the Indian girl. She's all right, man.'

Deidre Arnold was local, at some housing meeting, and agreed to come and take Andre back. She pulled up in an old estate car full of gardening tools.

'So this is your old flat,' she said.

'Dump,' Andre muttered.

Deidre raised her eyebrows. 'It looks okay.'

Andre opened the back door and climbed in.

Deidre looked surprised. 'You can sit in the front, if you want.'

Andre grunted and started fumbling with the seatbelt, stabbing the clasp against the socket. He used to boast about making the quickest, neatest spliffs in Hackney. He'd even demonstrated it to me, his nimble fingers rolling and folding like he was making Tower Bridge out of Rizla. Now the clasp kept banging the sides and wouldn't go in. He was muttering some of the words Mum banned from the house, getting louder as the clasp veered further and further away from its goal. Deidre Arnold looked at me with a question in her eyes. She obviously hadn't read

Andre's file with enough attention.

I lay my hand over Andre's, waited until he relaxed then guided the clasp home. It clicked into place.

'Yeah, thanks, bro.'

Andre shut the car door and stared ahead. Deidre Arnold started the engine and giving me a little wave pulled out of the estate and on to the road.

I set off home too. Twenty minutes, if the traffic was good, and I'd be back in my room with the Blackberry. I'd find an old-style charger somewhere. Mum had a whole box full of them.

The road was gridlocked. I stared out of the bus window at a bloke on the phone in the estate agents. In thousands of years, we could all have evolved super-brains. We'd swap memories or automatically repair brain damage like we do with our skin. Or we'd be telekinetic. I'd squeeze a few brain cells together and the Blackberry would lift off my bed, skim through the open letterbox and fly down the street towards me. Yeah, in thousands of years' time, we'd be able to do all that, but we'd probably still get stuck in traffic jams.

The driver announced that two buses had collided in Mare Street and opened the back door before the passengers wore out the bell. I was off before the doors were properly open, running through the churchyard, past the police station. Who was locked up in the cell-stink and aircon now?

I raced down the street, almost skidding to a stop outside my house and shoved my key in the lock.

'Oi!' Tish was leaning out of her bedroom window. 'Wait up!'

She disappeared. I could do it quickly, open the door, dash inside and bolt it shut. I could . . . except Tish would be banging and kicking until the police came for her.

She came running out her house. 'Let's see it, then!'

'What?'

'You're kidding, right?' She was frowning. 'You really weren't going to tell me, were you? Shame on you, Milo!'

'I don't know what you're on about.'

'The phone, Marlon! The one Sonya's gran gave you!'

'You been snooping on me, Tish?'

'Get over yourself.' Tish pushed past me. 'You know what they say about kettles. I was hardly going to stand there watching the thing boil, was I? I came down the corridor and heard you all in mid-flow.'

'Sneak!' I was smiling, though. Tish the spy, pressed against the wall, hand to her ear – that was funny.

'Just as well I did,' she said. 'Do you know how hard it was for me to keep it zipped on the train? I thought I'd give you your space, let you find your own words. But you, you miserable git, you were planning to keep your mouth shut,

133

weren't you? So what's on it?'

'I don't know. The battery's dead.'

'Let's see.'

I ran upstairs and fetched it. She squinted at the charger port. 'I've got one that'll fit. Hang on a minute.'

She was out of the door, back a few minutes later. We plugged it in in the sitting room, waiting for the battery to spark into life.

'I reckon it's her drugs phone,' Tish said.

'How do you come to that conclusion?'

'How can you not come to that conclusion?' Tish sounded excited. 'Didn't you listen to what her grandmother was saying? Sonya's mum was a druggie. She arranged for her daughter to go to Ibiza. She must have been taking stuff in or bringing it back. Actually, it could have been both.'

Sonya, a hardcore pusher? No. She'd sat right where Tish was now, leaning towards me, listening. Siouxza.

'Nice one,' I said. 'Titian Harding-Brooks. CSI Hackney.'

'What?' Proper Tish anger. 'D'you think her lovely blonde hair and her cute smile meant she couldn't carry a load of pills through customs?'

'I didn't say that.'

She picked up the Blackberry, holding it like she wanted to hurl it at me. 'That's what you want to think, though.'

'Forget it, Tish! It doesn't feel right, talking about her like that.'

'You wanted to find out why she chose you.'

'We decided it's because I'm not a numbhead. Remember?'

Tish didn't laugh. 'Let's see if I'm right, shall we?'

The screen lit up.

'No password.' Tish shook her head. 'Not exactly a pro at this stuff, was she?'

'Maybe she'd had enough of it all and stopped caring.'

'Yeah,' Tish said. 'Maybe. Right.' She checked the messages. 'Empty. No photos, neither. See?'

Tish's face was daring me to argue. 'Typical drugs phone. Nothing on there to get anyone in trouble. Let's see the contacts. Yeah. Diamond.' She moved closer to me. 'Can you see, Marlon?'

Yeah, I could see. Hess, Orangeboy. Orangeboy? *Tell Mr Orange* . . . Tish carried on flipping through the list. Rizz, Rodge. Stunna, Westboy.

'Stupid names,' she was saying. 'I wonder who thought them up. Maybe Stunna's pug ugly. Or Westboy lives in Essex. I'm going to have a look at their numbers. Maybe one of them's really stupid and got a landline – a nice little postcard to the police saying "Come and find me!" You never know.'

I watched her. Diamond's number was a mobile. And Hess's. And Orangeboy—

'Stop there, Tish.'

'What?'

'Orangeboy. Look.'

She looked at me, then back at the phone. 'Jesus, Marlon! Orangeboy. That's your number, right?'

I nodded.

'What's it doing on her drugs phone?'

'How do I know? You're the expert on these things!'

She prodded the screen. 'Orangeboy.'

'I get it, right?'

Tish sat back. 'What's this about? I've known you long enough to tell when you're hiding something. Talk to me.'

She crossed her arms, sitting there solid as a Buddha. I stared at the phone. No answers were flashing up on that cracked screen, but a voice was getting louder in my head, a streetboy voice with a message. *Tell Mr Orange, I'm coming.*

Tish poked my arm. 'You look like something's crawling across your face. And you're twitching, little brother.'

I tried to zone her out. I had to try and understand this first. Sonya knocked on my door. She came in my house and made me feel important. And she did it so well. Even thinking about it now made my heart twist. We went to the fair and she asked me to carry her pills. And then . . . The next bit wasn't planned. Now I had her Blackberry and a load of missed calls and some gangsta boy making threats on my phone. Mr Orange. Orangeboy. No coincidence, was it? Was he coming for me? And if he was, did I want to handle all this crap on my own?

Tish's fingers clamped the back of my neck. 'Vulcan mindmeld coming soon!'

I pulled her hand off. 'Be serious, right?'

She looked like she was going to say something but changed her mind.

'It's this,' I said. I dug out my own phone and played her the message on loudspeaker.

'Woah!' She shook her head. 'Deep!' She listened again with the phone pressed up against her ear. 'I don't recognise the voice.'

'Me neither.'

'Orangeboy. Mr Orange.' She lay my phone next to the Blackberry. 'What the hell have you got yourself into?'

'I don't know. I haven't heard anything since.'

'But now you've got Sonya's drugs phone. I wonder why her grandmother gave it to you.'

'I thought you heard the whole conversation.'

Tish scowled. 'No, I mean, I wonder if she knew what it was. The police must have asked her a load of questions too. Why didn't she give it to them? D'you ever see it before?'

'Don't know. And no.'

Sonya's phone was small and pink. I'd watched her put in my number. M-A-R-L-O-N. Not moron Orangeboy. Or

Stunna. Or Westboy. Or any of that other crap.

Tish said, 'Orangeboy. It's a weird name.'

'Yeah, I noticed.'

'What's orange?' Tish looked thoughtful. 'Well, there's a girl in my form, Lila. She uses a bucket of that fake tan stuff.'

'For God's sake, Tish.'

'Sorry, just thinking out loud.'

'Agent Orange,' I said. 'It was a poison in the Vietnam war.'

'You're not that toxic, Mr— Oh.' She frowned.

'What?'

'I don't know about Orangeboy, but there's a famous Mr Orange.'

'Who?'

'Haven't you seen *Reservoir Dogs*?'

I shook my head.

'God, Milo. Watch less sci-fi and more violence! All the gangsters have colour code names – Mr Pink, Mr White, Mr Blonde, and so on.'

'And Mr Orange.'

'Yeah. He's the undercover cop.'

'A grass?'

'Yes.'

They thought I was a grass? I told the police that the pills were Sonya's, but she had me on her phone as

138

Orangeboy before that, when I didn't know anything I could grass about.

I snatched up the Blackberry.

Tish looked alarmed. 'What are you doing?'

'This is all wrong. The more I think about it, all I'm getting is questions. Someone must have some answers.'

First on the list was Diamond. I jabbed 'call'. Silence. Number dialling. Connection. More silence.

I waited a second, then, 'Hello?'

The line went dead. I tried the number again, but it flicked straight to voicemail.

'What's up?' Tish was ready to pull the phone out of my hand.

'Diamond doesn't want to talk.'

'Try another one!'

'For God's sake, what do you think I'm going to do?'

Next was Stunna. Straight to voicemail. Westboy. Number not recognised. Diamond again. Dialling, dialling, dialling – connection! I held my breath. Right now would be a good time for those telekinetic powers. I'd make Diamond's phone stick to his ear until he talked to me.

A voice yelled, 'I told you not to call me again!'

I looked at Tish. 'Jesus, Milo! Quick! Put it on speaker!'

'Hello?' I used the voice Mum loved, no street. 'Hello! Wait, don't . . .' Dead line.

I tried him again. Voicemail.

I swapped the Blackberry for my own phone and kept the message short.

SONYA'S DEAD. PLEASE CALL ME.

My phone rang almost straight away. Tish grabbed it and turned the volume right up.

'Who are you?' The voice had a slight tremble to it.

'My name's Marlon. I was with her. When she died.'

'Is that a threat?' The voice was almost a whisper. Tish was nudging, trying to get her ear up close to the handset.

'No! We were at the fair. We were on this ride and—'

'Jesus! That was you? And her? I heard about that! What happened?'

'I don't know. She was alive and then she wasn't.'

A pause. 'Was that it?'

'What do you mean?'

'Did she have anything with her?'

Tish gave me her superior look. 'Tell him,' she hissed. 'Or he's not going to tell you anything!'

I said, 'What do you think she had?'

Silence. Tish nudged me so hard I almost tipped over.

'Yeah,' I said. 'She had pills.'

More silence. Tish was flexing her fingers like she was fighting to stop herself yanking the Blackberry out of my hand.

There was whispery sound, like a laugh. 'She asked you to carry them, didn't she?'

'Yeah.' The words bubbled out. 'Do you know why she

140

had them? Who gave them to her? Did she do the same with—'

Diamond ended the call.

Diamond. Diamond. Diamond. I was calling him from my phone, not even hiding my number. But Diamond didn't want to shine.

I tried Rodge. The number wasn't recognised.

'Now what?' Tish asked.

'I'll keep trying.'

Round about eight, I heard Mum bustle through the front door. I came downstairs into the kitchen as she heaved her Tesco bag on to the table.

'I can only manage "heat up" tonight.' She made a face at the bookcase. 'I'll have to turn Jamie Oliver to the wall. I can't handle that accusing look.' She fished inside the bag. 'Spaghetti and meatballs or Thai green curry?'

'Meatballs, please.'

'Okay. You nuke while I sort out plates.'

I slid off the cardboard sleeves and poked holes in the plastic. Mum opened a bottle of wine and poured herself a glass. She caught my look.

'The Never-on-a-Monday rule is there to be broken, especially after the last few days. I managed to skive off from the last seminar and I had a long conversation with Deidre Arnold instead.' She took a big sip of wine. 'She said it's a love-hate relationship between Andre and that Saleema girl. I'm beginning to wonder if it's the love bit I should be worried about. The one thing he never did was bring a baby home to me. And' – she laughed – 'I'm not expecting you to fill that gap neither, Marlon.'

Some chance! And she knew that. That's why she could laugh about it.

The microwave pinged. I stirred the spaghetti. Mum put down her glass, came over and kissed me on the cheek.

'Thank you for taking care of Andre,' she said.

'He's my brother.'

'Even if he can't always remember it.'

I closed the microwave door and reset the timer. Mum was looking at me over the top of her wine glass.

She said, 'I told Deidre the whole story about Sharkie and the car accident.'

'The whole story?'

'Yes. I think she was a little freaked out about the seatbelt thing.'

'She looked it.'

'She also wanted to know if Andre had any contact with Sharkie's family.'

'Why?' Mum should be as cheesed off as me about this one. 'Did you tell her that Sharkie's mum spat at you in the church? She wanted Andre to die, for God's sake!'

'No.' Mum's voice was steady. 'I didn't tell her that.

Because if it was the other way round, I'd be doing exactly the same thing. Do you know, when your dad died, I'd sometimes look at strange men in the street. I'd think "Why don't you drop dead so Jes can come back?" That kind of grief pulls all the good things out of you.' Mum was standing straight opposite me. 'I know I want to protect Andre, but perhaps it hasn't helped that he's lost contact with all his old friends. Not everyone was bad, were they?'

Not every one. But *nearly* every one.

It was a strange evening. It was like Mum had made a decision not to mention my fight with Yasir, but she kept sneaking looks at me when she thought I wasn't watching. I stayed downstairs with her and left both my phones in my room. We watched a tech show and moaned at the size of the competition prize, but we still picked out all the things we wouldn't mind having. Those bouncy blade things, they were top of Mum's list. Then Andre phoned, sorry for scaring Mum earlier. He'd made up with Saleema and they'd promised not to yell at each other any more. Mum gave me a half-smile and pretended she was rocking a baby in her arms.

We turned off the downstairs lights around eleven.

Up in my room, I checked both phones and called everyone on Sonya's list again. No one was picking up.

I must have dozed off because suddenly it was twelve

minutes past four in the morning and my phone was blasting that stupid Beyoncé song Tish loaded on. I grabbed it and checked the screen. It said 'Unknown'. I breathed out slowly, made myself hold the phone tighter, when my brain was telling me to drop it, turn it off.

The flashing stopped. A few seconds later it started again. I held the phone to my ear. 'Who's this?'

A laugh. 'Crap, isn't it?'

'Who are you?'

'Yeah, really crap, when that unknown number flashes up and you've got no idea what they're going to say.'

I threw back the duvet and went and looked out the window. The street was empty. What was I expecting, for God's sake? A kid with cane row staring up at me?

That voice. Proper-speaking, a bit wobbly, I'd heard it before.

I said, 'Is that Diamond?'

'I don't know what you're talking about.'

Of course. He'd have no idea he was Diamond to Sonya, just like Marlon, AKA Orangeboy.

I said, 'I didn't mean to scare you.'

'You didn't.'

My heart could power the Starship Enterprise. I bet his could too.

'Look,' I said. 'I'm just trying to work out what happened to Sonya.'

'Was that true? About her dying?'

'Yes. Sorry.'

'Jesus.' His breathing, then silence. 'So how did you get this number?'

'Her grandmother gave me her phone . . .'

'Her grandmother?'

'Yeah. Sonya lived with her. I went to see her.'

'So that was true. You could never tell with Sonya. She was good at saying what you wanted to hear.'

The streetlight clicked off outside. Diamond was probably sitting there in shadows in some other part of London. Maybe he'd been lying awake thinking it all over, hoping I was talking crap and Sonya was still alive.

He said, 'Her grandma gave you the phone.'

'Yeah.'

'Why?'

'I don't know. She just did.'

'Did she say anything else about it? Like, you know, why Sonya had it?'

'No. Just that she hadn't seen it before. Listen, you said something about pills. Do you know where she got them from?'

'I don't want to talk on the phone. Can we meet?'

My stomach pulled. 'You want to meet me?'

'Yeah. There's stuff about Sonya, but I don't want to tell you on the phone.'

I found a pencil and a back of a textbook. 'Where?'

'Do you know Brockwell Park? You go to Brixton and get a bus or . . .'

The streetlight clicked back on. It must have lit up my brain. 'No, mate. I'm not coming south.'

'If you want to know . . .'

'No.'

Silence. *Diamond*. He was probably the kid whose mum sent him to school fifty miles out so he didn't have to rub shoulders with London bad boys. But meeting him in some unfamiliar Brixton park with Sonya's phone in my pocket? Not happening.

I said, 'I'll text you the time and the place.'

'You have to bring the phone,' he said.

'Why?'

'You said my number's on it. There might be other stuff, a photo, or an address, or something.'

'There isn't.'

'You expect me to believe you?'

My eyes were hurting, and my brain starting to close down. He was right. There was no reason for him to trust me. 'Yeah. I'll bring the phone.'

7

The crapstorm heading my way from school still hadn't hit. Maybe the Year Eights had bigged up my ninja skills, or more like it, the teachers had issued instructions to leave me alone. Whatever the reason, three days had gone by and Yasir and the other idiots were staying out of my way.

Mum phoned me at four every afternoon to check how I was getting on. Today was no different. I finished the call, put my phone away and stared at the escalator chugging up to somewhere north of heaven, otherwise known to the thousands of happy shoppers as the top floor of Westfield mall, Stratford.

Tish said, 'Did you tell her where you were?'

'Yes.'

'Did you tell her you're with me?'

'Yes.'

'Did that make her feel better?'

'No.'

'Jeez! Your mum's got such an attitude!'

But she was smiling. She knows Mum really loves her.

'So what's the plan?' she said.

147

'Well, he's agreed to come east.'

'I'm surprised about that.'

'Me too. Though he sounded pretty cheesed off.'

Tish flashed her 'meh' face. 'He phoned you before sun up and *he's* cheesed off? Man, him and me seriously won't be making friends.'

We stepped on to the escalator. The music was full-on earache, all the hits from *Now That's What I Call Rubbish* then some Billy Paul. Just like a fairground. An old guy with a big rucksack jostled hard against Tish, clonking her on the chin with his bag.

Tish yelled, 'Oi!'

He glanced back at her, then carried on up, taking the steps two at a time.

I said, 'You all right?'

'Think so.'

I prodded beneath her chin with my thumb. 'This hurt?'

'No, Dr Marlon, it does not. But if you mention my secret chin hair to anyone, you'll be the one hurting.'

'Consider your beard safe with me.'

I smiled at her. She smiled back at me. I wondered if she was having the same thought. What if the rucksack guy was pointing us out?

No, Marlon, mate. Tish doesn't think she's in a Bourne film.

We stepped off the escalator. Tish said, 'Are we going right to the top floor?'

148

'Yeah. I thought it would be better to look down on people.'

'Like the Enterprise hovering above a new planet.'

'If you say so.'

'I'm just trying to get into your mind, Marlon. Reckon he's come alone?'

Hope so. 'I don't know.'

We crossed the walkway to the next escalator. The place was rammed. I'd wanted somewhere public, but this place was almost too full.

I said, 'What do all these people want?'

Tish shrugged. 'Two floors of Primark. Cheap leggings, Marlon. It's worth it. Though half the girls here don't need to be flaunting it in Lycra. Look at her! She's older than my mum!'

I was looking, but not where Tish pointed. Those boys over there, waiting outside Boss. Or the two kids by the nail bar. Or the one yelling into his phone by the pretzel store. One of them could be Diamond. Or his back up. The school kid stabbed at Victoria station, and the guy outside the trainer shop in Oxford Street . . . the streets were teeming with people then, and both of them ended up dead. But it was still better here than some shady corner of a south London park.

'I wonder if he's up there watching,' Tish said.

'He doesn't know what we look like.' *Well, I don't think*

so. 'There's – what – thousands of people here. Loads of them could be us.'

'And loads of them could be him too. Did he sound white or black?'

'I don't know!'

'I just thought we could narrow it down a bit. Maybe he's Bengali.'

'I don't think so.'

'Could be. Open your mind, Milo.'

Up and up. The only way we'd get higher was by suckerpad across the glass ceiling.

'That one,' I said.

It was the diner by the bowling alley, with red leather seats outside on the walkway and wooden tables and chairs inside. The waitress led us past tables of families loaded with shopping bags to the far back of the restaurant.

'Why here?' Tish said.

'So I can see who's coming in.'

'But we can't get out.'

'We can go round the tables or in the loos. These places usually have a security guard too.'

'You sure about all this?'

I didn't say anything.

Tish emptied coins on to the table. 'Chips and a milkshake. Just.'

'I'll get it.'

The waitress was back again. 'Marlon Asimov?'

Tish sniggered. 'Is that the name you gave him?'

'Yes.'

The waitress turned to someone behind her. 'Are these your friends, honey?'

If this was Diamond, it was spot on. The boy had pale hair, pale eyebrows, and his skin was a bit shiny and so fair you could almost see through it. We were probably the same age, but he wasn't filling his years so well. He was scanning me too. Then he noticed Tish, dropped his eyes and just stood there.

She said, 'Do you want to sit down?'

He did, same side as Tish, elbows cramped into his body.

The waitress said, 'I'll be back in a few minutes.'

Me and Diamond looked at each other, eyes saying the same thing. *Why the hell would Sonya have anything to do with you?*

The thing is, in spite of all the stuff your mum tells you, about kindness and sense of humour and patience, there is a league. Sonya was in Premier and that lot stick together. Sometimes someone from the lower level gets promoted up or someone at the top does something so stupid they're kicked out. People like me and Diamond, we didn't even get to wipe the mud off the top lot's boots. And Tish? She was a different league all together, one that played rugby or dodgeball or some Tish-type mashup of both.

I said, 'Thanks for coming here.'

Diamond nodded.

'What's your name?'

'Alex.'

'I'm Marlon,' I said.

'I know.'

'And this is my friend, Tish.'

He still wouldn't look at her. 'Can I see the phone?'

Tish gave him a shotgun look. 'You're in a hurry.'

Alex turned to me, his back to Tish. He'd obviously read a manual on how to wind her up.

'You said you'd bring it. I'm not going to say anything unless I know you're for real.'

Tish opened her mouth. I glared at her and she stayed silent.

I slipped the Blackberry out of my pocket and laid it on the table. Alex picked it up and turned it on, scrolling through the names. He stopped when he saw 'Diamond', looked at me, then back down again. Unless he thought too hard about it, 'Diamond' wouldn't seem too bad.

He said, 'Which one is you?'

'Orangeboy.'

He gave me a sideways look. 'Why?'

A suntan. A poison. A grass. 'Don't know.'

I said, 'Do you recognise anyone?'

'No.'

'I tried everyone, but you're the only one I could get through to.'

He carried on examining the Blackberry.

'You could have changed your SIM,' I said. 'Got a new number.'

Head down. 'Yeah.'

Stuck behind his back, Tish looked ready to explode.

The waitress was hovering again. We ordered, chips, milkshakes, a burger and just a coke for Alex. He obviously wasn't planning to linger. His coat was done right up to the neck, with a scarf tucked in too.

I said, 'Were you waiting for Sonya to call you again?'

Alex frowned. 'Maybe. But you couldn't always believe what she said.'

I sat back. 'The police thought I was her drug dealer.'

His eyes opened wide. 'The police?'

I carried on. 'They might draw the same conclusion about anyone on this list.'

'You're going to give this to the police?' His voice was tiny.

'No,' I said. 'I don't want to.'

Almost a whisper. 'You mustn't! You can't!'

You had to feel sorry for him. At least I had Tish to help me out; he looked like he had no one to back him up at all.

I said, 'I promised Sonya's gran I'd try and find out

153

what was going on with her before she died. I want to keep that promise.'

A tiny nod.

Tish moved closer to him. 'How did you and Sonya meet?'

Alex was fascinated by a cup ring on the table. I had to lean forward to hear him.

'My stepbrother was a year above her at school. They went out for a bit and she used to come to the house. She always used to talk to me. None of his other girlfriends bothered, but she did, even after they split up. She used to text me sometimes, or we'd talk a bit.'

The drinks came, and the chips. The burger was on its way.

Alex sipped his Coke. I tried the shake, a big, icy mouthful that made my face ache.

I said, 'And then what?'

Beyoncé. 'Single Ladies'. I reached for my phone.

'No,' Tish said. 'It's me.' She checked the number. 'Sorry. Need to get this.'

Alex said, 'Have you two got the same ring tones?'

'It's her joke.' I took another gulp of milkshake.

'If you say so. Go on, then. How did *you* meet Sonya?'

'She knocked on my door and asked me out.'

'Seriously?' Alex lowered his voice. 'Did she have the pills?'

'At the fairground. Yes.'

'Did you take any?'

'Just a quarter. She did as well.'

'She didn't.'

'What do you mean?'

Alex shook his head. 'That was part of it. She made you think she did, just so you would. You'd never done it before?'

'No.'

'No drugs at all? Me neither.'

The burger appeared. I took a bite.

'I didn't think I'd ever want to,' Alex was saying, 'but, you know . . . being with Sonya.'

I did know. I'd seen it, walking across the fairground with her blonde hair swinging like something out of an advert, the men double-taking, even the ones with girlfriends. Even the ones with little kids.

But it was more than that. It was the way she could tune herself into you.

I said, 'How many times did you go out with her?'

'Twice. The first time we just sat in the park and did the 'E'. Well, I did the 'E' and she pretended to.'

'And the second time?'

'We were supposed to go to the cinema, but she phoned me up and said she had a confession.' He took another sip of Coke. 'I thought she was going to say she was seeing someone else. But she told me she hadn't done the pill with me at the park. She said she really wanted to, though.'

'Then what happened?'

He glanced towards the door, dropped his voice even lower. 'We met up the next day and she had a bag of twenty pills.'

'Twenty?'

'She asked me to buy them from her. She said that some guy was hassling her and she needed the money quickly.'

'Did she say who it was?'

Alex was staring out towards the shopping centre.

'Alex! Did she say who it was?'

He shook his head, still looking out the way Tish had gone.

'It's all right,' I said. 'Tish doesn't know how to have a short conversation.' *And she was probably letting Shaun slime up to her.*

Alex said, 'No, she didn't say who it was.'

'Then what happened?'

'I called her a few times but she didn't call me back. I ended up flushing the whole lot down the loo. Then these other guys kept calling me, trying to make me buy more. They said I could make loads of money if I sold them on.'

'The same guys hassling Sonya, d'you reckon?'

He shrugged.

156

'Is this him?' I took out my phone and played him the message. *Mr Orange . . .*

Alex was shaking his head like something was stuck in his ear. 'There's nothing else, right? I have to go.'

'Please,' I said. 'She died right next to me. I need to know what this is about.'

He looked at me, then outside again.

'Just a couple of minutes,' I said. 'Until Tish comes back.'

He sat down, picked up his glass, put it down again.

I said, 'You kept your old number. Did you think she was going to call again?'

'She did.'

I said. 'What happened?'

'She wanted me to meet her in Brixton.'

'Why?'

'She said something happened to her mum and she was a bit upset.'

'Did you go?'

'No. I thought she just wanted to sell me more pills.'

'So that was it, then?' I said. 'She hooked up with us, we bought the pills off her and then we were supposed to sell them on. It doesn't make sense. You and me, we don't even do that stuff and I don't know anyone who does. What were we supposed to do with it all? Why would we go back for more?'

Alex rubbed at the moisture on the table. 'My stepbrother

157

used to be into it. She used to get them for him. When they split up, I think she hoped he'd still be up for it, but he went off to uni and wasn't bothered. Maybe she thought you knew someone who'd be interested.'

Ecstasy? That was never Andre's thing.

'So all these names . . .' I scrolled through the Blackberry's contacts. 'You reckon they were people she was trying to sell stuff to.'

'Must be.'

I stared at the contacts list. 'Stunna. I suppose you've got no idea who that is.'

'No.'

Seven or eight of us, two or three dates each. No wonder she knew the routine – what to say, when to touch me, when to smile. I looked down at my burger. The mayonnaise had glooped out over the lettuce and the bun was all greased up. Tish could have it if she didn't mind chewing round my teethmarks.

'Papa Don't Preach'.

Alex smirked. 'It must be you this time.'

I let it ring out in my pocket.

'She couldn't have been making that much money.' I was half-talking to myself. 'Her room wasn't full of stuff, or anything.'

'She said she gave the money to her mum. Her mum owed a bit of money and Sonya was helping her out.'

Jesus! Poor Sonya. How long had she had to deal with this stuff? Her grandma said she'd been caught once, but still took the risk. One of the few times Andre talked to me about his street life, he said that the longer you carried on, the more risky it got. If your rivals couldn't get you, they'd come after your sister, your mum, your cousin. And you'd end up in prison. Or dead.

I said, 'There were these boys in the fairground. They looked like they were hassling her. They could have been having a go at her mum too.'

Alex's face changed, as if he was seeing Sonya coming towards him. 'I don't know anything about that.'

'Alex?'

He stood up. Tish was striding back to us.

I caught Tish's expression; my words were automatic. 'Don't worry about her.'

I was lying. He needed to worry. When Tish thought somebody was messing with her mates, she turned into Godzilla and today, that somebody was Alex. He stepped back.

Tish stomped right up to him. 'Bastard!' She picked up her drink and hurled it.

Pink milk dripped from Alex's face, the lumps of ice cream slopping on his shoulder. Someone whooped. And hell, the nutter laugh was bouncing around the bottom of my stomach trying to make it up my throat.

'Tish?' The word came out like a hiccup.

Tish looked ready to follow up the milkshake with one of the skewers from the next table. The waitress rushed up talking at Tish, but Tish was yelling over her, fresh, hot words that would have made even Andre's ears burn. A couple of the munchers had their phones up too. We were a spectator sport, Tish cussing out this guy who looked like melted ice cream sundae and me standing there staring at them.

'Tish?' I took her arm. Two blokes in red diner t-shirts were hurrying towards us. 'What the hell are you doing?'

She looked at me. 'The bastard set us up.'

'Serious?'

'Yeah. Him. The guys who left that sweet message for you. They're on their way now.'

'How do you know?'

She tapped her phone. 'Tell you later. Let's just get out of here.' She scowled at Alex. 'The bill's on you. And every nasty, manky disease as well.'

I grabbed Sonya's Blackberry and followed Tish, weaving through the tables until we were out on the walkway. I clocked them straight away. Three of them, coming off the escalator. A skinny, brown-haired one, the kid with the bike. A tall one, hood up. And the last one, yeah. Cane Row. Our eyes met. He smiled and nudged his hoodie mate.

'Keep walking.' Tish linked her arm through mine.

'Security might get them, just for the hood.'

We needed to do more than walk. Security. Cameras. That would make them bigger and bolder. Thousands of eyes full of fear watching their bravado. They'd eat that right up.

'It's the phone,' I said. 'They're after that.' I looked round. They weren't far behind us now, sauntering, like it was all too easy. 'Alex must have let them know we had it with us.'

'You want to give it back?'

'No!'

'Right then!' Tish looped her fingers through mine. 'These are my streets. Let's go.'

Walkways and shops stretched ahead. And more escalators. We sped up, keeping pace side-by-side, not quite running. Suddenly, Tish was on the escalator, speeding down the steps, dodging the loaded bags. I tucked in close behind her. My heart was thumping and the music – seriously? – Jackie Wilson, 'Sweetest Feeling'! Dad showed me the video for the song. Jackie Wilson's singing on this old style telly and a couple are dancing, then the shoes start tapping and the tulips are doing the harmonies and—

I was thinking about that now? NOW?

Yeah. Or my feet would stop moving completely. And my feet had to keep moving because the thugs were on the escalator too, shoving their way through. What if they had a psycho stationed on every floor? What floor *were* we on?

We hit firm ground, bombing along the walkway.

'Tish!' I gasped. 'We need to get out of sight!' I yanked her towards a shop. 'In here!'

She screwed up her face. 'Dorothy Perkins? Are you mad?'

'For f—'

She was rushing on.

I could just give them the phone. All those other people must have changed their numbers. It was useless to anyone. Except, Sonya's gran had trusted me. She didn't pass it on just so that I could hand it straight over to the thugs who'd been hassling her granddaughter.

A quick look back. They were keeping up, three or four people between them and us. All of them had their hoods up now.

'Here!' Tish pulled my arm so hard, it nearly popped out the socket.

She veered into another clothes shop and now she was running, proper running, swerving past the rails of dresses and trousers and leggings. And I was right there with her, feet slamming, one, two, leaping the clothes on the floor, leaving the hangers swinging. A woman jerked out the way, but I felt the judder as I bumped her. I couldn't look back, couldn't say sorry. I had to steam ahead, through the tight-packed people, the toddlers and the buggies.

We were scrambling down the shop's escalator. I stumbled, catching myself before I hurtled on to Tish.

This must be the ground floor – must be! Unless Westfield had turned into a skyscraper. We raced through kids' clothes, spotty bikinis, racks of hair-bands – and a big wide door opening out to the concourse. The security guard at the door stepped forward.

Listen out! There's no alarm, mate! Don't stop us!

He reached out, his fingers brushing my sleeve, but he was too slow. A swift scan backwards. Faces were turned towards us, vexed, curious faces but none of them under a hood. Not yet. Though they must be on the stairs already. And the guard was on his walkie-talkie.

'Milo!'

Tish was sprinting towards the station. I was right with her, past Greggs, past Marks and Spencers, past Starbucks. At last! We were out of the mall.

I slammed my travelcard on to the reader.

Bourne would have leaped the turnstiles.

And I was along the tunnel, up the stairs and on to the platform, side by side with Tish. My heart could start an earthquake. My breath was razors. Tish's eyes were watering and she was bending, holding her stomach like an alien was ready to burst out of it.

'Not yet!' I gasped. 'Can't stop yet.'

Over the thud of blood, I heard the announcement. This

train. Right now. Get on! And there they were! Hoods, faces, chests, rising over the steps, powering towards us.

Tish spotted them at the same time, and it was like we pushed each other, almost *lifted* each other off the platform and through the train door, as it padded shut behind us.

The train whirred out of the station. I looked back. The thugs were gone.

8

Nine days, checking the phones and anyone who came near me. Once, when Mum had too much wine, she told me that she kept seeing Dad on the street for months after he died. She said it could be the back of a head, or the shape of a chin, or sometimes a walk, long, quick steps in bright red trainers that Dad might have worn. Now it was like that for me. Nearly every kid I saw had cane row or scruffy brown hair and all of them were wearing hoods.

Mum must have noticed I was acting a bit edgy because she started making even stronger hints about me joining a mentoring scheme. I said I'd think about it.

Any spare time I had, I was back with the phone. Even the sickest kitten couldn't have got more attention than that Blackberry. I kept trying all the numbers. Alex must have changed his SIM, probably for good this time, now he knew for sure that Sonya was never going to phone him again. The thugs must have known his number, maybe even known his address. The same way Sonya knocked on my door, they could have knocked on his. 'Call the boy. Make sure he brings the phone'. They weren't going to take no for an answer and Alex wasn't the kind of kid who had badman back up to call on.

Tish, though, was harder on him. According to her, you never grassed up no matter what. It didn't matter that he didn't know me. According to Tish, me and him were in the same boat and he shouldn't have told them where to come and get me. *Yeah, Tish. Remember how I told the cops about Sonya's pills?* Tish was styling it off like Westfield was just fun, though she was still looking round her when we were walking to school. Ever since that day, we always walked to school together.

Saturday morning, I woke up too early. It wasn't dreams, or if it was, I couldn't remember them. There was a feeling, though, like my brain was wriggling and the ripples were passing down through my spine to my nervous system. I was the same way when Andre was in the coma and I'd sit by his bed, thinking he'd never wake up.

As I came out my room, Mum was running up the stairs.

'My warm up,' she said. 'First keep-fit class in months and I don't want to embarrass myself. This came.' She handed me a small white envelope with MARLON SUNDAY written across it in black Biro. It was like the birthday party invitations kids used to hand out at primary school.

Mum ran back down the stairs and called up. 'If it's from school and it's bad, time it well when you tell me, okay?'

'Yeah.'

166

'Right. See you later. Though, if Supa-Zumba does everything it's supposed to, it may be from an oxygen tent.'

As soon as Mum left, I ripped a slit at the top of the envelope and pulled out a square of folded paper. The words were scribbled down in the same black pen. They told me the funeral of Sonya Wilson was at one o'clock next Tuesday, St John and James church in Brixton. I checked the envelope again – no stamp. It was hand delivered.

I took a picture and snapped it over to Tish. She replied straight away. 'COME OVER!!!!'

Down in her kitchen, Tish turned the note over and sniffed it.

'I reckon it's from her grandma,' she said.

I took back the note and held it to my nose. 'No. Can't smell any smoke or incense. And it doesn't look like a proper invitation.'

'I'm not sure . . .' Tish was picking her words carefully. 'I don't think people send invitations to funerals. It must be from her.'

'And she jumped on her bike in Streatham and came over to deliver it, did she?'

Tish snorted. 'She could have got a cab.'

'Be serious, Tish. It means someone's got my address and wants me to know it.'

'You think it's them?'

167

I nodded.

'You're going to go anyway?'

Thinking about it made my stomach churn. I'd been to Dad's funeral and to Sharkie's; there were all these sharp little memories rattling about inside my head. The Baptist woman muttering in tongues at Sharkie's. All the people dressed in black at Dad's even though Mum asked them to come in colour. This time there'd be the gangboys who thought I was a grass.

Yeah, Marlon. It sounds like it's going to be your funeral too.

Tish opened up the freezer and waved a Cornetto at me. 'Want one?'

'No, thanks. I have to go, Tish. It seems wrong if I don't. It's like they've won.'

'You could always go back to the police.'

'Are you mad?'

'No! I thought . . .'

'If you were there when they were asking me questions, Tish, you wouldn't even bother thinking.'

She peeled away the wrapper and dropped it in the bin. 'They had to ask you stuff, Marlon. You had pills and Sonya died.'

'It was the way they asked it, like I was just another Andre.'

'You're not. And they know that now.' She bit a chunk off her cone. 'If you decide to go, you need to be careful.

168

There's bound to be a copper or two on the lookout. Though even that scum wouldn't dare shank you in church.'

'I forgot about that.'

Another liaison with Viking and Sergeant Fat-Knuckle. I hoped the church would be so crowded I wouldn't see them. But I still wanted them there.

Life started to slide back into its old grooves. At school, the kids pushed past me like I was a stiff door. Mr Habato gave up on his sympathetic looks. There were no more missed calls, no messages, no answer when I tried any of the numbers on the Blackberry. And Tish split up with Shaun. Again. Same old, same old.

At first I wasn't going to tell Mum about the funeral, but Tish talked me round. It was on a school day and I'd caused Mum enough grief when I walked out of school after the fight. She came up with every argument there was for me not to go. I'd be upset. I wouldn't know anyone. I'd be the villain and they'd all be queuing up to tell me something. She said I was so young and I'd already been to two funerals; I didn't need to go to another one. Then she changed tack and offered to take a day off work to go with me. When I turned her down, she looked relieved, but still tried to persuade Tish to change my mind. That wasn't one of Mum's best thought-through plans, as Tish wanted details of everything that happened.

* * *

Tuesday morning. Funeral day. I needed music, but couldn't find the right tune. Shuffle bumped me from Percy Sledge to Richie Havens, warm and tender love to going back to my roots, then across to Freddie Hubbard and the song about sunflowers. I sat on my bed in silence.

Mum knocked on my door. 'Can I come in?'

She was dressed for work, her jacket draped over one arm. She handed me a mug of coffee, but her eyes were on the black trousers and jumper hanging from my wardrobe door. She sighed.

'So you're going, then?'

'Yes.'

She pulled the trousers tight to check the crease. 'These could have done with a dry clean. Have you got proper shoes?'

'There's my black trainers.'

'Trainers?' She sighed again. 'Are you sure you want to do this, Marlon? I don't want you to go through what I did at Sharkie's funeral. You'll be there, in front of all those people and I can't even be with you if something kicks off. What if her parents take it out on you? Grief does weird things.'

'She lived with her grandma.'

'How do you know that?'

'Tish found out for me. And then . . . we went round

there. To pay our respects.'

Mum punched her arm through her jacket sleeve. 'When?'

'That Monday. After the fight.'

'That's a big secret to keep.' The second arm was through and she shrugged the jacket on. 'And I'm not sure what to think about it. Did she know who you were?'

'I told her.'

'Grief! And?'

'She said she was glad it was me with Sonya.'

Mum blinked, then turned away from me, pulling at the trousers again. She scratched at some fluff only she could see. I waited.

'Okay,' she said. 'Go if you must, but only to the church, honey, not the cemetery. And call me as soon as you're done, okay?'

'Yes. I promise.'

Mum checked her hair in the mirror. 'And leave off your trainers. Put on your black shoes and pass an iron over those creases.'

'Okay.'

She kissed my forehead. 'Okay.'

I took the tube from Highbury. Every time it stopped, I wanted to jump out. On every platform, there was a kid in a hood, sometimes two. A tall white boy in a grey sweatshirt came and sat opposite me at King's Cross. He unzipped a small sports bag on the seat next to him and started rummaging inside. I had to keep looking, even if he noticed and cussed me. At last, he plucked out an old-style Gameboy, sat back and started working it.

I stared at my reflection in the window. Was this my future? An adrenaline freak-out every time I saw someone wearing a hoodie? I might as well lock myself in an attic and stay there until I was sixty.

I took out the Blackberry and scrolled through the names again. Rodge, Rich, Hess, who were they? Maybe it wasn't even that clever. Rodge was Roger, Rich – Richard. And Hess? Heston? And Orangeboy. *Me*. Did any of them know that Sonya had died? What if they were at the funeral? How the hell would I know?

Outside, the Brixton sign was slowing from a blur to solid words. I stood up, brushing knees with the boy opposite. He looked up, annoyed, dropped his Gameboy in his bag and stalked down the aisle to the door.

St John and St James was one of those massive Victorian churches built away from the main road, in the middle of a wild-looking garden. Bushes poked through the iron railings on to the street and butterflies flew between the clumps of flowers. I could still hear the horns and the bus brakes from the main road, but if I blocked my ears,

172

I'd be in the countryside.

An undertaker was standing by the gate, enjoying a fag. He didn't look much older than me. Did he ever think he'd end up doing this when he left school? An old man with a Zimmer frame clanked by on the opposite pavement; his bright blue and green trainers made him look like he was wearing someone else's feet. I nodded to the undertaker, pushed open the church door, and eased it closed behind me.

This church was brighter than the one where they held Sharkie's funeral. Sunlight poured through the windows and there were no statues of a bleeding Jesus nailed to his cross. I passed a little table with leaflets and collection boxes and slipped into a pew at the back.

The church wasn't full – not even half full. Rows of empty pews stretched in front of me because all the mourners were down the front. None of them looked like they'd been Sonya's friend at school. Not our school or any school. The crowd of crying girls with runny make-up – Tish had been wrong about that. There were no girls Sonya's age here at all. I looked at the walls, the windows, the candles, the backs of the heads in front of me. I tried to keep my eyes on all that, but in the end, I had to look down the aisle.

The coffin was white, with a bunch of pink roses on the lid. I never even knew they made white coffins. Inside it was the girl who'd tugged the curls on the back of my neck. It seemed so small. It could hold her body, but nothing else about her. Not her laugh. Not the big way she moved her hands. Not all the thoughts in her head. Nothing.

I had to keep it all inside me, bite my lip, make my breathing long and slow, force my chest, my throat, my eyes to relax. People were singing, 'All Things Bright and Beautiful' and it sounded like no one wanted to hear themselves. But Sonya probably wouldn't have cared. I didn't imagine hymns were her thing.

What music did she like, then?

One voice was stronger than others, making it sound like Sonya really mattered. I'd heard that voice before. Seven or eight pews down, I saw Mr Pitfield, our deputy school head standing stiff and upright, like his own cardboard cut-out. They'd never mentioned anything about Sonya in assembly, probably because all the older kids who'd remember her had left now.

The hymn was finishing. I mouthed the last bit – 'the Lord God made them all' – and sat down. Behind me, in front of me, either side of me was bare wood. It would have been good to have Tish here now. The priest was talking, telling us how Sonya's body must be honoured and that she'd rise again and need it once more. Was that going to make Sonya's gran feel any better?

There she was, in the front pew, wearing a black

headscarf. Her hand was in front of her face like she was wiping her eyes. Next to her, I couldn't quite make it out – man? Woman? The shape looked like a woman but the hair was shorn to stubble. Two blokes in suits sat behind Sonya's gran. If coppers were here, this would be them, though from behind they looked too short to be the sergeant and his sidekick. They shared their pew with a huddle of women, one with a weave that came down to her waist and another one wearing a green baseball cap. A few more people were scattered in front of Mr Pitfield and – there they were. It must be. It felt like a bubble of air had got trapped in my chest.

Side by side. One with brown hair, about my height, but thinner. Another one taller, first time without a hood. His hair was light blonde, pulled back into a ponytail. The one between them, his head was criss-crossed with cane row. It's a common hairstyle. Even I cane-rowed my hair last summer. And a lot of England had brown hair. But the three of them together, the tall one, the skinny kid, the cane row. God.

I'd done what I'd said I'd do. I'd come and I'd paid my respects, whatever that means. I'd made myself look at that coffin, even though I knew that wherever Sonya's spirit was, it wasn't in that box. Now I could go.

As I looked away from them, I saw that Sonya's gran had turned and was watching me. She nodded, as if she was saying 'thank you'. I nodded back. The shaven haired man-woman next to her turned round too. It was definitely a female, but I couldn't even tell if she was looking at me or way past me, because her expression didn't change. I'd seen that face in a photo before. Yes, it could be a smiling mother with creamy brown hair and her arms around her daughter. But this thin-faced woman looked more like the grainy picture in the newspaper. Bitter Rose, faded petals.

I was right at the back. I could walk out now. Yes, sneak away and leave Sonya's gran with her blanked-out daughter and the thugs who probably helped put Sonya in that box in the first place. How could I look Mum in the eye? She went to Sharkie's funeral even though she knew she had to face his family.

We were asked to kneel – everyone obeyed, including me. Including them. The priest was confident that Sonya was going to heaven. Then time for another hymn, one I hadn't heard before.

Mum never did the ghost thing, or heaven thing, when Dad died. She never tried to pretend that Dad was just on the other side of a one-way mirror, smiling on, even though she'd probably wished it herself. I'd heard her talking to Tish's mum, telling her she wasn't wasting all her energy on something that wasn't solid, when her boys were right there with her and needed her. But one day, me and Andre found a box of letters that Mum had written to Dad. They were

176

dated after Dad died. They were in envelopes with different addresses – a cinema, a restaurant, Homerton Hospital, where me and Andre were born. Neither of us wanted to read the letters. The addresses were enough.

The priest invited Mr Pitfield to talk. It seemed a strange choice. Even I probably knew more about Sonya than he did. He strode up like he was taking assembly and peered out over the church. He must have clocked me sitting there, because he paused for a second, before taking a note out of his jacket pocket and unfolding it. I felt sorry for the man. He had to be brave to go up there and speak. He'd probably passed Sonya in the corridor and told her to put her blazer on or warned her about wearing the wrong colour socks, but never even knew her name. The stuff he was spouting – a bright young woman, her future ahead of her, a painful loss. As much as he probably wanted to, he couldn't say anything special about Sonya. *About Siouxza*. He didn't *know* anything special.

If it was me up there, would I be any better?

Mr Pitfield finished and walked back to his seat, scrunching the paper in his hands. And just then, Cane Row turned around. Slow. Unsmiling. Checking me out. I looked right back. The two beside him, I didn't need to see the front of their stupid, thick heads. All three of them had been at the fair. And at Westfield Now they were here. *He* was here.

177

And his face. It stuck in my head after he turned back. I needed to remember him. He *wanted* me to remember him. Kids like him bigged themselves up by advertising their power. That meant their targets had to know who to be scared of. It was more than that, though, as if his face was playing snap with another face in my memory. Maybe I *had* seen him before. But so what? We were probably at some holiday scheme over the summer when Mum was working. There were kids from everywhere at those places. I probably passed loads of them all the time without even noticing.

That's because none of them were trying to screw me out.

Right. I'd seen him. He'd seen me. Now what?

Leave.

Someone else was talking; it was the woman with the weave.

Go. Now. You've got a head start.

She was gripping the pulpit and seemed to be pulling air into her lungs, like she was ready to sing. When she spoke, her voice was small and shaky, the stories coming out in little bubbles.

GO!

She'd looked after Sonya when she was a baby. Sonya loved pushing her toy dog on wheels when she was learning to walk. She used to sing 'Oranges and Lemons' and build fairy palaces out of bricks. I could see her, a happy child like the one in the photos, stumbling after her toy.

My eyes dropped to the coffin. Sonya's grandma and mother were there at the front next to each other, close, but apart. The woman started a sentence, then stopped and went back to her seat. The priest said a few more prayers, then the undertakers made their slow walk down the sides to the front. They lifted Sonya on to their shoulders without shifting the roses and walked down the aisle towards me. The procession would follow. Sonya, her grandmother, her mother, Cane Row and his thugs, so close that I could touch them.

You should have gone!

I bowed my head, so all I could see was shiny, black shoes and the undertakers' trouser hems.

'Marlon?' Sonya's gran was shaking her head at me. Her skin was blotched and pink, her eyes red and sore. Her daughter glanced at me, then ahead at the coffin. They carried on down the aisle, staying close to Sonya. Right behind, it was them, up front, like they were family.

Just slip down the other end of the pew and GO!

I watched them coming towards me, their hands crossed and heads bowed. Just as they passed me, Cane Row nodded towards me.

'Orangeboy. Sorry for your loss.'

What's your problem? I couldn't trust my voice to say it, in case it sprang out much too loud.

'Marlon.'

Mr Pitfield was beside me. A wrinkly corner of paper poked out from his pocket.

'Yes, sir.'

'Would you like a lift to the cemetery?'

'No, thank you. I'm going home.'

'Okay. I'll see you in school tomorrow.'

And I'll let you off for not being in today. He didn't need to say it. He virtually telepathed it.

The woman with the weave came up to him, accepting his offer of a ride. Mr Pitfield nodded and they walked away together. The last few people fell in place behind the procession. The men who should have 'copper' tattooed on their foreheads, the woman in the baseball cup, a trickle of others. And that was it, no one else. Just me in this big church with the light beaming through and the empty space by the altar.

Go! Now! While the coppers are about and everyone else.

'Are you all right?' The priest was back inside.

'Yes, thanks.'

He sat down beside me. 'Was Sonya your friend?'

'Sort of.'

The priest nodded. You were supposed to confess to priests, tell them the deepest, harshest things about yourself so they could have a word in God's ear on your behalf. It was tempting. Especially as this priest looked genuinely sad, ready to stay with me for as long as it took.

But I didn't have 'as long as'. I had to get away.

My trouser pocket vibrated, the left hand one with Sonya's Blackberry in it.

The priest stood up. 'Don't worry. Take your time.'

He walked back down the aisle and disappeared into a room behind the altar.

I slid out the Blackberry. One missed call – private. I looked round the church. What were they doing? Hiding behind a pew to see if I answered? Somewhere outside, Cane Row was stabbing in numbers, making his point. *I know you're in there. I know you got that phone. We're ready to take it.*

I glanced towards the closed door. Outside, the undertakers would be getting ready to go. They'd slide the coffin into the shiny hearse, shut the door and take Sonya to be buried. I tested the sentence over in my head. 'Take Sonya to be buried.' The thing was, it was just a sentence – words, nothing more. It was just as easy to believe that Sonya could be anywhere. On a plane to Hawaii, or strapped to a weather balloon floating over the earth, or standing in a queue with me, saying—

Balls it.

What?

Her voice in my head. *Balls it.*

I looked at the Blackberry, nodded towards the altar. Balls it. Thank you, Sonya!

The priest was still in his secret room. I powered down the phone and slid it in the back of my boxers. It needed a hard push and a wriggle to fall in place. I took a few careful steps. It felt like my balls were being slapped by a metal bat so I tugged up the waistband and readjusted. That was a bit better. Now all I had to do was walk properly and keep my face neutral. Yeah, I could manage that. I pushed open the door and stepped outside.

The hearses hadn't left yet. Two big wreaths were propped up in the back window, 'Sonya' in pink and white flowers, 'My Daughter' in purple and blue. No Siouxza. Mrs Steedman was talking to the woman with the weave while Sonya's mum was sitting in the back of a hearse. The driver waited by the open door until Mrs Steedman climbed in, then he started the engine and pulled away.

People were getting ready to follow. Mr Pitfield gave me a little wave from his Volvo; there were another five people in there with him. I couldn't see Cane Row and his henchmen anywhere. Why would they bother hanging round? They'd shown me who they were, let me know they could find me. And maybe they'd clocked the police and cleared off.

The last car pulled away. This was it. Done. I found my proper phone and called Mum. She answered straight away, pleased I was okay. We'd talk it over tonight. I checked my messages. Just three from Tish. She was going to—

The fist came out of nowhere. I was thrown against the church wall, my head slamming on the brick. Pain crackled though my skull. My phone dropped from my hand and it was under my feet somewhere, but I couldn't pick it up because they were either side of me, the skinny one, the tall one, heaving all their weight on to my chest, like they wanted to squeeze me to dust. I struggled to hook my arms round, to push them away. But they grabbed my wrists, one each, twisting. Soon they'd snap.

'Get the fuck off me!' My spit flicked on the tall one's chin. Good! It had to hang there, because he couldn't let go.

My phone was shoved in my face. Any closer and they'd jam it up my nostril.

The nutter laugh? Jesus! Not now! No! NO!

'Where's the phone?' Cane Row had made his entrance, damn sure they were holding me good and tight first. The morons twisted and pushed me harder. I was cracking apart like a jigsaw.

He said, 'You think we stupid?'

Yes!

Hands were pressing and poking into my pockets, under my jumper, the top of my waistband. *Not there! Please, God, not there!* My mouth filled with a sticky coffee taste; I swallowed hard to keep it down.

Cane Row stepped away and nodded. His thugs hurled

me back again. My spine hit the wall. And the Blackberry was shifting. One more jerk and it would fall down my trouser leg. I squeezed my thighs together. If it was worth this much to them, they sure as hell weren't going to get it now.

Cane Row's face loomed closer. 'Where's the phone, man?'

'You've got it! In your hand!'

Cane Row muttered something and hurled my phone into a bush. 'You think we're making joke?' He pushed his face into mine. The boy had a baby moustache. If I blew it, it could fly away. Heat was building up inside me, my hypothalamus revving up. Flight. Fight. Flight. Fight. He was so close I could smell him, breath, skin, hair. His eyelashes were long, like a girl's. He must have been a pretty baby. I bet his mum made him wear a little white dress and a bonnet. And, *shit,* out it burst – the nutter laugh. It launched so quick and hard, there was nothing I could do to hold it back. Tears ran down my face and my stomach muscles were cramping up. I ran out of breath. Stopped.

Cane Row stood there, calm. 'Yes.' His voice was quiet. 'Orangeboy thinks we're making joke.' He grabbed my chin tight, like he wanted to crack bone. 'The boy's gone dotish, just like his mashup brother.' His thumb and finger pressed down on either side of my mouth. 'You don't understand how this t'ing's working, Orangeboy.'

No! I don't understand! I was losing my thoughts.

I tried to shake my head, shift him. Nothing. Not even a twitch.

'Close your eyes, Orangeboy.' Cane Row was smiling, fingers pushing, pushing, grinding my cheek into teeth.

Suddenly the fingers shifted, pinching my nose, sealing up my nostrils.

'Imagine, boy. I'm a blonde gyal, yeah?'

My mouth opened, trying to suck in air. The idiots were laughing. Was this mad knobwit going to kiss me or something? His mouth was almost touching mine. Yeah, me and him, lip to lip in the churchyard. The laugh was stirring again. I forced it back.

Cane Row coughed. Suddenly, I got it. I tried to twist away, but the idiot-boys were clamping my face in place. The glob of spit flew out of his mouth and into mine, sitting on my tongue in a warm puddle. The back of my throat clamped tight, but my reflexes were fighting. Swallow! Swallow! Swallow!

I spat hard. Cane Row jumped back, missed it. I scraped my top teeth against my tongue, spat again and again. The idiots were honking like hyenas. Yeah, Marlon Sunday, the joke that kept on giving.

Think this is funny?

I tugged one arm free, launched myself forward and landed a hook. Cane Row listed sideways. There was cheering in my head, but I should have got him in the mouth! Knocked his teeth down his throat so he could never do this to anyone again.

His thugs pulled me back. A hand blurred through the air, the wrist bone slamming against my eye socket. The world muddled. I blinked hard, caught my breath, and kicked out; my foot connected with a shin. Proper shoes. Mum was right. They're much better than trainers. The air went still. Cane Row's jacket flapped open, showing a glint of silver. A knife? This psycho carried a knife to a girl's funeral?

'You think you're such a good boy.'

What?

The air whizzed. A punch landed in my gut, the soft bit, just below my ribs. My body went into spasm, breath pushed back in my lungs and stayed there. Knuckles skimmed my cheek, cracked against my nose.

No more! No more! But there could be much more. He'd made sure I saw the shank. They could still do it, kill me here, in the churchyard while Sonya and the flowers and all those people were on their way to the cemetery.

Cane Row suddenly looked behind him. He turned back, smirking.

'Tell Mr Orange, I'm coming.'

He let go of me, straightening his jacket like a banker getting off a train. He strutted off, the moron brothers right behind.

I sunk to the ground. It sounded like an alarm had gone off inside my head, one high note skewing the message paths telling me what part of my body belonged where. I had no arms or legs or hands. I was just pain and ache shifting through jelly.

'I'll call an ambulance.' The priest was crouching beside me.

They must have seen him. That's why they left off. Even Cane Row didn't want to tangle too much with God's messenger on earth.

That fat slug in my mouth – that was my tongue. I had to move it, tip against teeth, mouth pulling shapes to make words. It wasn't happening.

'And the police.' The priest had a phone. Where did he keep it? Did his robes have pockets? The laugh was swelling up. A ripple of pain in my – yes, chest, the thing that had my lungs inside. And the lungs, they hurt. If I stopped the breath coming out from them, I'd hold down the laugh. That hurt too.

The priest held me gently under my shoulders. 'Can you stand up?'

Utter focus, brain straining. The connections were shimmery but just starting to tick over. I made it up, but my stomach pulled hard. I had just enough time to lurch over and heave, my guts pulsing and pulsing, bile and emptiness. I took tissues out my jacket pocket, the ones

187

Mum said I'd need at a funeral. Not for this, though. I wiped my mouth.

The priest turned away until I'd finished. He said, 'Come back to the vicarage and I'll get you some tea.'

'No.' Just a mumble, but if I shook my head, my eyeballs would fly out.

'The ambulance won't take long, just a couple of minutes. Come in and clean up and we'll write down what they looked like.'

This man had never sat on the wrong side of a police table, never had the coppers staring him down, calling him a liar. Never had to push his nose into his sleeve in a stinking police cell or had some sergeant asking him if he'd slept with a girl who'd just died.

'No,' I said. 'Not the police.'

The priest stepped back. 'Those boys were at the funeral, weren't they? Do you know them?'

My head was shaking, maybe saying 'no', maybe joining in with the rest of my body. I tried to make my feet, legs, hips move together so I could walk away. If I sat down, I'd never get up.

The priest was beside me again. 'Can I call someone to come and get you?'

Lips in a circle, fat tongue tapping the roof of my mouth. 'No.'

'Okay. But come inside and sit down. I've got some

Savlon somewhere and you need some ice for your face.'

My mouth moved and a strange sound came out. The priest leaned closer and I tried to make the sound again. He looked around and I kept my mind on one thought. Keep standing. He was peering between two bushes.

'This one?' He held up my phone.

I nodded. As I shuffled forward, the Blackberry dug into my leg, like it wanted to remind me that it had all been worth it.

The vicarage was a few seconds away on a normal day. This must have been the slowest trip the priest had ever made, with me staggering and stopping after every tiny step. He opened the door and waited while I stopped to let the nausea pass.

He said, 'Do you want to clean up first?'

'Yes, please.'

The toilet was right next to the front door. I held on to the sink, waiting for the sickness to ease. I felt like I'd been run over by a lorry. I looked at myself in the small mirror above the sink. My eyes were a bit puffy and there was a bleeding scratch on my cheekbone. More blood was smeared beneath my nose. Mum would be stressed, but it could be worse.

I turned on the hot tap and let it run until I could see steam.

A knock on the door. 'Are you all right in there?'

'Yes, thanks.'

'Okay. Just checking you hadn't passed out.'

I put my mouth directly to the tap and sucked in a mouthful of scalding water, ignoring the burn on my tongue and inside my cheeks. I spat it out. Then again and again. I squirted a speck of soap on to my finger and rubbed it along my tongue, rinsed it and kept rinsing until the taste was gone. A splosh of cold water over my face and I checked myself again.

Cane Row had a knife. If the priest hadn't come, what next? A shank in my leg or my arm? A slash across the face, the knife point dug in at the corner of my eye and ripping its way down. *Mr Orange, I'm coming.* That was the message I was supposed to pass on. I wasn't Mr Orange then. Just Orangeboy. My head was too full of mush to work it out. I fished out the Blackberry and stuck it in my pocket.

'I've made you some tea!'

I could feel the priest waiting on the other side. I opened the door. 'Thank you.'

I drank the tea and rubbed the lotion on the sore bits. I also gladly swallowed the tablets, the sort that promised to kill pain quick. As I said goodbye, they were still to keep their promise. But my head fog was thinning out and one thought was coming out of the shadows. That thought was shaped like Andre. Sonya mentioned him. Cane Row mentioned him. My brother was living his street life for more than six years before the accident, enough to make an army of enemies. None of them ever came to the house. He'd moved out before he started getting into the bad stuff, but somehow that threat was always bubbling under. Mum even had locks put on the windows.

But how could Andre be Mr Orange? He'd always been clear about his views on snitches. Beef was sorted out in the street with each other and the police were the common enemy. This must be some misunderstanding, something stupid got out of proportion.

I left the vicarage and headed towards the main road, stopping every time my knees said 'enough'. I nipped the tip of my tongue between my front teeth, pushing hard enough to distract my brain from everything else.

Brixton was busy, like everyone who didn't go to Westfield came here. It was the south's version of Dalston, with the market and African clothes stores and those booths with Asian blokes flogging cheap phone cards. A Rasta guy in a tracksuit shoved a leaflet in my hand. Fred's frozen fish shop was now open for business. Shoppers hustled past me on the narrow pavement. Every time I got knocked, it felt like another bit of my insides ripped away.

Cane Row and his sidekicks could be anywhere. They could be making their way through the market or hiding by

191

the kente cloth or spying through the window of a patty shop. I stopped by the bus stop and leaned against the shelter. The bus opposite pulled away. They were there! No, it was just some kid talking on his phone. But what if Cane Row had put out the call and there was a whole army of little boys out to find me and prove themselves? The kid opposite could have just taken a picture of me. It would already be circling his networks.

A 159 bus pulled up. I got on quick, went straight to the top and sank into a free seat by the window. It was just me and no one else. As the door shut and we moved away, I breathed out. I still hurt, but not so much.

The bus was heading to Oxford Street, but I wasn't planning to go that far. One more bus and I was knocking at the door with the pots of twisted trees either side.

Deidre Arnold looked me up and down. 'You're . . . Andre's brother?'

'Yes, Marlon. Is Andre here? I tried his phone, but it was dead.'

'Yes, but you? You look – what happened to your face?'

'I was coming home from a funeral and some kids jumped me for my phone.' Truth, with lots of wrapping.

'Oh, good God! I'm so sorry. It's happened to some of our residents. They're seen as an easy touch. Is there anything I can do?'

Call up assassins. Set them on Cane Row.

'No, I'm all right.'

'Did you report it?'

'Not yet.'

'We always do. Not that anyone's ever been caught. Andre's out the back, I'll take you round.' She was still studying me. 'Are you sure you're all right, Marlon?'

'Yeah, thanks.'

I followed her into a bright, yellow kitchen, through a sliding door to a small conservatory and out into the garden. It was bigger than you'd expect, wrapped around three sides of the house like an apron, with a row of tall trees that made sure it was a secret from outsiders. Andre was sitting on a blanket by some rose bushes. He was with a long-haired guy in skinny jeans, the sort of bloke my brother used to cuss for cluttering up his favourite bars. They were lifting handfuls of compost from a bag to small plastic pots.

Deidre Arnold called, 'Rowan?'

Skinny-jean boy patted Andre on the shoulder and came over. His smile wavered, then he fixed it tight. 'You must be Andre's brother. I can see the resemblance.'

'Thank you.'

'No worries. Do you want to take over gardening duties?'

Andre was scooping up earth and letting it trickle through his fingers. He didn't seem to notice when I took Rowan's place. He filled another small pot and patted it down.

I sat down beside him. 'Hi, Andre.'

He didn't look up.

'What's going in?'

He pointed to the seed packets fanned out in front of him. 'Lettuce, tomato, pumpkin. I never knew they grew pumpkins here. I thought it was just America.'

He poked a hole in a pot of soil with his finger, tore the edge off a packet and shook a seed into the pot. He smoothed the soil over and passed it to me.

'This good, Sharkie?'

'It's Marlon.'

'How long it takes?'

I checked the packet. These were small, pale striped things, not the orange cartoon giants. 'It says "from early August".'

Andre planted another seed and another one, the pots lined up waiting for me to inspect. A radio played inside the house and a bunch of seagulls squawked on their way to – where? Probably Brighton or Southend. It was like a holiday, but in someone else's life. It was the life where your brother taught you the good stuff, where the only thing you found under his bed was his porn stash. Where you and your girlfriend go on a picnic and the other boys don't want to slice you up. Yeah, that was somebody else's life. But I had to deal with mine. That meant getting Andre to answer some questions. Carefully though, or he'd blow up and storm away.

I said, 'So you're a gardener now.'

Andre shrugged. 'The people say I have to do it to help my anger management.'

'Does it help?'

We looked at each other and in spite of it all I laughed with him. Andre was angry before the accident. Mum said he'd been born in a fury and never recovered.

The sun was heating up my back, especially the sore places that hit the wall. I took off my jacket and lay it on the ground. Rowan wandered over with tea and biscuits. He must have brewed it in a nuclear reactor because it was red hot. I let it linger on the patch of tongue where the gob had landed.

Rowan picked up a plant pot. 'This is the easy bit. When the plants grow bigger, we'll have to dig a hole and plant them out properly.' He stood up. 'I'll leave you guys to it.'

As he walked away, Andre sucked his teeth. 'The damn fool thinks I'm stupid! Course I know the thing's going to grow!'

It was a flash of old Andre, sparking up beneath the hat and shades. He muttered something else. I told him I hadn't heard. He pushed back the peak of his cap and let his sunglasses hang low, like he was challenging me with his carved-up face.

'I said them people shouldn't have bother. They should

have left me in the car, right there.'

'The man coming after you had a gun! Did you want him to shoot you?'

He didn't react. A good sign.

I said, 'If he had a gun, how come you and Sharkie weren't strapped?'

'We didn't deal with that business.'

'Yes, you did. Don't you remember the box in your wardrobe?'

'Stop talking at me, man.'

'We went to the bookshop. You and Sharkie bought a gun!'

'I don't remember nothing!' His hand shot out and walloped away the pots. Soil and seeds scattered across the grass. 'You didn't hear me?'

'Yes, I heard you.'

'So leave man alone!'

I waited for someone to run out to see what the yelling was about. But they must be used to shouting in a place like this; there was going to be a lot of frustration. I needed more than frustration, though. I needed information.

'Sorry Andre. I'm just trying to understand your old life. If badmen were coming after you, why didn't you just stop it all?'

Andre shook his head. 'Man, if you don't know, I can't

196

tell you.' He poked his stomach. 'It was here, right here. You're walking down the street and everyone's looking at you like you're a king. People move out your way and no man's going to say nothing to you. And if them others want to bring beef, we got each other's back.' He pushed his hat low, shades firmly against his face. 'You know who's on your side.'

The pumpkin seed in my fingers collapsed into a sticky mess. I hadn't realised I was holding it. I wiped my hand on the grass.

I said, 'What about the ones who weren't on your side?'

Andre picked up a wooden plant tag and poked it in and out of the soil.

'What happened if they came after you? What did you do?'

In, out, in, out.

'Things must have got bad. Do you remember that bookshop in Highgate? You were supposed to take me to the drama club, but we ended up there. I kept my promise, Andre. I never told Mum.'

The earth was bumpy with slits. 'I can't remember nothing, man.'

'I found the gun in your wardrobe. Maybe it wasn't real, but it looked it. You came and saw me holding it, Andre. It was the only time you ever hit me. Try and remember.'

He held the plant tag still, looking at me, his thoughts

197

secret behind those shades. 'No, man. A bookshop.' He laughed. 'I wouldn't go to no bookshop.'

'Okay.' I looked round. There was no one to hear us. 'What would you have done if you needed a gun? Where would you go?'

'If you make good money, you buy top range, not one of them little fireworks that could blow up on you. Maybe a smooth Mac-10, clean, no history. But me and Sharkie, we didn't get that type of money. We're not selling shots or knifing up big men in them estates. It was just me and my brother.'

Sharkie. His brother.

He was still talking, forgotten I was there. 'Me and Sharkie don't need nothing much.'

I said, 'Why?'

'Why?'

'Why would you – anyone – get a gun?'

He was shaking his head. 'The street's unpredictable, man. Me and Sharkie, we don't cross no one. We even call truce with some of them south London boys so they don't bother us if we went down their ways. Same thing if they come up here.'

'No one tried to make trouble for you, then?'

'I don't remember.'

'What about when you came out of hospital?'

'Yeah!' He slapped my leg; my nerves squealed. 'This

fool, he knocks on my door soon after I come back to the flat. He's telling me some stupidness, how he sold me something before and how I still need to protect myself. Man must look at me and thinks he sees a proper crip.'

His voice was rising again. I made mine extra quiet.

'Andre, I think something did happen. I need you to try and remember.'

Nothing.

'There's a boy, about my age. Maybe a bit older. I think I know his face, Andre. And he gave me a message. 'Tell Mr Orange, I'm coming'. I think you're Mr Orange.'

He dropped the plant tag. 'I don't remember nothing. Man, you just come here to stress me out.'

He stood up clumsily, turned away and limped towards the house. I tried to get up and follow him but my body screamed, nerve endings slicing into each other. He turned the corner and was gone. I lay back and closed my eyes.

'Pumpkin seed devastation.'

Rowan was standing over me.

'Yeah,' I said.

'Was it about Saleema?'

'No. Was there another bust up?'

Rowan laughed. 'No, they've given up on all the yelling. It's a bit more the opposite really. Her family's moving up to Humberside and taking her with them. Andre's pretty upset.'

'No, he didn't mention it.'

Rowan kneeled down and started scooping earth back into the pots, carefully teasing out the pumpkin seeds. 'You're looking a bit shattered, Marlon. Fancy another cup of tea?'

'No, I'm all right, thanks.'

I watched him refilling the pots, arranging the seeds in a pile next to them.

Rowan said, 'Andre's lonely. With Saleema gone, everyone here's older than him. There's no one else . . .'

Black?

'From his culture. He doesn't have any friends come to see him, though from what I heard, that's probably a good thing. But I think he needs to connect back with the outside world. Not just you and your mum, but a bit wider. He refuses to go to any support groups. I'm sure you can imagine the kind of things he says about them.'

Oh, yes.

'Got any ideas? Me and Deidre are a bit flummoxed.'

'I'll think about it.'

'Thanks.' Rowan smiled.

A couple of bees swerved between us and settled on the roses.

'Hey!' he said. 'It looks like we're in for some London honey.'

I watched them rummage through the petals.

'If it's all right,' I said, 'I will have that cup of tea.'

'No worries.'

'And is it okay if I stay out here for a bit? I'll redo the pumpkins.'

'Be my guest.'

When I left, Andre was in the TV room, deep into *The Simpsons*. It was the one with the blind man and the dope, one of Andre's favourites. He grunted 'goodbye' back at me, like I was someone he'd just met.

My timing was crap, bang into rush hour. I had to stand on the bus, propping myself up with the pole, rammed against the suits coming home from the offices. The woman next to me was checking the weather forecast for Athens on her Blackberry.

When Sonya checked her Blackberry, she wasn't finding out if it was sunny or not in her holiday destination. It was probably hidden under her duvet with her door locked, planning her outings with Rizz and Stunna and Diamond, boys like me who were more likely to kiss Princess Leia than get the attention of a girl like Sonya. All of us collected on her phone with a sad little nickname to remember us by. Cane Row wanted that phone badly, though, a tidy bit of evidence to link him to the drugs. Once the police got it in their labs, they'd do their best to trace the calls and track down the boys who'd she talked to – including me. Me and

Alex had already proved we couldn't keep our mouths shut. I didn't reckon that any of the others were heroes neither. At least now Sonya's Blackberry was safe, as long nobody checked why the earth was dug up under the rose bush.

Two more buses and a hundred hours later, I was at the top of my street. I walked down slowly, making the most of the air and the headspace. Tish had sent a whole load of texts demanding details about the funeral. I had to work out what to tell her. The full story and she'd be shouting about going to the police again. And then there was Mum. I'd checked my face at Andre's and it was swelling up instead of calming down. It was going to stress her out big time.

The house looked empty. It was probably a late session at the library tonight, an author signing or something. Maybe if I stuck my head in the freezer for half an hour, I'd be okay by the time she came home.

'Orangeboy?' Called so quietly, the plane going overhead almost drowned it out.

Before I could turn, an arm hooked around my neck, squeezing my throat. I was yanked backwards, off-balance, landing on the pavement.

My attacker crouched down next to me. His hood was up, pulled low over his forehead, and he'd wrapped a scarf round the bottom of his face. But I could see his eyes, with long eyelashes, like a girl.

He glanced up the road. I'd heard it too, a bus on its way down. His mouth was close to my ear.

'Tell Mr Orange, the time has come.'

9

I pulled myself on to the bench and slumped down, clinging to the plastic. Adrenaline and cortisol had kicked at my brain and run away again. I had nothing left to help me move.

The bus doors puffed open. 'Marlon?' Wheels and feet. 'Marlon!'

I frowned, trying to open my good eye wide.

'Tish . . .'

'Jesus, Marlon! What happened?'

I tried to speak; my throat still wouldn't work. I managed to stand up, one hand on Tish's shoulder and the other one on the side of the bus shelter. That dark splodge on the ground, was that my blood? I touched my face. The cut felt split open.

Tish said, 'Can you walk?'

No! Can't you feel me shaking?

'Come on, Milo! Just a few steps, right?'

One foot after the other, each step a jab in my gut. We crossed the road, me leaning heavily against Tish's shoulders.

'Where are your keys?' she said.

'Pocket.'

She fished inside my jacket, pulled them out and opened the door.

'Oh Jesus,' she said. 'Oh God.'

Somewhere in the back of my throat words started, but stayed stuck there. Cane Row must have had a plan – mash it up and mash it hard. They'd charged through the house like a damn army, kicking around our shoes, pulling down our coats, throwing all our pictures on the floor. I looked at myself, Year Nine, with my face stamped in. And my grandma, a year before she died, glass cracks cutting through her cheek.

I had to hold the wall to help me into the sitting room. They must have known this place was special, because they'd put in the work. They'd found my old kids' encyclopaedias, Dad's atlases, the posh Dickens collection Mum bought herself last Christmas. They'd bounced them like tennis balls and then just ripped the pages out. I picked up *Oliver Twist*. Its spine was all floppy and bent.

Tish was shaking her head, looking ready to cry.

I said, 'I'll get them.'

Tish looked at me. 'We need to call the police, Marlon.'

'No.'

'Yes, Marlon. You're not Andre. You're not a gangsta, remember?'

Yeah, I remembered. Because if I was, I wouldn't be standing here now. I'd be on the phone, gathering my own army, priming my weapons. This was beef, proper beef. When it happened, your mates came with you to sort it out.

Tish picked up an armful of our crushed books. 'This must be them, Marlon. Just give them the phone, all right?'

'No.'

'Things are getting too hot.'

'I haven't got it any more.'

'What?'

'I'm going to check upstairs.'

I pulled myself up along the banister. A mob of mini-men were setting off bangers in my head, one step, one explosion. All the upstairs doors were flung open. I could see into Mum's room; nothing looked disturbed. But my room . . .

The duvet and sheet were pulled off my bed and they'd emptied out the drawers into a mountain of pillows and covers. All my books, music, school stuff, everything, was piled up on top like the start of a bloody great bonfire. The vinyl, Lonnie Liston Smith, George Benson, The Jones Girls, flung across the room. Brothers Johnson, smashed.

'Look what that girl dropped you in!' Tish's eyes were wide and furious. 'All this crap landing at your mum's house, just because you were following your dick . . .'

'Yeah, Tish, I really need that now!' The dried blood was making my face stiff and my head was throbbing. 'And Sonya's dead, right? So leave it alone!'

Tish took a step towards me, like she was ready to have her own workout on my face. 'You still don't get it, do you? You still think she was after you for your sweet nature? You seriously think she had no idea that this crap could happen? Her mum was a junkie, Marlon! She knew exactly what came with it! No – she knew exactly *who* came with it . . . People who want their money. People who are never going to be nice. This was Andre's life, not yours. You're not a gangsta.'

Tish was right. No one could call me a gangsta. But the thing was, those morons had bashed up my mum's house. There was no choice. I had to do something.

Tish called 999. The police were coming, and an ambulance. I called Mum. She was already at the top of the street and must have run down to get here quick. She came through the door, looked at me, then the hallway. Then she tried to make me take the ambulance to A & E. I didn't want to go, didn't want to leave her. But I ended up shouting, not at her, but because I didn't know what to say. She looked like she never wanted to live in this house again. I should have told her I understood. Instead, I yelled at her to leave me alone. The police and paramedic looked at me as if I was the nastiest form of dog crap.

I tried to apologise, but she pretended I wasn't there, even when I was sat next to her on the sofa while we were interviewed. She kept looking straight ahead, her hands clasped in her lap. Every time I shifted, my body shrieked back at me. I checked the clock. Three more hours before the next batch of Nurofen. And guess what? They delivered up the Ol' Gil sidekick copper from that Saturday night. He took a couple of sips of the tea Mum made him and left the mug on the floor by his feet.

'It's hard on your mother,' he said.

I glanced at Mum. 'She's right next to me. You don't need to talk like she's not there.'

Mum sighed. 'Not now, Marlon.'

The copper nodded in agreement. 'Any idea who trashed the house, Marlon?'

'No.'

'It must have been the same guys who jumped you at the bus stop.'

Yes.

'Who were they?'

'I don't know.' *And if I told you, what would you do about it?*

'What did they look like?'

'I don't know.'

Mum sighed again, but didn't say anything.

'Black? White?' This copper must be part snake; he didn't need to blink.

'I didn't see.'

'Oh, come on! You must be able to tell if someone's black or white.'

'I'd just been to see my brother. I was coming down the road and someone grabbed me by the bus stop. He was behind me, I didn't see him at all."

'Did they take anything? Your phone, maybe?'

'No.'

The copper stood up. 'They smashed your room up good and proper, but they didn't touch the kitchen or your mum's room. Your TV's still here, and your mum's laptop.'

I nodded.

'A burglary with nothing taken. Weird, that.'

'Yes.'

'And you didn't see anything at all.' His hand was on the door handle. 'You know where I am if you can remember any more.'

Mum and the copper said a few words in the hallway, then the front door slammed. I heard her sliding in the bolt. She came in, closing the sitting room door, leaning her back against it.

'They're going to come and change the locks tomorrow. Then they'll send someone round to do a security assessment, though it seems a bit late for that now.' She sat next to me on the sofa and touched the dressing under my eye. 'It's not fair, is it? Andre came home looking like this more than once and I barely raised an eyebrow. The street fighting and the bravado, that was who he was. But I hoped he'd work his way through it and turn his mind to something else. But, you, Marlon. I never saw you as a fighter.'

'I'm not. That's why I look like this.'

She managed a little smile. 'But with everything Andre put us through . . .' She shrugged. 'It never came to this, did it? He never brought it into our home. Is there something you want to tell me, Marlon?'

'No, I'm all right.'

'Are you? It's since the girl died.' I must have flinched because she rested her hand on my shoulder. 'This isn't about her, God bless her. It's just – things have shifted. So much has happened to us, hasn't it? So much more than other people. I thought everything had calmed down now. I thought we'd gone as low as we could and were climbing up the other side.' She stood up. 'Maybe I should have moved out of London. I don't know . . .'

I stood up too. The top of her head only reached my chin. 'It's not your fault, Mum.'

'I'm scared for us, Marlon. I can't imagine climbing into bed and going to sleep. I don't think I can even close my eyes. You know how I love sitting in here and listening to my music, but I feel like we've been invaded. Just the thought of them touching your father's . . .' She wiped her eyes. 'Jonathan says we can stay at his. He's on his way already. It's not great for school, but we'll manage.'

'You go. I'll stay.'

Mum squeezed her eyes shut and rubbed her hands into her face. 'I can't leave you here.'

'If we both leave now, it feels like we'll never come back again.'

Mum was looking at the box of massacred atlases and the books slumping into each other because so many were missing. My throat was full of needles. All the 'sorrys' I wanted to say were tangled up in them.

'Maybe you're right.' Mum's voice was small and unconvinced. 'People get broken into all the time. I'll just have to man up and deal with it. I'll go and make us some hot chocolate. That's if they've left us a pan to boil the milk in.'

I slid myself on to the floor. My ribs bellowed. I picked up the Nurofen, but if I knocked back any more I'd dissolve when I touched water. I reached for the box of torn maps, took out the top one and flattened the pages out. Then the next one and the next one. I started marrying up the page numbers and joining together the country outlines. Spanish mountains. Bermuda. Scottish Islands and Highlands. Did Dad ever go to these places? Or were they just as far away as Ganymede or Io?

'Here.' Mum placed the mug on the coffee table. 'It's okay, Marlon. We can sort it out together. I think we should try and make sense of your room first.'

Jonathan arrived as we stood staring at the chaos. He took charge straight away. 'I'll take CDs. You and Jenny are on shoes and clothes.'

You had to admire the man; he must be furious with me, but he was holding it all in so he wouldn't upset Mum.

We all went to bed around midnight. I managed just a few blinks of sleep. Every time I moved it hurt like hell and when I finally dozed off I dreamed that a blue, furry monster leaped out of my wardrobe and bit my face. I sat up and turned on the lamp, popped out another two Nurofen and swallowed them with a gulp of water.

3.47 a.m. I looked out of the window. Parked cars, streetlights, the empty bus shelter. Tish's window was dark and her curtains drawn. As I was up, I might as well check the house again. When I was doing the rounds an hour ago, I'd found Mum in the kitchen, brewing more hot chocolate. We'd both nearly jumped out of our skins.

I shuffled downstairs again. The front door bolt was firm, so was the kitchen's now. That's how they'd got in.

They'd forced open a neighbour's decrepit side gate, vaulted the garden fence and come in through the kitchen door. They'd broken the glass, reached through and unlocked it.

Maybe Tish was right and I should have just given the Blackberry to the police, let them sort it out. But somehow that didn't seem right. Sonya's gran hadn't. It would have been like handing in Sonya herself. For the second time.

'Marlon?'

Mum was knocking on my door. I tried to open my eyes, but the left one felt like it had been stitched together by a lunatic surgeon who'd kneed me in the nuts at the same time.

She opened the door a crack. 'You don't have to go school today. I've left a message on the absent line and emailed them as well. You know what they're like. They'll probably still call me.'

'Thanks, Mum.'

'Shall I bring you up some coffee?'

'No. I'm okay, thanks.'

My door clicked shut. I eased myself up and looked out of the window. A bloke in a red sweatshirt was walking his dog. A bus slowed as it reached the bus stop. I inched myself around so I was sitting on the edge of the bed, catching sight of my face in the wardrobe mirror. Not so much beaten boxer as football in the face. A football with a couple of nails stuck in it. I stood up. My body was a circuit board of agony.

Coming downstairs, I smelled coffee and singed toast. Jonathan was scraping the burned bits into the sink.

'I think your toaster's on its last legs.'

'It's been like that for ages,' I said. 'You have to push the button so it pops out early.'

Jonathan turned on the tap swilling the crumbs down the plughole, back still turned to me.

'Jenny's having a bath,' he said.

Too much information. He faced me, eyes hard, mouth drawn tight. A happy face on a beach ball? How the hell could I ever have thought that?

'After you went to bed, I had to stop her from taking out a bucket and washing this whole house down. She said she felt contaminated.'

Who was this man, a guest in my kitchen, telling me how Mum felt? Like I wouldn't know?

'I care about Jenny,' he said. 'I don't want her to feel like this.'

I nodded. There'd been a tiny pause when he said Mum's name, like he needed to find the right breath. He had to keep so much inside him. I'd never thought about it before, but it was true. Jonathan didn't yell and shout at me, didn't even swear. Sometimes he must want to explode.

My heart was racing; I waited for it to smoothe out. 'I don't want Mum to feel this way either.'

He was studying me. 'So what do you suggest?'

'Perhaps she should stay with you for a bit.'

'She doesn't want to leave you, Marlon.'

'I know. But I don't mind.'

'You're welcome to come too.'

First one bad boy son, then the other. Most men would have disappeared in the first six months, but Jonathan stuck around for her. He made the invitation like he meant it.

'Marlon, I don't want to interfere in your life . . .'

Don't pause, Jonathan, because I can't fill in the gaps for you.

'If you know any way to make this better . . .' Jonathan's eyes softened. 'Please do, okay? And, for God's sake, please don't make it worse.'

Jonathan turned back to the sink.

When Mum came into my room later, there was a busyness about her. She was wearing make-up, earrings and the long red necklace Jonathan bought her for Christmas. She looked at the closed books on my desk then back at me.

She said, 'How are you feeling?'

'Like I've been run over by a tractor.'

She smiled. 'The way I felt yesterday, it could have been me behind the wheel.'

I opened my mouth.

She held up her hand. 'Don't say you're sorry. Or else I'll start to think you're guilty. Listen, me and Jonathan are going down B&Q. I've made a list.' She held up the page. 'Filler, picture frames, hooks, a new dustpan and brush, unless you've got it up here somewhere.' Another smile. 'I suppose we would have found it last night if you did. Then we're going to look round some door companies and see about replacing that back door, and maybe the front one too with something more secure. Can you think of anything else?'

I could still do with that assassin. I shook my head.

'Okay, hon. Try and have something to eat. Lock the door after we've gone and give me a call if you start feeling dizzy.'

'Yes, Mum.'

'And do some revision. Did I tell you about Aunty Cecile's business partner? She's from Congo so she speaks French. I'm sure she'll be happy to help if you need to practise conversation.'

'Thanks, Mum.'

'Okay, I get the message. I'll leave you alone now. There's still some glass in the hallway carpet, so be careful.'

After the front door slammed behind Mum and Jonathan, I snapped on the latch. I cleared the breakfast table and spread out my books. Down here, I wouldn't be tempted to look out of the window every time I heard voices in the street.

What should I start with? French. That was the hardest. Irregular and reflexive verbs or the page of Camus that Mum had photocopied for me? As I stared hard at the words, a fist flew towards me. My blood dripped on the ground. I blinked hard and looked down again. Paper, lines, squiggles and dots.

I flipped the French books shut. When that gutslime shoved me against the wall, my head banged twice, but there was no permanent damage. My neurons would zap back to life. Wernike's, Broca's, the inferior frontal gyrus, all the cogs would grind together again and help me – seeing, translating, understanding, a proper smooth brain action. What happened to me was nothing, not compared to Andre. His brain was a soft lump of dough inside a hollow ball that got whacked by a cricket bat. When he was lying like dead in hospital, all wrapped round with tubes and wires, all his connections were shaken around and pulled apart. His brain from his body, me from his best mate, new Andre from old Andre.

Old Andre, who left some hidden mark in the past that was rubbing off on me. If he couldn't remember what it was, I needed to talk to someone who did. And yes, didn't Rowan say that Andre needed to connect with old friends?

10

The Coburn estate was built by an architect who hated people. There were rows of terraced houses with identical porches and gardens without fences. These were surrounded by random-sized tower blocks, tall, modern ones, low flat ones and one of those old-style red brick ones with shared balconies. I checked off the names. Gaugin Court, Da Vinci Terrace, Botticelli Tower. None of them painters, as far as I knew, ever spent time in Hackney. Something thudded at my feet. It was a rolled up disposable nappy. A couple more were blocking the gutter in the road. Somebody in one of the top floors must have aimed for the bin and missed. Or aimed for me and nearly not missed.

I moved on, scanning the street signs for Picasso Road. Funny how the address just stuck in my head. Hogarth Road. More an alley, really. Gainsborough Road . . .

This place used to be famous for its own little army of hyped-up hood rats. Takeaway places never delivered here and someone set up a website full of pictures of the yellow police boards. But it was quiet now. The gang kids were probably all banged up or dead. There were a couple of posher-looking places here, too, set back from the road, behind big gates. I was on Picasso now. 20, 18, 16, a row of houses next to a new block of flats. Some people had planted up their front gardens with flowers. Those were the proper optimists, sticking their roses back in each time they were stolen. Or the estate psychos who knew no one was going to run across their lawns and nick their pots. Or force open their backdoors and mash up their homes.

Number 2. A basket of dead flowers was hanging from the porch. The lawn was tufty with bare patches – and God, lumps of dog crap had burned their way through the grass. I took a deep breath and walked down the path. The door opened before I reached the end and a girl stared out at me. She was probably eleven or twelve and her face was a bit narrower, but other than that she'd hardly changed in three years. It was Bronwyn, Sharkie's youngest sister.

'Is Louis there?'

'Who are you?'

'My name's Marlon, Marlon Sunday.'

She closed the door in my face. It opened again, almost immediately.

'Marlon Sunday?'

Louis White was wider than when I'd last seen him. Well, his shoulders were. He was wearing black tracksuit bottoms and a grey t-shirt wringing in sweat. His head and neck were dripping too. He rubbed a towel across his face and slung it round his shoulders.

'If I've come at a bad time . . .' I backed away.

Louis grinned. 'And leave it another three years? Come in, man. Come in!'

'Yeah. Thanks.'

I followed him into the front room.

'You relax here,' Louis said. 'I'll get Bronwyn to get you a drink while I just clean up.'

I sat down on the new-looking armchair. All that ibuprofen must have accumulated in my system, because I could bend my legs without swords slicing up my back. I checked out the room. Two things were hard to miss. One was the giant flat screen TV, tuned to Sky Sports on mute. The other was the frame full of Sharkie on the wall above the mantelpiece. There must have been about ten years of school photos mixed with some blurry barbecues and Christmases. All those Sharkies were grinning at the camera, never guessing that they wouldn't get to twenty.

It was the same thing with Sonya. Maybe once you died, your family had to keep staring at your face to make sure it stayed fixed. Mum had been the same way with Dad.

The biggest picture on Louis White's wall was Sharkie holding his baby, Joseph.

'Mum asked all the family to give up their photos.' Louis had changed into jeans and a hoodie. Yeah, he was definitely wider. 'She made one for me, one for Joseph and one for herself.'

'How is she now?'

Louis shrugged. 'Still angry. And your mum?'

'About the same. What about Joseph?'

'He's a big boy now.' He frowned. 'Him and his mum moved up to Manchester. There was a fire in their flat when they were out and she didn't feel safe here no more. She's with another guy now.' He looked me up and down. 'I know it's a cliché, mate, but I have to say it. You've grown! I never imagined that little squirt would become a tall man like you.' He leaned close; I smelled soap and freshness. 'What happened to your face? It looks fresh.'

'Some kids tried to take my phone.' *The short version.*

'Damn! You must have been flashing some serious hardware for them to clout you like that! Any idea who did it?'

'Not really.'

Louis's eyes were still on me. 'Tell the police?'

'No.'

'You should have.'

Louis White said *what*?

Just then, Bronwyn shoved through the door with two glasses of water, thrusting one at me. There was a clear mouth mark on the edge of it. Bronwyn smirked and slammed out again. As I put my glass on the floor, Louis rolled his eyes.

'Don't take it personally, Marlon. That girl wants to fight the whole world these days. She's been excluded from school for a week so I told Mum to send her here.' He smiled. 'It's good to see you.'

'I meant to come before,' I said. 'It was just . . . it never seemed right.'

'I'm glad it seems right now.'

Silence.

Louis scratched his ear. 'It seems to me no one was to blame. What happened to our brothers, it was just fate.'

'And the guy with the gun chasing them.'

'Yes.'

The silence grew thicker. We watched the figures darting around the giant screen. Baseball, just rounders with bright lights.

'You haven't asked about Andre,' I said.

Louis glanced at me, then back at the screen. 'Yeah. How's he doing?'

'Sometimes good, sometimes not so good.'

Louis nodded. 'That's the way these things are.'

A baseball player lifted his bat and swung it hard; the ball rocketed through the stadium. The camera panned through the cheering crowds.

'He's angry too,' I said. 'He can't go back to being the person he was. And I think he's angry with Mum because he reckons she prefers him as he is now.'

Louis turned to give me his full attention. 'Does she?'

'No.'

'And what about you, Marlon? How do you get on with your new big brother?'

'He thinks I'm Sharkie half the time.'

Louis sucked his teeth. 'That's deep.'

The ibuprofen was fading or the pain had moved up a notch. I shifted in the seat.

Louis said, 'What happened to you?'

'What do you mean?'

'Your face.'

'I told you.'

'No you didn't.'

His voice was louder than before, letting me see what he really thought. I was the kid brother of the guy who smashed his own little brother into a brick wall.

'You turn up here after three years with a bash-up face. You really expecting me not to ask?'

I was losing him. 'Something happened.'

'Like what?'

'I was with this girl and she died.'

'Serious?' He switched the TV off. 'Was she sick or something?'

'I don't know. It's not sorted yet. We were at a fair and one minute she was okay and then . . . then she wasn't.'

'Man, that's hard. For everyone.'

I nodded.

'You think it's her family coming after you?'

'No.'

He leaned back. 'Who, then?'

'There were these boys at the fairground. She said she knew them, but I think they were hassling her.'

'So this is why you're here?'

Out of the corner of my eye, twenty Sharkies grinning at me. 'I think it's something to do with Andre. I've asked him, but he says he can't remember.'

Louis took a deep breath in. 'And?'

'You know who he used to run with, who had his back.'

He nodded. 'You want to find out why someone's got beef with your brother.'

'Yes.'

'And then you're going to deal with it.'

I nodded.

He turned away for a second. When he looked back at me, he seemed to have wiped off any expression. 'This one got beef. That one got beef. Marlon, if I was going to pick beef with anyone, it would be you. My little brother's dead. Your brother was driving the car. That's big beef, man. Massive.'

It was like he'd dug an icicle in my spine. That friendly grin was a trap. He'd laid it down three years ago and had been waiting ever since. Out of my own choice, I'd entered

224

this wide man's house and was sitting here right next to him. There was a gun under that cushion. Or he was planning to use his own hands. Cane Row and his idiots were out on the stairs, ready to join in, because he'd set this whole thing up. My brother killed his brother. He was right. This was proper beef and now it was time for revenge.

I made to stand up, legs just working.

He said. 'Marlon. Sit down and listen.'

Ice water dripped through my vertebrae. I didn't have a choice. I sat. Louis tapped his finger against his palm. 'First thing. I don't have no truck with that beef business. I don't want to spend my whole life mad and fighting people. That's not going to bring Sharkie back.' Two fingers, tap. 'Second. Things are complicated now . . . You could say I've gone over to the other side.'

'What do you mean?'

'I'm a special.' Louis laughed at my confused face. 'In the Met. A special police officer. I'm doing everything your brother hated, and for free. I've been there two years now. After the accident, I started thinking. Whether I liked it or not, my life had changed and I wanted to control that change, you understand?'

No. I didn't. Sharkie's big brother, a copper? How did that happen?

'You're not the only one who's surprised.' In a tired way, Louis looked amused. 'D'you see my front lawn?'

225

'The dog crap?'

'Yeah, some local hero gets his dog to express his opinion in the middle of the night. Probably the same fool who pushes the Bounty bars through the letterbox. Brown on the outside and white in the middle.'

He didn't need to explain that one. I knew.

Louis stood up, holding out his hand. 'Marlon, you're a braver man than me, coming to make the first move. I appreciate it, yeah? But I've got to be careful what I get involved in. I've got to be above the law. Way above the law. D'you know what I mean?'

He shook my hand, shoving in a business card at the same time, before pulling me into a hug. Louis White, the hugging type – that was new. He didn't pick that up from the Met.

Walking through the estate, I tried to remember the streets I'd passed. Rothko Heights, Dali Court, Turner Tower. These ones were different. The terraced houses ended and I was on the main road with patches of grass and blocks of flats either side. So Louis was a volunteer copper. He was one of them. If he carried on, he'd be sitting across the table from me, calling me a drug dealer.

I'd have to get my answers somewhere else. Maybe I'd go back to Tish's churning through the internet. Or Mrs Steedman, she must know more.

Mondrian, Blake, Hirst. This definitely wasn't the way I came. But that was the railway bridge over there. If I followed it, I'd end up back near the station on the main road. *Or somewhere miles away in the opposite direction.* I crossed over to a small parade of shops, if you could call it a 'parade'. A newsagent was crammed between a boarded up chemist and a Paddy Power with a couple of old guys puffing fags outside. They nodded to me.

'Soddin' useless in there,' one of them said.

The other one laughed. 'That's 'cause you're backing donkeys, Mick.'

I bought a Coke and some Skittles in the newsagent and checked my directions with the woman behind the counter. As I came out, I spotted grey and blue, our school uniforms, on the path between two blocks opposite. I stayed by the newsagent, watching them. There was a boy and a girl, up close together and two other girls, lagging behind, laughing. They must have sneaked out for lunch. The three girls turned away, strolling up the road towards a Chicken Spot. The boy sauntered towards me, checking me out, before going inside the newsagent. I hadn't noticed him before at school. His hair was white blonde and that was bound to show up in a school like ours. He reminded me of a skinny version of Roy, the mad replicant from *Blade Runner*. Andre used to laugh at boys like him, who walked round like they were dons but hadn't done anything to prove it.

227

But it wasn't the blonde kid that made my heart beat. It was the girl. The one who'd been snuggling up to him, who'd looked back at me then quickly away again.

It was Tish.

11

Tish was at my door early next morning. Usually she shoots right through, mouth on overtime, but this time we just stood there, looking at each other.

'Scott Lester,' she said. 'He hasn't got no girlfriend, wife or kids. Satisfied?'

She shoved past me, her DMs stomping down to the kitchen. I followed her. She settled herself at the table and shook cornflakes into a bowl. When they were piled up into a mountain, she poured in milk and half a bowl of sugar. She pushed it towards me.

'You look like Darth Vader when the mask got taken off.'

'Thanks.'

'But the place is looking better.'

'Jonathan knows people. He got it all sorted quickly.'

'Good for him. Anything else happen?'

'Not really.'

'What do you mean "not really"?'

'I mean no.'

She clinked a spoon into the bowl. 'Because if things got worse, you'd tell the police, right?'

'Yeah. Officer Wiggum from *The Simpsons*, taking notes

on his invisible typewriter.'

'Very funny.'

'Even funnier that you think they'll listen to me.' I
pushed the bowl back to her. 'By the way, I've already
had breakfast.'

'I take it that's my answer, then.' She shovelled a big
spoonful into her own mouth and chewed, screwing up her
face. She tipped in more sugar and tasted. 'That's better.
You coming in today then?'

'Yeah. What else am I going to do sitting round here?'

'I could think of loads of things. But you're too well
brought up to do any of them. Where's Aunty Jen?'

'They're having a special session for refugee kids
later. She wanted to make sure everything was set up
properly.'

'Bet she's worrying about you, though.'

The landline started ringing in the sitting room.

I laughed. 'How do you do that, Tish?'

'Alien abduction telepathy.'

I answered it. Tish was dead right. It was Mum and she
was worried. I brought the phone back into the kitchen
with me.

'If you get any problems,' Mum was saying, 'and I mean
those teachers too, Marlon, call me. Okay?'

'It'll be fine, Mum.'

Tish narrowed her eyes into a Yoda face, pinching her

ears and pulling them out. 'Marlon. What wrong can go possibly?'

Tish didn't exactly drag me to school, more like we were dragging each other. Us and the school were both negative poles; as we moved closer, it pushed us away.

At school, the same old kids were hanging about by the fence, like they were waiting for their mates to lob over cakes filled with escape gear. The same horse-faced security guard was checking car passes. The same trains were shuttling to and from Liverpool Street on the bridge over the road. The two fat tennis players had given it a miss today, though. We sat down on the wall by the flowerbeds. Two Year-Seven girls next to us had an earbud each, plugged into a phone, chatting crap about some rapper. A tall Turkish kid slapped one of the Muslim girls on the arse, earning an earful of cuss for his troubles.

'So where is he?' I said.

Tish sighed. 'You going to make this your business, now?'

My face was getting warm. 'No. It's just what happens.' I tried to add a laugh to my voice. 'When you're both in the same school, you've got to have a skin graft that means you can't separate.'

Tish didn't smile. 'It's not like that with me and Scott,'

'How is it?'

'Casual.'

'Right.'

But she was scanning the playground, like she was on the lookout. She must have realised, because she seemed a bit embarrassed.

She said, 'I wish I could find words to describe this place.'

'It's a pod.'

Tish scuffed her DMs against the tarmac. 'Explain.'

'Imagine you're an alien scientist, you know ET, or something, but invisible. You're watching this world and making loads of notes in your super-tech laptop. But even with all the alien technology, you can't understand how it all works.'

'You're an alien?'

'I feel like it sometimes.'

Tish sighed. 'You and half the world, but they're just better at pretending to fit in.'

The bell rang. The groups split up and started drifting towards their tutor groups. Moses, from my chemistry class, had his arm around Vinnie's shoulders. They were having one serious conversation. Vinnie's head was nodding, until he saw me. He looked at Moses and they started laughing. They walked past and didn't say anything to me at all.

Tish nudged me. 'What's the matter?'

'Vinnie used to come round my house to play,' I said. 'He was my best friend in Year Four.'

'At least you *had* friends in Year Four,' Tish said. 'In my school, if you didn't have Baby Annabel, you weren't no one.'

'Wouldn't your mum get you one?'

'Yeah, she did after a bit, though dolls were supposed to be banned in our house. But I painted its face brown and dressed it like Missy Elliott. That didn't get me any friends neither.' She pulled my arm. 'Come on. We'll be late.'

The few kids in my tutor group who'd turned up for revision classes were poring over their books, or at least pretending to. Some of them might be sleeping with their eyes open, because I never saw them turn the page. No sulking lump of Yasir, though. That was good.

Mr Habato tapped me on the shoulder. I could see him trying not to look at my swollen eye. 'Focus, Marlon. And all will be well.'

I'm one eye down, Mr Habato. That makes it twice as hard.

In chemistry, Mr Laing was reviewing the periodic table. I ended up sitting bang in front. Moses was next to me and kept sneaking a look at my face. If I managed the B I was forecast, Mum's heart would sing. More than that. It would probably combust with happiness, burning out the other crap stuff I'd made her think about. All I had to do was concentrate. Focus! Everything else had to be a blur – Andre, Cane Row, Sonya, Diamond.

Diamond. Chemical symbol C. Allotrope of carbon. No free electrons.

233

The shiny, transparent boy waiting by his phone in case Sonya called. Instead he gets the call telling him he has to be bait.

'The properties of iron?' Mr Laing was asking no one in particular.

Chemical symbol Fe. Atomic number 26. Iron reacts with chlorine, bromine, fluorine. Reacts with oxygen in the air to make oxides and hydroxides.

Reacts with the oxygen in the body as haemoglobin in blood.

Part of the reaction when some knuckle dangler slams your head against a church wall.

Chemistry was about formulae. I had to know the rules and when they could be broken. I had to fill my head with properties and know what mixes with what. Someone had already done the experiments and made the mistakes. They'd sniffed a load of poisonous gases and set the explosions. I just had to follow the instructions and reach the same conclusions, remember what combinations were safe and what mixed up elements meant danger.

I couldn't see Tish at first break, lunchtime neither. She'd probably managed to get herself another detention. Or she could be squeezing up to the skinny replicant, Scott Lester. I needed a big brain blink to wipe that image. I spotted an empty chair in a quiet corner of the canteen, dropped my bag there and went up to the queue. There was just enough credit on my account for a ham sandwich and a carton of Ribena. I slid my tray on to the table and sat down. A few younger kids were gawping at my face. I screwed them out and they got up and left. I'd have done the same when I was eleven, if some knock-up-faced sixteen-year-old came and plonked himself next to me.

We had a flash new school building, fingerprint technology for lunchtime, but the same old acoustics, with every clank and shriek bouncing across the walls and off the floor. And the sandwich tasted like glue. Was it like this for Diamond? Or Stunna, or Rodge, chewing their lunch by themselves, thinking about Sonya? Or was I the saddest loser out of all of them?

I pushed the food away. My head hurt and the skin on my face felt like it was ready to snap. Maths revision class wasn't going to be happening for me. After this, I was off home.

My back bumped as the kid behind me pushed out his chair to stand up.

'Idiot!' The shout came just as water splashed over my shoulder.

I turned around. The blonde kid, Scott Lester, was standing behind me. His tray was flooded with water and a beaker was lying on its side.

He shook his head at me. I couldn't tell if he recognised me or not.

'Sorry, mate,' he said. 'The little dumbskull behind you

didn't look where he was going.'

The kid who'd pushed out his chair, spat out a swear word, picked up his tray and disappeared.

Scott Lester peered at my bag. 'It's all over your books, man.'

'What?'

My bag was open. That wasn't right. After chemistry, I'd put in my pens and my books and zipped it right up. I didn't have anything to steal, but after those idiots came in my house, I needed my things secret and safe. But now my bag was gaping wide with a beaker of water in it.

Scott Lester shook his head. 'Really, really sorry, mate.'

I gritted my teeth. 'Don't worry about it.'

It was all the more reason to go home. I wasn't going to do much maths revision with the paper all stuck together. I reached for my bag, but Scott Lester had got there first, picking through my stuff.

'I'll help you sort it!'

'No!' I knocked his hand away.

Other kids were getting interested now, leaning over their noodles and baked potatoes for a better look. A couple of teachers were glancing over too.

'What's your problem?' Scott's hand was still in my bag. 'I said I'm sorry.'

'And I said I'd sort it out.' I couldn't make my voice soft, not while his fingers were lifting up my books.

It's pens and chemistry textbooks, maths exam papers, scrap. It's not Mum's books, Dad's maps. What is the problem?

The problem was – I could feel it before it happened, like the heavy ache in your stomach before you throw up. Scott Lester was already reaching into my bag, already squeezing his face into surprise, already holding the small, see-through plastic pouch high so everyone could see it.

'It looks like your stash is safe, though!'

I was shaking my head. The scumbag was waving the pouch like he'd won a lucky dip.

'You know I've never seen it before!' My hands were on Scott Lester's shoulder, face close into his face. 'You put it there! You put it there!'

And the words kept coming, even though the principal was here and Mr Habato and they were making me walk away.

Of course they called Mum. And the police. The cops must have heard my name and smiled across at each other like they'd been waiting for this. Maybe they'd been laying bets.

Mum came striding over to the free chair outside the principal's office and squeezed my hand. If she'd been crying or punching the wall over me, she was hiding it well. She was wearing a grey skirt with a matching jacket and she'd straightened her hair and twisted it up into a bun. She had on the little silver earrings that Dad bought her when they got engaged. She looked smarter than most of the teachers in the school. She hadn't looked like that when she went to work this morning.

'Before we go in,' she said. 'Tell me the truth. Was it yours?'

'No, Mum. It wasn't.'

She was staring into me now, as if her brain was running through all the other times she'd asked me stuff.

'I could always tell when you were lying,' she said. 'You were always so bad at it. But after the fairground and the house, I'm not sure any more. I think you're telling me the truth now. And I really want to believe it.'

I took her hand. 'I've never seen that bag before in my life.'

'Right, Marlon. That's all I need to know.'

Last time I'd been in the principal's office, it had felt enormous. I'd been picking up an achievement certificate in Year Seven. Now it seemed much smaller, full of people sitting there waiting for us. They'd already had their conversations before me and Mum came in. The principal was sitting in a chair in front of his desk, as if he was really just as equal as everyone else. There was Mr Pitfield, Mr Habato, Ms Leisch, head of Year Eleven progress, the new tired-looking learning mentor and two coppers. New ones, black ones. Was I expected to open up to them? Feel extra guilt?

Everyone was in a circle, going round introducing themselves like they were alcoholics. Mum said who she was – Mrs Sunday. The only one whose first name got used was me.

'We all know why we're here,' the principal said.

Mum said, 'I don't.'

Everyone looked at her. She gave them a polite smile, like she was waiting behind her library desk to check out their books.

The principal's face adjusted to 'patient'. 'I apologise if I wasn't clear on the phone, Mrs Sunday. A bag of what appears to be strong cannabis resin was found in Marlon's bag.'

Mum nodded. 'I'm aware of that, Mr Sandalwood and impressed that you were able to recognise it. But what I am not clear about is whether my son is already assumed to be a drug dealer.'

Mr Habato's mouth twitched. He glanced at the principal and down at the floor. One of the coppers pressed a sneeze against his hand.

The principal said, 'We have a zero tolerance policy towards drugs in my school.'

Mum shot back, 'And we have a zero tolerance policy towards drugs in my house.'

Mr Habato tried. 'Of course, Mrs Sunday, we're not trying to suggest—'

Mum wouldn't let him finish. 'Three years ago, my eldest son, Andre, was badly injured in a traffic accident. As you can imagine, it was a tough time for us. First Marlon loses his dad and then that.' She had the group's attention. Even the principal didn't dare interrupt her. 'Andre was in a coma. Then he was so confused he tried to rip his tubes out. So they put him back into a medically-induced coma. After eighteen months and lots of rehab, we hoped Andre could live independently. That's certainly what he wanted. I didn't, but I couldn't stop him. He moved back into his old flat and some of his so-called friends slithered back on the scene and took over my son's home to sell drugs and prostitutes. All through these times, Marlon has been my rock. A few weeks ago, Marlon was witness to a tragic incident. It's my turn to be his rock.'

The coppers looked at each other. The older one said gently, 'Mrs Sunday, Marlon was found with a bag of skunk, very strong cannabis, on school premises.'

'Found?' Mum's voice had gone all deep. It was the voice she used when I was small and she was explaining to me why she should punish me. 'From the way the principal described it to me – and I'm sure I'll be corrected if I'm wrong – my son left his bag to go and get some lunch. When he came back, it had been opened and a boy rather conveniently spilled water in it. In spite of Marlon's protests, this boy stuck in his finger and pulled out a plum.

No doubt this boy has been questioned in front of two police officers as well?'

Silence.

The principal said, 'The other student involved has given his account of the incident.'

'So it's my son's word against his.'

Mr Habato gave a tiny nod. He didn't look very happy with the situation, shuffling his feet about as Mum turned her beam on him.

'Mr Habato, has Marlon ever come in looking like he's been smoking skunk?'

Mr Habato shook his head. 'All was well up until last month. We wrote to you about the fight with the other boy in the tutor group.'

'And I duly responded. But did Marlon look as if he was smoking skunk?'

'No.'

'Ms Leisch? What about my son's attendance and work?'

She gave an awkward little smile. 'Generally good, though he could improve his presentation.'

'That's not what I asked, Ms Leisch.'

Don't you know, Mum? She never answers the questions you ask.

Mum wasn't giving up, though. 'Ms Leisch, does Marlon's homework, his schoolwork, anything suggest he is smoking strong cannabis?'

'Not that I'm aware of.'

'Right.' Mum stood up, put her hands on her hips. 'My son behaves well, achieves well, has caused no concern until the tragedy a few weeks ago. But instead of finding ways to support him, you are accusing him of being a drug dealer.'

There was a tiny bubble of sweat on her temple. The principal cleared his throat.

'We are not accusing Marlon of being a drug dealer, Mrs Sunday. We would just like to find out how the drugs turned up in your son's bag.'

'That's easy,' Mum said. 'Check the CCTV.'

Mr Habato seemed to squeeze back a smile.

Mum continued, 'Last year you kindly informed parents that you were spending an impressive sum of money installing cameras for the protection of students and staff. Well, now use your investment to protect my son.' She touched my shoulder. 'I think I would prefer you to complete your revision at home, Marlon. Let's go.'

Mum stuck close by my side until we were out of the school ground. Beyond the security guard's view, she turned to me.

'Your brother was my sacrifice to the system. Everything his teachers said to me, I believed. I vowed never to make that mistake again.'

I reached out to hug her, but she stepped back, taking

242

my hands instead. I thought her hands would be strong and warm like before, but she was shaking.

'Guilt or no guilt, I've still got a mortgage to pay. I'll see you after work.'

'Thanks, Mum. Really, thank you.'

'You don't have to thank me, Marlon. All I'm asking is you don't let me down.'

She kissed my forehead. For once her high heels meant she didn't have to stretch.

'Look, a bus is coming!'

My hands dropped to my side as she let go. The bus driver waited for her, she waved and she was gone.

I should have traced my path back over the park, along the main road to the junction and down my road. I should have opened the front door with the new keys in the new lock, walked up the stairs past the gaps on the walls where the pictures had been and laid out my books. I should have blanked it all out and done what I promised – get on with my revision, not let Mum down.

But I was going to let Mum down even more if I didn't deal with this other stuff. Whatever had been going on with Andre, Cane Row had brought this to my home and my school. They'd pulled Mum right in. What was the worst thing that could happen if I didn't go home? Mum would have a go. What was the worst thing that could happen if I didn't sort this out? They'd flashed a shank at me at a funeral, torn up my house, held me down and hit me. I was the last man standing. If I let this rest, soon there'd be no one left.

I glanced back towards school. What the hell did I expect to see? Tish wasn't always going to be trotting after me. Not now. She was too busy trotting beside Scott Lester. But when she heard about what happened, she'd drop him straight away. She'd style it off, big time, but he'd be gone.

I looked over to the road where the bus had waited for Mum. I *was* going to trace my path back, but not towards home.

12

I leaned forward and let my forehead touch the train window. The speed increased and the train tapped out a rhythm that made my whole face ache. In a sick way, the pain felt good. It made me focus. See, that's what I needed, Mr Habato. Serious stress and a train ride.

I came out of the station and walked towards Sonya's gran's flat. The road seemed shorter than before, probably because I knew where I was going. A woman wheeling a buggy down the street crossed over before she reached me. I caught her eye as she passed by on the other side of the pavement; she looked away quickly. I was a tall, angry boy with a banged-up face – she could see me but she didn't want to. I drew myself taller, fixed my face harder.

As I stood by the entrance ready to try the pizza trick again, the door opened. I recognised the neighbour, Agnes.

'You!' She said. 'What happened to your face?'

'I . . .'

'It looks like someone beat you.' She shook her head. 'Don't bring trouble to Violet's door, you hear?'

Trouble was there, long before me. I slipped past her and ran up the stairs.

Mrs Steedman's curtains were still drawn, and I thought I caught the whiff of incense beneath the door. I lifted the letterbox and let it fall hard. Nothing. I let it bang again. A few seconds later, the door opened. Mrs Steedman was in a dressing gown that flapped open over an old shirt and pyjama bottoms. Her eyes were red and her oily hair was stuck to her head.

She whispered, 'Jesus! Your face!'

Yeah, thanks for the reminder.

'They jumped me after the funeral.'

'I'm so sorry. It was brave of you to come.'

'Someone sent me a note.'

She pulled her dressing gown shut. 'A note? Who?'

'I don't know. It was hand delivered to my door. And now some kid's planted drugs on me at school.'

'Oh my God. At school?'

I stepped forward, but she shook her head. 'Can I come in?'

'No, not now. You need to talk to Hayley. She knows them. You just missed her. She's gone to the cemetery. Do you know the City one, over near Wanstead?'

'Yeah.' Too well.

'You could go over there now. And, Marlon? Honest, I'm sorry.'

246

I stopped at the end of the street and looked back at the block. I couldn't quite work out which window was Sonya's. In my head, though, there was a shadow standing there watching me. And it wasn't Mrs Steedman.

The first time I came to City of London cemetery, I thought it was as big as London itself. I was in Mum's car, in a long line following Sharkie's coffin and my head was all churned up from the funeral service. I'd seen Sharkie's mum shaking and holding on to the pew and his dad, like a skeleton with skin stretched across it. Later Mum told me he died just a few months afterwards while visiting his sister in the States. We'd sat behind Sharkie's girlfriend, in her black, furry coat, rocking their baby in its buggy. Even though they were falling apart with grief, they'd turned their hatred on Mum as if she'd been driving the car that shunted Sharkie into the wall. And Mum soaked it all up so it wouldn't touch Andre.

This time it was just me walking through the Victorian archway that reminded me of a kid's drawing of a castle. There were thousands and thousands of graves. How did you find just one? There must be some logic to it all. Perhaps one part of the cemetery was the really old bit with all the Victorians and their pillars and angels, and somewhere else, all the newer ones were together. If I could find that out, I might find Hayley.

247

There was a café just on my right. Someone there should know how it worked. A punky-looking girl with a nose ring was wiping a table and an elderly couple were sitting like statues by the window. None of them looked like they wanted me to bother them.

There she was. Hayley. She'd pushed her chair back from the table, with her legs sprawling out underneath. Her eyes were closed and her head tipped up as if she was hoping that the sun would shine on her. A Sprite can sat on the table in front of her.

A warm human being would feel sorry for her. No matter what she'd done, she'd never have wanted this. But just seeing her there and thinking about her thuglet mates and Dad's maps and Mum's books, all torn to scraps, and Mum ready to abandon the house she worked so hard to keep after Dad died. Her little mate Cane Row spat in my mouth after her own daughter's funeral. Something sparked in me, hot and nasty. I walked towards her.

Hayley opened her eyes and gave a little jolt. I stayed where I was, looking at her. She stood up slowly and came towards me. Over her shoulder, the old couple were still looking out the window, but the punky waitress was watching us with interest. Hayley came right up close, so I could see the top of her head. It was scabby from where she'd hacked off her hair.

She said, 'What do you want?'

'Your mum said you were here.'

'So?'

'I want to talk to you.'

Hayley looked me up and down, face hard as concrete. 'Why should I talk to you?'

'You know who I am. I was with Sonya at the fairground.'

Hayley snorted. 'Do you want a medal for it?'

I breathed in. (Earth, Wind and Fire, 1971. The Need of Love, 1972. Last Days and Time, *also 1972, the first album on Columbia.*) I breathed out slowly, made myself relax.

I said, 'Are you going to where Sonya is?'

A tiny nod.

'Can I come with you?'

She shrugged and walked past me.

I waited, then I followed, a few paces behind. She didn't bother looking back to see if I was still there. We took a path round to the right past old crumbling headstones sticking out from beneath the bushes. And then rows of modern graves with photographs and gold and black inscriptions. Some were decorated with vases of plastic flowers or layers of green chippings. I almost expected to see a picture of Sharkie smiling back at me. They'd used his proper name, of course, Sylvester Amstell White.

Hayley had stopped walking. She was watching three squirrels chasing each other over the graves. Two more bounced out of the bushes, racing towards their mates.

249

'I hate the bastards,' she said, without turning around. 'Look at them! Rats with fluffy tails. I did community service in Springfield Park once. Every time the gardeners planted something, these thieving bastards used to come and dig it up. Did you ever go the conservatory there?'

'No.'

'It's at the top, by the white house. You could go in and see the fish. They were big, fat things. I used to take Sonya there when she was a baby, every Saturday, two o'clock. I'd try and teach her the words for things. The squirrels were always waiting for us outside, like, I don't know, little bouncers.' Hayley cleared her throat and laughed. 'Fearless little sods too. I'd stamp at them and shout at them and swear at them and they'd just stand there looking at me. And they'd follow us. It was their territory, wasn't it? And they were going to make sure I knew.'

One of the squirrels jumped on to a memorial stone, and stood there watching us on its hind legs with its front paws together.

Hayley laughed again and wiped her eyes on her sleeve. 'It's taking the piss out of all them praying angels.' She drew back her shoulders. 'I did care about her. I really did.'

'I never said you didn't.'

She walked away, quick this time. I stayed close, crossing a strip of grass between rows of recent graves. All the world had come to Wanstead. Chinese names, Nigerian, Polish,

English. Marcus Reynolds, born St Kitts, 3rd March 1929. Mary-Ann Grey, aged eight, her grave scattered with silver stars. I was an intruder here. How would I feel if some stranger stamped past Dad's grave without caring? Maybe that's why Dad made Mum promise a cremation.

Hayley stopped at the end of the row. Gerald Michael Steedman, born 22nd November 1945, died 1st December 1999. The words were etched on one side of a marble scroll. A bunch of pink roses were squeezed into a small, glass vase in front. No photograph.

'She's here,' Hayley said. 'With her granddad.'

She turned to face me. I held my breath. It was like her sneer was scribbled in pencil on tracing paper with her real expression all twisted up underneath. She bent forward, like she couldn't breathe.

'Sonya, I'm sorry!'

Suddenly I wasn't there at all. I was outside Mum's bedroom, listening to her crying until Andre dragged me away and tucked me back under my duvet. He'd sit on my bed and turn on Michael Jackson, but every time it came to 'I Want You Back', he'd press 'skip'. He said when Mum heard it, it made her cry more.

I made myself step forward and put a hand on Hayley's back. 'Please . . .'

Please what? Stop crying about your daughter's death? Stop making me feel sorry for you?

251

As she straightened up, I snatched my hand away.

'You think I'm shit,' she said. 'A shit mother who doesn't give a shit.'

It was hard to keep looking at her. Her face was tight and angry, but bits of Sonya – her eyelashes, her lips – and the old Hayley's long, hair and bright grin, I could see them underneath.

'I didn't say that.' I had to keep looking, show I meant it. 'But since I met Sonya, everything's gone mad. Those boys who came to Sonya's funeral, they were waiting outside for me. Then they came to my house and smashed things up.'

Hayley tugged a couple of droopy roses out of the vase. She pulled off the brown petals and wedged the flowers back in.

'D'you know what? It's been a bad couple of weeks for me too.' The sneer was back, drawn thick and dark. 'Mum might think you're some goody-goody, there for my daughter's last moment, but you told the Bill Sonya was a drug dealer.'

Heat was creeping up my neck. 'They were *her* pills.'

'You grassed up a dead girl! What a loyal friend you are!' She bent down and picked up a stone, squeezing it tight in her fist. 'She cared for me, no matter what.'

'What if she just wanted to be normal?'

'You know jack shit, Marlon. About Sonya, or me, or

nothing. Nothing about our family at all.' She pointed to the grave. 'You see him? He was just the same. Everyone thought he was so great, but what a bitter, nasty man he turned out to be. Even if I wasn't inside, I wouldn't have gone to his funeral. Just in case I ended up doing the cancan as the coffin went down.'

'But Sonya's here.'

'This was Mum's grave, for when she needed it, though I don't know why she wanted to be stuck with that bullying bastard, neither. We didn't expect . . . God, I hope Sonya's haunting him!'

She launched the stone; it looped in the air and cracked off a headstone. That was for someone's wife or dad, for God's sake!

I kept my voice calm. 'Why's the kid with cane row after me?'

She shrugged. 'Who knows?'

'Is it to do with my brother?'

She gave a big dramatic yawn. 'Told you. Don't know.'

'Who are they?'

'There's two of us standing here. Only one of us likes to run off our mouth.'

Head to the Sky, 1973. Open Our Eyes, 1974. *Those Earth, Wind and Fire boys were busy – at least one album a year.*

I said, 'What if I just give them the phone?'

253

She shook her head and seemed to fold into herself. 'You've got a phone. So what? It's just a list of names. Thing is, he knows where your mum works. He knows where your brother lives. He's been to your house.'

She crouched down, laying her palms on the new turf.

'No, Orangeboy, the phone's nothing much at all. The thing he wants most is you.'

The train home was busier, but I could have spread out a rug made of ten-pound notes and still no one was going to sit next to me. It didn't surprise me. I saw my reflection in the window. I looked like ET's uglier brother.

'The thing he wants most is you.'

At Liverpool Street, I waited ages for a bus, then walked down my street quickly, crossing the road well before the bus stop. I stopped. Someone was standing by my front door.

'I've been waiting for ages,' Tish said. 'Where have you been?'

'Cemetery.' The words came out sharp. 'You know, after your boyfriend set me up at school.'

'I heard about that. And he's not my boyfriend. I told you, it's casual.'

'It's'. Not *'it was'*. He was still present.

There were three locks to open now, new keys muddled up with the old one. If Cane Row and his buddies were waiting, they could have strolled over and beat me to a pulp while I was trying to open up.

'Why d'you go to the cemetery?'

'Why do people go to cemeteries, Tish. Work it out.'

I pushed the door open.

Tish said, 'I could go back across the road without telling you what I came for. And I will if you're going to carry on being a dick.'

Along the hall, down into the kitchen with Tish behind. I opened the fridge and took out some juice. Tish picked a couple of glasses out the dryer and plonked them down.

'I was going to meet you for lunch,' she said. 'But I was in detention.'

'Congratulations.'

'Thanks, Marlon.' She held her glass out to be filled. 'Do you want the info on Scott Lester?'

'What do you mean?'

'I know why he put the weed in your bag.'

'Why?'

'Want me to tell you? Then get off your high horse about me fraternising with the enemy.'

'What are you on about?'

'Your dickiness. About me and Scott Lester.'

'I'm not being dicky.'

'Hyperdicky with added dickiness. Promise you'll stop and I'll spill the beans.'

My face was hurting and smiling was really hard, like it was tugging something deeper inside. I held my hand up in a scout salute. 'I hereby promise that I, Marlon Isaac Asimov Sunday, will do my best not to make deliberately dicky comments about your casual relationship with Scott 'Weed-In-Bag' Lester.'

'Gee, thanks, Milo. But I'll tell you anyway. He did it because his brother gave him twenty quid.'

A pang of disappointment. 'Is that it?'

Tish cut her eyes at me. ''Course not. Scott's family used to live down Brixton way and his brother, Wayne, still hangs with one of the crews down there. That's one of the reasons his mum moved them north. Like that makes a difference.'

'Which crew is it?'

'Riotboyz or something.'

'Sounds like they're from a comic.'

'Yeah. Wayne should be. He's a bit moist and a bit thick and he does what he's told. Except the things he does aren't funny.'

'Like what?'

'Well . . .' She bit her lip. 'The thing at the church . . .'

'Scott's brother was there?'

'Yeah.'

'Tall? Blonde hair?'

She shrugged. 'I haven't had the pleasure yet.'

Him and the other moron, throwing me against the wall, holding me down for their psycho mate to spit on my tongue.

I said, 'How long have you known this?'

'Just found out. Didn't you see? I was waiting by your door to tell you.'

'Yeah. Sorry.'

'Thank you. Can I carry on?'

'Yeah.'

She sighed. 'The black kid with cane row – he's D-Ice.'

'What's his proper name?'

'Dunno. Didn't want to ask too much. D-Ice got the name from *Grand Theft*. He's the leader of some hood thugs or something. Scott says—'

'He says a lot, doesn't he?'

'Dicky comment alert! D'you want to know this or not?'

'Yeah. Go on.'

'D-Ice and Wayne go back a while, in south London. Then D-Ice was inside for a bit.'

'Prison?'

'Young offenders. Now he's out, he's building up his rep again.'

'Doing what?'

'Smashing other people's things. Smashing other people. And d'you know what he does when he really wants to muck with people's heads?'

'Yeah.' I swallowed hard as the lump rose up my throat.

'He spits – Jesus, Milo! No!'

Yes.

Tish was studying my face. She bit her lip, but didn't look away. 'Sorry,' she said. 'You didn't tell me that bit. It's foul, all of it.'

'But you're still hanging with Scott Lester, though.'

Now she looked away.

'I know,' I said. 'It's casual.'

'Yeah. But Scott's not into all that.'

'That?'

'Yeah. "That". And anything else if that's what you're thinking.'

Seriously?

But she was carrying on. 'He reckons his brother's a bit dunce doing that crap with D-Ice, especially now the gang's started dealing drugs, proper hard stuff. It was Scott who told me about them coming for you at Westfield.'

'What? He told you to warn me?'

'Not exactly. I mean, he didn't even know where I was. He just kind of said that his brother was going down to Stratford and they were going to get this kid from our school. The one who was with the girl who died.'

She looked at me, like she was expecting thanks.

I said, 'Hayley said something at the cemetery. The phone doesn't matter any more. She said he wanted me.'

Tish was biting at her lip again. 'Yeah. I know.'

'You know? What the hell do you know, Tish?'

It's . . . well, it's D-Ice's brother.'

'What about him?'

'Milo, his brother's called Tayz. He was—'

'Driving the car chasing Andre and Sharkie.'

So this was it. Tayz was banged up and D-Ice was carrying on what his brother started.

But I still didn't know why they were coming for Andre.

Mum got home around eight, bringing a bag full of takeaway. She said it was the least she could do after abandoning me at school. Abandoning me. That's all she said. Nothing about the skunk and the principal and the police. I wasn't going to bring it up either, not while she was looking relaxed. I wanted her to stay relaxed, so it was easier to ask her some questions. She was the one who'd had to deal with the police, who'd spent most of the time by Andre's bedside. She'd done her best to protect me and keep all the horrible stuff away from me. Now I was older, maybe she'd tell me more.

She put the bags down on the work surface. 'Vietnamese okay?'

'Great.'

We could never eat much Vietnamese when Andre was here; he liked his food plain.

Mum said, 'I've got us summer rolls to share, because the soup's pretty filling.'

I peeled the cling film off the plastic containers and took out bowls and side plates. I laid them on the kitchen table while Mum poured the chilli dip out of the little plastic tub into a glass dish.

'When you were younger,' she said, 'I was always such a stickler for eating at the table. None of this plate on knees business.'

I pulled back the chair for her to sit down. 'Not just when I was younger, Mum.'

She laughed. 'Me and your dad laid down some rules for when we had children. No baby talk, no beating, no front-of-the-telly eating.'

'Did you keep to them?'

'You should know, Marlon!'

'I don't remember baby talk. But I do remember Dad trying to teach me Klingon!'

She gave a proper laugh then, with all her face and body. 'Yes, he proposed to me in Klingon. I thought he was choking on his salmon!'

I dipped my roll in the chilli sauce, watching Mum's expressions change. It was sadness, not disappointment. I could manage that.

Ask her now! About Andre and Tayz. What did Andre do?

'The thing is,' Mum was saying. 'We did wonder if we'd

made the right rules, especially when Andre started playing up. We thought about moving away, right out of London. But then we decided that wouldn't change Andre. It would probably just isolate him even more. And as soon as he was old enough, he'd just get on a train and come back again.'

Did Andre break some other rules, Mum? Some special rules between him and Tayz? The questions were bursting out my head but I couldn't open my mouth to ask them. There was too much sadness in Mum, like she was talking about Andre but thinking about Dad.

Summer rolls done, Mum was pouring the broth on to the noodles. I added my chicken, bamboo shoots and herbs.

Mum smiled. 'Your dad passed on the chilli too.'

The soup was hot and bright-tasting, but the chicken was just a little bit dry. I put down my spoon. Mum was scraping seeds out of the chilli with her knifepoint.

I said, 'Do you miss Dad?'

I wasn't sure if she'd heard me. She sliced the pepper into tiny broken rings and scattered them on her soup. She had a quick taste.

'Ahhh, perfect!' She looked thoughtful. 'I miss how we were, yes. God knows how we would be now. You never know.'

I tried to hook into the pictures scrolling through Mum's head, of her and Dad, then fast-forwarding ten years. In my head, not much changed.

'It's strange to think you hardly knew him at all,' she said. 'But there's so much of you in him. I see it every day.'

'Do you see him in Andre?'

Mum sighed and wiped her face with a piece of kitchen roll. 'Fifty-one-year-old women should not eat pepper. Andre has your father's stubbornness, and after everything your brother went through, I'm bloody glad of that!' She chuckled. 'He's also testament to your father's sci-fi obsession. I bet no other kid starting Rushmore that year had Han and Luke as their middle names.'

She went to the fridge for a bottle of fizzy water and poured glasses for both of us.

'But you escaped with minimal damage. And that was down to me. If Jes had his way, you'd have been . . .'

'Calrissian Wookie?'

'Possibly. Or some obscure character from *Blake's 7*. But then I had to make that big compromise, didn't I?'

'Mum, please don't remind me!'

She took a mouthful of water and almost spat it out again laughing. 'I wish we could have captured the priest's face . . . "I christen you, Marlon Isaac Asimov – except she pronounced it 'Arse-imov' – Sunday." And of course, I couldn't stop giggling. And that started off Aunty Cecile. Your father, though – he was well vexed. How could this woman not recognise his heartfelt tribute to the greatest science-fiction writer in the world?'

Mum, sitting there, her face all crinkled up and laughing like I hadn't seen for so long. It should have been four of us sitting around the table sharing jokes, but one was dead, one changed. There was only me and Mum left. And a few miles across the river, some little psycho hoodrat was plotting to make Mum's life dissolve again.

Maybe Mum did know why Tayz was after Andre, but now she was smiling. I imagined Dad in her head, fuming and real, while the baptism guests tried not to crack up.

Ask her now?

'It could have been worse,' she was saying. 'Your dad could have preferred Phillip K Dick!'

No. Not now.

I said, 'Perhaps I should be prouder of my name.'

'Oh, Marlon! I've never believed that you weren't proud of it. Your father thought Asimov was a great man and we were both sure that you would live up to it.'

After supper, we watched *The Matrix*, the film Mum swore Dad would have loved. Dad died the year before it came out so she said that made it easier. She could think about him without thinking about seeing it with him.

We said goodnight still smiling, without the tightness from the last week or so. As I went upstairs, I thought about blurting out all the churning mess in my head. But then I saw Mum's smile fading, her eyes blinking hard the way she does when she's trying to hold back anger and tears. I'd ask her tomorrow. Definitely, tomorrow.

In bed, I turned off the light and closed my eyes, Ramsey Lewis on low. Music was drugs, or that's what one of the books said. It stimulated the amygdala and poked at your moods. We'd played Andre's favourite songs to him when he was in the coma, but all it did was wind up Mum with those rappers spitting lyrics full of words she hated. She'd turn it down every time a nurse came in.

Ramsey Lewis was on his piano. Instrumentals were good, when your head was so full up. You didn't need anyone else's words.

A couple of buses rolled past and a helicopter was hovering low for ages. What were they looking for? An ant under a bush? A car pulled up, bass booming, joining the big noise party. I peered out between the curtains. Tish was leaning over talking to someone in the front seat. I couldn't quite see who it was. I didn't need to. She slammed the door shut and went into her house.

13

Mum left the newspaper on the breakfast bar. Just in case I missed it, she'd drawn a big red circle round the words *and* scribbled a note. *Now let's get on with our lives.*

A seventeen-year-old girl who collapsed at a fairground last month died from an undiagnosed heart defect.

I read it twice. It was nothing to do with Ecstasy. Nothing to do with me. Mum wouldn't have to face TV news shots of her son going into court with a blanket on his head.

Jonathan had spoken to one of his expensive lawyers the week after Sonya died to try and reassure Mum that the police couldn't charge me with anything to do with Sonya's death. Neither me nor Mum had been convinced, not really. And there was still the drugs charge – the pills had been sent away for testing. But maybe they wouldn't bother taking it further now. I bet Jonathan was already on the phone to the lawyer pressing for 'no further action'.

It was weird getting this from a newspaper. Usually, Tish was way ahead with the news. Ages before anyone else, she'd be knocking on the door or banging out texts to me, but there'd been nothing, not since last week, when she broke the news about D-Ice and Tayz.

I cut out the article and stuck it in my pocket. The glow inside me was still hot. If Sonya was still alive, things would have been different. But not in a good way. What if we'd had our picnic in the park? More pills? More promises? Was I meant to be like Alex, buying off her just so I had a chance to see her? No. She'd knocked on *my* door, searched *me* out. I still didn't get it. D-Ice knew where I lived. He didn't need a honey trap to draw me out. I wouldn't have expected him. He could come for me any time. So why did he send Sonya?

Since Tish told me about Tayz, I'd got stuck into my own research. It felt weird doing it after all this time. Soon after Andre's accident, Mum said that she'd tell me the basic facts as long as I promised not to dig any further. She knew the way things worked, she'd said – the more stuff I found out, the more I'd be looking for revenge. It would go back and forth, battle after battle, until everyone was dead or in prison. I must never enter that world. It didn't take much to open the door.

Sorry, Mum. When Sonya knocked, the door bust apart.

The *South London Recorder* had a big article: *Twenty-first Century Al Capones*. The article was pretty crap and I reckoned the journalist was making up half the quotes. There was a picture though, a big, blurry face in shades of grey. This was Tayz, the guy who mashed Andre's mind, and killed Andre's best friend.

Tayz was one of the Riotboyz, a 'Face' — one of the flashmen with the cars and clothes, showing the other kids what they could do. Him and his youngers ran an estate up Brixton Hill. There was a quote from a social worker who said that she couldn't go and visit families in some of the blocks unless she went with a copper. If you weren't known, you weren't getting in.

The gang did all the usual stuff — street crime, drugs, beating up dealers and picking fights with the Brixton Spikes in the estate opposite. Apparently, they sent doctors from the local hospital over to Afghanistan because they'd become experts in treating bullet wounds.

Tayz's crew were big on filming themselves. In most of their videos, they were shouting lyrics about all the crap they did. One video was just a load of photos of guns and knives, a machine gun, a pistol, machetes, everything, with loud grime rap and sirens in the background. At the end, the music stopped suddenly and a pair of trainers came into view. It looked like they were covered in blood.

The bloody trainers showed up in a blog called 'Crack Attack', set up by some sort of south London vigilante called Lambo. He reckoned that his estate was full of guns, from crappy little starter pistols drilled out to take live bullets, to MP5s and submachine guns like the proper military. According to Lambo, someone even tried to get hold of a rocket launcher. His blog hadn't been updated for more than a year. I wondered why he'd stopped.

I clicked on another photo, squinting up close to the screen and making my eyes water. Tayz was in profile and he wasn't alone. The other boy's eyes were boring right into the camera, like even in 2D he could mess you up. I knew that face. Cane-Row. I checked the article. The face had a name. Peter Juan Diego Marrliack, better known as D-Ice. Peter. It didn't help. The harder I tried to remember him, the more he squirmed away. This is how it must be for Andre every time he looks at me.

But I couldn't forget him either. Eight hours later, in daylight, it was like D-Ice's face was tattooed under my eyelids. But I'd try and keep at least one promise to Mum. I'd revise, even if I had to look at my books through the prism of D-Ice's mug. I'd take Mr Habato's advice and focus.

I sorted through my revision books, laid out my pencils, highlighter, scrap paper, stopwatch. I slipped an old exam paper from out of my folder and scanned the list of questions, picked up a pencil and started writing.

By three o'clock, my head was almost too heavy to nod to the funky stuff I'd put on to keep my mood light. Any more tea and it would be squirting from my pores. I'd worked through four questions, four more than I thought I'd get through and my notes were just about readable.

I stood up and yawned. I needed to get out and freshen up my brain.

Or go back online. Follow more links.

No. I had to get out.

I checked the windows and secured the back door, then did the front locks and pushed to make sure they'd caught. I walked up towards the main road, crossing over at the junction by the estate agent. The school dam was just bursting, flowing through the local streets. I'd been part of that grey and blue stream. Now I stood by myself between a car and a lamppost, not even getting my feet wet. Nearly a thousand kids, good, bad and pug ugly, new ones, trying to style off their nerves and the familiar older, stupid faces. Yasir and Melinda were over there, throwing cusses at each other. Louise, the Year Nine maths genius, passed right by me, eyes straight ahead, chewing at nothing.

And there, right there, Scott Lester, with a group of thicko worshippers. He was trying on a swagger and a grin, like he was the King of Clapton. He needed to look in a mirror and see he was just a skinny blond kid with a big mouth. If he didn't see that, Tish *must*. She knew better. Or maybe not. She was there, racing through the tide. I raised my arm, but she didn't see.

'Scott! Wait up!'

If I stood in front of her, she would have run through me like a ghost. She was so hooked up to him.

So what you are standing round watching for?

She'd stopped half a street away, crowds of kids weaving in front of her, so she kept disappearing. Scott was clear enough though. His mouth was stretched open in a giant yawn. One of his mates barked and they all laughed. Some kid, his face all cramped up with acne, *barked*? At Tish? If Tish had heard him that kid would never make another sound again.

She reappeared at the edge of Scott's gang, stopping there, with her hands on her hips. *You see something funny?* I didn't need to see her lips to know her words. Scott was throwing a few words back, a smile on his lips for his mates' benefit. He seriously thought he could out-word Tish. Idiot!

But there was a shift in the group, six boys on one side and Tish on the other. I edged closer, not so close that she'd see me. Scott was moving towards her, mouth going like he was giving it some. Tish stepped forward and pushed him. Just a tiny push. Scott stopped dead still, all his mates too.

Too much Tishness! He won't understand! I had to get to her. That little runt Lester was just waiting for a chance to big himself up in front of his numb-brain mates and Tish was writing him the invitation. I started moving, still watching Scott and Tish staring at each other. Yasir yelled something obnoxious and a semi-circle moulded

270

round them. The air was grimy with the buzz of kids expecting action.

I shoved my way through a group of Year Sevens. It was like the fairground again, everyone tight in their knots, no one getting out the way. Want to swap cuss? Yeah! I was up for that!

I stopped, still a few feet behind Tish. Scott's hand was on her shoulder. She was letting him keep it there! He was saying something in her ear and now the creep's hand was sliding down her back.

Too low. Too low!

And they walked away, Tish's arm slung around Scott Lester's shoulders. Something must have happened, a short circuit in her brain. She must *see* what Scott was like! He was there, right in front of her! That knobwit almost got me flung out of school!

But she still held on to him and walked away.

I moved back through the dregs trickling away from school. Soon I was by the letting agents, then turning off the main road into my street. *What's the crap with Tish, anyhow?* She'd always done her own thing. I'd need a NASA computer to count the number of times she'd asked my advice and ignored it.

But Scott Lester?

Yeah. Scott Lester. Get over it.

As I came close to my house, my hand dropped into in

my pocket. The keys felt good and heavy. It was automatic now to glance towards the bus stop. It was occupied. A black jacket, brown skin, cane row. A skinny white kid with a bike leaning against the shelter.

We never turn off our flight or fight mechanism, but I didn't want to do either. I just felt angry.

I had to breathe, set my face right, deal with this. He was Tayz's brother. I was Andre's brother. That made us equal. There were only two of them today. Not quite equal, but better than before.

I took my hand out of my pocket and walked straight towards them. 'What do you want?'

D-Ice smiled. 'The 242 to Tottenham Court Road.'

Skinny Boy sniggered. I checked him out – no Lester resemblance. Scott's brother must definitely be the other tall one. He patted his scruffed-up hair. 'You're staring, darling. Like what you see?'

I copied Skinny Boy's smile. 'No, mate. You're too ugly for me.' Back to D-Ice. I lost my smile and stretched my shoulders back and wide. 'I'm asking again. What do you want?'

I'd got the tone right. D-Ice's smile flipped into a scowl as he stood up. He was shorter than me; no wonder he needed his two helpers.

He nodded across the road. 'Let's go.'

I took a step back. 'My house? You must be mental!'

'You ain't got nut'n I ain't seen already.' He moved towards me, lifting the hem of his sweatshirt. His blade was tucked down his waistband.

I looked around and the street was empty. If he stabbed me up here, no one would come. Though, even if the place was busting with people, if it was the busiest shopping place in London, the busiest Tube station at the busiest time, who *would* come? In the end, it didn't matter if we were on the street or in my house, he'd made the rules and he was always going to win. For now.

D-Ice said, 'We moving, then?'

The three of us crossed the road, looking like old mates to anyone having a nose out their window. Down my path and the scumbags laughing as I fiddled with my three keys.

D-Ice said, 'All this in our honour?'

Skinny Boy found that hilarious, just like a good sidekick's supposed to.

I shut the door behind them and took them down to the kitchen. Skinny Boy sprawled back on his chair. D-Ice sat upright, legs wide, like his balls were bigger than the earth. I stayed standing, leaning against the fridge.

I looked D-Ice in the eye. Full on, no wavering. 'Is this about our brothers, Peter?'

D-Ice was keeping his face blank.

I said, 'Your brother's going to come out, what, in two, three years? Andre, he's always going to stay like he is.

Sharkie, he's going to stay dead. Whatever you're coming for, I don't see no point.'

'You think I'm coming? I'm already here.' He spat on the floor, a blob of froth on Mum's tiles. I made myself look away. 'See? Marking my territory.'

He leaned forward, quick. My brain was on red alert. I flinched. D-Ice sat back again, smiling.

'You're going to work for me, brud.'

I laughed. 'No, mate. You're mad!'

Skinny Boy copied me in a stupid squeaky voice. 'No, mate. You're mad!'

I pushed my back into the fridge, bending my fingernails hard against the smooth surface until they hurt. It would almost be worth it, springing forward and getting one mad punch in, but they'd be back on me quick, laughing as the blade slipped in and my blood dripped across Mum's kitchen. Or the knife might be just a part of it. Short kid with a big mouth, he'd be first in the queue for a gun.

Skinny Boy stood up, so sudden his chair fell back. 'Need a slash.'

He stalked out of the room, like the place was his, footsteps thumping up the stairs.

I said, 'He better not mash the place.'

D-Ice stretched. I stood there watching him. This boy wasn't tall and shouldn't make heads turn in the street. His clothes, all brand – must be, though they hung off him like someone bigger had tried them on first. But he made those dumbwit boys hold me down. He made Sonya sell his drugs. Journalists spouted hundreds of words about kids like him, like they were Satan's nephews mixed with Jay Z. That's what made D-Ice and that lot strong. They got on a bus and no one met their eye. They leeched off that.

He made a big show of looking round, nodding approvingly. 'It's a nice place, this one. Your mum's got style. She cook good too? Maybe when this is over, we can all have dinner.'

If I reached up, I'd feel the blender on top of the fridge, just a lift and arc away from the top of D-Ice's head. A good quality blender, Mum said, because it was heavy, metal and glass. The moment of contact would be messy and happy.

'I saw you at the fair,' I said. 'When I was with Sonya. What were you doing?'

D-Ice smiled. 'Looking for a ride, brud.'

Blood, glass and bone all over the kitchen floor. I'd still be grinning as the cops came and took me away.

D-Ice shifted position, leaning right towards me. 'You're going to work for me.'

'No, man. I'm not.'

Even as I said them, the words felt loose, rattling inside my head without fitting properly. Upstairs, there's my books, and exam papers, revision and notes. After that? A Levels. More books and exam papers, more revision and notes. More time listening to kids talking crap and teachers who don't want to be there. After that? Maybe I'd scrape a university place and wind up with loads of debt. And then what? Mum always said that there was no pressure, take it slowly, discover my dreams and then follow them, though the dreams I was having now, I didn't want to go anywhere they were taking me.

Sorry, Sonya, I'm never going to be a brain surgeon.

D-Ice was grinning, like he could see right into my thoughts. I shook my head and spat out a cuss that made big-ball boys like D-Ice feel less than a man. He jumped up, Skinny Boy suddenly beside him. That must be the quickest piss in history. They jammed me hard against the fridge, Mum's stupid pineapple magnet screwing into my back. Just holding me there, not hitting me, nothing. My stupid brain squirted out its fear drugs anyway. D-Ice could probably smell it.

'You have to understand proper.' D-Ice's mouth was up close to my ear, making sure the words didn't escape. 'This ain't negotiable. What Mr Orange started, you gotta pay back.' He stepped back. 'Consider your interview successful, Mr Sunday. You will be hearing from us soon.'

They sauntered out of the kitchen and the front door slammed shut. I pushed myself away from the fridge – bad move. I fell towards a chair and dropped on to the seat. They swaggered into *my* house, filthy fingers on *my* walls.

They must reckon they have an open invitation. Skinny Boy was strutting around like his name was on the deeds. I levered myself up. *Strutting around . . .* Where I couldn't see him.

I stumbled into the sitting room. All the surviving books were still on their shelves and my laptop was by the sofa. I ran upstairs to my bedroom. Old vinyl covers were spread across my bed, just like I'd left them. The books on the heap by the floor – I'd left them there too. Into Mum's room. Her curtains were wide open and her grey fluffy slippers were side by side near her bed, same as every morning.

Her bed – Jesus. No. A thick, sharp stink. Not this! The bastard must have – what? Kneeled on Mum's bed? Stood on the side and aimed?

It's pee. It could have been worse.

Seriously? I'm happy because he didn't crouch down and take a dump on Mum's pillow?

I pulled off the top throw. It had gone all the way, down through the duvet. The boy must have a bladder like a horse. The bottom sheet was soaking, the mattress too. Mum was going to kill me. Or even worse, she'd cry and never stop, because her disappointment would keep filling up. I breathed in hard, tightening my throat. Not one foul molecule from Skinny Boy's rotting kidneys was going to slip into my body.

I yanked everything on to the floor, fingers nowhere near the damp. Now what?

Wash it, you idiot.

How? You'd need an industrial-size washing machine to fit that lot in and a mile of radiators turned up to furnace. I opened the window wide and fanned fresh air in. Next stop, the bathroom. I filled the bath with hot water, sloshed in Radox, Persil, shampoo, anything. As the bubbles frothed up, I turned off the taps and dumped in the bedding.

Back to Mum's bedroom, with rubber gloves and bath cleaner. I sprayed the mattress, scrubbing at it with a brillo pad, sniffed – chemical lemon, nothing else. Now a blast from Mum's hairdryer, on the highest setting. The mattress looked dry, but there was no way in hell I was going to touch that faint, greasy stain to find out for sure. Mum was bound to notice that. I flipped the mattress over.

Straightening up, I breathed out. It felt like the first proper breath I'd taken since I'd walked into the room. I stretched, sore skin tugging across my bones and took another deep breath. This was it. Things had moved up a level. No matter what Tish said, I had to move up a level too.

I went back downstairs slowly. What did moving up a level even mean?

It's obvious. You need protection.

And where's that going to end?

Behind a load of rolled up wire and bars, with a landing full of D-Ices hyping their rep.

This was what Mum had worked so hard to keep me away from, extra hard after she lost Andre. But I hadn't chosen this world. A portal had gaped open and sucked me in. If I didn't do something, it was going to swallow me up. Mum too.

In the kitchen, I opened the drawer, looking for the long knife right at the back. I ran my fingers along the narrow blade. It was completely blunt, but that didn't matter. It was how I styled it off. All I needed was a sly flash, just like D-Ice.

But was that enough? What if they were coming at me? What if it was me or them? What if I had to use it? I needed more than style. That knife, right there, jammed between two wooden spoons, metal handle, metal blade, made in one piece. I held it. It was cold in my palm and didn't quite nestle. It wasn't designed for that – it was meant to be used. I let it clank back in and slammed the drawer shut.

Mum called around six. She was going out for a meal with Jonathan and was thinking of staying at his place. If I didn't want to be home by myself, she'd definitely come back, no problem. If she heard the relief in my voice, she didn't mention it. The story I'd concocted about her mattress made *Inception* look easy. *I went into your room, Mum, because it's the quietest. I thought I could revise better. Then I made myself some coffee and knocked it over* . . . Like she would have bought that.

There was still a tang of something in there, but I shut the windows and locked the front and back doors.

I was half-watching some programme about a building scam when the door knocked. I peered through the spy hole and opened up. Tish slid past me. Tish, who'd let Scott Lester's hand slide down her back.

'You all right?' Her face was serious.

'How come you're not wrapped around Scott Lester?' A joke that didn't sound like a joke.

'I am,' she scowled. 'He's invisible. I heard you had a visit today.'

'Where was your boy's brother? Standing guard outside?'

She wrinkled her face. 'Wayne was in the copshop all day. He was cycling on the pavement and punched some poor bloke who told him off.'

'You seem to know a lot about Scott Lester's brother.'

She rolled her eyes. 'Do you want fight words, or do you want to tell me what happened?'

'You seem to know already.'

'No.' Her voice was steady. 'Tell me.'

I did, watching her mouth wrinkle in disgust.

'They walked right in here and did that? That's rank! What're you going to do now?'

I took a deep breath. 'Let them know next time's not going to be so easy.'

'What d'you mean?'

'Protection.'

'Jonathan's getting alarms put in?'

'No, Tish. Something else. For me.'

'You what? You mean – a blade? Serious?' She shook her head. 'By some miracle, you got away with the pills. If they catch you with a knife, Marlon, that's a different story.'

'I thought you liked bad boys, Tish.'

She didn't smile. 'I don't like dead boys. Or prison boys. Or stupid boys.'

'It was just an idea.' I sounded like a sulky ten year old. 'He's after me for something Andre did and he's not going to stop.'

'What did Andre do?'

'It's like you said. Mr Orange, in the film, he was the grass, right?'

'What about all that street honour stuff? And what would Andre grass about anyway?'

'No idea. I tried asking him, but he said he can't remember anything. If I ask him too much, he freaks out.'

'What does D-Ice want?'

'He says he wants me to work for him.'

'What? You?'

Thanks, Tish.

She was shaking her head. 'Yeah. I suppose I get it. You'd be his little dog, Marlon. You'd have to trot after him and let him spit in your mouth whenever he asked.' She gave me a half smile. 'Translated into your world, he's Jabba the Hutt and you're his Princess Leia.'

'Yeah, Tish. I'll put on a gold bikini and strangle him.'

Her smile flickered. 'Marlon, I don't want you to get caught by Jabba in the first place.'

Silence. One that needed words in it.

Tish said, 'What have you done about Aunty Jenny's bed stuff?'

'They're soaking in the bath.'

'You're not going to wash it or nothing?'

'I thought it might jam up the machine. Mum put the sofa covers in the old one and killed it.'

Tish stuck out her lip. 'Impressive. For a boy. Most of you would shove it in and watch telly while the thing exploded. Bring the stuff over to our place. We've got a massive thing that Mum bought when she was going through her dyeing phase. You could fit the whole sofa in there. It does the drying too.'

'Yeah? Thanks!' This was proper Tish, proper friend Tish. 'How long d'you reckon it takes? Two or three hours?'

'Something like that. It'll be ready by the morning. Aunty Jenny will never know the difference.'

'Thanks, Tish. I owe you a curry.'

'With pudding.'

'We can have it tonight, if you want.'

She grimaced. 'Sorry, Milo. Got other plans.'

With . . . I nodded.

'Right!' She was all brisk. 'Get some bags, the biggest ones you can find and we'll load up. Mum's in with her book group tonight so she'll keep an eye on it all.'

'Won't she ask questions?'

'Everyone in her group brings a bottle of wine. She'll be well distracted.'

We dragged the sopping wet bedding over and loaded it into the washing machine. Tish was right. Aunty Mandisa was too busy organising plates of snacks and glasses to challenge my spilled coffee story.

Tish didn't see me out. She was getting ready for her big date.

So now it was back to me and the telly, playing the remote control like a pinball machine. A cupcake ice-off? Another Hitler doc? A cook slicing off a hunk of salt beef and a fat man eating a giant sandwich with barbecue sauce sloshing around his mouth. And . . . I pressed 'mute'. I could hear something. It sounded like a little silver whisper and a knocking sound. Yup, in my head, the knife was calling to me.

I turned the telly back up and kept flicking through the

channels. Nature programme, nature programme, history of something I wasn't interested in. I might as well do something useful. Dad's maps were under the stairs now, their new home after the break-in. I emptied the box on to the sitting room floor and spread out the world atlas with the big pictures of the two hemispheres. Dad collected maps for as long as I remembered, spending weekends tramping to antique markets across the country. Neither me nor Andre had any idea why, especially as Dad's first love was science-fiction. The other side of the world versus the other side of the universe. I ran my finger along the coastlines. Tasman Sea. Pacific Ocean. Pitt Islands. Cook Islands. What was life like there? Everyone must know all your business from the day you were born and before. If someone was out to get you, there'd be nowhere to run, nowhere to hide.

It wasn't any better in London.

The landline rang. It was nearly eleven o' clock. Damn! Mum must be on her way back, after all. She'd be well-vexed to find a bare mattress.

I picked up the receiver. 'Hello?'

'You hear me?' The voice faded between the rush of traffic. Serious traffic.

'Andre?' *God! It was!* 'Where the hell are you?'

'With my good friends.'

My heart pounded. 'What friends?'

'Good friends, boy!'

'What friends? Are they with you?'

A cuss word and the line went dead. I sat there for a moment. Andre had always made his own moves, with his own people, kept his circle tight. *Good friends?* Saleema? Some other bloke from the home who couldn't look after himself?

And the other option was . . . I jumped up, grabbed my phone and rushed into the hallway. I was slipping on my trainers, making the call at the same time.

'Andre?'

He picked up straight away. Where the hell was he? The middle of the M4?

'Yeah? Who's this?'

'It's Marlon. Your brother.'

'My phone say it don't know you.'

'That's because you never save my number.'

'You're Marlon?'

'Yes, Andre! Where are you?'

'Don't know, man.'

'Your friends, where are they?'

'Don't know. They just give me this number and tell me phone it.'

Jesus! 'Okay, I'm coming. But I need to know where you are.'

'I told you. I don't know.'

Andre sounded calm, almost happy.

'Andre, these friends . . .'

'Good friends.'

'You knew them before?'

'You keep asking me these questions. None of your business if I know them before. They come and take me out, man. Proper take me out. You coming?'

'Yes! But I need . . . Can you see a bus stop?'

'Yes, right here.'

'Okay. What does it say?'

'I can't see it properly. Wait.'

A big breath out and the sound of hydraulic brakes, voices.

'Driver says this is Tesco, Old Kent Road.'

'Okay, Andre. Just stay there. I'll be with you soon.'

How? Private jet? Teleport chamber? I'd be too late for the Tube and a bus would take all night. I dug in my pockets. I didn't have enough money for a cab to the top of the road, let alone south London. I'd have to call Mum and explain.

My fingers were rubbing against something else in my pocket; I took it out. It was Louis White's business card.

The roads were jammed, even at this time of night. I kept calling, making sure Andre stayed there. Louis White didn't ask for explanations, not at first. It was only after we crossed

Blackfriars that he glanced across at me.

'You going to tell me more?'

Choices. Lie to this man I'd got out of his bed to help me. Tell the truth to this man who was as good as police.

'What do you mean?'

A frown. 'I mean who abandoned your big brother on Old Kent Road?'

'He gets a bit confused. He said he went out with friends.'

'His friends dumped him on the street?'

'I don't know.'

'Really?'

'He didn't say.'

'Maybe I can ask him myself,' Louis said quietly. 'That looks like him there.'

Yeah, that was him, lounging on the bench, arms spread across the back like he owned it.

As we pulled up, Louis said, 'Don't introduce me.'

'Sorry?'

'If he doesn't recognise me, don't introduce me. Now doesn't seem the time.'

'Sure.' I opened the car door. 'Thank you.'

Andre didn't seem to notice me until I was standing close up. He wasn't wearing shades and in the shadows his face looked smooth and easy.

'Andre? It's Marlon.'

'Yeah?'

'Your brother.'

Andre propped himself up, squinting at me. 'Yeah, yeah.' He stretched his hand out to shake mine. 'I thought you were a ghost, man. My boys said you'd come.' He pointed to Louis's car. 'That the cab?'

'Yeah, that's the cab.'

Andre's breath stunk of alcohol and there was a smokiness on his clothes. As he bent himself awkwardly into the back seat, the smell filled the car. Louis's eyes fixed on the rear-view mirror.

I said, 'You okay, Andre?'

'No! Where's the thing?'

'By your hand. Just there.'

Andre patted the seat, found the seatbelt and slotted it in.

Louis said, 'Ready to go?'

Andre closed his eyes. 'Yeah, let's go.'

It was a quick drive to Andre's home. Louis rang the doorbell while I stirred my brother awake. Even though I tried to be gentle, Andre woke up flailing and angry, twisting and yanking at his tubes like he was still in hospital.

'We're here,' I said.

Andre pushed his face into mine. I breathed in the booze and smoke.

He growled, 'Who are you?'

'Marlon. Your brother.'

Andre stumbled out and stood holding on to the car door. 'Marlon?'

'Yes.'

Andre looked thoughtful. 'Marlon.' He smiled, reached into the back pocket of his jeans and pulled out a piece of paper. 'Marlon. My friends sent something for you.'

He pushed the paper at me and wobbled away, past Louis and a night worker talking in the doorway and into the house.

Louis walked back towards the car. I shoved the paper in my pocket.

'The people aren't happy,' Louis said. 'Andre promised he'd be back at midnight.'

'I'm surprised they didn't call my mum.'

Louis raised his eyebrows. 'Is that how it works? If he doesn't behave, your mum gets a call?'

I slid the seatbelt across. 'That's how Mum wants it to work. When he first went there, she used to phone the place so much they promised to call her if anything was wrong.'

Louis pulled into the night. 'So life changed big time for Andre?'

'Yes.' For all of us.

I turned away, pushing my nose against the window. Louis must have got the message; he didn't ask anything else, not even when we pulled up outside my house. I

289

checked out the bus stop and the shadows by the front door as I climbed out of the car. Empty.

'Thanks.'

'Yeah.'

Louis's car didn't move until I opened my front door, like I was his girl he'd just dropped home. As I closed the door, I heard the car shoot off down the road. Right there in the hallway, I pulled the crumple of paper out my pocket and stretched it flat, examining it closely.

It was a drawing, a crap one. Just in case you couldn't work out the pictures, there were words to help. Three coffins, side by side, *Crip Boy* under one, then *Mummy*, then – they didn't call her Sonya. Just reading the word they used made me feel sick. Below, in big scrawled capitals, *RIP*.

I squeezed the paper in the palm of my hand, hoping hot blood and sweat would churn it to a pulp. I locked the door and bolted it, then went down to the kitchen. I opened the drawer, lifted out the knife and slipped it into the waistband of my trousers. It didn't feel good, but it felt right.

14

The clock said 8.13 a.m. My trousers were on the floor by
my bed. That scrap of paper was still in my jeans pocket.
The knife was still under the mattress.

Down in the kitchen, I poured myself a bowl of
cornflakes, took a couple of mouthfuls and put down my
spoon. Adrenaline was up and busy again – I was going to
run out of it soon. But not just yet. I needed it badly. Last
night, I'd made a decision. I wasn't going to bother Mum or
Andre any more. Only D-Ice knew what was in his head.
Instead of him coming to me, I was taking my questions
straight to him.

Stepping out, blade ready for my call – it should be easy.
That was the way it seemed to the world, something you
slung in your pocket in the same way you zipped up
your fly. But man, in real life . . . First, where the hell did
I hide the thing? If I shoved it in my back pocket, would I
cut off my own balls if I sat down too quickly? Or what
if some eagle-eyed copper spotted the handle poking
out the top? I switched it to the front jeans pocket. Yeah.
Better. Easy to reach. I opened the front door and walked
up the path. No. The blade was shifting up and down

against my leg, like it was laughing at me.

I went straight back inside, yanked it out and dropped it on my bed. A posh silver kitchen knife on a black duvet, like a photo in a magazine. *Great gangsta thought, mate.*

I pulled open my cabinet drawer and spread out the two pieces of paper. The article about the seventeen-year-old girl who'd died, the girl I'd sat next to and laughed with. Siouxza. And the rubbish drawing. Andre and Mum and Sonya in their coffins. I went over to the mirror and studied myself, narrowing my eyes until my face blurred. I was Andre, no, I was D-Ice, standing here, looking at himself. I made my shoulders loose and sucked in my belly until it was hard. I pulled up my zip and flipped the hood over my head. There was an inside pocket. The knife fitted perfectly. Stepping forward and back, forward and back, I could just see the knife moving, but only if I was staring hard. I had to look back at people, stop them staring at me. Screwface – yeah, I could do that as good as D-Ice.

My hand brushed the jersey. Solid metal was just the other side, a handle tapering into a sharp tip. I let my finger rest on the point.

Streatham used to feel like a new country, but now I had my landmarks. I passed the house with the dead tree in the middle of the garden, the lamppost with the laminated lost cat poster strapped to it, the spiky bush on the corner. I lay my palm flat against my outside pocket. The blade made my walk different, quick, but heavier, with a swing. But still, it was only coming out of my pocket if it had to.

If it had to?

In self defence. If they went for me first. Or I thought they were going to.

That's it?

Yes. I wasn't going to start a knife battle I couldn't win. But that heaviness in my pocket, the sharpness skimming my fleece – that felt good.

No worry about security this time as the lock was gouged right out. I took the stairs, two at a time up to the fourth floor, my heart going like a power drill. Outside the flat, I drew myself up to my full height and knocked.

Hayley had to be in there. I felt it. She wasn't going to wriggle away from questions this time. She was going to tell me where to find D-Ice. I lifted the letterbox and dropped it again. Yes! A movement behind the kitchen window. I dropped my hand into my pocket and hammered the letterbox, the knife bouncing with every jolt.

'Now you're one of the problems.'

Agnes was standing by her door with a tall, wide man next to her. Neither was smiling.

'You and all the other boys,' she said. 'In, out, in out. Causing everyone trouble.'

The man came right out to show me he knew the gym well. His big hands could shape a fist and cause damage.

Agnes shook her head, slowly. 'I thought you weren't like the other ones.'

'They're all the same.' Agnes's giant friend stepped closer. 'You better go home, boy.'

This bloke, he could block out the light. He could crush my voice box with one hand. But I had something he didn't expect, that little silver whisper in my pocket, calling a bit louder now. Yeah man. You keep staring me out. My fingernail tapped the knife handle.

Agnes moved in front of Muscle Man and touched my shoulder. 'Stay out of trouble. Go home.'

Tap, tap. Nail on metal. I glanced back at the window; a curtain edge shifted.

'Please,' Agnes said. 'For Violet's sake. For her granddaughter's sake. Just go.'

I turned and ran back down the stairs.

The bus home from London Bridge was empty and I was the only one on the top deck. I lay down my jacket carefully on the seat next to me. I felt cooler, lighter. I touched the pocket with the knife, feeling its edge beneath the material.

My phone vibrated. It was a text from Mum. More like an essay, really; Mum kept in punctuation and didn't do abbreviations. She and Jonathan were making the most of the good weather and heading out to Kew Gardens and I was welcome to come along. All the way across London for grass and flowers? With Mum and Jonathan walking along hand in hand, too. After all these years, that still felt a bit weird.

The words kept coming. This time, another essay about revision. She must have used up her whole month's text allowance in a few minutes.

As the bus turned the corner to the station, the driver announced that it was terminating early. I could walk the rest of the way, fifteen minutes max. I shrugged into my jacket, feeling the metal drop, and made my way downstairs. Out on the street, I took a quick look round to see who was checking me. No one. Funny how quickly my body worked itself out – the right stride, the right arm movement, the right expression, face blanked, eyes on the road ahead.

The main road was jammed as usual, with buses and bicycles fighting the cars. Somewhere over the other side of London, Mum was holding hands with Jonathan in a greenhouse full of palm trees. Closer to home, Tish was probably hugging up to Scott Lester. And somewhere else, D-Ice was rubbing his hands and smirking, sure everything was going his way. Yeah, he could think that for now.

I cut through the alleyway by the corner shop and headed straight across the zebra crossing. As I stepped out, a car slowed down and the driver pressed his horn hard.

What was this idiot's problem? No. I couldn't look. Catch eyes with the wrong person when you're carrying and you can end up in trouble. I had to keep walking. The car crawled round the corner beside me and stopped. My stomach blipped. D-Ice and Skinny Boy had wheels now?

The window rolled down. There was just enough space to fit a gun barrel. And me, I was just standing there, like I had a bull's eye painted on my chest. It was going to happen here, in broad daylight. My brain was clear, but my feet wouldn't move.

The window carried on all the way down. A uniform? A copper! Bastards! In an unmarked car, and all. I could laugh. Andre always said the feds were legal gangsters. I jammed my hands tighter in my pockets.

You're going to push that blade through your kidney, mate!

Sweat was popping on my forehead. But I could style this off, Andre-style. *Breathe out slowly. Let my shoulders relax back even more.*

The copper started laughing. 'You don't recognise the car in daylight?' The car door opened; Louis White was grinning, just like his little brother. 'Or was it the uniform?'

I couldn't answer. It was like I'd been unplugged.

The car door was still open, but the grin had disappeared. 'I won't be doing your brother no favours if I let you walk around with that knife on you.'

Seriously? Were they issuing coppers with x-ray contact

lenses now? Or maybe he was just bluffing.

The knife handle was cold in my fingers. 'No one asked you for favours.'

'You did. Last night.'

I shrugged. 'It won't happen again.'

I turned and started walking.

Louis shouted after me. 'Where are you off to?'

I stopped. 'Home.'

'With a knife in your pocket and a bad-boy look on your face?'

I shouldn't have knocked on his door. I should have run when he told me he was a copper.

'Get in the car, Marlon.'

'You taking me down the station, *special* constable?'

'Don't tempt me. Now get in the car.'

'And if I don't?'

Louis opened his door, came round and stood dead opposite me. 'I'll follow you home and sit outside your house.'

It was me that looked away first. I hadn't put in the same hours of screwface practice as my brother. I took my time to climb in the car and shut the door.

Louis said, 'You done?'

'What d'you mean?'

'The rude boy stuff.' Louis slid the keys into the ignition and turned to me. 'I've seen it done enough times before and a lot more convincing. My little brother, that was his speciality.'

Nice one, Louis. There was no reply to that.

A bus was coming up behind – and another one, both of them ones that stopped by my house. If I'd waited, I could have been on one of them, heading down my road.

I said, 'Aren't you going to be late for work?'

'I've finished. I thought I'd come and see you.'

'You were going to turn up at my house? In your gear and everything?'

'Worried what the neighbours would think?' Louis laughed. 'Could be worse. Could be one of my mates turning up to tell your mum you've been stabbed.'

I opened the car door. 'I'll walk.'

'Grow up, Marlon.' Louis turned the key and released the brake. 'Got a knife on you? You're going to end up with one in you.'

The man was talking like a TV advert. I just had time to shut the door before the car shot into the traffic flow. *Grow up? Okay!* I was huddling down in my seat. I pulled myself upright and planted myself solid. I still wasn't filling as much space as Louis, but give it time.

I said, 'How d'you know about the knife?'

'The sun's shining and you've got your jacket on. Your hand's in your pocket. And the look, Marlon, and the walk. Every would-be younger in London's playing it like that.'

So I was styling it right.

'Don't look so proud,' Louis said. 'You really want to look like a thirteen-year-old boy trying to be a badman? Them boys are jumpy, Marlon. Quick to put a bullet through friend and rival.'

I forced a laugh. 'I'm not from the countryside! I don't need the scare tales.'

'Scare tales?' Louis glanced at me. 'What's scary is the stuff you don't hear. Most of the time, it's one hyped-up little kid sticking it to another one in some shoved away end of Edmonton. Who cares?'

Louis sped through a light on amber, and turned down a side street. 'Why are *you* carrying a knife, Marlon?'

'You seem to know so much. You tell me.'

'Lose the damn act, please. Or else I can't help you.'

'Help?' A proper laugh this time. 'Remember the church? I didn't see you doing much help then. Your mum's face was right up in my mum's face. Right up!'

Louis pulled into a bay outside a chicken place. 'I'm sorry about that. But we were grieving. It's got nothing to do with what's happening now.'

'We were grieving too. First my dad died. Then there was Andre. You never even came to see him in hospital.'

Louis stared out the front. He was still holding the steering wheel. 'It was complicated.'

The blokes in the Lickin' Chicken were setting up for

the afternoon, wiping the counter and tables, sharing a few laughs and jokes. Maybe that was the way to a simple life. Open a chicken shop.

'I'm sorry about the church thing,' Louis said, quietly. 'I always have been. It doesn't mean I'm going to stop asking you, though. Why are you carrying a knife?'

'Andre said coppers never go off duty.'

His jaw twitched, like he was squeezing his teeth together. He turned to look at me. 'This is nothing to do with me being a copper! Three years I don't see you, Marlon. Then you turn up on my doorstep with a bashed up face and next thing your brother gets abducted. You don't have to be feds to ask questions.'

A motorcycle shot past us, way over speed. Louis kept looking at me.

'See? Off duty. So, Marlon. Why are you—'

'You tell me something first. About Tayz and his brother.'

'Tayz?'

'Tell me.'

'So that's why you're walking round Hackney looking like you're ready to shank a man.'

'Just tell me.'

He unhooked his seatbelt and sat back. 'Tayz is in prison with three years still to go. He's not likely to come out early, neither.'

'I read that he's running things from there.'

Louis shook his head. 'Them journalists have been reading too much *Godfather*. Tayz isn't running nothing. He's just a little trout in a big shark pool, and a stupid trout too. Dangle a razor blade in the water, and he'll think it's a worm and swallow it.'

One of the chicken-shop guys had come out and was washing down the front window. He was putting everything into it, like it didn't bother him that the street dirt and the traffic were going to mess it up straight away.

Louis started the car again. We drove for a while in silence. It was familiar territory – the new, bright blocks, the old, flaky ones, the mosque, the halal butcher and a random organic fruit and veg place. Once we'd passed two more turnings, it would be my street. Louis slowed to a halt in the stalled traffic.

I said, 'Doesn't it make him more dangerous if he's stupid?'

'Dangerous or dead. It could go either way.'

We inched forward.

'Thing is, Marlon, after my brother's passing, I didn't want to think about this crap again. But I've been fooling myself. You ever seen that film *Avengers Assemble*?'

I nodded.

'There's this bit where they tell Bruce Banner to get angry and Hulk up. The rest of the time, they've been telling him to keep Hulk down. Remember it?'

'Yeah.'

'So you wonder if he can Hulk on demand and get really wild and furious. But he says he has a secret.'

'Yeah.'

'Do you remember what it is?'

'Yeah. He's always angry.'

'Right.' Louis tapped his head. 'That's me. And Tayz. And his brother. And probably you, too. Always, always angry.'

Forward again, so we were almost touching the bumper in front. A cyclist squeezed past my window so close his cheek nearly smeared the glass.

Louis glanced over at me. 'Some of us hold the anger down. And in some of us it bursts out in all the wrong places. Then it's like we want to destroy the whole of New York City.'

The lights changed ahead. We didn't move.

Louis was on a roll. 'Problem is, the anger keeps passing down and passing down. This one does this and that one does that, so this one has to go and fight that one. One has a knife, so the other gets a strap. So what are we going to do, shoot and stab each other until no one's left?' He sighed. 'Sorry, Marlon. It just hurts me. And it hurts me more to think you want to be part of it.'

'I don't.'

The car in front was inching back until it was almost

kissing Louis's car. Louis was watching it hard. As the other side of the road cleared, the driver swung round into a tight U and sped away.

Louis pummelled his heart. 'Okay. Breathing again. Right, I'm prepared to believe for now that the knife's a one-off. Anything else you want to ask me?'

'Know anything about Tayz's brother, D-Ice?'

'D-Ice? Is that what he calls himself?'

'What do you know about him?'

'His real name's Peter.'

'I know.'

'You've been Sherlocking. He's been inside. Do you know that too?'

I nodded.

'Deduce what for?'

'No.'

'He tried to set fire to a woman's flat.'

'Jesus! Was anyone hurt?'

'The place was empty, thank God. It belonged to Sharkie's girlfriend, Marlon. One of her neighbours spotted him shoving burning paper through the letterbox and called the police straight away. She never returned home and a month later she moved up to Manchester. Who could blame her?'

The air in the car was getting stale. I opened the window. We were moving again, crawling behind a Hackney Homes van as motorbikes whipped past our sides. Any breeze coming through stank of exhaust.

Louis said, 'Are you okay, Marlon?'

'Yeah. Tayz ran with the Riotboyz. What about D-Ice?'

He sighed. 'Stupid, stupid boys, them lot up in Brixton. When they're seven, they're playing football together in the playground. Five years later, they're trying to slash out each other's veins and none of them know why. *I* don't know why, even when our brothers were part of it.'

I said, 'So them and the Spikes are still fighting.'

'The little ones, yeah, shanking up each other and distracting from the big men's activities. The big guys, they've got to work together, especially the ones at the top, clubbing together to keep out the chancers. There's only so many crackheads to go round in any one territory.'

This was nothing I didn't really know. 'So the gangs are all linked up.'

'Kind of. And kind of not. Boys on all sides have some family connection, brothers, half-brothers, nephews, whatever, in different places. Sometimes they're together. Sometimes they're against. Remember those girls shot outside the New Year's party in Birmingham?'

'Yeah.' Mum had printed out the story and thrown it at Andre.

'One of the girls, it was her brother that shot them. Complete waste of life.'

'And D-Ice?'

'D-Ice.' He shook his head. 'I feel like I'm boosting his rep just by calling him that. Him and Tayz had different dads and their mum got left with both of them. The poor woman must have had it hard, first one boy working the streets, then the next, like two little dons. Then Tayz got put away and it all crumbled.'

'What happened?'

'The council came down hard on their mum. Breach of tenancy, et cetera, et cetera, and no one was going to mount a petition on her behalf. She's off the council list and she's a teaching assistant in a primary school. You can't even rent a puddle in London on those wages. She had to move away.'

'Where did she go?'

'Liverpool or somewhere round those ways, where she had family. Far, far away from her sons. It was like she completely wiped her hands of them.'

While my mum was holding on to us as tight as she could.

'So Mum's gone, and big brother Tayz is banged up in High Sutton. D-Ice hasn't got no one, no one to look out for him or even make him a decent meal after a hard day on the frontline. I reckon social services tried to do their best, but I couldn't see him playing good boy in any foster home. He ended up in a hostel in Bromley. You ever been in one of those places?'

I shook my head. But there was one by the bus stop in Dalston. I'd seen the shrivelled men outside with their cans in paper bags.

I said, 'How long did he stay there?'

'Two weeks. Then set fire to Michelle's flat.'

'You know a lot.'

'You can find out a lot in three years if you keep looking.'

We pulled on to the roundabout.

Louis said, 'That enough information for you?'

It felt like the car was full of water pressing against my chest. It was hard finding breath to answer him. 'Yes.'

Turning off the roundabout, a black cab whizzed past us in the bus lane, swinging out again to avoid a bus. Louis shoved his brakes on. The knife jerked.

Louis said, 'Tell the police.'

'What?'

'I'm not stupid, Marlon. I can see what's happening. Your bashed-up face, the thing last night, it's telling me the story. If you're not careful, you're going to get sucked in.'

I stared out of the window.

'So you reckon you can handle this yourself.'

'I have to.'

'Let me help.' Louis indicated, slowed, stopped.

'No.'

'You don't trust me, do you?'

'You're a copper. You're one of them.'

I had the door open and was out of the car quick. Behind me, an engine started up, but I wasn't looking around. A police car screamed past me down the hill. I needed space – breath space, thought space. I walked quick, feet coming down hard.

When Tayz went inside, D-Ice was left to deal with things. It was too late to get revenge on Sharkie, but there was always Sharkie's girl and their baby son. After that, he must have spent two years or so stewing in his cell, working out the best way to get back at Andre. Then he must have imagined me at home, my mum okay, no stress. Perhaps the thing with Sonya was an accident. She must have been buying drugs off him to help pay off her mum's debt. Me, Alex, the rest of us, all helping Hayley Wilson balance her books. Except, what if Hayley hadn't stopped buying and the debt had got bigger? What else did Sonya have to do? D-Ice, he found new ways to use her. He had me in his sight and aimed Sonya my way.

But plans changed. No one could imagine that Sonya would die.

Another cop car shot past. And a van. The world was full of them, lights flashing, sirens shredding the air. What if I had to go past them? Right. I'd do it all quiet and casual, open the door, go straight into the kitchen and put the knife back in the drawer. I folded myself in, hunched my shoulders, kept my eyes on my feet, left, right, left, right, forward.

All these police. It was like one of those call-outs on CSI.

In a year or so, Louis White would be sitting inside a car like that, a proper paid up Met man, him and his copper mates.

What if he's grassed you up and they're all waiting for you?

No, he hadn't called anyone while I was with him.

Wait. They were all parked there, outside Tish's. *Tish?* Jesus! Scott Lester must have—

No! They were outside *my* house. Mum? No, she was with Jonathan, in Kew Gardens. Andre! Those scumbags had made their move on Andre! *Give the boy a message, a strong one!* They didn't have to do much. Just take him somewhere busy, down the Underground maybe, and leave him. A big, black guy, stressed out, yelling, people thinking he's a nutter. Stumbling about all confused, calling for Sharkie or Mum while the trains rushed in and out and the people pushed past him. If he tripped, if he tumbled . . .

That drumming noise, my feet pounding downhill, the rush of the wind on my face was like a Tube train shooting through a tunnel, the brakes screeching through my head to a collision. I was going to collide too, with the coppers standing in my way. They needed to move, needed to stop shouting at me . . . Shouting at me?

I braced myself, stopped. Their hands were on me straight away, pulling my arms back, patting my pocket, pulling out the knife.

It could have been the same cell, with the same freezing air blasting the same stink up my nostrils. Mum on her way again, the solicitor poised again, like I was in a sci-fi time loop. Even the poster on the ceiling hadn't changed. I knew the number to call if my drug use was stressing me.

I sat on the edge of the bed. Earth, Wind and Fire? Flares and jumpsuits, glitterballs and spaceships. I didn't need that now. My brain was twisted up, like it was full of sparking cables. I closed my eyes, tried to smoothe it, make my thoughts mould one into another, until there was only one thought. One boy. D-Ice. He'd made his plan to mash up my family's life. It was time to stop him.

Mum was in the interview room. Just one glance before turning away from me.

I didn't start this, Mum? Don't you understand? Or maybe there was something else in her look that she didn't want me to see.

She was sitting next to a young Indian-looking bloke in a suit. He jumped to his feet and held out his hand. A careful handshake, probably showing the cameras I'm not pressing anything into his palm.

'Hello, Marlon. My name's Chattura. I've been asked to represent you.'

Mum glared at me. 'Jonathan thought we could do better than the duty guy this time.'

Chattura managed a half-smile. 'Let's have a little talk before the police interview you, if that's okay.'

A little talk. Like I was a five-year-old caught eating Play-Doh. I looked past the solicitor. 'Mum?'

She was shaking her head.

Chattura clapped his hands together, then rubbed them. 'Let's get on.' He took a pen out of his top pocket and checked the notes on the file in front of him. 'You understand what's happening, Marlon?'

Mum was wiping her eyes with a tissue.

'Yes!' Fizzing cables. 'Some idiot lied to the police and said I hurt Mrs Steedman.'

'Who?' Mum was frowning.

Chattura ignored her. 'When the police came to arrest you, they say you behaved "aggressively".'

'I didn't.'

'Were you running towards them shouting?'

'Yeah, I did that. I thought something had happened to Mum . . .' Mum looked at me, then at the floor. 'Or my brother.'

'Why?'

Because these dickwits said it would.

310

Mum sniffed and dabbed her nose. 'We've had police cars come round twice. The first time was when my husband collapsed in the street. The other time was when his brother . . . Andre was in a car accident. He was in a coma for a month and his best friend was killed.'

Chattura made a note. 'Thank you, Mrs Sunday.' Back to me. 'And when they were searching you, they found the knife.'

I nodded.

'I think we have a big problem here, Marlon. But let's deal with the alleged assault first. Do you know the alleged victim?'

'Yes.'

The pen was dead vertical in Chattura's hand. 'How?'

'I knew her granddaughter, Sonya.'

Mum turned to stare at me. 'That girl again?'

Chattura frowned. 'Carry on, Marlon.'

'I was with Sonya, when she died at the fair. There was something wrong with her heart.'

I could say the words now, like I was describing a TV programme. I wouldn't dream yellow or taste mustard or smell fried onions, not if I kept it all in a distant part of my head.

Chattura said, 'Her neighbours report seeing you there earlier today.'

'Yes. I knocked but nobody answered.'

'And then what happened?'

'Her neighbours came out and I came home.'

'Do you know if anybody was in the house?'

'No.'

'You didn't rush in and knock Mrs Steedman to the floor?'

'No! Her neighbours saw I didn't.'

Mum still wouldn't look at me. She leaned towards the solicitor. 'Who reported the assault?'

'Hayley Wilson, Mrs Steedman's daughter.'

What?

Mum frowned. 'She's . . .'

I had to talk to the side of Mum's face. 'She's Sonya's mum.'

Mum let out the same kind of laugh that was brewing in my throat, cross and funny mixed. '*She* named *my* son as the boy who pushed an old woman to the ground in her own house. I'm surprised the police even bothered to show up. It's ridiculous!'

Chattura shook his head. 'Ms Wilson is not claiming that she saw it. She alleges she heard her mother shout and ran into the hallway in time to see the suspect disappear. She thought she recognised you, Marlon, from the back of your head.'

The nutter laugh was bubbling too close. If I let it break through, they'd have to sedate me.

Mum said, 'What did this Mrs Steedman say?'

'Very little. Her daughter claims she was too shocked.'

Mum took a sip of tea and breathed out loudly. 'And that's the evidence they used to arrest my son. The back of his head.'

Chattura leaned forwards towards me. 'Hayley Wilson said you were obsessed with her daughter, Marlon. She said you turned up at her home and demanded to see pictures of her. And you went to Sonya's funeral, uninvited.'

A quick breath in from Mum. 'Bitch!'

I jolted. That word was banned from our house, locked out in the street with 'retard'.

Chattura gently cleared his throat. 'Please, Mrs Sunday. Marlon, she's alleging that you hassled her at the cemetery until she took you to her daughter's grave.'

Hassled *her*? Her little friends abandoned my disabled brother in the middle of the night by a busy road! They broke into my house, punched me, drew a knife on me! That's the real story!

You going to tell it then?

You're kidding. Look what happened the first time you were here.

They all knew the story they wanted to hear. It wasn't mine.

Chattura's pen moved silently; it must be an expensive one. 'Where were you at two o'clock this afternoon?'

'With the police.'

'This is not a joke, Marlon.' If Mum had her knife back, she'd have thrown it at me, point first.

'I know. I was with a policeman. Louis White.'

Mum's eyes widened. 'Louis *White*? Sharkie's brother?'

'Yeah, he's one of those volunteer coppers. I went to see him a few days ago, to see if he'd visit Andre. He was on his way back from work and gave me a lift.'

Chaturra said, 'Was the knife on you?'

'Yes.'

Mum was perched on the edge of her chair. She twisted her shoulder towards the solicitor, like she was going to shove him out of the way and get on with the interrogation herself.

'What knife was it, Marlon?'

'The small one. From John Lewis.'

'Why did you have my onion knife in your pocket?'

'I don't know.'

Even if I summoned up the feelings I'd had that morning, I couldn't put them into proper words that she'd understand.

'There must have been a reason, Marlon. Or were you planning to pop round a friend's house and make them a quick salad?'

Chattura drew his chair closer to me, blocking out Mum. 'Let's concentrate on facts, please. Take me through what happened, in your own words.'

I breathed out slowly. 'I was doing my revision, or trying to. I couldn't think properly, so I decided to go for a walk.'

Mum snorted. 'All the way down to south London?'

I ignored her. 'I got jumped by some kids at the bus stop recently. I thought the knife would help me feel safer.'

Mum scraped her chair, but said nothing.

I carried on. 'Louis White saw me. He was in his car, on his way back from work. He kind of worked out I had the knife on me. He told me how stupid I was and gave me a lift to the top of my street so I could go home and get rid of it.'

'And that's it?' Chattura said.

'Yes.'

'But you did go to south London.'

'Yes.'

'Why?'

'Because . . . because after the fairground I wanted to go there.' I looked at Mum. 'After Dad died, did you ever go to the places you'd been with him?'

'That's different. We were together for fifteen years.' She came and crouched down in front of me, her hands on my knees. 'Don't look away from me, Marlon.'

I didn't, because I knew she wanted me to see everything she felt. I owed her that at least, for bringing her here again. Maybe if I looked really hard, I'd see something more.

Mum, do you know what Andre did? Did he grass?

'When you went down to Streatham,' she was saying. 'Was the knife on you then?'

I looked away. Mum stood up slowly and went and sat down in her chair.

'The police interviewed Hayley Wilson and her mother.' Chattura sounded like a teacher taking control of a classroom. 'There was absolutely no mention of a knife. No mention at all.'

It was past eight when the copper punched in the code and opened the door back into the public waiting room. A thin woman with a baby buggy full of plastic bags looked like she'd settled down for the night. A drunk bloke had claimed his space too, slumped over two seats. And there opposite him, was Jonathan. He jumped up, looking seriously grateful his wait was over. He put one arm around my shoulders, pulling Mum into him with the other.

'I wanted to come in,' he said. 'But they wouldn't let me.'

Mum sighed. 'You didn't miss anything special.'

Jonathan gave her a surprised look. He didn't know her as well as he thought. The sadness and anger in her words were so obvious.

He turned to me, his face full of concern, real concern, not just trying to look good in front of Mum. 'What are they going to do?'

'Bail,' I said. 'I have to go back in a month.'

Jonathan nodded. 'Chattura's good. The best they had available.'

Mum and Jonathan stopped at the Indian place at the top of the road for a takeaway. I headed straight home. I was stinking like a blocked drain.

I slammed the shower on as hot as I could bear, soaping hard and kneading the shampoo through my hair, two, three times. I creamed my skin with Palmers, breathing in the thick, sweet smell. This was me, Home Marlon, who ate summer rolls and watched *The Gadget Show* with his mum. And Cellboy Marlon? Washed down the plughole? No, he'd turned to steam and stuck to the walls, waiting for a chance to drip back into me.

'Marlon?' Mum was knocking on the bathroom door. 'Food.'

'Coming.'

As I passed the sitting room, I heard Mum and Jonathan talking. I carried on straight down, to the kitchen. They'd got me lamb curry. Mum knew it was my favourite. I spooned in a couple of mouthfuls straight from the foil container, then covered it and stuck it in the fridge. I gulped back a glass of orange juice. It cut right through the meaty fat taste. I poured another one to take upstairs.

Outside the sitting room door, I fiddled with the handle loud enough for them to change their conversation if they wanted to. Home Marlon. Thoughtful and considerate.

Mum was sitting next to Jonathan on the sofa and his arm was around her.

She said, 'Not eating?'

'I'm not really hungry.'

She nodded. 'Me neither.'

I sat down on the armchair opposite them, like I was being interviewed. Music was playing quietly, one of Jonathan's classical CDs. If Mum was by herself, she'd probably be blasting The Rolling Stones.

Jonathan's face seemed to shuffle around a bit, then him and Mum glanced at each other.

'We've been thinking,' he said.

My teeth clamped down on my lip. Announcement time. The big move to some village in Kent. Or, they were getting married. Jonathan was already holding Mum's hand like he wanted to put a ring on it.

Jonathan checked with Mum again. She nodded.

'I've asked Jennifer . . .'

For her hand in—

'. . . if I can take you out of state education. It's too late for your GCSEs, but your A Levels . . .'

I had to hold it in. If I broke out laughing now, Mum would kick me out of the house and probably down the street too. They were going to send me posh! As if gangboys didn't have cars or travelcards or phones or internet. Like

318

you drop off the end of the world if you cross the Hackney border. *And don't you know, Jonathan, things happen in posh places too?* Tish's friend got caught hiding a gun under her bed. Her boyfriend reckoned no one was going to trouble a rich girl in Barnet.

Mum was looking cross already. 'Haven't you got anything to say? This is the biggest chance you'll ever have.'

Jonathan stroked Mum's hand. 'Let him get used to it, Jenny. A whole new school, new home . . .'

'Home?' I sounded like an angry dog. 'You mean boarding school?'

'No.' Jonathan smiled. 'You're coming to my house. It's not too far away, so you can still see Tish. And there's four bedrooms. You can have a friend or two over whenever you like.'

Friends? New posh ones from private school?

'It might help things.' Jonathan's words petered away.

'Well?' Mum looked stormy.

'Yeah.' I nodded hard. 'A good idea. A great idea.'

'It is,' Mum said. She didn't sound like she was relieved. Just certain.

I said goodnight, went upstairs and lay on my bed in the dark. Soon I'd be Posh Marlon, with all the other rich kids, in Jonathan's big house in Camden. I shoved on my headphones. Bill Withers.

* * *

I must have fallen asleep, because when I opened my eyes the house was completely silent and there was no strip of hall light beneath my door. Mum – and Jonathan – had gone to bed. I sat up. A mug had been left on my bedside table, hot chocolate, still a tiny bit warm. That must have been Mum, while I was sleeping. A driver braked hard outside. Voices, then bass-heavy speakers as the car pulled away. It was none of my business, but I was wide awake now.

I had a clear view across the road. Tish was trying to open her front door. She managed to drop the key and as she bent over to pick it up, everything fell out of her bag. She crouched down, rubbing her hands across the ground, then sat back on her heels, face in her hands. I closed the curtains and sat down on the edge of my bed. *Leave it five, ten seconds. She'll sort herself out.* I checked again. She was still there. I slid on my trainers and crept down the stairs. Keys? Yeah, got them. I closed the door quietly and crossed the road.

Tish had moved to the doorstep. She watched me come towards her, her face full of shadows.

I said, 'Need a hand?'

She shook her head. 'Going to pick the lock with your knife, then?'

Her breath stank of alcohol and there was a slight wobble to her.

'You been drinking?' I tried to keep my voice easy.

'You been jooking?'

I stepped back. 'D'you need help or not?'

Tish's head was back in her hands and she was rocking to and fro. I crouched next to her and touched her back.

'Tish? What's wrong?'

She shrugged off my hand. 'Just leave me alone.'

It was just words, not the Tish tone that really meant it. I picked up her lipstick and travelcard and put them down on the doorstep next to her.

'Thanks.' She was still now, staring at the ground.

'Where's your keys?'

She waved towards the flowerbeds. I peered between two flowerpots, slipping my hand through the cobwebs and dirt. My fingertips brushed the metal. 'Got them.'

I slid the key into the lock.

She said, 'Not yet.'

'Okay.'

I sat down next to her. Her make-up was smeared from crying. If I was a girl, I could hug her, with no worries about the wrong bits of our bodies brushing past each other. No questions about whether it was just a hug or something else. No stupid thoughts about Scott Lester hugging her too.

She was looking at me. 'The knife thing. Why?'

'Because if I didn't, they'd keep coming back. And every time it would be worse.'

'And d'you think that's changed? It's like you've laid down an extra challenge.'

'You don't understand. You don't know what it's like when someone throws you against a wall like they want to kill you.'

'You're wrong. I do.'

'What?' A prickling in my stomach. 'When?'

'Tonight. When I was having an even crappier evening than you were, Marlon.'

She pushed herself up, seemed to buckle and sank down again.

'Are you okay?'

'Do I look okay?'

I slid closer and put an arm round her. It was automatic. She gave me a quick, surprised look.

'No, man!' She leaned into me. 'Keep it there! We can even swap over halfway if you like.'

'What happened, Tish?'

'What happened?' Tish shook her head, her hair brushing my chest. 'What happened is Wayne Lester's mum didn't get rid of him when she found out she was pregnant. It sounds a bit harsh, but he's just nothing. Not worth air, space, nothing. He's got a brain you can probably see through, but he thinks he's a big, bad man. That's a crap combination.'

My mouth opened too quickly. 'Is Scott like that?'

'Can't you just forget about him?'

'He dumped weed in my bag, Tish. He nearly got me chucked out of school!'

'I know, Marlon, but it wasn't personal. His brother pushed him into it. Scott's just . . . I don't know. He'll probably get chucked out himself and move on somewhere else.'

'Does that bother you?'

She shrugged. 'Me and Scott, that's finished with anyway.'

'Oh.'

'You're crap at lying, Marlon. So don't even bother.'

She shifted away from me.

'Sorry.' I moved my hand so my fingertips just touched hers. 'Tish, please tell me what happened.'

'Okay.' She looked at me, face set. 'I'll tell you. I don't want you to say anything, not while I'm talking, not afterwards, not ever. Can you manage that?'

'Tish . . .'

'Please.'

'I'll try.'

'Try as hard as you can, Marlon. Right?'

'Sure.'

She rested her hand on my knee, gently, like she didn't want to leave a print.

'Scott asked me round his house for something to eat. His mum was going to be there, all right?'

'I never said – '

'Your face did! And even if she wasn't, I can look after myself. Me and Scott haven't done anything like that, and it's not part of the plan. Got it?'

'Yeah.'

'We got back to Scott's around half five and his mum *was* there, though she kind of looks – I don't know – like she's been run over.' Tish laughed to herself. 'Wayne was on his sodding Xbox killing people. His eyes kind of lit up when he saw us and he started making really gross comments, about what he thought we'd be doing and stuff. Even Scott didn't like it so we went out again, round one of his mates.'

She smiled, her voice lifting. 'It was good fun, Milo. We were watching some stupid zombie film and his mates were making these cocktails with fizzy wine and brandy. No one from school was there, so I didn't have to think about who was going to be whispering about me tomorrow.'

'They don't—'

'They do talk about me, Milo. I know they do. Don't waste your breath. Anyway, problem was, I'd left my coat at Scott's. We got a lift back from one of his mates who said they'd hang on and drop me home. Scott was having a laugh in the front seat and couldn't be arsed to go up and get my coat. He threw his door key into the back and told me to get it myself if I wanted it so much.'

I pushed my teeth together. How was I supposed to keep my promise and say nothing, no matter what?

'Wayne must have been looking out the window.' Tish hugged her knees to her chest. 'Because he knew it was me. As soon as I opened the door, he grabbed me and pushed me against the wall. He said he had something for me.'

I swallowed hard. It was so bright in my head; the front door opening, the skanky coward lurking ready to grab her, Tish's back slamming against the wall. I flexed my hand, stretching the tendons until they hurt.

'I told him I didn't want nothing he'd got. He just laughed and said something really nasty. Then he tried to give me this note thing. He said D-Ice told him it had to go to you. I'm not his sodding postman and I told him that.' She paused, looked straight at me. 'Then he said, if I didn't bring it to you, he'd bring it himself. He'd have the others with them and they'd be tooled. They'd make sure it was an evening when Aunty Jen was in.'

I'd promised. Silence. Though my heart was going like I was climbing a skyscraper and I'd plummet off and die if I didn't keep moving.

'I couldn't help it,' she said. 'I know it was stupid, but I spat at him. I was just so mad. It was a really good gob. It got him right on his nose bridge and slid down the side. It was almost like getting him back for what D-Ice did to you. Then his hand came up like he was going to hit me.'

This must be how the bad things happen. You knock on the door, see Wayne's thick face. He's so close to you, and you just reach in your pocket and feel the weight in your hand, and the blade skims through the air . . . and the blood makes you happy, just for that moment.

'Their mum came out her room,' Tish said, 'and said in this really little voice, "Don't, Wayne." Wayne kind of laughed and let go of me. She stayed there until I got my coat and ran out.'

'Did you tell Scott?'

She shook her head. 'I couldn't. Not with his mate there and everything.'

'You must have been all stressed out. How come he didn't even notice that?'

'It was dark in the car and the music was really loud.' She stood up. 'That's it, Marlon. Nothing else to say.'

Yes, there was! Like how come Wayne fucking Lester can slope back to his Xbox and get away with it? I saw the stupid grin on his stupid face, as he thought he was the biggest thing going. Why wasn't it him sitting in a police room with the coppers pulling him apart?

Tish touched the top of my head. 'You can see me in, if you want.'

'Sure.'

She twisted the key and nudged open the door. 'You all right in the dark?'

'Yeah.' Should be. I'd been coming here since Tish moved in when I was five.

We crept along the black-purple hallway and up the stairs. I tripped on the first one, stopped, waiting for Aunty Mandisa to stick her head over the banister. Nothing. Up, following Tish, guided by the wall. She pushed open a door on the top landing and clicked on a sidelight.

It was my first time in her room since – God, when was it? I must have been eight, or nine. The blue cloudy ceiling – she'd kept that, though there was some weird collage of Desmond Tutu heads in a corner. The sheets of silver holographic paper pasted to the wall, that was new. There was a set of drawers spilling out, just like the one in Sonya's room. All girls must have them. And a pinboard on the drawers – photos of Tish, her mum, some old cartoon strips.

'Marlon?'

Her eyes were red and the mascara was caught in balls at the end of her eyelashes. There was so much space between us now.

'I've got the note,' she said. 'If you want it.'

'Yeah.'

Out of her jeans pocket, into my hand. A small, crumpled square. I unfolded it.

I said, 'Did you look?'

She nodded.

It was pencil again. The girl, that was supposed to be Tish. And the boys, what they were doing to her, made me want to throw up. I screwed it up and shoved it in my pocket.

She was looking at me, chewing at her lip. I moved towards her and took her hands. We were nose to nose, closer than I'd meant to be. She breathed out and I could feel it on my skin. She was warm too – it radiated off her, over me.

I let her hands go. 'I'll sort it, Tish.'

'Yeah.'

15

Jonathan's car wasn't outside. Mum said he left early to start sorting the move. Apparently, the house could be let out really quickly, but it might need a lick of paint first.

Mum had the blender down and was churning banana with milk, making her point between pulses. There was a flush of energy to her, like everything was pulled back into her control.

'And you have to keep at the revision.' Whirr, rattle. 'There's all the more to prove now.' Rattle, rattle, rattle. 'You will never, ever go to that woman's house again, Marlon. Ever.' Whirr! 'And if they try to contact you, tell me immediately. Do you understand?' She glared at me. 'Well?'

'Yes.'

'Good. And I'm going to sign you up for one of those mentor schemes whether you like it or not.' She plonked a glass of smoothie in front of me. 'If you can't talk to me about what's going on, we're going to bloody well find someone you will talk to.'

Just a few feet away upstairs, there's a picture in a drawer, a coffin with your name on it. Right next to Andre's. And Tish. I can't find the words to tell you what they say they'd do to her.

'Mum? When Andre—'

'Oh, good.' Mum said. 'I was expecting a call back from one of the rental agents.' She went up into the sitting room to answer the phone. She was back a second later.

'It's one of your friends.'

'What?'

'Tell them to call back on your mobile. I'm waiting for a whole load of calls.'

Friend? Since when did anyone call me on the landline?

She was topping up the blender, humming to herself. She turned and smiled at me.

'Sorry, hon. Just be quick, okay? I need to keep on moving, because if I stop, that's it. I've stopped.'

I nodded.

She'd dropped the phone on the sofa. I picked it up. 'What do you want?'

'Man, it's just, what do they call it? A courtesy call. Let you know how good that girl is.'

The blender below, pulse, stop, pulse, stop. In that room there, by myself, I pushed my shoulders back, touched my side where the knife should be.

'And your mum.' D-Ice chuckled. 'Does she look as good as she sounds? No wonder you carry your little toothpick. I'd want to make sure my mum was safe too.'

'I heard your mum got chucked out.' My voice was low and even. Perfect. 'Because of your brother.'

330

'Tayz didn't do nothing! It's your brother with the big, stupid mouth!'

'What did Andre do?'

"You owe me and you owe Tayz. The longer you leave it the quicker the debt spreading. I know how you like church. The one near you, by the police station, go there and see."

The line went dead.

I replaced the phone in the dock and looked around. Home Marlon could stay here and have more smoothie, but it would be like *Star Wars* when the walls start grinding together, staying here with everything coming at me and no place to go.

Trainers on, phone in pocket, I called downstairs. 'I'm just popping out.'

Mum appeared at the bottom of the stairs, scowling. 'Didn't you hear what I said earlier about revision, Marlon? You have to take this seriously.'

'I need some more notebooks and I've run out of Post-Its.'

Mum's face didn't soften.

I said, 'Do you need anything while I'm out?'

'You can check in at the dry cleaners and see if my jacket's ready.' She checked her watch. 'I need to leave this house in exactly twenty-five minutes. God help you if you're not back.'

'Sure.'

It was another warm, heavy day. The main road was clogged with traffic smog. The police station door was open, but no one was coming in or out. I walked down the path between the police station and the church. There was no metal in my pocket, but my body kept the stride. It felt good, the slight sway in my shoulders, my height raised to the max, hood up, passing the barred, basement windows.

The church was ahead, its side door covered in cardboard from where the homeless bloke had moved into the porch. An old woman was sitting on the bench by the war memorial, her feet sweeping the fag butts and breadcrumbs.

Right. Now I got it. I saw who they'd sent.

Hayley Wilson was standing by the faded poppy wreathes. She was still wearing the combat trousers, like she'd slept in them, and her black tracksuit top was zipped up to her chin.

She took a big draw from her cigarette, watching me coming towards her. 'Thought you'd be wearing a top hat.'

There was a big red button in my brain with Hayley's name on it. It was next to the ones labelled 'Yasir' and 'Lesters'. Press it and my fingers snapped into a fist.

I said, 'What d'you mean?'

'I hear you've got a new circus trick. Juggling with knives.'

I pushed the backs of my fingers into my palm until the

knuckles hurt. 'They caught the bloke who hurt your mum yet?'

Hayley's face blanked out. 'Who knows?' She took a final puff and dropped the butt next to a poppy wreath. 'This way. Stalker.'

Yeah, an enormous red button with 'Press' in glowing, gold letters.

She sat down on a low stone wall. I sat down too, keeping a big gap between us. The grass behind was edged with old tombstones. Was D-Ice close by checking me out? If I started looking round, she'd clock it and know I was nervous.

'So?' I managed to look straight at her.

She took another pack of cigarettes out of her trouser pocket. 'In a hurry? I thought you liked spending time with me.'

'Don't flatter yourself.'

She opened the pack and offered me one. 'Sure? I don't usually have enough to share.'

She was enjoying this, prodding me.

I said, 'I thought you'd be saving your money for Sonya's gravestone.'

A tiny ripple ran through me as the words came out. What would I have done if someone said something like that to Mum?

'You really think you're better than me, don't you?'

Hayley's face looked paler against the black top. 'If you're so righteous, get off your arse and tell them coppers down there what's happening. Go on! Go and be a good citizen!'

Another flutter inside me.

'I'm not pretending I'm anything different.' She spat the words out. 'I'm shitty, I know it. But you with your hood on, your strut on . . . I saw it! You're living the dream, aren't you?'

The heat crept up my face. 'So you're proud of it then, getting Sonya to sell drugs for you.'

"I didn't do that.'

'You didn't stop her!'

'No, I didn't stop her.' Her voice was almost lost in the traffic.

'Why not?'

Her hand moved around the pocket of her combats. She pulled out a lighter, stared at it for a couple of seconds, then shoved it away again. 'See all that stuff they're doing to you? How they prod around and find your weak spots?' She touched her head. 'Well, welcome to the club!'

The scabs. The stubble.

'Your hair?' I said. 'D-Ice did that? Why?'

'Because he could. My hair was like Sonya's, except I didn't dye it any more. It was long.' She held her arm against her side and touched her elbow. 'Down to here. Just as well I don't earn my living with my looks, eh? Though there've been times I've been tempted enough. I owed them money and Sonya helped me pay it back. Her and that little crew of loverboys buying bags of pills off her every time she fluttered her eyes at them.'

'You let her do that!'

'How far would you go to help your mother, Marlon?'

Carry a knife?

I said, 'Maybe I can get my head around that. But the thing with Sonya and me, that was different though. It was like she was looking for *me*. Not anyone. Me.'

Hayley laughed. 'Because D-Ice's clever, mate. Not your common or garden thug. He knew you'd answer.'

A flock of pigeons flew over the war memorial, landing clumsily on the grass. They'd spotted a fresh batch of breadcrumbs. Hayley stood up, rummaged in her pockets again. What else had she got in there? A couple of sofas and a fridge?

I said, 'The guys like Alex, maybe she knew them already, knew what she was getting. But she didn't know me at all. I could have had a grudge and wanted to make her pay. She could have said no to coming for me.'

'She did. They told her what else they'd do to me and she changed her mind.' She dropped something in my lap. 'D-Ice said to keep it switched on.'

It was a Blackberry, a cheap one with a scratched screen.

* * *

I picked up Mum's jacket from the dry cleaner and arrived home just as she was getting ready to race out of the door. I went straight upstairs, spread the revision books across my desk and turned on my laptop. I sat down on my bed and typed my brother's name into the browser. I'd never looked him up before. My life had always been too full of him, his street life, his accident, his recovery. It was like my family was plugged into our own matrix and Andre was the Architect, controlling our whole world, part of everything we did and thought. I didn't need to go looking for more.

As I tapped 'Enter', the screen filled with results. I started with the accident. It was weird reading about it this way. It felt too clean. A few sentences about the location and the journalists making sure they reminded their readers that Andre Sunday's street name was Booka. They might as well have a loud, shiny title yelling 'Gangster!' Then a few words about the passenger, Sylvester 'Sharkie' White, who died at the scene. Just half a column here and there, nothing about Mum running out of the room to throw up when the police came to tell her about Andre. Or Andre's face cut up or his thigh bone nearly exploded. Nothing about how his memories keep buffering or how he couldn't stop crying when he first tried to walk or how he didn't cry when he found out that his best friend died. Nothing about how Mum went in every day to feed him from a beaker because he couldn't grip a mug.

There was none of that – but there was one thing. The car that hit Andre was stolen. By the time the police came, the driver was gone and – surprise, surprise – there were no eye witnesses. All they found was a bashed-up Hyundai and a few silent onlookers.

But they still found their way to Tayz. Someone must have opened their mouth and pointed the cops in the right direction.

Was it Andre? My changed-up forgetful brother?

Whoever it was, they lit the fuse. A few months later, D-Ice's life went bang. After Tayz was arrested, the police raided his Mum's flat and found money, weed, knives, a gun. She lost her home and D-Ice was kicked out.

Jesus, if me, Mum and Andre had been in a council place, that could have been us. Who knew what Andre used to have in his room? But we weren't in the middle of an estate, we were here, in this road, with tidy hedges and Tesco deliveries and the bus going up and down. I sat back. If I could get into D-Ice's head, what would I see? *Booka the grass's little brother, he's got everything. And me, D-Ice? Family split up and stuck in some crappy little room dodging the homeless mental cases.*

D-Ice could have gone after Andre, but that was no challenge. Andre's life was never going to be the same anyway. D-Ice wanted to mash up my life, just like his had been. And it looked like nothing was going to stop him.

I'd told Tish I was going to fix this, Louis too, but I was sinking further underwater with nothing to pull me up. Soon I'd hit the rocks at the bottom with just the dark and heaviness above me.

I blinked again and again, quickly, letting in little flashes of light, pushing myself back to the surface. If I gave up now, D-Ice won. Was he better than me? Stronger or cleverer than me? No, he was just a wannabe hoodboy bringing his arguments into my home. That stuff must have happened to Andre all the time. The only difference was that Andre knew the game, he understood the street rules. I was still learning.

If Andre was in my shoes, what would he do? If talking didn't work and a knife didn't work, if the street was getting hot and unpredictable, what would he do?

My fingers were on the keyboard again. Just three letters, enter.

As I clicked through the results, the idea got bigger and redder inside my head, shaped itself into the parts. A trigger, a barrel, a grip.

Things must have got hot like this for Andre, even if he said he didn't remember. I did. It was the first and only time I was let into Andre's street life. He used every threat he knew to stop me telling Mum. After going into special detail about all the lies he was going to spring on her if I ever opened my mouth, he moved on to the guilt stuff.

I shouldn't upset Mum, he said, because she was still upset about Dad. And it had worked.

My brother was supposed to pick me up from school and take me to my drama club in Holborn. Instead, he pulled up in Sharkie's car, music blasting, shades on, so every kid in school could see. That was his gift to me, he said. All the bigheads would see who they had to deal with if they tried anything on me. I never told him how wrong he was.

Straight away, I saw we were going nowhere near Holborn. I knew the route we were taking – Holloway Road, up past Archway towards the hospital where Dad spent hours having his chemo. We carried on up the hill to the back streets of Highgate, parking outside a bookshop. All the way there, the music was turned up to make my ears hurt, especially as the speakers were right behind my head. They must have been talking about things they didn't want me to hear.

As soon as we reached the bookshop, the music slammed off. Sharkie nudged Andre. 'Your turn, man.'

'Yeah, yeah, I know.' Andre grinned at me. 'You want a comic or something?'

'No, man. I'm too old for that crap!'

Sharkie and Andre looked at each other and started laughing.

Andre opened the car door. 'Right, little bruv. I'll get

something more grown-up for you, shall I?'

As soon as the door shut, Sharkie stopped smiling. He leaned forward, his fingers on the steering wheel like he was waiting for my brother to come running out with a sack of money.

I said, 'What does Andre need from a bookshop?'

'Books! What do you think?'

We sat there, ten minutes, fifteen minutes, with Sharkie staring at the shop window like he was trying to laser it down with his eyes.

The door opened and Andre came out, holding something wrapped up in a Tesco bag. He nodded to Sharkie.

'Let's go, man.'

The package was shut away in the glove compartment. As soon as we hit the main road, the bass was blasting out behind my head again.

I didn't bother asking about the grown-up thing he'd promised me, but I couldn't stop thinking about that package, something solid and real from my brother's other life. It wasn't Andre's, it was Booka's. Later that week, I hunted out the box in Andre's wardrobe. It was an old trainer box, the first pair he'd had sent over from America. The trainers were long abandoned, but I knew he kept the box for special things. After Dad died, he'd put Mr Potato Head in there, still in the flappy paper Jacksons' collar. I was too busy unwrapping the Tesco bag to hear Andre come into the room behind me.

G.U.N. Three letters typed into a browser. Man, if I was in America, I'd be sorted. Over there, it's like everyone's playing real life cowboys and Indians, with special weapons designed for the kids to join in. You could even get a picture book for small kids to big up their pistol-packing parents.

Back in England, most of what I found was in government reports and newspapers. There were definitely guns around. Some came over from Eastern Europe, other ones were converted in workshops. Anyone out of the area must reckon that Hackney's the Wild West, where every nightclub, park and pub basement's bulging with shooters.

I clicked out and deleted the history. Even if that was the case, guns cost money. What was I going to do? Turn up at some dodgy club and wrestle the weapon out of the hands of a partying hard man? I had fifteen pounds and some shrapnel. Jonathan always said I could ask him for anything. *Hi, Jonathan. Fancy contributing a few hundred towards a weapon?* No matter what excuse I gave to him, Mum was still going to ask questions. There was someone else, though. I took a picture of the Blackberry – *Got my own now* – and zapped it over to Tish.

At seven o'clock, I crossed the road and knocked on Tish's door. She opened straight away.

I said, 'Thanks, Tish.'

She closed the door behind me. 'You can start your own Blackberry museum soon.'

Neither of us laughed. She handed me an envelope. 'A hundred and twenty.'

I slipped it in my jeans pocket. 'Thanks. I'll pay you back.'

'Take your time. Dad'll send another top up next term. It doesn't seem much though. You hear about kids like D-Ice making thousands each week. I reckon he'd want a ton more than that if he's going to leave you alone.'

'I'll offer it as a first payment.'

'And then what?'

You carry on lying to your best friend. 'I don't know. But it gives me time.'

'Time for what?'

'To sort something else out.'

She frowned. 'Yeah, like what?'

'I don't know yet.'

For a moment, I thought she was going to snatch the money back.

She turned into the house. 'Let's talk about it downstairs.'

I followed her along the purple veiny corridor to the kitchen. Her laptop was open on the breakfast bar.

I said, 'Research?'

'Recipe. Your mum's gone off to work, hasn't she?'

'Yeah. There's a reading group at the library tonight.'

'So you haven't eaten then.'

'I wasn't really hungry.'

'You will be.'

I perched on one of the breakfast-bar stools. Tish was slicing garlic cloves like she was auditioning for *Masterchef*. Her knife was just smaller than the one that had been banging round my pocket. It cut through the garlic like it was mashed potato.

'You're good at that,' I said.

'Don't sound so surprised.' A quick glance at me, then back down. 'I would have starved if I couldn't cook. Mum's been off teaching her courses since I started secondary.'

'Doesn't it bother you that she's away so much?'

'We get on much better when we see less of each other.'

Another clove and a bunch of herbs. Tish set the garlic to fry. I breathed in the smell. My hypothalamus was definitely twitching.

She shook a packet of pasta at me. 'Bow ties all right?'

'Yeah. That's my favourite.'

'Mine too. I don't know why, because they're all made out the same stuff.'

'Sometimes your brain mixes things up,' I said. 'Like when you think a green sweet's going to be mint or lime. If it turns out strawberry, it freaks you out.'

'Er . . . and?'

'Your brain expects twisty pasta to feel different when

it's in your mouth and it makes you think it's got a twisty flavour.'

'A twisty flavour?'

Pasta shapes. The perfect conversation when you're waiting for a psycho to call you up.

Tish was still talking. 'I heard it was the sauce. You use different ones for different sauces and your brain gets used to it. Or' – she made her eyebrows twitch up and down – 'it's the type of wheat. Durum's the best.' She laughed. 'See, Milo? In the great kingdom of geekdom, I am a queen and you're a mere sock washer. I just hide it better.'

And I'm thinking of buying a gun.

'Yeah,' I said. 'You win. Where's Aunty Mandisa?'

'On a date.'

'Your mum goes on dates?'

'Sometimes.' She plonked herself down on a stool. 'Do you want to carry on talking about my mum's love life? Or pasta shapes? Or shall we talk about D-Ice and Tayz?'

Or the fact that I'm lying to my best friend to get money.

I said, 'What about them? I didn't think there was anything else to say.'

'Der! You've got a hundred and twenty quid cash in one pocket and your own drugs phone in the other. Worth a conversation, I'd say.'

'We've already talked about it.'

'No,' she said. 'We haven't. Even as I was counting out

the twenties, I knew you were feeding me a load of crap. Which I hasten to add, isn't what's being served on your plate later.'

I didn't smile.

'Okay,' she said. 'I get it. You've gone all hard and screwface.'

'Maybe it just isn't funny.'

She gave a little shrug. 'I'm well aware of that, Milo. It's just, I don't know. I feel a bit scared.'

Tish, scared? Or at least, admitting it. It was as likely as Spock playing saxophone.

I said, 'I'm sorry, Tish. I didn't know you'd get caught up in all this. But I've kind of got a plan now.'

'Yeah,' she said. 'That's why I'm scared. Not for me, but for you. It's like you were Geek Marlon . . .'

'Thanks, Tish.'

'No, Marlon! That's good! That's who my friend was. You *were* Geek Marlon. Now you're Marlon-with-a-Knife. What next, a street name?'

'Like I said, I have a plan.'

'Jesus, Milo!' She was looking at me like I'd suddenly sprouted tentacles. 'You're not going to do their stuff for them, are you? You're not using my money for your starter fund!'

'No.'

She leaned towards me and poked me in the chest.

My bruises flared. It was like being electrocuted. 'Tell me the truth.'

'I can't.'

'Go to the police. Like whatshername said.'

'Hayley was taking the piss. You know that. Where's my proof?'

'The drawings.'

'Funnily enough they didn't sign them, Tish. And the thing is . . . I know you're part of this and you've helped me and stuff and I really appreciate the money, but this is my thing to sort out.'

'Right.'

She jumped off the stool and went over to the cooker, standing with her back to me, stirring the pasta. 'I almost got beat up because of you.'

'I know. I'm sorry. But you could have just . . . I don't know . . . taken the note from him. Gobbing at an idiot like Wayne Lester, well, it was only going to wind him up, wasn't it?'

She spun around. 'You just don't get it, do you?'

'What?'

'Oh, for God's sake! Just get the knives and forks!'

She strained the pot of boiling pasta into the sink, standing in a cloud of smoke like a genie. I thought of her last night, rocking to and fro, her head full of that revolting drawing.

'Sorry, Tish. That didn't come out right.' I went towards her. 'Do you want to see the Blackberry?'

'I know what a bloody phone looks like!'

'I'm sorry if I—'

She nodded towards the drawers. 'Knives. Forks. And juice.'

'Do you know what, Tish? I'm trying to make things right between us!'

'Well, you're doing a bloody bad job.'

I set the table while Tish mixed the sauce in with the pasta. She slopped the bows into two bowls and slammed them on the breakfast bar. We sat down next to each other and started eating.

I said, 'This is really nice.'

'Thanks.' She didn't look at me.

I took the Blackberry out of my pocket and lay it down on the table. It was a cheap pay-as-you-go, a few years old. But it was charged up and ready for action.

I said. 'I'm trying to deal with this the best way I can.'

She lay down her fork and rested her chin in her hands. Her eyes could have pierced holes in concrete. 'By lying to me?'

'What do you mean?'

'Even better. Lying to me *and* treating me like an idiot. Double crap.'

I let my fork clink into my empty bowl and took it over

to the sink. I rinsed them, but didn't go back to the table. 'Why do you think I'm lying to you?'

'Because I am not an idiot.'

I said, 'I reckon I should just go home.'

She slid one little bow into her mouth and chewed for ages. 'Sit down, Milo. If you were going to go, you'd have done it by now. Tell me honestly, why do you need the money?'

I sat down. 'I'll tell you if you promise not to freak.'

'Can't promise.'

'Then I can't tell you.'

'For God's sake! Just spit it out!'

'Okay. If you really want to know, I want to get a gun.'

'This is a joke, right?'

I shook my head.

She pushed her bowl away. Most of her food was still in it. 'Going to get a poncho and sombrero to go with it?'

'Hilarious, Tish.' I stood up. 'You wanted the truth.'

'You had the pills, you got caught. You had the knife, you got caught. You're going for the full hat trick then.'

'Is that the best you can do?'

'I've given you my damn birthday money. What else do you want?'

'I thought you'd understand. You know, like the way you understand about Scott Lester.'

'Nice dig, Marlon.'

I scooped up the Blackberry and tucked it in my pocket. 'D-Ice said he was coming for me and he meant it. I reckon Andre grassed on his brother, and that's how they found Tayz and arrested him.'

'That was years ago. Why's D-Ice coming for you now?'

'He was inside. He'd tried to set fire to Sharkie's girl's flat.'

'Oh my God.'

'So you understand why I need to protect myself? And Mum too.'

'No, that makes it worse. And don't drag Aunty Jenny into this. It's not like she'd agree with you. You're just going to end up with two black boys shooting each other over beef. Don't you see, Marlon? It's just the same old, same old.'

'You don't understand at all.'

I turned around and walked out.

Tish stayed where she was. 'When you're stuck in some crappy young offenders' place, I'm not coming to visit you, right? Right?'

Yeah, Tish. Right.

I slammed Tish's front door so hard I was surprised the house didn't collapse. I couldn't go straight home, not now. Tish twisted hard, then she gave one more pull. No amount of jazz flute, or saxophone, or 'Lovely Day' was going to smoothe it all out. Yeah, if the world was good and proper and everything was always what it should be, she'd be right. I'd go to the police. D-Ice would be arrested and we'd all live happily ever after. But D-Ice didn't live in a good and proper world and he didn't respect the rules of anyone who did. Unless he was locked up forever, he was always going to come looking for me.

I checked the Blackberry, making sure the volume was turned full up and started walking towards the main road, just one foot in front of the other until my head was clear. The thing with Tish was, she wanted drama. If something was ready to kick off, she had to be right in it, but when it all got too hot, she backed away. It was the same with all those swagger merchants she hung with. They chased her, they got her, she ran away. She'd wriggled her way into this thing with Sonya and D-Ice and then – then – just to add even more stress, she got snug with Scott Lester. It was like she'd been deliberately trying to wind me up.

It wasn't the way it usually happened with her and her boys. Shaun, he'd been after her for ages until she'd said yes. Same with Jeevan, same with Sav. And every time, she'd go through it with me in detail, like I was supposed to tell her what to do. So why Scott Lester? The first I'd heard of him was when we went to see Sonya's gran together. Tish reckoned he was the kid at school who could get her some pills. Then she never mentioned it again. She'd have told me if she took E, just for the aggro. Bring on the crap storm! That's Tish.

But was she ever going to tell me about Scott Lester at all if I hadn't seen them together?

I was at the top of the hill by the estate agents. Its shutters were pulled down, but the Chinese takeaway was open and a woman was leaning on the counter staring out at the road. The bollards must be looking particularly special tonight.

When Scott Lester dropped that skunk in my bag, Tish still stuck by him, even though she knew what his brother did to me. She told me they were coming down to Westfield to get me.

Hang on!

I stopped walking. The Chinese takeaway woman was looking at me now, probably hoping I'd move out the way of her view. She'd have to wait a bit longer. If I moved too quickly, the thought would slip away.

Tish knew about Diamond grassing us up because Scott Lester told her. Soon as Scott called her at the diner, she told me. Every single thing he told her, she told me. The reason she was mixed up with Scott Lester was because he told her stuff and then she told me.

Damn.

That slophead Wayne Lester got nasty with Tish because of me. And I'd never even said thank you to her. I'd done the opposite and made her think it was her fault.

Call now! Say sorry!

My phone rang. Not the Blackberry, my proper phone. *Tish?* Mum. No, it was Jonathan on Mum's phone. He started talking straight away, his words pushing into each other. I only heard three of them.

Mum.

Fire.

Hospital.

Jonathan had jumped in his car in Camden and was at the hospital in half an hour. He'd keep me informed, he said. 'Informed', like I was one of those friends you only just about stay in touch with. He *informed* me that Mum was there for observation and that he was turning off his phone to talk to the doctor. He didn't tell me the other stuff, but I could check that out for myself as the Overground stopped at every station in London and stayed there twice the time it needed to. What happened if you breathed in a load of smoke? There were chemical reactions. Mum would have a lung full of carbon dioxide or even cyanide, every breath loaded with poison. The heat would burn the inside of her throat. Her lungs would block up with soot particles. She could even suffocate. My mum was lying on the hospital bed, gasping and gasping, with no breath coming through.

Mum, tied up in tubes and drips. Like Andre. Like Dad. Jesus! Stop after stop. And then I had to get the Tube.

This was meant to be a hospital, but it looked like a prison. Nothing from the outside made it seem like a place where people went to get better. Jonathan told me to come to A & E and it wasn't hard to find. The queue of people waiting to be seen snaked right out the door. Some of them weren't even getting to reception by midnight, let alone in front of a doctor. I squeezed between two women who glared at me like I was cutting the queue and found a spare chair. There weren't many. It was like an airport in a snowstorm.

I couldn't find the right way to sit, as if a shoal of piranhas kept changing direction in my stomach. Now and again, one swum up to my stomach lining and took a big bite. Everybody else looked like they were hunkering down for the night. A couple of people a few rows away had even brought a packed lunch. The old man opposite was bent over pressing his arm against his stomach, as if his guts were falling out. The woman with him was completely still, her eyes closed. Next to me, well, I don't think this guy had seen a shower for a while. He was sitting bolt upright, his fingers moving like he was in front of a keyboard only he could see. Everybody was in their own bubble of misery.

I looked at the rows of shut doors on the other side of

the waiting room. What if they'd moved Mum and no one was telling me? She could be in an ambulance heading to a specialist burns unit. Or Jonathan could have booked her into a private place and made her promise not to tell me. I checked my phone. He wasn't keeping me informed.

Text Tish. Tell her.

Really? After tonight's barney?

I stuck on my headphones and closed my eyes. John Coltrane.

A hand on my shoulder. I made the saxophone fade away.

'Marlon?'

It was Jonathan. Where was—? Mum was here. Right next to him. All those disaster films I'd seen . . . In my head, Mum should be all smudged up and covered in ash. She wasn't. She was Mum. Except her eyes were twitching, like it hurt her to open them. She rubbed at her throat, blinking hard. Her left hand hung by her side, all bandaged up.

I stood up. 'Mum?'

I went to hug her. Her hair smelled of smoke. If she was wearing Palmers, it was lost somewhere beneath. And her arms stayed by her side. She didn't hug me back.

I let go of her. 'What happened?'

She touched her throat and her eyes squinted like they wanted to close.

Mum?

Jonathan said, 'Let's get out of here.'

He put his arm around Mum and led her out. I followed behind.

We headed to Jonathan's place. Mum sat in front of me, her head and the backrest making a strange-shaped shadow. The only time she moved was when Jonathan turned on some music. She leaned forward and switched it off, saying something to Jonathan I couldn't quite hear.

He said, 'Do you want to know what happened?'

He was facing forward, but definitely talking to me. Yes, I did want to know. I needed to know, though every bone in my skull was grinding into each other.

'Well. Do you?'

Mum's hand moved and touched Jonathan's knee.

'I'll tell you anyway,' he said. 'Three boys came into the library after the reading group finished and your mum was tidying up. The security guard wasn't happy, because he saw what they were.'

'Jonathan.' Mum's voice was a whisper.

Mum?

'This isn't about race, Jenny!' Jonathan slammed on the brake, almost jumping the red light. 'This is about attitude. And only one of them was black. But your mum, Marlon, she believes in people. Far more than they deserve.'

Mum, this isn't your fault.

A car behind us hooted as the light switched to amber. We moved on.

'Anyway.' Jonathan sounded calmer. 'One of the boys said he needed a book for his homework and Jenny persuaded the security guard to let them in.'

Not! Mum's! Fault!

'And that's when it started. In they came, bashing the place about, yelling stuff at your mum. Shall I tell him what they called you?'

Mum's shadow moved.

'Okay. I won't. But I'm sure, Marlon, you know the words I mean.'

You know I do! And I'm going to sort it out, right? More than you ever can.

'They were clever. While Jenny and the security guard . tried to deal with two of them, the third one sneaked off to set the fire.'

Mum sniffed. Jonathan reached over to her. I stayed still, my fists full of car seat.

'They ran off,' Jonathan said. 'Jenny tried to pull some of the books out of the fire until the security guard came with a fire extinguisher.'

I said, 'Was there much damage?'

The indicator clicked left into Jonathan's road. And the Blackberry! Now it was adding its own noise, buzzing in my pocket like an angry fly. I flicked it on to silent, gripping it tight.

'Damage?' Jonathan said. 'Think about it! Of course there was.'

Jonathan parked outside his house and went round to open the car door for Mum. He took her good hand and helped her out.

'It's been a long time since you've been here, Marlon,' he said.

'Yes.'

He went into the house first to switch off the alarm. I touched Mum's arm.

'Are you okay?'

She sighed. 'I can't really talk. My throat hurts.'

'Will the library be all right?'

'I don't know, Marlon.'

She moved away and went in ahead of me.

Jonathan's place smelled of cleanness. I don't mean that in a good way. He paid someone to brush up his dirt and spray the place full of freshener. Was he expecting Mum to do that for him when we moved here?

When we moved here. New house, new school, new room, new Marlon. In Jonathan's world, you drove your stuff a few miles along the road and everything was all right. He didn't realise that stuff follows you. It stalks at fairgrounds and spits in your mouth. Despite what the press says, gangboys do cross postcodes, especially if they think they've got good reason.

'I'm putting on the kettle,' Jonathan said.

Hot chocolate! That's what Mum wants. Not, tea!

'Do you want anything, Marlon?'

I want to check the phone. I want Mum to look at me like I'm real.

'No. Thanks.'

Jonathan was standing in the kitchen, Mum between us. 'Are you sure there's nothing you want?'

His eyes bored into me.

'I think I better go to bed,' I said.

Nobody moved.

Jonathan said, 'Do you know anything about what happened tonight?'

I shook my head.

'That's such a pity.' Jonathan rubbed his hands together. 'A terrible pity.'

Right, Jonathan.

'Okay, then. You're in the room on the first landing, next to the airing cupboard. Remember it?'

'Yes. Thanks.'

He nodded again. Mum didn't move at all, didn't even look at me.

I should have taken my trainers off. I was treading street dirt into Jonathan's carpets, but I didn't think about it until

I was outside the room. Anyway, it wasn't like he'd be brushing out the carpets himself. I opened the door. Jonathan was right. It had been a long time since I was here, two years or more. The room hadn't changed, though. Grey walls, grey curtains, grey bedclothes, a wall-length wardrobe and a desk. I turned on the sidelight by the bed and slipped off my Nikes, pulled out the Blackberry and stared at the message.

Let's go to work.

Yeah, D-Ice. You're so clever.

I'd checked out *Reservoir Dogs*, all of them in their shades and suits, with a strut and a strap. Mr Orange was in the middle, at the front. He got shot dead at the end.

I had a dream. A girl was hiding her face in my neck, her blonde hair tickling my skin. Her fingertips were stroking my cheek, but it was like she was painting a picture. My face was all wet, red streaks dripping down my chin. But I let her carry on.

I woke up, pushed off the duvet and lay there, ready to reach out for my music. But the stuff I wanted to hear was a few miles away. At home. Straight away the grinding started again, inside my head, working its way through my body, like all the soft stuff was turning to metal.

I put on yesterday's clothes and went downstairs. Mum was sitting at the table drinking coffee, wearing a dressing gown that must be Jonathan's. Her bandaged hand was resting on the table next to her newspaper.

'I made a pot.' Her voice sounded nearly normal, just quieter.

'Thanks. Do you feel better?'

She sipped her coffee.

I said, 'Where's Jonathan?'

'He had an appointment.' She shut the paper. 'I'm not going back home, Marlon.'

'What do you mean?'

She shook her head. 'I mean that I'm done.'

I sat down. 'Everything's at home, Mum. Everything. Dad's things too.'

'I know, but—'

'Maybe after a couple of days, you'll feel better.'

'No. I won't.' She took another sip of her coffee. She was drinking it black. Usually it looked like she'd mixed it with half a pint of milk. 'Can't you see, Marlon? I can't be safe at home. I can't be safe at work. Wherever I go . . .'

She was crying. She wiped her face on the dressing gown's sleeve. I should hug her or get her some tissues. I should say sorry over and over again like I was trying to fill a big bucket of sorrys. But Mum was like Sonya at the fairground, when she'd put up the forcefield around herself. For the first time I could remember, Mum looked like she didn't want me anywhere near her.

I sat down and filled my cup with coffee, keeping my hand steady as I stirred in a shovel load of sugar.

Mum said, 'When I was a kid, my grandma used to brandish this book at me. Dante's *Inferno*. Heard of it?'

'Yes. Mrs Littoli used to go on about it.'

'It's a lovely little number.' She tried to smile. 'It's full of people having the hell tortured out of them. According to Granny, the ninth and deepest plane of hell was reserved for traitors, especially little girls who were rude to their grandmothers. They'd get buried up to their necks in ice forever.'

I tried to smile as well. 'Your gran was a bit hardcore, wasn't she?'

'You could say that. I used to have these dreams that I was stuck in my mum's big chest freezer with only my head sticking out. My body was getting colder and colder until I couldn't feel it any more. Then I'd stop struggling.'

I drank back the whole cup of coffee and poured more. She was watching me.

'Do you still have those dreams?' I asked.

She rested her forehead on her hand. Her fingers were pointing to a strand of white hair, dead centre above her nose bridge. When I was little, she used to send me on search and destroy missions, pulling them out.

'Marlon, I'm trying to tell you something.' She leaned towards me and put her hand on my arm. 'I want you to understand. I have to let the past go. And I don't want to feel guilty.'

'Guilty?'

'Yes.' She waved her arm. 'About this. About being here. About leaving Dad's stuff behind. About making you move here.'

'Mum?'

'Yes?'

'Is there anything else?'

'Like what, Marlon?'

'About Andre's accident. Or the stuff that happened afterwards. Is any of that making you feel guilty?'

She rubbed her eyes. 'Nearly everything about Andre's life makes me feel guilty.'

'But anything specific. Do you know how the police found out that Tayz was driving the car?'

She looked away. 'By doing their job. That's how.'

'The car was stolen. There weren't any witnesses.'

She moved back away from me. 'I told you. Now I want to stop feeling guilty.'

'Mum, you don't have to feel guilty. Not if it was Andre that told them. It was him, wasn't it?'

She sighed. 'No, Marlon. It was me. Andre said something in the ambulance. I didn't quite understand it, but I told the police anyway, even though I knew Andre would hate me if he found out.' She slammed her good hand down on the table making the teaspoon jiggle in the sugar. 'That damn street code! It's rubbish! One boy dead, another one mangled up and I'm supposed to keep my mouth closed? The only way I could face Sharkie's mother in that church was because I knew that the murderer would end up behind bars. And it was me who made sure he got there.'

And then Mum started to cry, big, proper tears.

I stirred in more sugar and took a large gulp, lifting the cup to my mouth, then even higher so Mum couldn't see my face. The hot coffee, the sugar, the caffeine, was kicking up my neurons and deeper inside, the adrenaline was spitting out through my blood. Andre was born angry. Mum was right. I was angry too, but I just hadn't seen it before. But now I knew it. I felt it. It was like one of those action films where the hero lights the fuel trail. Me, I'm standing at the end.

I stood up. 'Mum, you shouldn't feel guilty. None of this is your fault.'

'No.' The word sounded like it came from across the street. She bent down and stared at her newspaper. There were more white hairs, right at the back where she couldn't see them.

I meant it though. My mother should never, ever feel guilty. She was the only one who'd done everything right. Now I had to go out and do everything wrong.

I went upstairs and pulled on my hoodie. I stashed D-Ice's Blackberry in the pocket and made sure Tish's six twenties were still lining my jeans pocket. The plan, the bit I couldn't tell Tish was simple. Meet D-Ice and show him I was serious. He had to understand. This beef was dead.

For the first thing on my list, there was only one place I knew I could go. It was back up the road to the bookshop.

Four years ago, I'd sat in the car trying to look through the window into the shop. The time had come for me to go through the door. For some people, four years is nothing. They look the same, live in the same place, they're still getting into bed with the same person. For me, it's the difference between Andre strutting his funk around east London and eating baby food through tubes, the difference between being a twelve-year-old kid in the back of a car and knocking on a stranger's door and negotiating a strap.

Four years. People move on, especially in that type of work, but I'd looked online; I didn't see anything about a gun haul in a Highgate bookshop. That would have made headlines. Less than a year ago, it seems like the gun guy had been looking to Andre for repeat custom. So he could still be in business. I had to hope.

So you're going to rap on some stranger's door and ask for a weapon?

Yes.

If I opened that shop door like Home Marlon, I'd come

out with an armful of *Star Trek* annuals. I had to be Cellboy Marlon, Marlon with pills in one pocket and a blade in another. Marlon who looked like he had one thing on his mind.

As I left the house, I looked into the kitchen. Mum was still sitting there, newspaper open. I don't think she'd even turned the page.

Cellboy Marlon, turn away. Leave.

I closed the door quietly and walked away from the house. Jonathan's street was on one side of a small square with a fenced off garden in the middle, no buses or Tesco vans. No one was going to park up their car here shaking the place with bass. I reckon everyone knew everyone, but no one knew me. The thing with London is that the noise and the mess are always nearby. I walked past the posters for the square's garden fête and I was back in the middle of it.

Rush hour was supposed to be over, but no one had told Camden. Even the bus stop looked like it was getting ready to hold a gig. I checked the Blackberry. Blank. I bet D-Ice was timing it, knowing that I was on the edge and waiting. He probably thought I was going to roll over panting too.

I had to jostle to get on the bus. Other times I would have let it pass and waited for the next one, but not this time. When that Blackberry started speaking, I needed to be ready. Pocket heavy. Protected. The driver kept cramming them in. A backpacker bloke was swaying beside me, his buckle clipping my shoulder every time the bus stopped. A young mixed race girl was busy texting while her kid sat in its buggy making faces to itself. I was just 'normal' to them, on some boring journey. I managed to push in my earbuds. The playlist landed on Billy Paul, the one with the Martin Luther King sample in it. I skipped over it. I didn't need to hear that dream right now.

Stop, start, stop, start, all the way up past Archway and along Highgate Road. The windows were open, but no breeze was coming through. My t-shirt felt like a sticky new skin under the hoodie. I checked the Blackberry again. Nothing. The bus emptied out, but I didn't sit down, pushing the bell as soon as I recognised the street.

These were the posh houses. Four years ago, it didn't look any different. And the bookshop was still there, the only shop in a short row of terraced houses. An old bench was chained outside with a couple of boxes of old books on it.

Buy the lot of them and take them to the library. That's going to make Mum smile again.

The window was full of posters so you couldn't see inside. If I wanted to go to a steam fair two months ago, I'd have been sorted. But that wasn't what I wanted. I wanted to walk into the shop and come out strapped.

I tried to peer between the posters to check who was

inside. All I could make out was more books. I leaned against the window, the glass cold against my back. The place could have changed hands over time. Tish looked that stuff up. She'd find out who built the place, who put up the shelves and who cleaned the windows. Tish wasn't here though and soon my phone was going to be buzzing with new information. If I was going to face D-Ice and end this beef, it had to be now. I put up my hood and swung open the shop door.

Inside was small and dark. The shelves were crammed with books and boxes of magazines were heaped against the corners. Mum would have loved it in here, running her finger along the spines and pulling out her finds. A woman was watching me from behind the counter. She was probably about Mum's age, but she'd let her hair go white and cropped it short so she looked young and old at the same time. Her eyes went from my trainers up to my hood and it was like her face stuck. She looked at me, searching for my eyes under the shadow of my hood. I turned away and stared at one of the display books. A man in old-fashioned army gear was kissing a woman in a long white dress, jammed between a medical textbook and a French dictionary. Maybe the weapons were hidden behind special titles.

The nutter laugh was rising. I squashed it flat.

The woman behind the counter, what was she? The gunman's wife or mother? She turned a page of a magazine

367

on the counter, but she was still looking at me. She could be like one of those women in Westerns with a shotgun under the desk, the barrel pointing straight at my knees. Or a bit higher up. Was there a code word or a handshake? Did I ask for a certain book?

That's Home Marlon thinking too much. Cellboy Marlon, you need to act.

I spun around and she flinched back.

Straight away, she tried a smile. *She's someone's mum who likes books.* 'Can I help you?'

Just say 'no, thank you' and leave. 'You know why I'm here.'

She swallowed. I saw her throat move.

'No,' she said in a tiny voice. 'I don't.'

Oh God! I'm so sorry, so sorry, so— Cellboy Marlon *doesn't apologise. This is what he wants. And this woman, she'd already made her mind up about you when you walked through the door.*

I went up to the counter, a proper saunter, so she had time to think about me coming. Keeping my eyes on her face, a good swagger stare, I swept the magazine off the counter. It flipped open on a page full of blue dresses.

'You know why I'm here. Where is he?'

She glanced down at her magazine, all heaped up on the floor.

Pick it up for her, man!

Something crossed her face, like in her head she was reaching across the counter and thumping me, angry about being scared.

In the same little voice, she said, 'He told me no one was going to come through here any more.'

"Cept for me. Where is he?'

Two hands on the counter, pushing myself up like I wanted to cover her in shadow.

'Please . . .' She turned round and unlocked a door behind her. I looked through into a store room full of more shelves and boxes. She opened a back door out on to a small car park with a flight of steps leading to a flat above the bookshop. As soon as I was out, she slammed the door behind me, probably flattened herself against it, double locked it. Maybe even shut the shop itself, until she was sure I'd gone.

I'd done that. Just by walking in. *And knocking her magazine away.*

The flat looked completely normal. I don't know what I expected to see – twenty-stone bodyguards, or something. But it was the sort of place where anyone lived, especially the sort of 'anyone' who didn't hawk arms. I climbed the stairs Cellboy Marlon style, two at a time, like the place was my own, drawing myself up tall at the top. I stopped, holding my breath. There was no sound from inside. I rang the bell and the door opened straight away. The woman had probably phoned ahead to let him know.

The guy was the same height as me, skinny, and about twenty years older, though that could just have been hard living. His head was shaved and the stubble was like a giant bruise. I scanned his face – yeah – he looked like the woman below. A brother, maybe.

He pushed his tongue against his cheek, and looked me up and down. 'Who are you?'

'Booka's brother.'

'Who the fuck's that?'

Behind him, a baby started crying.

'Jesus!' He was looking at me in disgust. 'You woke up my kid, man.'

'Sor—' I coughed it short. *Remember, Cellboy Marlon doesn't apologise.*

'Booka,' I said. 'Drove into a wall and killed his mate.'

Stubble Head nodded. 'Yeah, yeah, I remember.' A smirk. 'Left him spazzed out.'

Cellboy Marlon. Screwface fixed tight, holding it down even when your fists are clenching.

I said, 'He told me come and see you.'

'Why?'

Another scream from the baby. Proud daddy ignored it.

'Wants to take up your offer of help.'

'What help?'

'My brother said you came to see him.'

'I see loads of people.' Stubble Head grinned. 'I'm good that way.'

This was school times a million. That one person who had power over you, prodding hard, waiting for you to hit back so they can slap you down. You had to wait, swallow it all, don't give them the pleasure.

I said, 'You brought him something.'

'Yeah. Flowers.'

Behind him, the baby screamed again and carried on crying. Stubble Head was too busy peering over my shoulder to notice. He probably thought I'd come with back up. His eyes returned to me.

He said, 'You want flowers, then.'

Flowers?

He rolled his eyes. 'Flowers. Like the ones I took your brother.'

'Oh. Yeah. Flowers.' Arms. Stubble Head's special code.

He said, 'How much are you spending?'

'A hundred.'

'What?' He coughed out a laugh. 'You're not getting many fresh tulips for that.'

'I'll have whatever's in stock.'

He didn't move from the doorway. 'Prove it.'

'Prove what?'

'You're Booka's brother. I don't know you from Jesus.'

'Serious?' What the hell did he expect? A doorstep DNA test?

'Yeah. Serious.' He started to close the door.

'Wait.' I fumbled in my pocket for my phone.

'In your own time!' He leaned against the doorframe, whistling as he watched me.

I flicked through the pictures and found one of me and Andre on the Southbank last year. 'This do you?'

A smile flickered across his face and he opened the door wider. He was whistling again. It was 'Who Will Buy?' from *Oliver!*.

The hall was short and narrow with rooms leading off. I squeezed past a loaded coat stand and a shoe rack full of slippers, pink shiny ones, Batman ones, a pair where you slipped your feet into Homer Simpson's mouth. The sitting room door was open and for a second I locked eyes with a girl there, bouncing a baby in a seat. She mouthed something at me, her face wrinkled up with disgust.

What have I ever done to you?

'In here.' Stubble Head opened a safety gate into the kitchen.

The room was tiny and neat, though they'd managed to fit in a giant fridge covered in baby photos. Big tins of baby milk powder were lined up on top of a microwave, like they were waiting for someone to play target practice. Bang them all down and you win your girl a prize.

It was just me and Stubble Head here in this little space. I pulled myself even taller, let my shoulders loosen, one hand in my pocket, the other one on the table.

I said, 'I know a hundred is scant, but maybe an air gun, or something . . .'

He was so quick, I barely saw him. His hand thudded against my chest, throwing me back against the edge of the door.

'Don't start running off your mouth, you get me? You turn up here with no warning and I still let you in. Keep your face closed, right?'

I didn't need to speak; my heart was hammering out Morse. *Pump, pump, pump.* He stepped back, held out his hand and tapped his palm. I passed over the money. He held up each note to the light, then rolled them into a tube and stuck them in his shirt pocket.

'Stay here.'

He clicked open the gate and was off down the corridor. I heard the girl's voice and the baby crying, then he was back standing by the door. He shoved a small, wrapped package at me. It was soft beneath the newspaper, like a bundle of rags. I squeezed it tighter and my fingers closed round the narrow metal barrel of a gun. A hundred quid wasn't getting a Glock or something decent. For that price, it was going to be dirty as hell.

It didn't matter. I was holding a gun.

Stubble Head was watching me.

Jesus, this is what it feels like, when you want to stroke it and drop it at the same time. This is it, with your heart beating like it's ready to burst. This is your mum finally giving up on you. This is Tish crying in some miserable visiting room. This is Andre trying to get your name right at your funeral.

And this is Clint Eastwood and Ray Liotta and Samuel L Jackson in his suit and shiny 'fro. And Morpheus in The Matrix, *like a king in his coat and shades, exploding the agents and saving Niobe and Zion.*

This is me, now.

I started to pull back the newspaper.

'What the hell are you doing?' Stubble Head glared at me. 'Why don't you just sign it 'Dickhead' and shove it on the counter of the nearest copshop? Prints, man!'

'I need to check—'

'What? If it's a suitable quality?' He smirked. 'What you going to do? Nip along to the corner shop and buy a better one if mine ain't good enough?' He held out his hand. 'Give it back, then.'

I slipped the package into my jacket pocket and pushed open the child gate.

Does this gun have a safety catch? Is it on?

The sitting room door was closed now, but the muffled sound of some kids' programme was leaking through underneath. Stubble Head planted himself by the front

374

door, hand on the latch. Tattoos ran from his thumb up his arms, blue and green lions stalking up to his shoulder.

He leaned towards me. 'Well, Little Booka, put them in water as soon as you get home and don't forget to add a teaspoon of sugar for longer lasting blooms.' Leaning closer still. 'And I tell you what, if anything leads back to me, I swear on my kids' lives I'll be coming for you. Now bugger off.'

I walked away, arms swinging, slow stride, like only my time mattered. Steady, steady, though I wanted to run as fast as I could. The door was closed behind me, but if I went back and pushed my eye against the spy hole, I reckoned there'd be another eye on the other side. *Keep going!* Down the steps, through the car park, on to the street. The package was jiggling in my pocket, knocking against my side. The whole world must see it, through the jersey, the newspaper, the rags.

Is it loaded?

I had to keep walking, round the corner and get out of sight. I slid my hand in my pocket and touched the lump of newspaper. *Jesus. A gun.*

Hood up, chest high. Hold it together.

Except right now, the Blackberry was going off and D-Ice was waiting for me to pick up and talk.

16

For the first time, a number came up. He must have picked up some crappy little pay-as-you-go all for me. I pressed 'accept'. My chest felt like it was being lassoed. 'What do you want?'

D-Ice was in a car. I heard the music and a siren blasting by.

'We're going to work.'

Someone laughed in the background. Probably Wayne Lester not ready to believe that the joke was already stale. In the street there, by myself, I made my face hard to make sure my voice came out right.

I said, 'What do you want?'

'Your first assignment, brud. 313 Torrance Road in Brixton. Man's called Cory, leaving his yard at midday. Midday, you get me? You need to get your little dick over there now.'

'Why?'

'Man's a grocer. You're picking up food.'

'Then what?'

'Wait. Until I come.'

The line went dead. I breathed in and out slowly.

My plan was simple. I'd already got the gun. It was bulking out my pocket like it had swallowed a sack of steroids. Next, meet D-Ice. That part of the plan was happening too. Except it wasn't *me* going to find *him*, I had to do his errand first. Had to. He was in a car. If I said no, he could get to Andre, my house, Mum, quicker than me.

He wanted me to collect 'food' – ammo maybe, or pills. I had just over an hour to get to Brixton. I checked the map on my phone. Torrance Road was up the hill from Brixton station, bang in the middle of Riotboyz' territory. I touched my pocket. Yes. The gun fitted so well.

The side streets in Highgate were empty. All the good citizens must be out at work, running their banks or law firms. I turned back on to the main road. A girl was by the bus stop, busy on her headset chatting about some boy who'd spent money on her sister. If she had X-ray eyes and could see in my pocket, she'd be having a whole different conversation.

Just thinking about it set my body alarms off again. And that was sirens, right?

I looked up the road. It was an ambulance, probably heading to Whittington Hospital. There were buses behind it too. If I made it down to Highbury, I could jump the Victoria Line from there. Everyone knew you didn't take drugs on the Tube, not since the Met started the sniffer patrols. But what about guns? Could the dogs sniff them too? Stubble Head looked like he dealt a bit of hash on the side. What if they smelled that?

A bus pulled into the stop. The girl stood up still yabbering, swiped her Oystercard and went upstairs. I stayed where I was and the bus pulled away. There was a cab with a light on behind it. That was better. Twenty quid would get me some of the way.

'Marlon!' A white car stopped so close I saw my knees in the paintwork.

Here? Now? *Seriously?*

It should have been funny. I stared down at the pavement then back at the car.

'Can I drop you off anywhere?'

'No. I'm all right.'

Jonathan's eyes narrowed. 'Are you waiting for someone?'

'No.'

'Marlon, please just get in the car. We really need to talk.'

More sirens were shooting up the hill, a cop car this time and a motorbike. For a second, Stubble Head flashed into my mind, face to the wall, hands cuffed behind him, giving the cops a full-on description of the boy who'd bought his last gun. Jonathan was heading south and time wasn't on my side. I opened the car door and climbed in.

Jonathan's car had that perfumey smell, chemical pine and hardcore air conditioning. Someone on the radio was talking about farming. I could just hear their voice above the whoosh of cold air.

He said, 'Jenny said you'd gone out.'

'Did you come looking for me?'

'Yes.'

I let the word gap grow bigger between us.

He said, 'I went to your old house.'

Old house?

'Jenny said you might be there, but you weren't.'

No, Jonathan. I went to a crappy bookshop to buy a gun.

'I'm on my way back from a client in Muswell Hill. I wasn't even looking out for you. Serendipity, eh, Marlon? A happy chance.'

I slunk down in the seat, clasping my hands together, the left one holding the right one back from pulling out the gun and checking the safety catch. What if the next time Jonathan slammed on the brake, the trigger knocked against my back and I shot myself right here, in the car, next to him. *Serendipity, eh, Jonathan?*

Jonathan's voice became sharper. 'What were you doing here?'

I forced my hands still. 'Seeing friends.'

'Oh. I didn't know you had friends this way.'

He must have noticed the way Mum looked at me sometimes, when she wanted to check that the words she was hearing matched the truth. But Mum had a right

379

to look at me that way. This man didn't.

He said, 'Where do they live?'

'Who?'

'Your friends.'

'Highgate.'

A cyclist swerved in front of us on the roundabout. Jonathan beeped and the cyclist gave him the finger.

Jonathan shook his head. 'Suicide case.'

There's a gun in my pocket if he really wants a way out. But the mad cyclist had interrupted Jonathan's questions. I had to keep it that way.

I said, 'You wanted to talk.'

'I want us both to talk. Your exams are important, Marlon. And no matter what you think of me, I believe you're important. I know you're a caring, bright young man. But something's changed. Last night . . .'

'I wasn't there.'

'But your mum was.'

'Are you blaming her?'

'No! I am not!'

'You said it was her fault, for letting the boys in. The security guard could see what they were, remember? But my mum let them come in.'

A woman with a buggy was standing by a zebra crossing on the pavement. She waited until Jonathan stopped completely and started to cross.

'I did not blame Jenny!'

'Sounded like it.'

The woman had crossed, but we were still sitting there. I glanced at the dashboard clock. I'd lost quarter of an hour already. The car behind hooted and Jonathan pulled away.

'She's signed off work, for two weeks at least. She can take much longer if she wants to. I've told her that she doesn't have to go back at all.' I felt Jonathan looking at me. 'There's going to be a formal police investigation, Marlon. The council take these things seriously, you know.'

Heavy silence.

Jonathan said, 'Look, I don't want to interfere or anything . . .'

We were nosed up against a dustcart. The workers were taking their time moving piles of rubbish bags from outside the shops. I opened the car door.

'Marlon?'

'Sorry, Jonathan.' But the words didn't make it out of my mouth.

I headed down a one-way street, traffic heading back the way I'd come. Jonathan kept to the rules; he wasn't going to follow. The canal was up ahead. East took me home, to *my old house*, and the other way to the Tube station. There was no time for buses. I'd have to risk the sniffer dogs of Brixton.

* * *

The Tube was packed down to Stockwell, then it emptied out. I kept my hand on my pocket, scanning the platform every time we stopped. No police, no dogs, nothing. I came up the escalator in Brixton, watching, listening, but the only uniforms were on the Underground guys. It was 11.45 a.m. I could make it.

Brixton air was pressing down on me and the street was too wide and too full. Everyone else looked like they knew they should be there. The guy trying to flog incense, the people pushing at the bus stops, the crowd going in and out of the market behind the station – all of them belonged. It was only me, standing there like I'd been beamed down from the moon, with 'North London Fresh Meat' in glowing letters above my head.

'Brother!' A tall guy in a grey suit wanted to hand me a Nation of Islam leaflet. I took it.

'You know Torrance Road?' I said.

'Torrance Road?' He pointed up the road and told me where to go. He shoved a handful of leaflets at me. 'Be lucky, brother.'

I couldn't run, not with all these people to push through and if any cops were around, they'd want to know what my problem was. Especially if they worked out where I was heading. So I walked, head down, quick. Was this the path Sonya had followed, up the hill to get her bag of pills? Thinking about it made the world sharper. The grey splats of chewing gum, every crack and yellow line, every empty chicken box and drinks can, I saw them all. The old guys drinking outside the cinema, looking like they were made from rags and dust. Did Sonya pass them too?

It was 11.55 a.m. I had five minutes. I was at the top of the hill and there across the road, was a carpet warehouse, a big bully building by the parade of small shops. The Nation of Islam guy told me the street I needed was right opposite. It was. I was standing on the corner of Torrance Road. I dumped the Nation of Islam leaflets in a bin, turned in and stopped. I had taken my first step on to Riotboyz' turf.

The thing was, it wasn't like this place had been lifted out of some war zone and dropped in south London. Some of the houses looked all right, worth a load more than Mum's, though nowhere near as much as Jonathan's. But you could imagine a sniper on a roof or behind a curtain, fingers itching to light you up. There was definitely something here, waiting.

My foot clunked metal, an old Coke can. What did I expect? An IED? Three minutes to twelve. I had to move. The houses started at '1', and didn't run on for too long, so I was heading for the tower blocks at the end. It was always going to be the tower blocks, and now I was starting to recognise them. On one of the YouTube videos, some kid with a scarf on his face was lifting up his jacket to flash his strap while a load more kids cussed out some other gang in the background. It must have been filmed by that block, there, with the bright blue security door and grey tiles around the entrance.

I put my hand in my pocket, squeezed the newspaper tight, tighter, until I felt the hardness underneath. Clint Eastwood, Samuel L, Morpheus.

I walked on.

I was by a ramp down to some underground garages. Yes, this was the block. I looked up at twelve or thirteen rows of balconies, like steps. Plastic bags waved from railings, because in someone's wildest imagination, London pigeons were scared of crinkling plastic.

Midday. Bang on. I reached forward to push open the door.

'Boy! What d'you want?'

The voices were above me. A clump of ash landed by my feet and at the same time I smelled weed. It was as strong as if they were blowing it through a funnel up my nose. The security door burst open and they surged through.

Pull yourself up! Shoulders back! Right now. Right now!

But my body wanted to squeeze itself into a matchbox.

Tall! Blank out your face. Fill your space! Now! NOW!

They were behind me, in front of me, around me. One of them moved up close, his face in mine. He was thirteen, fourteen at most. His hair was mown down with two tracks above his ear, dead, straight parallel lines. I pressed my hand against my pocket and screwfaced right back.

The boy said, 'You gonna answer me, bred?'

'Come for Cory.' My voice was as steady as his barber's hand.

The boy turned to an older Turkish-looking kid with a bitty beard. 'Cory? He work for D-Ice?'

The older nodded.

And he's upstairs, hand on door, waiting for me.

They hung back to let me go. As I moved towards the door, I heard shuffling behind my back and I was shoved forwards.

I spun round. 'What's your problem?'

'You.'

The blonde hair, the slow, scummy smile. Wayne Lester. Denthead. Moron. Grinning, because hitting me in the back was the cleverest thing he'd ever done. Almost as clever as trying to shove paper in Tish's mouth.

You know what, Denthead? I've got a gun in my pocket.

I wiped my shoulder where his hand had been, keeping my eyes locked on his. 'Leave it, Lester. I want Santa, not his elf.'

He moved, but I was quicker. My fist swiped across his cheek, not hard enough for him to fall, but it hurt. His eyes watered. And that made me smile. He was ready to move again, but suddenly he looked around. It was just me and him.

He stepped back, rubbing his cheek. 'See you on the way back down.'

I patted my pocket. 'Yeah. Can't wait.'

Into the foyer, straight and strong – *Samuel L* – though my legs felt like they were made of Cheestrings. The lift door opened. It was empty, but the thing looked like a crate on a string. I took the stairs, two at a time. The stairway was the same as Sonya's, different coloured tiles in random patterns, like the architect was a Lego fan. Someone was coming up just behind me. I stopped. The footsteps stopped. I moved on, so did they. I looked back. The stairway was empty.

The footsteps are yours, you idiot!

I reached the first floor landing; everything was silent. Second floor landing – empty too. Third floor, it was the same. All the noise and action was going on behind the closed doors. I was outside 310, a corner flat with a window box with more fag ends in it than plants. Cory's flat was at the end behind a security gate fitted between the balcony wall and the flat. And there was another grille across the front door too. You only got in that place if the person inside wanted you to. And you weren't coming out without their permission neither, in whatever state they decided.

I took out my phone and sent a message to Tish, with the address where I was. She couldn't check it until lunchtime. If I came out, I'd text her again. If I didn't, she'd know where to find me.

Samuel L? Right. He'd storm in shooting, not stop to text his mate first, especially when the clock's saying five minutes past. Cory could be gone. He could be on the phone to D-Ice cussing me out. He could be standing behind all those bars, waiting to show me what he thought of lateness.

I checked across the balconies and down below. It was all quiet. I slipped my phone back in my pocket, waited for my breath to slow down and went right up to the first security gate. There was a doorbell by the side; I rang it.

The grille across the front door swung open, then the door itself. A girl looked out at me, her bright blue haircut like a helmet. She scratched her forehead and the whole thing moved.

'What d'you want?'

I said, 'I've come for Cory.'

She glanced back inside the flat, looked at me and sucked her teeth.

'Man, you've got bad timing.' She called behind her. 'Cory?'

She was shoved aside and a bloke came out, barefoot, in boxer shorts and vest. He looked vexed.

'What d'you want?'

I stroked my pocket. 'D-Ice sent me.'

'What for?'

'Food.'

'Who the hell are you? The Riddler?'

The girl said something, close to Cory's ear. Now he looked double-vexed. 'Next time, man calls for me, tell me! Let him in.'

I breathed out quietly. If Cory didn't know about me, this couldn't be a set up. She swung out of the door. Her dress stopped where her thighs started and she moved her hips like she was trying to polish a car with them. I dropped my eyes and watched her knees coming towards me, Cory's bare feet following behind her. As the girl opened the gate, he pulled me in so quick I almost tripped over. The gate clanged shut behind me. Tayz must know that sound well.

'Lock up!' Cory ordered.

The key scraped against metal behind me. I followed Cory into the flat, waiting in the doorway. No one was inviting me further in, but I didn't need to go any further. Just there, with the front door open behind me was enough.

The hallway was empty, all white walls and wood floors. A radio was on in another room, with a guy advertising insurance like it was the next *Terminator* film. Under that, silence and shut doors.

Cory said, 'I heard something happened to the blonde girl.'

I nodded.

'And you're taking her place? It was much better looking at her, man. You know I don't normally take orders past midday.'

Another nod.

'But Brandy didn't pass me the message about you coming. Just this time, you get me? Usual sixty?'

'Yeah.'

'Settling up?'

I was supposed to bring this man money? I shook my head, looked bored.

Cory scowled. 'Man needs to settle. This time's the last one, okay?'

I nodded. 'I'll tell him.'

'And he has to talk to *me,* right? Girl there thinks she's running things.' He waved his hand outside. 'She don't run nothing, right?'

'Yeah.'

'Remember that. I'll get your things.' Cory opened a door – I saw a wardrobe and a bed – and closed it behind himself. The light behind me blocked out. I moved forwards for the girl to pass, but she stayed behind me, so close I heard her breathing

Her hand!

She said, 'You're D-Ice's task boy now?'

Her thigh, rubbing against mine.

'That stupid boy, Wayne. Got a promotion, has he?'

Her hand on the side of my thigh, stroking me. Jesus! Was this the way it worked?

'Stop it!' It was supposed to be a whisper but my mum probably heard it from Camden. I glanced at the bedroom door.

'Go on,' she said. 'Call him.'

Both hands now, slipping beneath my jacket. I spun round and pushed her away. Her eyes narrowed.

'Touch me again, and I'll call Cory myself. I'll tell him where you're trying to put your hands. Man!' She was holding up my phone. 'Old-style!'

I swiped it back from her hands. 'What's your problem?'

She rolled her eyes. 'I ain't got no problem. But you, I can make sure you have big problems. What's in your jacket pocket?'

'None of your business.'

'Yes it is.'

She reached forward. I grabbed her wrist, but her other hand had already swooped.

'Brandy? What's up?' Cory was standing in the doorway staring at us. He flung the pouches he was holding back into the room and slammed the door shut.

Brandy paused, hand in my pocket, then pulled out the bundle of newspaper.

'Looks like I found something for you, Cory.'

Words formed. 'It's nothing.'

But Cory was tearing at the newspaper. 'This better not be . . . I told that little runt, don't no one walk into my house with a strap. You hear me? No one.'

Voice! I need you now! 'D-Ice didn't tell me nothing.'

Cory's voice was low. 'It ain't my business what he told you or not.'

The torn up newspaper dropped to the floor.

'You come with an arm, you're making trouble. And I can give you trouble. Lots of trouble. So much damn trouble that your mum ain't ever going to recognise you again.'

The thing was wrapped in a piece of old curtain, but the silver barrel was poking out. As I leaned forward to look, Cory laughed. 'Jesus Christ!'

He opened his hand and the gun dropped to the floor. It landed with a little tap. A proper gun, that would sound heavier. This thing, it was nothing like proper. Stubble Head must already be on the phone to his mates, having a laugh about wrapping up his kid's cap gun and taking a hundred quid off some idiot who knocked on his door. I felt the heat rising up my neck, spreading across my face. If it could burn me all up so I was just a pile of smoking dust, that would be better than being here now.

I could feel Cory and Brandy staring at me. I kept my eyes on the floor.

Cory's feet came up close. 'I should beat you just for the insult!'

I glanced at the front door; it was shut. And beyond that were Cory's two security gates.

I made myself look at Cory. 'Nothing wrong in taking care of myself.'

Cory nodded slowly. 'You don't need to, because I'm going to take care of you.'

Brandy clapped. She was ready to pull up a seat and chew popcorn. Cory, he was what? Ten, fifteen years older than me. Whatever he was going to try, I wasn't gonna make it easy. He was still in vest and boxers, so it wasn't like he was hiding a weapon. My hands balled into fists.

Music blasted from a phone somewhere behind one of those doors. Brandy's hand snapped to her mouth.

Cory frowned. 'What?'

'It's that Whiska kid.' She wasn't quite meeting her man's eye. 'He said he was on his way.'

'Man, you need to tell me, Brandy! Tell me! You!' He shoved me towards the door. 'You must be feeling lucky. Get out! And tell Tayz's idiot brother – bring me my money, you hear? And after that, we're done.'

He slammed back into the bedroom.

Brandy bent over to pick up the gun, showing me more skin than I needed to see. 'Here's your shooter, Woody.'

I sucked my teeth and slipped it in my pocket. Brandy pushed past me, poking me with the key as she passed. She opened the front door, kicked the security grille wide and unlocked the gate on to the shared balcony, blowing me a kiss as I went through.

I walked away quickly, turned the corner and stood there, by the lift. I took the gun out my pocket. It was pathetic. If the trigger even worked, a flag with the word 'bang' would probably drop out the barrel. This was my protection, the thing that made me strong enough to go through those metal gates and come out again. My Travelcard weighed more.

Stubble Head must have been saying his prayers hard last night, because this morning he'd opened his front door and there I was, topping up his family holiday fund. He saw what I was, same way Hayley did, Tish did, even Jonathan. He knew that if he wrapped up his kid's toy, there was no way I was going back to complain. In *The Matrix*, Neo's offered a red pill and a blue pill. The red pill is the one that strips away the fantasy world. Now I'd swallowed the red too. I could see what Stubble Head really was – a pathetic, bullyboy joker.

I opened the flap to the rubbish chute and let the gun drop in. It clicked as it hit the side of the chute and then nothing. It landed with no noise, lying in a mashup of food slops and tins. I heard a *thunk* in the chute as another bag of rubbish was dropped in from the floor above.

But this thing hadn't ended yet. D-Ice was still out there and he was coming for me. I wasn't a gangsta. I wasn't

Andre and I couldn't walk in his shoes. The red pill told me I was Marlon on a south London estate with no money, no gun, nothing. Right now, D-Ice must be on his phone checking the progress of his drugs and the report from Cory wasn't going to be glowing. I'd failed in the biggest way there was. Cory's shop was closed to D-Ice. No more deals, no more credit. Beef on beef on beef.

I had to get out.

The lift door opened and I was in there. It smelled like someone had smashed a bottle of cider against the walls. The doors shut and the lift jerked down. Maybe D-Ice was on his way here now. Maybe he was waiting nearby. I had to get to the ground floor and out that door, back over to north London. And then? Yeah. I'd tell someone, Louis maybe. Tish was right. I couldn't handle this myself.

Second floor. *Keep going down. Down!* The lift stopped and the doors slid open.

'You got something for us?'

17

The young one with tramlines kept the lift doors forced open. Two more minions were slouching by the stairs, hoods pulled up over their caps. One of them had a brute-faced Staff puppy tugging at the lead. The dog barked, wrenching at its lead, towards me.

All of them, their eyes were on me. The faces, the pose, the dog, they knew the way to work it. This is what stressed the teachers and the shopkeepers and the passengers on buses trying not to catch their eye. And yeah, it was seriously stressing me, even though I knew that the real place their posing mattered was here, with each other.

The Turkish-looking thug-boy was doing the talking. 'You need to pay your tax, man.'

I said, 'No mate. I ain't got nothing for you.'

He cocked his head. 'You been to Cory. You're gonna have something.'

I shook my head.

A yawn, big and wide in my face. 'Check him.'

They moved quick, pressing around me, the small space filling with the stink of smoke and sweat. The dog lead wrapped around my legs, its bulk pushing against me.

Hands rammed in my pockets, pulling at my jacket. One of them fished out the Blackberry and threw it over to the boss. Another one found my Samsung.

Their leader held up the two phones. 'Man's been to the Grocer, he ain't got nothing else?'

'This.' The twenty pound note, Tish's money. The thug who robbed it flicked up his cap. It was Wayne Lester, mighty Wayne Lester, officially an adult, running with these little boys.

He was nodding, like he was trying to jump-start his head. 'Maybe we aren't looking in the right place. That right, Marlon?'

He came towards me. In his head, he was walking like Mike Tyson. In my head, he needed his nappy changed. *Nutter laugh! Nutter laugh! Nutter laugh!* Then my head was full of red, hot and thick, blotting out everything around me. I could have been walking down the road! I could have been waiting by the platform for the train heading north, checking on Mum, trying to explain! I could be saying 'sorry' to Tish. These idiot thug-boys were stopping me. I breathed in, breathed out. My eyes stayed on Wayne Lester, his grinning face, his jacket pockets, his fists.

His head was bowed, like the thoughts piling up were too heavy. 'I like your girl,' he said. 'She took me and my brother, same time.'

A picture flashed in my head of Wayne Lester's mum,

tired and giving up. My mum in Jonathan's kitchen, she'd had that exhaustion too. But I was here in this place now, with these kids cheering Wayne like he was their champion. I remembered how my face made the bookseller woman swallow in fear. Yeah, I knew how it worked too.

'No, mate.' I shoved Wayne Lester's chest and he slammed against the lift wall. The whole thing shuddered. 'You're talking about your mother with you and your brother.'

One of the gang kids whooped, but as the words came out, I wanted them to disappear. Lester's mum didn't deserve that.

The dog was shrieking and twisting on its lead like it was Wayne's biggest supporter. Wayne's arm swung back, then blurred towards me. *Snap!* His knuckles slammed against my cheek. My teeth clipped my lip. The blood tasted deep, like there was a pool of it, filling my mouth. Another great achievement, Wayne!

Someone must have given a signal because the dog was yanked away and the lift door creaked shut. Me, Wayne Lester, the Turkish kid, nose to nose, eye to eye, in this shaky box. I had to hold my breath. The sweat, the cider, the closeness, made my stomach swerve.

Ground floor. *The door's going to open. They're going to push you out, with a punch just for show.* Dream on. We carried on down.

The lift shook to a stop and the door opened into half-darkness. I was shoved out into the centre of Hell. The place stank of rot and burning and there was even an old chest freezer like the one Mum used to dream about. I imagined the lid thumping down on me, heavy blackness, ice creeping into my bones. Rows of concrete pillars held up a roof that looked almost too low to walk under. The floor was concrete too, with heaps of rubbish and leaves and charred bits and ash spread across it like a rug. I was in the underground garages, though most of them had been broken into and some of them had no doors at all. I couldn't see any cars in one piece. Abandoned garages, where no one came.

The thugs had multiplied; seven or eight of them now, jostling each other and the Staffie had been brought along too, to join in the fun. Its owner was small, eleven, maybe, twelve at most. He'd wrapped a scarf round his face so all I could see was his eyes. He flicked back his jacket, making sure I saw his blade, bringing the Staffie up close so it could sniff me.

And suddenly there was just one thought in my head.

I don't want to die.

Not here in this filthy bunker, with kids who didn't even know my name.

I tried to broadcast it strong and loud, up the slope and out on to the street. I wanted it to float north from Brixton, radiate east. I wanted Tish to feel it, Louis to feel it, even Jonathan to feel it.

I DON'T WANT TO DIE!

Then don't!

No one was busting in here to take me to freedom. No Trinity, no Neo, no shades, no leather. I had to take control. These little bastards fed off fear. It was time to bring on the famine. I turned on the screwface and relaxed my body like I could swagger out any time I wanted.

The Turkish kid was doing the tiger walk, up and down, up and down, then round behind my back. I made myself still, not even a twitch, though I felt like I was going over the top of the highest big wheel in the world.

Wayne Lester strutted forward, hands spread out like he was some Mafia kingpin. 'Cory's girl said you tried to rob him.'

I looked him straight in his ugly face. 'Take your pills, Wayne. You're hearing voices.'

Turkish boy's turn. 'What you got from Cory?'

I blinked. A good, slow one. 'Nothing.'

Wayne Lester grinned. 'Reckon he's going to stick to his story?'

I heard a sound behind me. It was the scratch of tape being pulled from a roll.

What?

Wayne Lester tugged at my jacket. I slapped his hands

away, then charged. My fist balled into his stomach. As he bent double, my forehead crashed into his nose.

There were shouts and laughter, mad barking, the strange garage echo filling the place with demons. Wayne was shoved aside and the dog leaped towards me and was yanked away. As I twisted and kicked, the demons were on me, pushing me from one to the other like I was keeping time. Sometimes my fists connected, a face, a jacket, another hand. Mostly I touched air.

Mum eating hot pepper and fanning her mouth.

I wasn't going to die here.

Andre nudging pumpkin seeds into the warm soil.

No. Not here.

Tish, way back, making the school hall squeal when she looked like she was cutting off her own arm. Yeah, she should have won that talent contest.

And Dad, just a tiny bit. Reading something out of his Asimov books in a robot voice.

Not here.

My brain was getting that message big time, pumping it through my body. I tried to see inside myself, imagined a supernova filling me with mad energy. It simmered in my arms and legs as I lashed out, punching and thrashing. But it wasn't enough. There was one of me, a mob of them, a dog. They were on my shoulders and back, kicking out my legs so I fell on to the crappy floor. The dog's teeth pierced my arm. It squealed as someone booted it away and my arms were pulled above my head while two of them kneeled on my legs. All of them were shouting, making jokes, grins on their stupid faces, their phones flashing so they could add my picture to their gallery. Of course they were happy. This time it wasn't them.

The Turkish kid was bending over me, making sure I could see him. He was holding a big roll of gaffer tape. He unwound a length slowly, ear bent towards it like he was savouring the noise.

'Think we should send his mum a present?'

More jeers, using Mum's name like it was something nasty as one of the kids sliced the tape with his knife. My wrists were gripped hard and the tape sealed my mouth. There was no place for my breath to go. I tried to open my mouth, just a little, but my lips were stuck solid. My lungs were screeching, and I was sweating now, my forehead slick with it, my t-shirt rancid. My eyeballs were pressing out their sockets, my hypothalamus setting off the klaxons. I wasn't drowning. I was suffocating.

I had to sort out my breathing, or there'd be shut down. I closed my eyes, breathed in slowly through my nose, out again. Thick air squelched through my system. Out, in, slowly.

Hands unzipped my jacket. My eyes snapped open. The Turkish kid stretched out another length of tape like a garrotte. Wayne Lester heaved the jacket down my arms, got it over my fists and threw it on the floor. My legs, my arms, my back, my head were banging on the concrete as I tried to get free. The hoodrats loved it, yelling out their pathetic jokes. Fingers flipped up the edge of my t-shirt, pulling it high. My trainer was wrenched off, clomping against a pillar. Then the other. A kick thudded into my ankle. My tendon quivered and a dull hit of pain shot up my leg. My mouth filled with saltwater. I couldn't throw up now. I'd drown in my own sick.

The Turkish boy waved the loop of black tape. Just out of sight, I heard them pulling out another stretch. I was dragged up so I was sitting and my t-shirt was tugged off, my hands pulled behind me. Air against sweat, hot and cold at the same time. Wayne Lester started taping me up, my chest and arms together, my hands wedged behind my back. More and more, from my neck down my stomach, like he wanted to make me into a mummy. He wrenched it tight from behind. A cheer! Because that's so funny! So damn funny! My pores squeezed together, my skin rubbing against my ribs. Their fingers were in my waistband, nails cutting grooves in my skin.

They're taking off my trousers because . . . They're going to . . .

Oh, God. That tape. They'd loop it through my legs, making sure it's tight. They wouldn't stop until they heard me scream. And then they'd pull it tighter. And after that? Over my nose.

I WILL NOT DIE!

I was thrashing and twisting, like I was plugged into a pylon. The Turkish one called something and one of them bent right down close. A knuckle cracked against the bone beneath my eye. My head was full of fireworks, cosmic ones, the star inside me sending out sparks. But I didn't stop moving.

Suddenly, there was silence. Wayne Lester crouched next to me, a grin on his face, his eyes distant, as if he was having time with his own personal Holy Spirit. He was holding a knife, pointing it to the ceiling, like an offering to God.

A voice yelled, 'Go on, Les! Shank him, man!'

And the demons' chorus. 'Shank him! Shank him! Shank him!'

Tramlines passed him a spliff. He took a big pull and handed it back, hand relaxing, so the knife drooped down, point resting on my chest.

'Shank him!'

As he lifted the knife, the world crashed in. It screeched and roared, blasting through the garage. A chip of concrete flew off a pillar.

Trinity? Neo?

Wayne Lester drew back. The Turkish kid was on his

feet, his soldiers, *his snipers* up and around him. He kicked me as he ran past, but I was just nothing as they surged forward to this new enemy. Another bang. *Bullets?* The echo bounced off the pillars. A car engine roared, a wall of shouts and cussing, all merged into one ear-mashing din.

I rolled on to my side, my tender ankle hitting the concrete. The nerves went into seizure, each twitch digging in more pain. Trying to blank out my ankle, I took a deep breath through my nose and curled into a ball. I brought my knee up until it was by my face and rubbed my mouth against it. Maybe the sweat helped, but it didn't take much until the end caught and my gag came off. I sucked in air, dust, everything. Now for the rest of it. I wriggled hard, scraping my back against the gritty concrete. My fingers stretched behind me, pressing and prodding, nails scratching until they found a loose corner. I pulled and a flap of tape dangled free. I tugged it, the tape unwrapping around my belly. Even though my wrists were a bit looser, I couldn't reach round to take it behind. I breathed out hard. The tape shifted on my chest. I eased my thumb underneath a layer, twisting, making more space, the sweat and dirt and stickiness sliding against my skin. Thumb out. Two fingers. Three fingers. Yes! My whole hand slipped beneath it, tearing it off, skin and hair coming too. But it didn't matter. I lifted the cocoon of tape over my head and gave one last tug to unpeel it from my back.

Free.

I crawled forward, pumping so much sweat I should have been gliding like a slug. My t-shirt was crumpled in a pile of mulch. I grabbed it and put it on, huddling down by a pillar, squinting into the smoke and gloom.

A car had stopped at the bottom of the ramp, doors flung open and for a second, one bright second, I was back in *The Matrix*. Trinity and Neo, storming in, guns blazing.

I blinked the dust out of my eyes. This was Brixton, I was by myself and *I* had to get myself out. This was my chance. My trainers were gone, but that didn't matter. Nothing on that floor would give me more pain than I already felt.

'Caught you, man!'

My t-shirt was grabbed from behind, the neck cutting into my throat. My breath stopped, my mouth gaping as my windpipe clamped shut. I staggered, pulled backwards, trying to twist my way free. Every move made my neckline dig further. I tugged at the tight fabric until the air seeped back in, filling my lungs with sour-smelling smoke and hot oil. My bad foot bounced across the floor – God! Every neuron spouted fire. My foot, my legs, my chest, my nose. Marlon Sunday, the human dragon. *Nutter laugh coming!* I closed my eyes, crunched my teeth together. Mum held Dad's hand and closed his eyes. The last thing he ever knew was that she loved him. My last few seconds would be in this rancid basement, face down in a pile of tyres and burned-out paper.

Suddenly, there was silence. Not proper silence. The screeching still echoed in my head and my heart sounded like it had been wound up until it nearly broke. I was dumped in the dirt by the car door and the neck of my t-shirt went slack. As I turned to check out my captor, his knee shot up, hitting my chin. My head snapped back, my teeth clicking together. The face grinning down at me belonged to the idiot boy, Dill, the one who'd used Mum's bed as a potty.

Adrenaline and noradrenaline smashing against my amylgada. Want a chemical reaction, Mr Laing? That's hate.

'Move from there and you're dead.'

The stupid bit of me, the bit that wasn't shaking in pain, laughed. The boy had been waiting to say that all his life. He needn't have bothered. I couldn't move anyway. My body had split into different parts, all of them in agony and confused about what they were supposed to do.

Dill pushed past me and stopped by the front of the car.

A voice, loud and vexed. Wayne Lester's. 'Man ain't got no tax. You made a promise, brud.'

More shouting. The dog was getting busy again too.

'D-Ice, man! You told us the boy would be loaded! His pockets ain't got nothing!'

'We bash up the boy and deliver him.' Wayne Lester

406

again. 'We keep our promise, but you don't keep none of yours. The deal was we help you out and we get something, right?'

Shouts of agreement.

'Looks like you ain't got Riotboyz' back.' Wayne Lester waited for his crew to stop whooping. 'Looks like you're only looking out for D-Ice.'

'What are you trying to say, Wayne?' D-Ice's voice, calm and quiet.

'I'm saying that we don't need you, *Peter*. I'm handling things now.'

'Man better not step closer.' D-Ice, like he's telling off a child. 'Man needs to know his place.'

I tried to edge forward, to see. My body started yelling abuse at me. I stayed where I was.

Wayne Lester was laughing. 'Yeah, man needs to know his place. Which man? The man right here, doing the business or the one come racing in here like *Fast and Furious* in his little yellow car. You got a baby on board, man?'

Another voice. Tramlines, maybe. But most of them sound that way, half boy, half man, thick London street.

'Yeah, D-Ice. Your trousers are hanging low, man. You got Huggies under there?'

More barking and laughing, lasting extra time with the echoes. Someone made a baby noise.

'You're all brave, man.' D-Ice's voice sounded like it had a laugh in it.

'Nuh. We know real life.' Wayne Lester's mouth carried on running. 'Cory ain't going to deal with you no more. You came in here in some little girl's car, trying to big yourself up. You told us the boy would be loaded and he ain't got dick. You're just mouth, D-Ice.'

'Serious?'

The hard shriek of a gun shot. My ears rippled with the explosion.

'Les, man?'

'Fuck! He shot Les!'

As I was hauled up, I saw the boys trying to pull Wayne Lester to his feet. He was clutching his arm, his eyes wide and his mouth hanging open. Dill shoved me into the back of the car and the door slammed shut.

'Sharkie?'

What the hell?

'Andre?'

My brother was in the back seat, staring at me.

The front doors opened and the car shot backwards up the ramp. I gripped the seat.

'Sharkie?'

'Andre! It's Marlon! You need to get out of here!'

Andre reached over me and yanked down the seatbelt. 'Put it on!'

'What? You think a seatbelt's going to make us safe here? We need to get out! Now!' We lurched to a stop at the top of the ramp and in the fog below, the boys were rising. D-Ice twisted round, so I could see his face between the front seats. He nodded down towards the gun barrel he was pointing towards us.

He grinned. 'Welcome to the Batmobile.'

He turned back and the car sprung forward, my neck jolting as we sped back down the ramp. I took the seatbelt from Andre and pulled it the rest of the way over me, my t-shirt rubbing the sore places where the gaffer tape had been. I clicked it in place.

'Man's fast,' Andre said.

We jerked to a stop. D-Ice and Dill rolled down the windows, screaming cusses as the gang jumped out of the way, pulling Wayne Lester with them. Then backwards again, we shot out into the road, cutting a tight curve and screeching away. The radio blasted out of the speaker behind my head telling me about tickets to the Summer Ball in Streatham.

D-Ice turned around again. 'You see them? You see how they're running like rats?'

'Stop the car!' My voice was loud, beating down the music and the engine.

D-Ice shook his head. 'Watch the noise, man. You know he ain't too keen on fast rides.'

Next to me, Andre was whispering to himself, banging his fingers into his palm.

'Andre,' I whispered. 'What are you doing here?'

He gave me a confused smile. 'These are my friends, man.'

'No! They are not!'

Andre pulled the cap over his eyes and turned away from me. My older brother, my big bad gangsta of a brother, that's all he had to offer. And the thing was, he'd damn well started it all! If him and Sharkie weren't doing their little runnings, if he'd stayed indoors and just got on with being normal, I wouldn't be here. And now he'd just gone into himself and left me to deal with it.

Everything that'd happened today, I'd got through. Stubble Head, Cory – Jesus, that tape. All of it. My whole body hurt. Any time I turned my head or my foot jolted or my back knocked the seat, it felt like needles were stabbing my thalamus, but I was still here. With no Andre, I could probably get through this too. But that was how it always happened – the world spun around Andre. No matter what plans you made, Andre ended up part of them and everything got a whole lot more complicated.

The car slowed down as we turned on to the main road, the radio switched low. Even D-Ice wasn't going to risk a cop stop now. These days, no Lambeth policeman was going to stop a car just because it was carrying four black boys, not without a good excuse anyway, but maybe I could give them that excuse. I looked hard. There were no cop cars at all. I tried to lock eyes with other people in their cars, passengers on the buses, but no one wanted to see me.

I leaned forward. 'What's my brother doing here?'

Dill sniggered. 'Hanging.'

'Drop him somewhere safe and we can sort this out.'

D-Ice met my eyes in the mirror. 'You mashed up my deal with Cory. How are you planning to sort that?'

'Let my brother out and I'll tell you.'

'No, man. Mr Orange needs to be right here.'

Andre didn't know! It wasn't him! It was . . . No. He never needed to know about Mum.

We turned into an estate and both the speed and radio were notched up again. Dill banged out a counterbeat on the dashboard. Beside me, Andre was rocking backwards and forwards like the way he did when he came out of hospital. First it was muttering, then the rocking and the finale was the full on screaming freak out. I didn't need that right now. I took a deep breath and stroked his arm.

'We'll be there soon,' I said.

'We need to slow down, man.'

'I know. We're going to.'

And we did. Right down. D-Ice swerved to the side of the road, landing by a parade of boarded up shops. The music snapped off. The engine hummed. My heart pounded. Andre's knees bumped into the back of Dill's seat.

Andre said, 'We're going to the river, yeah?'

D-Ice said, 'Check out Booka. He's the man with the plans.'

Dill laughed.

'Let my brother go.' I kept it calm, for Andre's sake.

Dill poked Andre's knee. 'You're here on your own free will, aren't you?'

Andre didn't answer; I don't know if he'd even heard. I leaned over him and tried to open his door, shaking it hard. The door was stuck fast.

D-Ice shook his head. 'Child locks. When you don't want the baby to escape.'

I sat back, fingers still gripping the door handle. 'The boys in there were making out that you're the baby.'

'Yeah.' He twisted round, grinning. 'The baby with the gun.'

The car was still and so was Andre, like time had stopped until the right thing happened. And what was the right thing? I wanted time to stay stopped until I worked it out. I had no weapon and no backup; my brother had beamed into his own dimension. In films, prisoners talked to their captors, tried to build trust with them. D-Ice was never going to trust me, but at least I could get him talking. I forced my eyes away from the gun.

'Does you mum call you D-Ice?' My voice was clear and slow. 'Or is it Peter Juan Diego Marrilack?'

Dill sniggered and looked from me to D-Ice. 'One dayglo? What's that about?'

D-Ice lunged at Dill. 'You dissing me?'

'No, man!' Dill didn't sound so certain. 'One dayglo. It just sounded—'

'Get out the car!'

'You're joking, mate. It's my sister's!'

'Which sister? The one in Enfield? I like the one in Year Nine. How old is she, Dillboy? Thirteen, yeah? She's looking like a big woman now.'

For a second Dill sat there, then shoved open the door. He called something nasty to Andre and stayed by the kerb as D-Ice pulled away.

Yes! One down, one to go – one plus gun.

We were almost back at the garages under Cory's tower block, like D-Ice wanted to taunt them some more. An old woman was walking her dog past the ramp. Other than that, nobody was about. Not even a police car, an ambulance, nothing. If anybody heard the shooting earlier, they weren't reporting it. They probably hoped everybody had shot each other dead.

D-Ice turned down the music. 'So you know my name.'

I waited.

'You think that's some kind of magic power? Like say my name and I'm yours?'

We carried on past the entrance to the garages, screeched

into a U-turn at the end of the road and sped back the way we came.

I said, 'So now what? You planning to drive around all day?'

D-Ice glanced up at his mirror. Hard eyes with girl's lashes. 'Marlon Isaac Asimov Sunday, you're mine. Ain't no magic to it. I saved your life. You owe me.'

'I don't owe you nothing.'

Another U-turn and back again, like D-Ice's trainer was superglued to the accelerator. Andre thumped my leg. A bolt of pain. I held the shout in the back of my throat.

'Sharkie, man. We're nearly there, yeah?'

'Yeah! Just hold it down!'

'Them little boys were going to tape you up.' D-Ice slowed down to make sure I heard the words. 'First your mouth, then your hands, then your feet, then your tiny, little dick. They were going to thief your drugs and sell them back to Cory. A nice little scam, yeah?'

'How do you know?'

'They're my boys.'

Not any more.

I said, 'What happened when Sonya went to Cory?'

He was watching me in the mirror. I could see the back of his head and his eyes at the same time, hating him from both sides. I wished my hate could burn through and meet in the middle and make his head burst.

'She was authorised. Anyone touch a girl like her, every mandem in London's tearing through the estate. Guns, dogs, everything. But you . . .' He was grinning. 'Whatever I tell my boys, they do. Roll you into one of them garages and leave you. Season you up with a pinch of oil and cook you. Anything.'

'You sure about that? It looked like there was a mutiny down there.'

Out of the corner of my eye, I saw Andre lift his fist again. I managed to catch it before it dented my thigh.

Andre shook his hand free. 'Answer me, man! We getting out now, yeah?'

D-Ice revved the engine hard. 'Yeah. Booka asked a question! Answer him!'

'We're nearly there, Andre.'

Andre sat back and closed his eyes.

I leaned forward to D-Ice. 'Whatever you do now, isn't going to change the past. We're both stuck with what our brothers did. It doesn't mean we have to carry it on.'

He sucked his teeth. 'I told you. You're my boy. You don't know what 'boy' means? They don't teach you slavery at school?'

Yeah, they did, but not all of it. Mum told me that slaves ran away, or died trying. Some of them turned against their master or didn't get caught in the first place.

I said, 'You used Sonya to get to me.'

'You're the brother with the brain.'

'What was the plan with her?'

'I made sure that girl was going to pull your strings like Pinocchio. Just one flutter of those eyelids and you were ready to carry pills for her. She'd make you steal from your own mother, if I said so. I could make you do anything.'

Like lie to my mother. And bring her into the police station with her head full of old history.

I said, 'I didn't put your brother in prison, Peter.'

D-Ice pumped the accelerator; we shot forward and stalled. He turned round, gun pointing towards Andre. 'No. He did. Grassed up a brethren.'

Brethren?

Andre's mouth was moving, but no words were coming out.

'Our brothers were friends? When?'

'Way back. You don't remember? Until Booka started checking out Tayz's girl. If he kept his eyes to himself, Tayz wouldn't have come looking.'

'Sharkie was killed because Andre was looking at some stupid girl? Man, this is pathetic.'

The car was getting smaller and hotter. We were sealed tight and my mouth tasted like old newspaper. D-Ice revved the engine, stalled again.

D-Ice was still talking. 'Your mum's one of the good

ones, yeah? She helps the kids and the old people in her library. And she's got herself a posh, white man, as well. Wonder what your dad would think of that?'

He'd . . . he'd be happy for her. Yeah. He would.

D-Ice pulled away, driving slowly. I tried the door again, still locked. We were back by the garages again. Somewhere on the balconies, between the flapping bags and security grilles, the snipers might be watching us. The car stopped. D-Ice turned so he could give me the full on stare between the seats.

'Your mum's there by Booka's bedside, every day, making him swallow his baby food. Then when he come out, her posh boyfriend make sure Booka get the best care. *My* mum, the police went through her place like a hurricane, man, and then she got kicked out. Not even her church people offered up a roof for her head. No place to stay, no money and the school she's working in makes sure she's not welcome no more.' He jerked his thumb towards Andre. 'Your mum was there. Mine couldn't even raise the pennies to come and see me inside. All those hours, cramped up in my pad, I kept seeing this picture in my head. I was walking to the place with all the mentals like him. I was knocking on the door. I had my blade ready for when they called him. But that was too easy, man. I wanted to mash up your family like you mashed up mine. And the best way? Through Mummy's little angel.' He smiled at me, shaking

417

his head. 'A blonde girl in tight jeans knocked at your door and the halo snapped.'

Andre pulled my arm. 'We're here! Let's get out!'

'Leave it, Andre!'

He tugged at the door handle. 'Now! We need to go now!' His hand flailed, whacking me in my bad eye. My arm sprung up and I hit him back. His cap fell off and his sunglasses dropped loose on his nose-bridge. His left eye was bloodshot, drooping, the skin folded into the thick scar that led up to the shiny patch of scalp. No matter how much his hair grew, it was never going to grow back there.

He was looking at me with shock in his eyes. Slowly, he jammed his cap back on. My stomach was going off like a fire extinguisher.

'Andre?'

He was rocking again, muttering something under his breath.

D-Ice whooped. 'Halo, man! It's on the floor and you just pissed on it.'

Suddenly, the car was in motion, faster than such a crap little box should ever go, shooting down that ramp like we were going to take off, except our path was blocked with concrete pillars. Andre was yelling, his head in his hands, his voice all mixed up with garage echo, the engine, the mad noise inside me as everything thudded and shook. The car screeched into a tight turn.

Andre punched the back of the driver's seat, 'Jesus, Sharkie! No, man! No!'

He turned to me and slammed his fist into my thigh. My nerves screamed out, my reflex bouncing to hit him back again, my brain kicking in just in time. My teeth clamped down on my tongue and I tasted more blood.

Andre's screaming. Comfort him. Tell him everything's all right.

But it wasn't. We were shooting back up the ramp. If I opened my mouth, it was going to be all adrenaline and nutter's laugh, bubbling up like hot porridge. We spun round again, me colliding into Andre like we were on a fairground ride.

Spinning on the Dizzy Drum, fingers snatching at each other, a flash of pink jumper, a smear of mustard—

Flying back down the ramp, the pillars getting big, big, bigger, Andre clawing at the seatbelt pulling tight across his chest, fighting it as it sprung back. Me, both hands pulling at the door, the music battering my ears. We screeched around the pillars, then raced back up to the road.

Brain pause. Now!

List it. What do you need to do?

Undo Andre.

Free myself.

Get out of the car. Open Andre's door.

Pull him out and leg it.

D-Ice had a gun, but he was driving. Just one good punch, that's all it needed, and in the last few weeks I'd had practice.

That was all I had to do.

I leaned forward. The gun was between D-Ice's knees. My hand felt for the catch to Andre's seatbelt. There it was.

'No! Keep it on!' Andre slapped my hand away.

'No, Andre,' I whispered. 'We have to get out.'

Andre gripped the catch, fingers rigid. 'It's him!'

'Andre!'

We were firing down the ramp again.

D-Ice turned and yelled, 'You enjoying the ride, Booka? Want me to go faster?'

Andre shook his head. 'It's him! It's him, man!'

'Who, Andre?'

'Him!'

Of course! The wall, the mighty impact, the crack of glass as his best friend hit the bricks. My brother was back in his hospital nightmares. He didn't see D-Ice. He saw—

'Tayz!'

D-Ice's eyes in the mirror, wide and confused. I heard my own voice, mixed with Andre's, shrieking. But it was too late. The pillar filled the windscreen and the whole world turned grey and dirty.

And then we hit.

I rocketed forward and snapped back. Every gasp of air

was shunted out of my lungs. The engine ticked over for a few seconds, then cut out. I rubbed the back of my neck, almost surprised my head was still attached to it. D-Ice? He was slumped forward. The gun must have fallen beneath him somewhere, but I wasn't planning to find it. As I watched him, his hand twitched.

'Andre?'

He was still, eyes closed, the sunglasses dropped in his lap. His hand was still protecting the seatbelt clasp.

'Andre. Come on!'

His eyelids flickered and his chest was going in out.

'Andre?'

I tried to move his hand, but it was solid.

'Man, we need to get out.'

He didn't answer. There was movement in the driver's seat and D-Ice made a sort of snorting noise. If he'd blacked out, it wasn't going to be for eternity.

'For God's sake, Andre!'

I grabbed his hand and tried to lever it off the catch. His grip was loosening, yes! It was nearly free and – he punched me. Not much force behind it, but enough to feel his fist leave its shape in my chest, joining the dots of pain into one big picture. Nerves sizzled and inside my head flashed white. I blinked hard.

He frowned at me. 'You hit me. Now I hit you back. We're even.'

Even? Nowhere near! But not now.

I checked outside. No one around yet. But news on these estates spread quickly. The boys could be on their way back down, bringing Cory with them. And I could smell petrol.

'Andre?'

A nod.

'The locks open from the outside. I need to go out the front so I can let you out, all right?'

Another nod.

D-Ice was still hunched down, though he was definitely breathing. I reached round the bottom of the passenger seat looking for the knob to fold the seat forward. There it was. I twisted, pushing the seat horizontal. I sneaked a look at D-Ice.

A gun was pointed right at me.

D-Ice said, 'Open that door and I blast you.' The skin was torn on his forehead and blood was dripping down his face.

I lifted my hands in the air. 'Right. Okay. You've won. I'll do whatever you want me to. Just let Andre go.'

Because soon my brother was going to catch that petrol smell too and if he had a full on panic session, we were never getting out.

D-Ice shook his head. 'Too late.'

He held the gun with two hands. The big gangsta boy

was going to shoot me dead. I didn't drop my eyes. When he pulled that trigger, I was going to be looking at him. My face was going to repeat through his dreams, the same way Sonya's did in mine. Our eyes locked, then suddenly he opened the driver's door and he was gone. I breathed out so hard I thought I was going to spit my lungs out. Maybe he had no more ammo, maybe he couldn't front it any more. Right now, it didn't matter.

'Andre! We're done here! Let's go!'

My brother was chuckling. 'That damn pea shooter! It can't do nothing.'

'It doesn't matter. He's gone.'

'No, man. He's there.'

'What?'

Andre was right. D-Ice was there, by the driver's door. His hand moved . . .

'Andre! Get down!'

I flung myself over him. The door clicked open, I closed my eyes – and nothing. I sat up again. No D-Ice, but the smell was in my throat straight away, grimy smoke coating my mouth. A ball of rags was burning on the passenger seat, and as I watched, flames caught an old magazine in the footwell. Bullseye. The faces turned black as purple and green flames started curling up.

And you're just sitting there looking at the pretty flames?

Andre flexed his shoulders. 'Man, you're trying to bust

423

my back.' He sat upright. 'I'm smelling smoke.'

'I know. Undo your seatbelt and we can get out.'

'Smoke, man! Smoke! There's a fire!'

Andre's arms were thumping around, the whole car shaking. I ducked past him, squeezing through into the front seat. The flames were rising, the burning squeezing behind my eyes. I shoved the driver's door wide open, the gust of air fanning the flames higher.

'Sharkie!' It was like the cry was trapped in the middle of his body.

'Hang on, Andre!'

My foot caught in the front seatbelt and I fell forward, cracking my knee against the concrete. There was pain – well, there must have been, but my brain had built itself a dam. No pain allowed through until later.

I yanked open Andre's door, caught his wrist and held it. The flames were jumping up the front seats, bending over towards him.

'Andre,' I said. 'This is Marlon.'

His eyes were watering and his nose was running. He opened his mouth to say something, but it was just a small gasp. He coughed and wiped his eyes.

'Marlon?' A whisper.

'Yeah. It's Marlon, your brother. We're getting out, okay?'

The front seat was on fire, the tips of the flames touching the roof. But the heat would be heading down too, through the hose to the tank, down the end of the fuel line.

I slammed my hand on the clasp and the seatbelt split apart. 'Jesus, Andre! Quick!'

As I tugged him out the muddle of seatbelt, his weight sent us crashing on to the ground. I scrabbled away, pulling him behind. Something popped and a wave of heat washed over us.

Andre turned back. 'The car's burning, man! Let's go!'

Thanks for that, Andre! I could have laughed if my lungs weren't so scorched up. We stumbled up towards the ramp and daylight, me and my brother holding on to each other. If either of us let go, the other one would fall down.

'Mr Orange, I said I was coming.'

D-Ice stepped out from behind a pillar. His gun was pointed at Andre.

And that was the second I saw it, him and me running slide races in an adventure playground. I was five or six. Dad was still alive but getting ill and I think Mum ordered Andre to take me out. There were four of us, two teams, D-Ice and Tayz versus me and Andre. We made an obstacle course on the slides and roundabouts and football pitch, yelling and challenging each other until it was dark. Did D-Ice remember it too?

I searched his face. There was nothing but anger.

I stepped forward. 'Peter? We didn't make this crap. We don't have to carry it on.'

Andre laughed. 'Don't worry, man. I've seen little boys like that before. Them guns are fireworks. It don't mean nothing.'

'You're wrong, Booka.' Now D-Ice's eyes were on me. 'It means a brother for a brother.'

His finger moved.

'No!' I lunged sideways, pushing Andre out of the way.

Bang.

18

Blood. Dark splatters of it across the dirty floor. Behind me, the front of the car was burning bright, flames shooting out a shattered window.

I squinted through the smoke, eyes stinging.

D-Ice was leaning against a pillar, staring at the mush of blood where his fingers should have been. I was staring too. It looked like his hand wasn't going to hold anything ever again. His jaw was moving, like he was talking to the wreckage at the end of his wrist.

Cheap guns, thin metal starter guns drilled out to take proper bullets – the things Andre called fireworks. The heat and force was too much and if the gun didn't blow up on first shoot, it was only a matter of time. Bang! Taking a few fingers with it.

D-Ice slid down a pillar on to the dirty floor.

My own fingers hung loose and heavy, like they were going to drop off my palms. My insides – slush, liquid, gas – no solid stuff at all.

That was sirens. If they were coming here, they were too late. I'd just be another dirty stain on the concrete.

Suddenly, my fingers were lifted, my hand held tight.

Andre's eyes were red and streaming. 'Marlie! You okay?'

I shook my head. He sat down next to me, squeezing my hand. My head sunk on to his shoulder. I closed my eyes and realised he was singing, just under his breath.

The Jackson 5. 'I Want You Back'.

We didn't move until the sirens shrieked to a stop.

19

We take two cars. Andre's in Jonathan's, in his usual place behind Mum. Two months later and this is the only car he'll get into and even then he'll still kick off. I hold my breath as he sits down and tugs the seatbelt. He clicks it in place, leans back and I reckon he's closing his eyes beneath his sunglasses. I shut the door after him, careful not to catch the bunch of flowers on the seat.

'Meet you there,' Mum says.

Me and Tish travel with Louis. In spite of Jonathan doing his best diplomacy work, Louis and Mum still can't work out what to say to each other. Andre's changed, but at least we still have him – Louis and his mum and Sharkie's son have got this big hole where Sharkie should be. It takes a long time for words to fill a gap that size.

Mum's still vexed with me. I accepted a caution for the pills and it'll go on my college record. That's just the start. There will be a court case about the knife. There's no charge for the skunk in my schoolbag though. The CCTV showed Scott Lester fiddling round my bag. No one could ask him anything about it – his family upped and left, leaving a load of rent arrears and nothing else.

Jonathan's paying out for a hotshot lawyer who's convinced him I'll only get a community order for the knife. She's going to persuade the court that I was in shock and my family and friends were threatened. I'm one of the good ones, she'll say, a hard working student from a decent family. An angel with a snapped halo.

I wonder what words the court will use for D-Ice. The papers called his brother 'an arrogant thug' and I guess the same headlines will come out again for D-Ice. I don't want to think about him, but it sticks in my mind, the blood and rubble left of his fingers. For now, he's locked away again, on remand. They searched the place he was staying and found more drugs, knives and a replica gun. Even the biggest hotshot lawyer would have trouble getting him off that one.

The lawyer told me something else and I need to let Tish know. But that can wait. We're here now, passing beneath the mock-castle gateway into the massive cemetery. It's funny how so many prisons have that same type of architecture. We pull into a space across from Jonathan's car. Mum's holding the door open for Andre; the flowers come out first, followed by the rest of him.

Tish says, 'You all right?' She's talking to Louis.

'Yeah,' he says. 'This is weird, though.'

'As long as your mum's not there,' Tish says. 'Weird's all right. I just don't fancy violent.'

Louis reckons he's giving up the police stuff. He has to stand up in court and say he didn't report me for having a knife. He reckons that if the situation happened again, he'd do the same thing and he's not sure if he can toe the police line. He's offered to do some workout stuff with Andre and he's put his name down to be a mentor to try and stop boys going into gangs.

He's also tracked down D-Ice's mum. He wants to go and see if she needs any help. I want to meet her too, try and find a way we can put all of this to rest.

We all follow Louis. Me and Tish, Mum next to Jonathan and Andre up ahead, until we get to Sharkie's grave. There's no picture, but when you read the dates you remember that he was only nineteen. Mum's watching Andre, clenching and flexing her fingers, but he looks pretty calm. There's already a bunch of fresh flowers in a vase and no room for Andre's, so he just stoops and lays them across the grave, then turns and walks away. Mum almost jumps the grave to get to him, but Louis is there first. Whatever they're saying to each other is just for them, but they carry on walking, side by side, back towards the café.

I've warned Mum that me and Tish have something else to do.

'Right,' she says. 'Don't be too long.'

The squirrels are back out today, doing parkour across the monuments. It takes me a while to find Sonya's grave and there still isn't anything to say she's even there.

I say, 'The lawyer told me Sonya's gran gave a statement.'

Tish's eyebrows are up straight away. 'About?'

'Everything. She knew about the drugs, but she was scared. Not for herself so much, for Hayley and Sonya.'

'Do you reckon Hayley will tell the truth?'

I shrug. 'Maybe.'

'Did the police find Sonya's Blackberry?'

I laughed. 'Right under the rosebush where I left it. Lucky, there hasn't been too much rain.'

'It didn't grow into a Blackberry tree?'

'No.'

But maybe they'll track down some of the other people – Stunna, Westboy, Diamond – who had their own stories about Sonya to tell.

This place is weirdly full of life. That seems right for Sonya. Trains speed past, the mowers are humming and the main road isn't far away.

'Are we done here?' Tish's palm brushes against mine, our little fingers pressing together. We let them stay that way. 'Is it hot chocolate time?'

'Yeah,' I say. 'Good idea.'

Tish goes on ahead and I close my eyes and I see her. Not Sonya. Siouxza. Thick, blonde hair, pink jumper, a quick smile. Then she's gone.

And now it's just me, standing alone.

Acknowledgements

So many, so many. So I'll start at the beginning with the instigators: Dreda Say Mitchell, Frances Fyfield and Arvon.

Next the incubators, who read, reread, advised and read some more: Nathalie Abi-Ezzi, Katherine Davey, Jenny Downham, Liz Graham, Sarah Lerner, Anna Owen, Aisha Phoenix, Elly Shepherd, Charlie Weinberg – and thank you, Eva Lewin, for linking me in.

Over to the experts – and, my, you have no idea how much you need them until you realise how much you don't know. The folks below advised me on everything from police, legal and inquest procedures to gangs, living with a brain injury, inside of a police cell and those 'big date' clothes. So, gratitude to: Annetta Bennett, Anita Bey, Chinyere Inyama, Chloe and Amelia's mum, Deniz Oguzkanli, Heather Ransom, Martin Porter, Randal Porter and Tendayi Kerr.

To those who stuck their heels in to support me and got me this far: my patient, encouraging agent, Caroline Sheldon, Lucy Donoghue, Jane Lane, Miranda Macaulay, Natalie Martin, Odina Nzegwu and Sheryl Burton.

Thank you, Hodder team, for fabulousness, coffee and cake including: Emma Goldhawk, Nina Douglas and Anne McNeil.

Patrick, your extensive knowledge of funky vibes is a thing of wonder, as is your extensive address book. Your help with the re-enactments involving onion knives in the kitchen are also deeply appreciated.

And finally, a big heads up for Denise C. for the emergency loan of a keyboard, without which another deadline would have whooshed by.

Discussion Points

◈ *'Don't admit, don't deny, shut your mouth like the FBI . . .'*
Marlon is caught between what his brother has taught
him and what his mum is urging him to do. Should he
have told the police that the pills were Sonya's? Should
Mum have told the police what Andre said? Why are
people criticised for 'grassing'?

◈ Sonya, Marlon, D-Ice, Mrs Steedman and Tish put
themselves in danger because of loyalty to their friends
and family. Do you think you would have done what
any of these characters did? Why or why not? How far
would you go to defend the people you love?

◈ The book is set in London, but the story can mean
something to people everywhere. What resonates with
you and your surroundings?

◈ Sonya tells Marlon that he could be a brain surgeon and
he laughs at her. Do you think this is possible for
Marlon? If not, why not?

⊕ Louis ends up unable to continue as a Special Constable in the Metropolitan Police. Do you agree or disagree with his decision? Have you ever had an encounter with authority that has made you question what you'd thought was right or wrong?

⊕ *'Not cool enough, not clever enough, not street boy enough for anyone to take notice.'*
What groups or cliques have you come across in your life? Are you considered a member of any group? If so, how do you think people see you?

⊕ Music is important to Marlon, especially as it gives him a link to his father. What does music mean to you? Are there songs that remind you of friends or family? What song would you pass on to the next generation and why?

⊕ What will you take away from this book? Was there a particular message you have responded to?

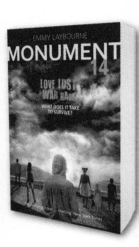
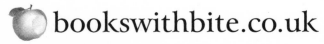